D0711485

GETTING WHAT SHE WANTS

Sophie's green eyes sparkled beneath the moonlight as Lance inched closer to her. Her back was pressed against the wood molding of the doorway, her delicate face angled upward so she could look into his eyes. Her mouth drew him, made him ache.

"I want the whitewashed look for the kitchen floors," she said.

"And Victorian accessories throughout."

"Absolutely."

He lowered his head toward her. "Craftsmanship is important to you?"

Her voice grew softer. "Only the best."

"It sounds as if you know exactly what you want."

A small smile curved Sophie's lips, triggering sensations inside him. "I do. Things that will last forever," she whispered. "But I'm not sure I can afford everything I want."

His chest squeezed as he feathered a strand of hair away from her neck. "Cost too high?"

Sophie nodded and licked her lips. "I'm afraid so."

He cupped the base of her head in his hand, his entire body tightening at the way her breath whispered out. Hunger, denial, and need bolted through him. He forgot they were talking about her house and furniture and flooring. The cost of wanting her was too high.

The price of not having her was even more painful.

Unable to control his tortured body's response to the flutter of desire in her eyes, he lowered his mouth and claimed her lips.

Sleepless in Savannah

Rita Herron

LOVE SPELL NEW YORK CITY

LOVE SPELL®

September 2003

Published by

Dorchester Publishing Co., Inc.
200 Madison Avenue
New York, NY 10016

ISBN 0-505-52544-5

The name "Love Spell" and its logo are trademarks of Dorchester Publishing Co., Inc.

Printed in the United States of America.

Visit us on the web at www.dorchesterpub.com.

Sleepless in Savannah

Chapter One

"Listen, Sophie, just follow the seven sacred rules for trapping a man." Maddie Summers-Holloway quirked an eyebrow, a hint of mischief in her sparkling brown eyes. "Then you'll snag Lance and we'll be sisters-in-law."

Sophie Lane laughed, squinting at her reflection in the mirror of the green room. Now that Maddie had been married an entire month, she was the expert. "Right. I'm sure he'll fall for those old tricks."

Not that she wanted to trick anyone into marriage. She didn't. She simply wanted Lance to fall in love with her the way she had fallen for him. And she had caught glimpses of moments when she knew he was attracted to her. That kind of chemistry she couldn't have misread.

But he'd blown her off with as much gusto as she would blow out her birthday candles a few days from now; anything to make the flaming evidence of aging disappear.

Thirty and still single.

1

At least she had a few good eggs left, or so her doctor had said at her last physical. *That* had made her feel *sooo* much better.

Maddie gave her a sympathetic look. "Hey, they might work. Lance is attracted to you. He just has some commitment issues to resolve. I swear, he still feels compelled to uphold that stupid bachelor pact Chase and my brothers made when they were kids."

Sophie sighed and sipped her diet Coke. She could understand young boys making an agreement never to get married, even writing it down, but to renew it as men? Even though they were worried romance might interfere with their work schedules and newly founded business, the pact was ridiculous. "At least Chase tore his up for you."

"Yeah, tearing up that pact was a beautiful thing." A dreamy glow settled into Maddie's eyes—the elated, happy look only newly married women possessed.

The look Sophie wanted for herself.

She leaned forward, searching for laugh lines in the mirror, but discovered frown ones instead, then pivoted the chair toward Arial, her makeup artist. "Do you think I need more powder around the eyes?"

Arial shook her head, her carrot-colored hair bobbing. "Too much, and it settles, uh . . ." Arial's expression turned to horror as she realized her faux pas. "It makes you look too made-up."

In other words—old.

Sophie winced. She didn't need a reminder. The ominous onset of the big three-oh had precipitated her willingness to trick Maddie's brother Lance into this date. After all, nothing else had worked so far.

Desperate desires called for desperate measures.

She was *not* desperate, she reminded herself. And

this would be the very *last* time she offered her heart up to be broken by Lance.

After all, he'd only agreed to appear today on the "Dating Game" episode out of guilt for treating her so poorly a few weeks ago. Why, the insufferable man had accused her of digging up sordid secrets about his family to air on TV just to spike her ratings. As if she would do such a thing.

Although she had conceded to a little minor manipulation today—the dating game was rigged so Lance would take home the prize.

Her.

Once he won, they'd embark on a romantic weekend getaway to Cancún. She hoped to dance her way into his heart on the beach, into his bed in the bungalow, and maybe into his life forever before the return flight home.

Maddie's wedding ring glittered as she finger-combed her auburn hair, and envy curled in Sophie's belly. "Rule number one:" Maddie chirped, "Bait the hook with a juicy worm."

"You mean I'm fish bait?"

"Right, translation—dress and act like a sex siren."

Sophie fluffed her own short black spiked hairdo, wondering if she should let her hair grow. Or dye it red, or let it go blond the way she used to wear it in Vegas.

A shudder gripped her.

No. Someone might recognize her from her past, and that could mean trouble: the kiss of death for the *Sophie Knows* show and the decent reputation she'd built for herself. Short and black would have to do. And if Lance didn't like it . . .

"Rule number two: Dangle the bait."

"Translation?"

3

"Shake your booty in his face and tease him mercilessly." Maddie tapped her metallic blue fingernails on the arm of the chair. "You won't have any problems there. Once Lance sees how fabulous you look in that string bikini, he'll be so tongue-tied he won't be able to resist you."

Sophie eyed her derriere in the mirror. Those extra five pounds she'd gained from pigging out on chocolate kisses would not help her case. "I'm not counting on it."

"Then move on to rule number three: Give him a nibble, then yank the line."

"Let me guess. A little kissing is allowed, even a little tongue, but no heavy petting."

"You're getting the hang of it."

Sophie chewed her nail. "Where did you get all this sage advice anyway?"

"*Cosmo*, of course."

Sophie pursed her lips. Of course, *Cosmo* knew everything about dating, sex, and relationships. "Okay, what's rule number four?"

"Make him swim in circles to catch the bait." Maddie wiggled her hips. "See, wiggle your butt and prance around with your boobs half falling out, but don't let him touch them . . . yet."

"You are incorrigible, Maddie."

Maddie was on a roll now. "Rule number five: Make sure his teeth are sunk in, then reel him in. Translation: Getting half-naked and sweaty is allowed, but no consummation. And six: Once you reel him in, keep the line tight. That means keep him sated."

"Ahh, the fun part." Sophie sighed, her stomach fluttering. It was almost airtime. "I just hope we get that far."

"Me, too." Maddie grinned. " 'Cause rule number

seven is to drop the line, rebait the hook, and find another fish."

Sophie sighed. "Right. A girl has to know when to cast another line."

"But you won't have to," Maddie argued. "He'll fall in love with you in Cancún. After all, you're beautiful, smart, and wonderful, Sophie; how can he resist?"

Sophie forced a smile. "Let's hope he never figures out that I set him up to be my date."

Maddie pressed a finger to her lips. "Don't worry; it'll be our little secret."

Their little secret?

Lance Summers had just emerged from the bathroom when he heard his sister talking to Sophie Lane about him.

The little sneak.

Fuming inside, he leaned closer to the doorway, watching as she bent her spiked dark head in collaboration with his darling kid sister's curly russet one. So, troublemaker Maddie and her cohort in crime, Sophie Lane, had set him up. He should have known the two conniving females would turn his acceptance as a bachelor for her silly dating game show into a scheme to get the two of them together. Now that Maddie was married, she'd embarked on a quest to get everyone around her hitched.

What else did Sophie have up that silk-clad sleeve of hers? Were she and Maddie already choosing wedding rings and china patterns? Did she have a limo waiting outside, ready to rush them to the church? Were they naming *his* children?

Sweat broke out on his brow and dribbled down his cheek.

Lord help him.

He was not ready to relinquish sole custody of his remote or forgo Sunday football for a relentless day at the mall, purse holding, while his wife tried on countless expensive outfits that he couldn't afford.

Footsteps clattered across the green room and he ducked behind the open doorway, determined not to get caught spying. Sophie pranced out the door, sashaying her voluptuous little body past like a sex siren purring his name, beckoning him to follow along like a bewitched innocent trailing along behind the Pied Piper. Maddie sauntered beside her, the two of them huddled together in hushed whispers, no doubt negotiating the details on the demise of his treasured bachelorhood.

He waited until they'd rounded the corner before he emerged, silently congratulated himself for not falling under her spell, and wiped the sweat from his brow as he formulated his own plan. They might think they'd outsmarted him, but he had been dodging husband hunters since college. Right now he had to focus on the company he and his brother, Reid, had just gotten off the ground; he could not be sidetracked by exotic dark eyes, red-hot lips, and a pair of sexy legs that belonged to a certain talk-show host.

He liked quiet, sensible females who didn't draw attention to themselves.

He had to remain in control.

And every time he got near Sophie that control shattered like a sheet of glass struck by a bulldozer.

The jazzy music that signified the beginning of *Sophie Knows* piped through the sound system, and he jogged across the hall to the room where the other contestants were waiting. Two other sets of bachelors had to endure the taxing ordeal of the dating game before he was forced through the torture.

He found his competition for round three pacing nervously.

"I'm Lance Summers, bachelor number three." He extended his hand in greeting.

The tall, scrawny blond offered a wimpy handshake. "Bachelor number one, Bailey Boxlighter."

"Rory Dalton." The dark-haired football type pumped Lance's hand, nearly breaking his fingers, as if brute force would prove his manhood. "Bachelor number two."

"Listen, you guys." Lance extracted his numb appendages, barely resisting the urge to shake back the feeling in them. For God's sake, he was six-two himself, almost two hundred pounds, not some kind of pantywaist. Who did this cretin think he was?

"What's up?" Boxlighter asked.

Lance jerked his thoughts back on track. "I was wondering if one of you would trade spots with me."

The blond frowned, his tanned forehead glowing bronze in the harsh lighting. No, almost orange. The guy must use that fake tanning cream. In fact, he'd missed a spot on his forehead.

"Why the switch?" the football hulk asked.

Lance shrugged, fighting the urge to brag that Sophie wanted him so badly she'd set him up. No sense rubbing it in to the other guys that they hadn't stood a chance. *He* didn't have to show off to prove his manliness. "Uh, I . . . I hate the number three." A lame excuse if he ever heard one, but he was groping in the dark without a flashlight. "It's my unlucky number."

The blond wrinkled his nose. "What are you, some kind of numerology freak?"

Lance shrugged. *Braniac.*

"I'll trade," the football hulk said. "I'm kind of

7

superstitious. Three's my jersey number."

Lance chuckled to himself. "All right, buddy. You take the third chair and I'll take the middle one."

"Do we need to tell the producer?"

Lance shook his head. "Naw, they don't really care what number we are." Besides, he didn't want to take the chance on Sophie discovering the switch.

"All right." Rory grinned. "And thanks for changing man. I feel lucky tonight."

The guy's cocky grin irritated Lance. The hulk wasn't getting the date through his charm. Still, the switch would mean *he* was off the hook, so what difference did the guy's attitude matter?

Now, on to the next part of his plan—disguise his voice and offer terrible answers so Sophie would never expect the switch. Then he'd be off the hook and free to get on with his bachelor life.

Just what he wanted.

The assistant producer peeked her head in the room and motioned for them to follow her. The orange-faced blond checked his reflection in the mirror, then licked his finger to tame a cowlick that had sprung up in back.

The football player flexed his muscles in a boxer's warm-up motion. "I'm ready."

Lance gritted his teeth as protective instincts for Sophie surfaced. Did he really want this lug to go out with her?

Sophie fought the quiver of nerves that tightened her chest as she congratulated the second couple. "Shandra and Dwayne will be heading off to Barbados in the morning. And we'll see them back next week to hear all about their romantic getaway."

Applause rang out and the audience cheered as she and the happy couple waved to the crowd. So far, their remake version of the *Dating Game* show had been a huge success.

Now she would take the hot seat.

"Ladies and gentlemen, for our third couple, the producers felt it would be a nice segue into the singles series we're running this week if I take part in the game."

Laughter bubbled through the audience.

Sophie played into their excitement. "I'm going to be asking three bachelors questions of my own; then I'll choose from one of them. Our camera crew will follow along on the date and you'll get to see firsthand if our dating game leads to successful matchmaking."

More applause, and the cameras panned the audience, where Sophie's assistant polled the crowd for comments.

The producer reviewed last-minute instructions with Sophie while another crew member miked her as she settled onto the stool on the right side of the floral divider. Neon-green letters spelled out THE DATING GAME in cursive lettering, while yellow daisies dotted the black silkscreen. It was very seventies, very retro. She felt as if she should be wearing go-go boots and a miniskirt.

Tense, she wet her lips and pulled her questions from her jacket pocket. The low sound of voices and men's shoes shuffling onstage echoed from behind the screen as the bachelors situated themselves in their assigned chairs. She pictured Lance's handsome strong jaw and wondered how he'd dressed for the occasion. Had he worn those faded jeans that hugged his muscular butt and that white shirt unbuttoned at the top with the cuffs rolled up? Or a dark suit that would accentuate those sultry coffee-colored eyes? Or maybe he'd decided to be daring and had sprung for some tight leather pants?

A frisson of desire danced in her belly at the thought. She had wanted Lance forever.

Well, for at least the last six months, but it *seemed* like forever.

The producer signaled showtime and the lights darkened onstage, one dim camera light zeroing in on her. "Welcome back to *Sophie Knows*," Sophie said. The females in the crowd started whispering their choices behind their hands. Were they admiring Lance? Choosing him for her weekend tryst?

The music zinged to a close and Sophie pasted on her bright entertainment smile. "All right, bachelor number one. What is your idea of a romantic date?"

Bachelor number one's chair rattled. "First we'd start off with an afternoon shopping spree, where I'd buy my lady a sexy party dress. Something slinky and expensive." The audience murmured their approval. "Then we'd take a nice moonlight drive in my convertible to a cozy little Italian place on the beach. And afterward . . ." He let the sentence trail off, his voice low and seductive. "Well, afterward we'd have dessert. But it wouldn't be in the restaurant."

Low laughter and whispers echoed throughout the audience.

Sophie twisted in her seat. She hoped Lance would have an equally romantic answer. In fact, she'd save him for last. "That sounds wonderful. Now, bachelor number two?"

"Order in pizza and watch the Braves game on the tube."

Sophie frowned, guessing by the audience's silence that they were unimpressed as well. Oh, well, it didn't matter. She'd already made up her mind. "Bachelor number three?"

A deep voice rumbled out. *Lance?* "We'd start off with an afternoon picnic in the mountains, then explore the woods together, wade in the creek. That night we'd sleep under the stars, cuddled together in a sleeping bag for one." He chuckled. "Except we probably wouldn't do much sleeping."

The crowd clapped. Sophie tingled all over as she imagined making love with Lance out in the open beneath the moon and stars. Tangled legs, sweaty bodies, and panting breaths, soft touches and erotic kisses . . .

She didn't need to ask any more questions.

But she had to play out the game. "All right. Bachelor number two, I'll start with you this time. If you could be an animal, what would you choose to be?"

"A wolf."

"So you could chase women?"

"No, so I could run free in the woods."

Hmm—commitment issues. Strike him out of the game. "Bachelor number one?"

"A cat, so I could curl up in a woman's lap at night and have her rub my back. Then I'd lick—"

"Wow," Sophie cut him off, "thank you, bachelor number one." If Lance wasn't careful, that first guy was going to knock him out of the game. "Bachelor number three?"

"A bear." His voice echoed with innuendo. "So I could wrap my arms around you and give you a bear hug. And we could hibernate all winter . . ."

Catcalls and laughter erupted, and Sophie's face heated. Who would have thought Lance would be such a ham on camera? And his voice sounded even deeper than normal. Huskier.

"All right, let's start with bachelor number one again."

"Honey you can start *and* end with me anytime."

The audience played along, enthusiasm building with their laughter.

"What food best describes your taste in women?"

He moaned suggestively. "Ice cream. I like my women sweet, dripping in chocolate sauce."

Oh, my.

"Bachelor number two?"

"A good burger. Nothing like simple, plain, and hearty."

What a dud. The coproducer waved at the clock.

"Number three." Lance.

"Hot tamales. I want my women spicy and hot."

Sophie shivered; once again the crowd murmured their appreciation.

"Last question, gentlemen. If you were going to choose a romantic gift for your lady, what would it be? Let's start with number two this time." *And get it over with.*

"A toaster."

Had he really said a kitchen appliance? What was wrong with this guy? "You think a toaster is romantic?"

"Well, it would save time in making breakfast the morning after."

Silence stretched after his answer as Sophie contemplated the meaning. In a Mars–Venus sort of way, she supposed it was a suitable answer. More time for lovemaking, less for cooking.

"Bachelor number one?"

"A fur coat." His voice grew lower. "Of course, she'd be naked underneath."

Judging from the whispered innuendoes and uproar of the crowd, the bachelors must have started male posturing or flexing their muscles behind the screen. Maybe she should have sneaked a look at the other two candidates before she decided on Lance.

After all, bachelor number one's answers were pretty romantic. "Bachelor number three?"

He cleared his throat and spoke in a low tone that sent her senses spinning. "I'd buy her a see-through negligee. Something silky that would brush her skin just the way I want to caress her with my fingers." He paused, then continued in a breathy voice. "And it would be red. Red-hot for the passion we'd feel in each other's arms."

The crowd roared, several women shouting out, "Pick him! Pick him!"

Sophie released a shaky breath, dabbing at her neck where perspiration had started to bead. The peppy music picked up, leading into the break, and the camera focused on the ticking of the clock, signifying that she had two minutes to make her decision. Then the camera zoomed to the audience, where her assistant polled the crowd.

"Psst."

Sophie folded the sheet of questions into a triangle in her hands.

"Psst, Sophie."

Out of the corner of her eye, she spotted Maddie to the left of the stage jumping up and down, waving frantically at her. *Come here!* Maddie mouthed.

Sophie frowned, indicating the clock hands winding around on the wall. There wasn't time. Worse, the producer was shooting daggers at her with his eyes as if to ask why Sophie had given Maddie full reign behind stage. Arial rushed to the edge with her makeup kit, but Maddie snatched the kit and ran toward Sophie. Teetering on her heels, Maddie paused beside her and leaned close, dusting Sophie's nose with powder.

Sophie covered her lapel microphone with her hand. "What is it? We're due back on air—"

"Lance is supposed to be bachelor number three, right?"

"Right."

"Well, he's not."

Sophie pushed Maddie's hand away as she grabbed the lipstick. "He's not what?"

"He's not number three." Maddie's eyes narrowed as she gestured toward the screen. "He's number two."

"Two?"

"Yes, two as in do—"

Sophie shushed her, the truth dawning. "That sneak."

"He must have caught on to us." Maddie hitched out a hip. "And he switched places!"

A fist squeezed Sophie's heart. Because he didn't want the date with her.

His answers to her questions reverberated inside her head like a cannon blast. He'd said he wanted hamburger. That he wanted to run free like the wolves. That he'd buy his girlfriend a toaster.

He was throwing the game on purpose!

"You should pick him anyway, just for revenge. Prove to him the sacred rules work." Maddie wagged the lipstick in Sophie's face. "This is not just a battle of the sexes anymore, girl; it's war. Down-and-out, dirty, full-fledged war."

The air caught in Sophie's lungs. *When life deals you lemons, make lemonade.*

She'd always tried to live by that motto.

In fact, she'd been trying to make lemonade with Lance, but he'd squeezed the last drop of hope from her now. Like a dried-up piece of fruit, her heart cracked and burst. She was a broken shell spitting nothing but shattered seeds.

The drumroll signified time for her to wrap up the

show. The producer gave her a venomous look.

"Remember rule number two," Maddie said in a hiss. "Dangle the bait and watch him squirm. So shake that booty and tease him mercilessly." Maddie shook her butt for emphasis, dotted Sophie's lips red, then teetered offstage.

Sophie's mind raced as the clock wound down and the buzzer exploded into the tense silence. "The audience is divided forty-forty between bachelor number one and three, with ten percent voting for number two," Sophie's assistant announced. "Who will win this romantic trip with our sexy host?"

The camera zoomed back to Sophie. What should she do?

Lance had given such god-awful answers to her questions. How could she pick him and not look like an idiot? Even the audience had pegged Lance as a loser.

But could she spend the weekend on a romantic getaway at a topless beach with a complete stranger?

Chapter Two

Tick-tock. Tick-tock. Tick-tock.

The clock counted down the final seconds. Sophie squirmed. She could not keep chasing a man who didn't want her. Lance must have seen beneath the surface and realized she wasn't the woman she portrayed herself to be. He had seen the flaws, maybe even knew her secrets. . . .

It was time to cut the line.

The buzzer sounded. Her assistant's voice broke through the blurred haze that had once been her brain.

"Okay, Sophie, will it be bachelor number one, bachelor number two, or bachelor number three?"

She felt the cameras focus on her again. "It was a hard decision, Eden, but I'm going to choose bachelor number three."

The crowd applauded. Music played for several seconds, giving Sophie's heart time to lob and settle. Finally her assistant waved for quiet. "It sounds as if the audience agrees with you. But let's meet the other bachelors first." Eden gestured toward the screen. "Bachelor number one is a model for a local sportswear company, has his own yacht, and lives on Skidaway Island. Meet Bailey Boxlighter. And he is yummy!"

The crowd whistled and cheered. Sophie pasted on a smile as he rounded the corner. No man should have such flawless skin and perfect teeth. She'd dated a model once who was so obsessed with his looks, he couldn't eat for checking his reflection in his wineglass. And she could have sworn she'd seen Bailey's face on the cover of a porn magazine in Vegas. If it was him, the man was so, um, *large*, he was deformed.

He kissed her cheek, then nibbled at her ear. "Sorry, Sophie; it would have been fun."

"You had some wonderful answers," she said, sensing a hurt ego more than true disappointment. He was obviously accustomed to women swooning over him.

The very reason she liked Lance. He was down-to-earth, real, caring—at least he cared about his siblings, but unfortunately not her.

Drat, she had to forget Lance Summers.

"And now bachelor number two. This hometown boy owns his own land development company here in Savannah. Meet Lance Summers."

Lance stalked around the screen, his wide shoulders encased in a denim jacket that made him look the rugged bad boy she knew him to be. This time her smile made her cheeks ache, but she had to save face.

"Better luck next time, Lance."

He nodded, then gave her a quick peck on her cheek, not quite meeting her eyes as he stepped aside. She was surprised he wasn't gloating. No man could have faked such bad answers except Lance. Which proved that if he ever set his mind to it, he'd probably be the most romantic man in the world.

But he was not to be hers. Some other woman would receive the pleasure of his adoration.

"And now, fellows, your consolation prize," Eden said. "The *Sophie Knows* show is giving you a six-month membership to the Savannah Singles Service."

Sophie beamed a look at Lance. "Hope you enjoy."

He frowned as if she'd sentenced him to hard labor. "Thanks a bunch."

A drumroll sounded, breaking into the tense silence that followed his reply. Sophie held her breath, mustering up fake enthusiasm as her assistant introduced her date.

"Our winning bachelor, number three, is an ex–football player for the Atlanta Falcons. He retired to Savannah but has recently agreed to join the coaching staff at the University of Georgia in the fall. I'd say Rory Dalton made a touchdown today!"

The crowd erupted into laughter, but Sophie inhaled as the ex–football player stalked toward her. She'd thought Lance was a big man, but this guy's shoulders looked like watermelons, his legs were the size of tree trunks, and when he picked her up and swung her around, her bones squeaked in protest. With a growl in her ear, he slid her to the floor, threw her backward over his arm, and settled his mouth on top of hers.

Good Lord almighty, he was going to swallow her whole and try to score right there on stage.

Lance was sweating profusely, due to the heat wave, he assured himself, not to the fact that the hulk was kissing Sophie. Still, protective instincts emerged, tempting him to intercept the man's pass, but he forced his feet to remain glued to the floor. He couldn't make a fool of himself on TV, not for a woman who was completely wrong for him.

Besides, he had fulfilled his obligation to Sophie and her show, and beat her at her own game. Now he could focus on his business, which he and his brother Reid had barely kept out of the red the last year, and forget the guilt that had dogged him for being rude to Sophie in the past. Plus, now that Maddie had gotten hitched to his best friend, Chase, Lance was finally free to enjoy his bachelorhood without worrying about a menagerie of sex-crazed men chasing his little sister. Sophie was too sophisticated, too showy, too much in the limelight, too perfect for a guy like him. He would never fit in with her TV producers and society-elite friends. Although sometimes at night he craved the soft curves of a woman's body pressed up to him, the idea of marriage made him nauseated. And Sophie had *marriage* written all over her.

Then why did he have this twisting, gnarling ache in his stomach as Sophie curled her hands around Dalton's arms?

Protective instincts, nothing more. She was his kid sister's friend, so naturally he felt the urge to call a penalty on the man for illegal maneuvers, but Sophie was a grown woman and could do whatever she pleased. Even if it meant pawing and humping onstage.

He cleared his throat in disgust, and the two finally broke apart. Sophie was breathless, her face flushed, her eyes wide as she staggered upright. He barely resisted the urge to assist her so she wouldn't fall down, and glared at the whisker burn on her cheek. Damn, had the man been raised by wolves?

"Well, it looks like Savannah won't be the only place with a heat wave; the steam is going to rise in Cancún," Sophie's assistant said with a twinkle in her eyes. "Our lucky couples will leave for their romantic getaways tonight. And on a special Saturday show we'll take a sneak peak to see how they're doing; then next week, we'll air special footage of each of their adventures." She paused. "If you'd like to vote on which couple you think might turn their dating match into a long-term relationship, log on to our Web site. Next week we'll find out which predictions come true."

The following few minutes blurred as the other couples and losing bachelors gathered onstage to throw kisses to the crowd. As the music wound down, chaos descended. Maddie and a number of production assistants rushed onstage to meet the bachelor and congratulate Sophie and the other couples, all chattering noisily and shrieking over the upcoming romantic excursions.

"Oh, my God, I can't believe we're going on a cruise," one of the women tittered.

"And I'm flying to Paris." The second woman moaned. "My dream."

Rory shook his hand, this time so hard Lance ground his molars. "Sorry you had to lose, man. I could give you some tips if you want."

"He could definitely use some pointers." Maddie inched up beside him. "My brother seems to be striking out with women all the time."

He struck out on purpose. Maddie knew that, didn't she? Lance narrowed his eyes at her while two cameramen pulled Rory to the side to sign autographs.

For cripes' sake, if he'd wanted to win the date,

he could have. He knew how to be romantic.

"What answer persuaded you to pick Rory?" Maddie asked Sophie.

Sophie tilted her delectable little head in thought. "The negligee. I love sexy red underwear."

Oh, good Lord. Did she have to plant that mental picture? Besides, Sophie didn't need a skimpy seethrough negligee for her to be sexy; she could seduce a man wearing a damn feedsack.

"What do you think about the consolation prize for the losers?" Sophie asked.

He was *not* a loser. "I'm not much for those singles clubs."

"Too bad you didn't win the date," Maddie said with an evil twinge to her voice.

"Listen, girls," Lance said, deciding to fess up. "I overheard you talking backstage and realized this was a setup, so I threw the game on purpose."

Sophie's dark eyebrow arched. "Really?"

"Face it," Maddie said. "You don't have a romantic bone in your body."

"Rory beat you fair and square," Sophie added. "Besides, bachelor number one was my next choice. You were dead last in the running."

Her words sank in, along with an image of her wearing that sexy red negligee for Wolfman. Lance had been *last* on her list? "Look, Sophie, I was just joking around. But you should be careful of this guy—"

"I don't need your advice on my love life," Sophie said.

Maddie thumped her foot up and down. "I can't believe you're being a sore loser, Lance."

His temper flared. "I lost on purpose."

Maddie rolled her eyes. "Right."

"Because you didn't want to go out with me." Sophie jabbed his chest with her finger for emphasis, but hurt softened her voice. "Don't worry, Lance; you didn't need to throw the game. I wouldn't go out with you if you were the last man on earth."

"The last man on earth?" Reid Summers laughed over the jukebox strains of country music blaring through Smoky Sam's. "She really said that?"

Chase tightened his hand around his beer mug. "Hell, yes, can you believe it? After she practically begged me to go on the show."

"Maybe she planned to turn you down all the time and she wanted to embarrass you on TV."

"That would be cruel."

Reid wiggled his eyebrows. "I bet she could be wicked."

Lance didn't like the look of lust in his brother's eyes. Reid would flirt with anything in a skirt, morals be damned. He'd always been fun-loving and cocky, but at least he kept Lance sane by not letting him get too serious about anything. Especially a woman.

"Besides, what are you so pissed about? I thought you didn't like Sophie."

"I . . . I never said I didn't like her."

"But you don't think she's attractive?"

Attractive? Sophie was a sex goddess. "Uh, I never said that. Exactly."

Reid grabbed a handful of peanuts from the bowl on the bar. "I'm not following, bro. You like her and you think she's attractive, but you don't want to date her?"

"No. Yes." Lance turned up his beer and drank greedily, trying to make sense of his reaction when none of it made sense to him. "Hell, I wouldn't have minded a date or two"—*and a night or two in her bed*—"but . . . Sophie's too sophisticated for me."

"You don't like sophisticated women?"

"It's not that, but . . ." What the hell was it? "She runs with a different crowd. TV producers, jet-setters, you know. They're not like us."

"Ego can't take the rich and famous, huh?"

"Yeah, that's it. It's not like I care if she runs off to Cancún with this guy and they get it on." His stomach churned.

"They might even end up getting hitched."

"Probably what she wants." Lance crushed a peanut in his hand. "If Maddie has her way, she'll arrange the wedding for them before they return from their trip."

Reid drew a slashing motion across his throat. "Maddie knows how to go straight for the jugular."

"Yeah, just look at Chase. Instead of being here with us, he's probably carting Maddie's packages around the mall."

"Letting her lead him around like a puppy on a leash."

"Purse holding and paying for expensive shoes and shit he can't afford."

"Sucker."

Lance winced. "I'm not falling into that trap."

Reid lifted his mug for a toast. "Here's to bachelorhood."

"Bachelorhood."

"To singles clubs."

Lance frowned. "A different woman every night."

"No panty hose draped over the shower rod."

"No loss of the remote control."

"If you can't be with the one you love, love the one you're with. And you don't even have to share the bed all night."

Lance grabbed another handful of peanuts and

tossed them down his throat, nearly choking on a splintered shell. He normally slept better alone, and he needed a lot of sleep. In fact, he was legendary for being able to fall asleep anywhere, anytime.

What about Sophie? Did she prefer having the bed to herself?

Or was she loving the guy she was with and sharing her bed with him?

Chase Holloway closed his eyes on a sigh as Maddie licked a path along his neck, then lower to his belly. He'd never been in such heaven.

"I love you, Chase."

Chase curled his hands into her riot of curls. "I love you, too, Maddie. Damn, you get hotter every day."

"It's this summer heat wave."

"No, baby, it's you."

Maddie lapped at his navel. "Thank you for going shopping with me today, honey. I'm sorry Lance and Reid gave you a hard time."

"They'll get over it." Chase's gaze raked over her seductive outfit—a French-cut black leather bustier with black fishnet stockings. "Anytime you want to go shopping in that lingerie store is fine with me."

Maddie traced a finger along his inner thigh, teasing. "Is that the reason you gave up beer drinking with the boys for me?"

Chase's body tightened into a big, quivery mass. "Sweetheart, beer drinking is way overrated."

Maddie laughed softly and closed her hand around him, torturing him with her touch. Chase moaned and dragged her up to cover his body, then flipped her over and took her mouth, tasting the fiery sweetness that made his wife so hot. Seconds later he slowly untied the ribbons securing the garment together at her chest, then nipped at the rosy tips of her breasts, suckling and laving her as his hands explored the rest of her body. Maddie was always supple and giving, and so damn erotic he would never get enough.

To think he'd once feared marriage would be confining—hell, now he wanted to confine *her* on occasion. He pushed her hands above her and pinned her to the bed, teasing her with his aching sex as he kneed her legs apart. Sometimes he wanted to tie her to the bed and keep her there so she would never leave him. He was so damn afraid he'd wake up one morning and be all alone, that he'd once again be the outsider, that all the good things that had happened to him the past few months would have been only a dream. Those nights, he'd wake up in a cold sweat, remembering that orphanage, the holidays he'd gone hungry.

Panic would literally rob the breath from him. Then, right there in the middle of the night, he'd have to take Maddie to make sure she was real. And thank God, Maddie always responded, always loved him back with the same heat and passion that she had the first time they'd made love. In fact, their heat seemed to grow hotter, more intense every day. . . .

He raised his head and gazed into her eyes, memorizing every precious inch of her, from her fiery auburn hair to that pouty lower lip to the way the two of them lay naked and entwined. He felt exposed, raw, but he didn't care.

Maddie traced a finger along his jaw. "You have that look in your eye again."

She always seemed to be able to read him.

"I guess I'll have to make it go away," she whispered. A sultry smile spread onto her face as she pulled him to her.

Chase was lost as he popped the snaps at her crotch, then rose above her and slid inside her slick heat. Maddie's moan shook the walls, her wild abandon unleashing his hunger. For the next few minutes he simply buried himself inside her, letting her love wash away any lingering doubts that what they shared would suddenly disappear. She clutched his arms, then clawed at his back as he drove himself deeper, her throaty whispers urging him harder, faster, until they both panted and kissed each other hungrily, their bodies slapping in rhythm as they rode the crest of their love. He felt himself coming apart, sensations spiraling out of control, and lowered his head to flick his tongue across the tips of her breasts again, licking and circling each hardened peak as she stretched her stockinged legs wider, circling her ankles around his hips. Her hands gripped his buttocks, pulling him into the heaven he craved, and he fought to hold off the pleasure. His loud suckling noises echoed through the air as she gasped and writhed beneath him, her sounds of pleasure triggering his own release.

Seconds later he brushed her hair from her cheek as she curled into his arms. They were both still trembling from the aftermath of their lovemaking. An uncharacteristic bit of emotion swelled in his chest. He'd never let emotions get to him before he'd fallen for his best friend's little sister. "Maddie?"

She traced a bloodred fingernail down his chest, teasing him again. "Yeah?"

He had to clear his throat to speak. "This has been the best few months of my life."

"Mine, too."

His voice grew low, huskier. "Don't ever leave me."

She smiled and slid her arms around his neck,

then cupped his face and kissed him again, this time slowly, tenderly, filled with love. He finally relaxed.

"I just wish everyone could be as happy as we are," Maddie whispered.

Chase quirked a brow at her. "You're talking about Sophie and your brother?"

Maddie threaded her fingers through his. "I don't understand Lance. He's never treated a woman the way he does Sophie. I thought they'd be so right for each other."

"You can't fix everyone's life, sweetheart."

"But Sophie is so wonderful," Maddie argued. "She doesn't deserve to be ditched by him."

Chase shrugged. There was no winning with his wife when she had her mind made up. *Poor Lance.*

Maddie poked out her bottom lip. "And she's leaving tonight with that football player for the weekend."

"Maybe she'll connect with this guy," Chase suggested.

"But he's not the one. And he might hurt her. And it's all Lance's fault, because he's so stubborn."

Chase angled his head to look into her eyes. "And you know all there is about love?"

She licked her lips. "I know when it feels right."

His expression sobered as she palmed his erection. "That feels right."

"Yes, it does." She cuddled into him. "And when I see Sophie and Lance together, it just feels right."

"If it is, they'll figure it out."

Maddie tapped her finger on her chin. "Maybe. Or maybe they need some help." She sat up, her beautiful breasts bobbing. Chase's sex leaped toward her.

Maddie caught the movement and laughed softly. "Hold that thought while I make a quick phone call."

Uh-oh. "What are you up to now, Maddie?"

Maddie punched in her brother's number and handed him the remote. "Here, occupy yourself until I get finished."

Chase chuckled and leaned back against the pillows, but one hand snaked out to knead her breast. How had he gotten so lucky? Not only was he in the bed with a beautiful, delicious woman who loved him, but he had the remote in one hand and her naked breast in the other—what more could a man want?

"Tell me what you want," Lance said to Sophie.

You. Sophie bit her tongue and rubbed her hand along her cat's back, taking refuge in the fact that at least she had a live-in friend, even if it was a feline.

"Sophie? I need to know exactly what you have in mind."

A long, slow, lazy afternoon in bed with the ceiling fan swirling above us to cool us off.

Thirsty from the heat, or maybe her mouth was dry from looking at Lance, she grabbed a diet Coke to occupy her mouth. *Tell me what you want.* Lance was referring to the renovations to the Victorian house she'd purchased in the historic district, not making love to her—which was all *she* could think about. He'd shown up five minutes after she'd arrived home from the show, primed and ready to discuss her house while she had less than an hour to gather her suitcase and head to the airport. She'd packed ahead of time, choosing a silver bikini, strapless sundresses, slingback sandals, and thong underwear, all of which she'd planned to use to lure him into loving her.

But now she'd be wearing those things for another

man. And if her first impressions were true, she'd be fending off Rory's thirteen hands.

Worse, Lance had made the choice; he'd rather clean out rusty pipes than be with her.

The irony of the situation and his timing didn't escape her. He'd chosen to work this weekend because she would be gone, meaning he wouldn't have to see her. The message had come through loud and clear, and although she was hardheaded, she had finally gotten it. Even her cat seemed to sense Lance was trouble. He'd snarled and hissed ever since Lance had walked in the door. Protective of his mistress. At least somebody was.

"Since when did you get a pet?" Lance asked.

"Maddie brought him over. He was homeless."

"Sounds like Maddie, always trying to pair up orphaned creatures."

She winced. Had Maddie told him about her past? "Maddie's going to drop by and feed her. Be sure not to let her outside," Sophie warned. "She's been declawed and can't protect herself."

Lance frowned as the cat hissed at him. "She certainly looks like she can take care of herself."

"Looks can be deceiving."

His gaze caught hers, tension rippling between them. But Sophie quickly broke the moment. "I've made a list," she said, resorting to what she hoped was a professional tone as she handed him the clipboard where she'd detailed her plans for the house. "I may not be able to swing everything I'd like right away, but I want an estimate anyway. The basics have to be done first, the kitchen needs updating, the bathrooms repaired, retiled, and painted, and if I can afford it, I want to add a breakfast bar in the kitchen."

Lance paced across the room, examining the space

as he ran a finger over the original wood molding. "All right. I'll put together an estimate while you're gone; then I'll start on the bathroom. You'll want the necessities taken care of before you do any cosmetic work."

"Right." She flicked her bangs from her eyes. "I thought you had work crews to do this kind of thing."

"They're finishing that subdivision on Skidaway now. While Reid is overseeing them, I thought I'd start here."

"Great." The man could be in love with the wood grain, but not her.

"Okeydokey. I guess I'll leave you to it, then."

Lance paused and looked up at her. "You don't want to sit down and go over things? I'll need to know what type of fixtures you have in mind, if you want tile in the bathroom, and what kind of wood you'd like to use if you want to redo the flooring in here and the rest of the downstairs—"

"Just look at what I've noted and do the basics for now. I'll decide about those other things when I return."

"Right."

Sophie hugged Jazzy good-bye, then breezed past Lance, trying desperately not to brush against his broad chest as she squeezed through the small doorway. It didn't work. Her breasts rubbed his chest and her thigh met his jeans-clad leg, sending heat bolting through her like a lightning rod. "Oh, and see if you can enlarge this doorway. It's entirely too small for this house."

Especially with you in it.

Lance's muscular hands wrapped around the edge of the clipboard. "All right, we'll talk when you return."

"Great." Sophie smiled brightly. "That is, if I'm not too exhausted. I may need a day or two to recover. A weekend with Rory in Cancún is bound to wear me out."

His smile faltered slightly as she sailed out the door, and she hoped his mind had started spinning with the implications of her comment.

Let him think she was having a wild love affair, for all she cared. The camera footage that would air next week would corroborate her story.

And she would *never* admit any different.

Chapter Three

After Sophie left, Lance studied her list. The two-story Victorian house had been built in the 1800s and was supposedly haunted, although he didn't believe in ghosts. It still had much of the original plumbing and wiring, along with the original wood floors, crown moldings topping the ten-foot ceilings, and fretwork on the wraparound front porch. The dining room still boasted velvet wallpaper in a French design, but it was peeling and faded, and the entire house needed painting. Although the kitchen needed modernizing, the previous owners had installed central heat and air, which would eliminate one major cost, and the wood stove in the kitchen and fireplace in the den and all the bedrooms probably offset high heating bills. When Sophie wasn't using a room, she could simply close it off.

But once he ripped up the chipped bathroom tiles, he might find damage to the subflooring. He was glad she'd picked tiles and left them for him. And if the stains on the kitchen ceiling were what he thought, Sophie might need a new roof. He'd get his men over as soon as possible to replace it.

At least she'd gotten the house for a song. Many of the older homes in the historic district had fallen into more serious disrepair, and had been auctioned off. There were also special state-funded incentives for buyers to renovate the houses with stipulations that the owners adhere to the guidelines issued by the Historical Society.

He jotted down questions to ask her when she returned and sketched out the general plan, then decided to walk through the rest of the house before he tackled the bathroom. With Sophie out of town, he might go ahead and tear out the back doorway. He could finish repairing it before she returned, alleviating the need for her to spend the night in the house without being able to lock the doors. Of course, he'd stay over so he could keep an eye on things. The last thing he needed was for Sophie to be robbed because he'd left her place open. Or for that psycho cat of hers to escape and get hurt.

The phone rang and he hesitated, wondering if he should pick it up. It might be Reid.

No, Reid would call his mobile phone. It had to be Sophie, and he was not her answering machine.

Three rings, four, and then the message machine picked up. "Hello," Sophie said in that sultry voice that drew his insides into a knot. "You've reached Sophie Lane. I'm sorry I can't come to the phone, but you know the drill; leave a message."

He told himself to leave the room and not listen, but his feet refused to cooperate. Seconds later another woman's voice echoed over the line. "Sophie, hon, this is Deseree. I saw the 'Dating Game' show, and man, what a catch you found in that jock. You were smart not to choose that dud bachelor number two. Did he have some awful answers or what? He must have crawled out from under a rock."

"I was faking it," Lance muttered.

"Anyway, I can't wait to see the footage of the date on TV."

He rubbed a hand over his face. Neither could he.

"Anyway, I'll try your cell phone. Have a great time!"

Lance hissed between his teeth. Sophie was probably already having a great time, indulging in more hanky-panky with the hulk.

Shaking off the images the caller had conjured in his mind, he took a quick walk through the den, his gaze landing on the country sofa and furnishings. He'd been shocked the first time he'd visited; he'd assumed Sophie would have chrome and glass and white leather, but the furnishings were homey, comfortable. Of course, she had mentioned that most of the furniture had come with the house and that Maddie would help her with the decorating. Would she update the furniture with contemporary pieces or would she opt for antiques and a welcoming atmosphere?

It didn't matter, he told himself. This was Sophie's house. She could do whatever she wanted. He just hoped she didn't ruin it with some ritzy-looking faux marble or cover the pine floors with cheesy shag carpet.

He stepped into her bedroom and hesitated, feeling like a voyeur as he skimmed over the four-poster canopy bed with its satiny white comforter. The bed itself looked decadent, everything in the room in its place, except for the red teddy lying at the foot of the bed as if it were waiting on a lover.

It was not only crotchless but see-through as hell. She might as well wear a piece of saran wrap.

Worse, the scent of Sophie's perfume, some kind of light floral mixture that reminded him of roses, wafted toward him, stirring sensations that he had no business feeling for a woman he didn't want to want.

His body hardened anyway. The traitor.

Had Sophie forgotten the teddy? Had she meant to take it with her to Cancún? And if she had forgotten it, would she crawl into bed tonight totally naked?

Rory would definitely want to get naked this weekend, Sophie thought. She drummed her fingers on the dash as she drove to the airport, desperately trying to think of excuses.

"Sorry, Rory, but it's the wrong time of the month."

Lame. Besides, some guys didn't care. And he might even use it against her and remind her that the chances of her getting pregnant were nil.

"I forgot protection."

But what if he produced a box of a hundred condoms? And even if he hadn't brought a stash, Cancún, the love nest of Mexico, probably sold them by the case. For all she knew, the maids might leave packages on the pillows at night along with the chocolates.

"I'm not allowed to sleep with you because of the show."

Yeah, right. Like he'd believe that.

"I had too much to drink and want the first time to be really special."

She could hear his sultry reply—"Honey, I'll make sure it's special."

"I'm allergic to sand."

"I'll spread a towel down on the beach."

Sophie's cell phone rang, cutting off her inner diatribe. She glanced at the number and grimaced. Her mother. Was Deseree in trouble again? Had she been arrested? Or did she need more money?

Willing herself to remain calm, she clicked the button to answer. "Hello, Deseree."

"Honey, I saw your show; it was wonderful!"

Sophie merged into the exit lane in the late-evening traffic. "Thanks."

"What have you done to your hair, though? I barely recognized you."

That was the idea.

Her mother tittered on before Sophie could respond. Thank heavens.

"Chopping it off like that, dying it that stark black. I did so love your long golden locks." Deseree hesitated on a gust of expelled air, and Sophie pictured her tilting her Virginia Slims up and daintily taking a puff. Her mother was always worried about her image, always wanting to look sophisticated and demure. Odd, considering her chosen profession, or maybe that was the reason she paid such close attention.

Sophie had never quite understood Deseree. And Deseree hadn't exactly been mother material.

"I needed a change," Sophie explained, not wanting to hurt her mother's feelings by explaining that she was trying to disguise herself. The last thing she wanted was to be recognized as her old self. She had a new career, a new start in life.

Sophie's secrets were not to be revealed.

"And that man you chose, wow, I haven't seen biceps like that since Larry Filch."

Her mother's on and off live-in lover during Sophie's freshman year. Sophie had marked her years in school by her mother's various boyfriends—she couldn't quite call them relationships—and her various apartments, which she couldn't quite call home.

The very reason it was so important to her to buy a house and settle down with one man.

"Yes, he's handsome," Sophie said in a guarded tone as she changed lanes. What was her mother up to? Did she want Sophie to fix her up with a man?

"I bet you're going to have a fabulous time in Cancún."

She doubted that. Not unless she got over Lance really quickly.

"Anyway, I called to see if Lucy arrived."

Her erratic sister? "Lucy's coming to see me?"

"Oh, dear, she hasn't called."

Sophie rolled her eyes, then braked for a red light. Was Deseree actually worried about one of her offspring? Now there was a switch. "No, but I'll try her cell," Sophie said, sensing trouble. And she'd find out what mischief Lucy was up to now.

"You should see the latest moves she added to the Dazzling Diva act. Your sister has become quite the Vegas star. Everyone is talking about her, even the talent scouts."

Guilt niggled at Sophie. She had started Lucy into the showy lifestyle, but now that Sophie had gotten out, she owed it to her sister to help her do the same.

"Do you know why Lucy's coming?"

The expelling of breath signified another dramatic drag on her cigarette. "Something about that singles series you're doing. Lucy wants you to work her into one of the shows, but she'll have to explain the details."

Sophie's premonition of bad luck intensified. "Deseree, I'm almost to the airport and I need to phone Lucy before I board. I'm hanging up now."

"Wait." Fingernails tapped across a hard surface,

and Sophie's stomach tightened. That could mean only one thing: her mother had another agenda.

"Listen, hon, I hate to ask you this, but the rent is due and I'm a little pinched. Could you just spot me a few dollars? I promise I'll pay you back the end of the month."

Sophie sighed. But the fact that her mother wanted money at least meant she wasn't up to her old tricks again. That is, unless she'd taken up buying expensive presents for the new man in her life.

Did Sophie really want to know? No.

"All right, I'll put a check in the mail from the airport."

"Thanks, honey. You and Lucy have fun next week. And enjoy your romantic weekend. Don't do anything I wouldn't do."

Her mother's parting words echoed in Sophie's mind, resurrecting memories of her childhood. *Don't do anything I wouldn't do.*

As if there were anything her mother *wouldn't* do.

Sophie grimaced and hung up, then punched in Lucy's number. Deseree was definitely trouble, suddenly trying to ensconce herself in Sophie's and Lucy's lives after being virtually absent all those years.

And Lucy, lovable as she was, exploded through life like a train wreck. Sophie's only hope was to talk to her little sister and try to circumvent disaster before things snowballed out of hand.

But first, she had to find out exactly what scheme Lucy had up her sleeve this time. . . .

Lance had already torn out the back door and checked for termite damage, then covered it with polyurethane in case it rained. Tomorrow he'd pick up the supplies he needed to replace the door casings. He wiped his neck with a towel. It must be a hundred degrees outside.

What was Sophie doing? Lying on the sugar-white sandy beaches of Cancún with the hulk? Letting him rub sunscreen all over her silky bare skin and getting sand in all the wrong places? Joining the nude sunbathers at the adult beach so they could gawk at her voluptuous figure?

Worse, once Sophie had sucked the hulk into her web of desire, would she decide he was worthy of a walk down the aisle?

He cursed a blue streak, banning the images from his mind as he attacked the master suite bathroom. He did not care if Sophie wound up marrying the hulk.

No, not one bit.

Marriage gave him the willies. Why, at Maddie and Chase's, he'd had to take antacids to keep his breakfast down. And owning a house was another trap—his own parents had been so in debt with their own when they'd died that Lance had had to forgo college in an effort to work, take care of Maddie and Reid, and get the house in good enough condition to sell.

Jazzy loped up beside him and glared down her pink nose, green eyes scrutinizing. He ignored the cat and ripped at the pipes with a vengeance. He'd focus on completing these renovations as quickly as possible and avoid her as well. He might not want marriage, but he couldn't help but *want* Sophie in other ways.

What man with any degree of testosterone wouldn't want Sophie Lane?

The way her big eyes danced with mischief screamed sex appeal. And though he normally preferred long hair, the way that short spiked black hair swirled around her ivory skin made him itch to claw his hands in it and muss it up. And those voluptuous breasts . . . God, they would swell in his hands. . . .

He turned the wrench with gusto, but a screw fell out and the pipe cracked, then literally broke in two in his hands. "Blast it all to hell."

The cat screeched and darted out of the way, skidding on the floor as she barreled around the corner. Water gushed out, pelting Lance in the face and drenching his clothes.

He fought the onslaught and reached down to turn off the water, frowning when he noticed the pipe had already been welded in three different places. Someone had done a shoddy job of temporarily glossing over the earlier damage to the house, most likely to make the sale. What other cosmetic repairs had been done to the place to hide major problems?

It reminded him of most marriages he knew. All appeared well on the surface but who knew what problems lay below. Take his parents' relationship. His father had been a well-known doctor, his mother a doctor's wife. They had both seemed happy.

Then they'd died.

His life had been snapped in two. He had been afraid the courts would put Maddie and Reid into some foster home, so he'd taken over the responsibility of raising them, but he'd been young himself.

Of course Maddie and Chase seemed happy. But their relationship was still in the honeymoon phase. Once that passed . . .

He didn't want to think about it. And he couldn't imagine himself married. He'd probably only disappoint Sophie if he got involved with her.

She'd want sophisticated, the jet-setter type. And he was nothing but a homeboy, a construction worker/developer who liked working with his hands, not hobnobbing in front of a camera.

The fact that she'd use her own date as a TV show proved they weren't compatible. She would make a spectacle out of her personal relationship with Rory in front of thousands for everyone to see.

Including him.

Which absolutely proved that a relationship between him and Sophie would never work. If he ever chose to get romantic with a woman, he wouldn't make a public spectacle of himself or their relationship. He'd woo her in subtle, simple ways. She wouldn't need a cameraman or voters on her Web site to tell her he was the one.

She'd know it every time he touched her.

Sophie tried to call Lucy on her cell phone, while she maneuvered her car through the traffic. Her diet Coke sloshed on the console, and she swiped at it, grateful when her little sister answered. Lucy was breathless and laughing as if she weren't alone. It sounded like Lucy was doing better in the love department than she was.

"Lucy, sorry if this is a bad time, but I'm on my way to the airport. Deseree said you were coming to Savannah."

"I am. Listen, Sophie, I have a new business on the side, and I want you to plug it on your show."

Oh, gracious, what was her sister into this month? "You're not taking the Diva act on the road?"

A man's teasing voice echoed in the background. "No, but that's not a bad idea."

"It's a terrible idea; I told you to think about something more reputable. Dancing may be fun now, but as you get older it'll get old, too. Aren't you tired of men gaping at you, thinking you're easy just because you dance?"

"I'm only twenty-six, not an old lady like you." Lucy was nothing if not a smart aleck. "And I don't think I'll ever get tired of men gaping at me."

Sophie ignored her sister's barb about her being old. The big three-oh left plenty of time for fun and men, but she had to be responsible, too. The man's husky purr sounded louder, as if he had moved closer to the phone. Surely her sister wouldn't have answered if she were in bed.... "Lucy, who is that guy?"

"Oh, it's just Elvin; he's helping me dress for the show."

The nude dancer from the Pleasure Palace? He'd looked like a druggie to Sophie. "Please don't tell me that you and Elvin are involved."

"No, of course not. We just like to have fun together. You do remember how to have fun, don't you, Soph?"

"Of course I do." Sophie pinched her eyes together and bit her tongue. Her big-sister lectures would fall on deaf ears. "Deseree said something about you adding new moves to the act. You're not stripping, are you?"

Lucy's laughter bubbled over the line. "No, Soph, but if I did, it wouldn't be a big deal."

"Yes, it would; you're not going to strip."

"Okay, then I need to make my new business work."

Lucy logic. "All right, tell me about this new venture or whatever it is."

"Well, last week I went to this thing called a Sleepover party and I decided to sell their products. My gosh, the discounts I get on the merchandise will make it worthwhile."

A car horn blasted, drowning out half of Lucy's words, and Sophie skimmed the shoulder, trying to avoid hitting the Land Rover. Lucy had said something about sleeping over at a party? "What are you talking about?"

"It's like selling Tupperware. You have home parties and demonstrate the items for sale. It's so much fun!"

"You're going to sell Tupperware?" Now, that she had to see.

"No, it's not Tupperware. It's gifts for singles."

Hmm, like aromatherapy products, CDs?

"Romantic gifts," Lucy continued.

"Like cards and bubble bath?"

"Er, yeah, we have cards and bubble bath and candles, among other things to enhance a relationship."

"Well, that does sound like it might work for the show."

"I know! Think of the great advertising."

"But why come here?"

"Because two of the girls here have the local market cornered, and you're featuring the singles series. It'll be the perfect way for me to launch into a new territory."

Sophie steered into the airport parking lot, then hopped out, holding the phone to her ear with her shoulder as she grabbed her suitcase. Static cut in, clogging the connection just as a plane took off with a roar over her head. "I'm losing you, Lucy, but you can come, on one condition."

"I knew you'd agree."

"Only if you promise not to mention the Diva act, or that I was ever a part of it."

Lucy whistled over the phone. "Are you sure you

don't want to let people know? You were a star in Vegas, Soph. Fans still remember you here."

Exactly what she wanted to avoid. "I'm positive. I have a new career now. If the press gets wind of my past life, it could ruin things for me."

"All right," Lucy agreed. "My lips are sealed."

"Good, you'd better keep them that way." Sophie hung up, checked her watch, and jogged toward the terminal. If she didn't rush she'd miss her plane.

Not that she was anxious to be with Rory, but she couldn't miss the date or her TV version of her romantic getaway wouldn't air. Then Lance Summers would never know what he had missed.

And she definitely intended to show him what a wonderful time she had had without him.

Even if her face cracked in two from all the phony smiling.

Chapter Four

Lance tossed and turned all night on Sophie's lumpy sofa, wishing he'd let one of his hired hands handle this renovation job, but for some reason he hadn't wanted to relinquish the project to anyone else. Maybe he didn't trust them to preserve the historical details. Or maybe he was afraid one of his work crew would wind up in Sophie's bed.

No. Sophie had nothing to do with it. He liked doing renovations; that was how he'd gotten his start in the business.

He rolled sideways, wincing as a pain shot through his lower back. Sophie's four-poster queen-size bed beckoned. It had to be more comfortable than the faded sofa, which was too short for his legs and too hard on his lumbar region. But her room also smelled like Sophie, and he could not imagine sliding between her sheets without imagining sliding Sophie beneath him, and that was not going to happen tonight or any other time in this century.

Damn it, he couldn't sleep, and he had to have at

least eight hours or he'd be a bear tomorrow. It was hot as Hades in the house, too, almost as bad as outdoors. Once he'd replaced the flooring and roofing, he'd have to check the air conditioner. A rumbling sound from the attic made him jerk his head up. Ghosts? No, old wiring, faulty plumbing, that psycho cat. The wind maybe?

Was the wind blowing in Cancún? He wiped at a bead of sweat on his face. Was it as hot on the beach as it was in her house?

The image of Sophie entwined in his arms set him to pacing, the uncomfortable couch forgotten as he prowled from one end of the room to the other. Was she in bed with Rory Dalton now? Letting the hulk run his stubby hands all over her delicate body, teasing her until she came apart in his arms? Playing naked and getting hot and sweaty with the waves crashing in the background as she cried out in orgasm?

He stopped and threw his hands over his head, trying to drown out the images.

A low whistling sound echoed from above, giving him pause again. Was someone in the house? He climbed the steps, glanced in the spare bedroom which was empty, then crossed the hall to Sophie's bedroom. Darkness swallowed the room, moonlight spilling in through the sheers draped from the ceiling to the faded carpet. He hoped Sophie would want to rip up the ugly carpet and showcase the original flooring.

He stepped forward, intending to examine it, but halted at the sight of that big black furball sprawled in the center of the magnificent bed. The furry animal lifted its head and hissed at him, claws bared (declawed or not, they looked ominous), teeth shining white in the dim moonlight.

Lance backed away, knowing he couldn't trespass into Sophie's territory with her feline protector armed, ready to pounce and do him bodily damage. Jazzy obviously didn't like him. Or maybe the house was haunted, as he'd once heard, and the whistling sound was the ghost, and the cat was reacting to it, not him. Animals were supposed to be able to sense ghosts.

The idea was ridiculous.

But the very first time he'd come to see Sophie here, she'd mentioned the legend of the star-crossed lovers. Legend claimed that during the Civil War, an injured soldier took refuge inside these walls. After the woman of the house had doctored the soldier's injuries, she'd taken him as her lover. But the soldier had been called back to war, and she'd never seen him again. Her anguished ghost supposedly roamed the house, waiting for him to return. . . .

Lance did not believe in star-crossed lovers. Maybe he didn't believe in love at all.

Reminding himself that the next day loomed with more backbreaking labor, he headed down the staircase, crossed to the sofa, stretched out, and closed his eyes.

An hour later he lay staring at the ceiling, counting the cracks and watching a spider spin a web in the left-hand corner. If he were at his apartment, he'd be sleeping like a baby. Or would the phone be ringing from that singles service? When he'd stopped by earlier, the message machine had been blinking out of control, the messages all from husband-hunting women.

He had never had insomnia in his life. Construction work, especially hands-on physical labor, normally wore him out.

Was the hulk wearing out Sophie now? Keeping

her awake with long, slow kisses? When they returned to Savannah, would Dalton try to move in on Sophie for good, make a permanent place in Sophie's bed for himself?

Would her cat like Dalton and allow *him* to venture into Sophie's bedroom?

His Southern, big-brotherly breeding kicked in. Maybe he should do something. After all, Sophie was Maddie's best friend; he'd hate to see anything bad happen to her. And some men did take advantage. . . .

I wouldn't go out with you if you were the last man on earth.

Her words tormented him.

And Maddie had doomed him further with her comment: *My brother needs help in the romance department.*

He closed his eyes, praying for sleep to claim him and end the torture, but images of Sophie in that sexy red negligee she'd left on her bed played behind his eyelids in the dark.

"I still can't believe we're here," Rory said in a husky whisper.

Sophie nodded and sipped her champagne. Cancún meant moonlit beaches, white powdery sand, the summer breeze blowing gently off the ocean, strains of piano music floating through the sultry air scented by tropical vegetation, and gourmet meals served by candlelight with endless complimentary wine—essentially, the resort was the most romantic place Sophie had ever seen.

Unfortunately her bones possessed no romantic inclinations at the moment.

Especially toward Rory Dalton, with the multiple hands and one-track mind.

"Smile for the camera."

Rory pulled her into an embrace and they posed. Sophie donned a smile that she hoped fooled everyone who would watch the show. They finished their wine, Rory toasting the trip, she praying it would soon be over. They had already sipped margaritas at sunset, taken a romantic stroll along the sandy shore, been serenaded by a Spanish quartet, enjoyed the evening show, and dined overlooking the majestic waters in the open-air pavilion.

"How about a dance?" His floral green shirt shimmered beneath a full moon that was meant for lovers. That, or werewolves ready to feed on the innocent.

Not that Sophie was completely innocent.

He caressed her neck, nibbling at her earlobe. Sophie told herself the camera was rolling, that Lance would see this footage and think she was having the time of her life, completely *over* him, and that nothing obscene could happen in the middle of a crowded dance floor in the outdoors.

Rory pulled her into his arms, but the scent of his cologne hung as heavy in the air as his testosterone. The man must be part ape. Sweat beaded on his forehead, dark hair escaped through the opening in the top of his Floridian shirt, and he had been salivating for the last hour. She should toss him a bone, but didn't want to lead the man on.

"Sophie, thanks for giving me the opportunity to share this trip with you."

He really was being nice, Sophie reasoned. It wasn't his fault she had been stupid enough to want Lance. Maybe she was being overly cynical.

"You're welcome; you won fair and square, Rory."

"I'm totally taken with you; you know that, don't you?"

She feigned laughter, playing along. "Where did you go to charm school?"

He pressed his body into hers, the force of his arousal punctuating the fact that he was all male, and that she might have misjudged his charm for a come-on. His hands slipped from her waist to cup her butt, and she tensed, another smile tightening her mouth as she offered a fake smile to the camera.

"This is the most exotic place I've even been," she said, hoping to turn the conversation to tourist mode. "The waves crashing in the background, the scents of flowers floating around us, the balmy air . . ."

He licked her neck, his pointed tongue circling her breastbone as he dipped lower. "If you think this is erotic, let's go back to my room."

Oh, gracious, he thought she'd said *erotic*?

"Er, Rory—"

"I can do things to you, baby, you've only dreamed about."

With another man. "I do believe you're working the camera." Sophie swayed as he spun her around, brushing his fingertips across the tips of her breasts in the process. He was nothing if not a smooth mover.

His sultry gaze lingered on her cleavage. "Will they join us later or will we be alone?"

His cocky boldness amazed her. "Excuse me?"

"If you want the cameras along, that's fine. If not, well . . . that's all right, too." His finger snaked out to trace a sensual line over her lip. "Either way, I promise to satisfy."

Sophie fought the urge to bite his finger. "We have a long weekend, Rory; let's not rush things."

His smile faltered slightly, but he recovered quickly. The man was accustomed to playing the game and winning. "All right. For now, I'll have to be content to hold you in my arms. But tonight I'll dream about finally getting you alone."

Sophie remembered Maddie's rules for trapping a man and wished she had brought flannel instead of this strapless red sundress. Worse, so far Maddie's rules were working with Rory—the more she dangled the bait in front of Rory and yanked it back, the more Rory chased it.

First thing Saturday morning, Lance had ordered a roofing crew over to check out Sophie's house. The sooner he finished with this place, the sooner he could get some shut-eye.

He had not slept a wink the night before.

And for a man who'd always been able to fall asleep standing up, that was criminal. He'd counted sheep until dawn, then made coffee, met the plumber at six, and had ripped up all the cracked tiles from both bathroom floors by noon. By two o'clock, he had replaced the subflooring, by three he was sweating bullets and irritable as hell. Then Maddie burst through the doorway, chattering and making his head spin as he tried to keep up with her.

"What are you doing here?" he finally asked between breaths.

"I came to feed Jazzy. I promised Sophie I'd check on her while she was gone."

The cat glared at him, tail swishing like a windshield wiper blade. "Uh, I guess I could do that, since I'm staying here anyway."

"You're sweet to offer, Lance, but I didn't think you liked cats."

"I like 'em fine." Except this one didn't like him. "Where did you find it, anyway?"

Maddie frowned, then stooped and picked up the

black furball. "Poor baby was scrounging for food near one of the unfinished houses on Skidaway."

And Maddie couldn't resist bringing her home.

Maddie glanced at her watch. "Oh, my gosh, look at the time. *Sophie Knows* airs any second. They're doing a special Saturday show just so we can watch Sophie's date."

As if he'd forgotten. "I guess you'd better run along then."

Maddie's eyes veered toward the TV mischievously. "But I don't want to miss it." She grabbed one of Sophie's diet Cokes from the refrigerator, then teetered toward the television set as if she owned the room, and plopped into the faded recliner with the cat purring in her lap. "Actually, I'll watch it here. My next appointment isn't for an hour, and it's around the corner. It'll be faster than driving all the way home and backtracking."

"Of course." Lance grunted, wondering what exactly Maddie was up to. Did she plan to tease him by making him watch Sophie's date on TV?

He stormed into the kitchen to begin repairs, refusing to give her the pleasure. But seconds later the head of the roofing crew called for him, so he ambled back to advise the workers on the job. He couldn't help but glance over at the television. And then he couldn't look away.

Sophie, decked out in a bright silver string bikini that left little to the imagination, was running along the most beautiful beach he'd ever seen, the sun kissing her silky porcelain skin, the wind tossing that short black hair around her face, while Rory Dalton chased her across the white sand.

Laughter spilled through the speakers as Rory tackled her from behind. His big hairy hands slid down Sophie's bare back as he cradled her in his arms and they hit the ground. Sophie squealed and pretended to battle for air, her cries for him to stop tickling her causing Lance's stomach to knot.

The camera skimmed past them for a second to feast on a distant beach as the newscaster commented, "Right now, Mr. Dalton is trying to persuade our own Sophie Lane to stroll down to the nude beach, folks. Will she give in and shed that bikini, or will modesty convince her to bask in the sun, where our cameras can capture her every movement?"

Lance silently cursed. While the thought of Sophie on the nude beach with the hulk sent him into fits, the thought of watching her every movement scantily clad and teasing Dalton to undress her with her racy laughter and flirty smile was just as painful.

Modesty was not a problem for Sophie Lane. Hell, no. Hadn't Sophie dragged his innocent little sister off to a nudist colony for the weekend before she'd married Chase? Hadn't she fixed Maddie up with the producer of an S-and-M show?

The woman definitely wasn't modest. If so, she'd cover up her near nakedness with a beach wrap.

"They look like they're having so much fun," Maddie commented. "He's such a hottie."

Lance flexed his muscles beneath his dirt-covered jeans and water-splattered workshirt. He wasn't exactly out of shape himself. But maybe he should work out more.

"When I get home, I'm going to vote on whether or not they'll make it."

He cleared his throat to speak, but the cat quirked beady eyes toward him.

"Do you think Sophie and Rory will wind up tying the knot?"

He shrugged. His stomach was in knots; that's

what he thought. "I've got work to do." The camera flashed back to Rory, who was plucking at the tie to Sophie's string top.

"Just think, Lance," Maddie said, smiling up at him, "if you'd won the date, you could have been there, sunning and and dancing with a beautiful woman, instead of here digging up the floor and replacing pipes."

He cast her an evil look and left the room. He didn't need her derisive comments; the sewage smell reeking from his clothes and his lack of sleep were perfect reminders. And if he were chasing Sophie, he'd catch her and they'd make love, which would be fantastic—but then she'd want marriage and that would be fatal.

"Tune in Monday to see just how far Sophie and Rory take their relationship," the announcer said.

Lance cursed beneath his breath. It was going to be a long damned weekend.

If Rory Dalton didn't peel his hairy, sweaty body off of her, Sophie was going to scream.

"Smile for the camera."

How could she smile when she was running for her life? Besides, her lips felt glued to her teeth in misery.

"Come on, Soph, let's go to the nude beach. You don't want tan lines, do you?"

Sophie feigned innocence. "I can't, Rory. I have my audience to think about."

"Your audience will love you for it."

"I don't think so." She jabbed where she thought it might hit home. "You make concessions for your fans, don't you?"

He nodded, then cupped her chin in his hand. "Sure, I understand. But when this weekend is over,

I want us to really be alone. Then we won't have to worry about a cameraman or your fans."

But I still have to live with myself.

He lowered his mouth and kissed her, not giving her time to protest. Sophie tried to relax. She wasn't betraying Lance by being with another man. In fact, she should give Rory a chance, because Lance didn't want her. But nothing about Rory's kiss aroused her.

Maddie's rules flitted through her head—*Give him a nibble; then yank the line.*

She eased back and he draped his arm over her shoulder. She wasn't playing games with him, but still, her refusal to climb in bed with him so readily seemed to spike his interest.

Would her distance from Lance entice him to come around?

She and Rory walked back toward their neighboring hotel rooms. Music and laughter floated around them; two lovers lay cuddled inside a hammock by the pool, laughing softly.

Sophie's heart ached to have that connection with a man. But as she said good-night to Rory, she knew that it wouldn't happen with him.

Maybe it never would with anyone.

Lucy Lane was well aware her sister worried about her, but what the heck was all the fuss? Lucy and Sophie had managed fine on their own since they were teenagers, had shared an apartment in one of the most exciting cities in the nation, dated constantly, and had nightly tips literally coming out of their ears, er, their bras.

Then Sophie had gotten this bug up her butt that their dancing act wasn't respectable, that she wanted to have a "real" career, to get married one day, and she had run out on the show and their life in Las Vegas.

If Lucy had her way, she'd convince Sophie to return to the Vegas show. She didn't particularly want Sophie to get married either; then Lucy wouldn't see her much, and things would never be the same between them. Lucy would be alone—more alone than she was now.

She hated being alone. Hated the dark at night. Had even brought her nightlight with her.

Granted, their Diva act was thriving, and Lucy had brought down the house a few times, but she missed her sister desperately. Although she was proud of Sophie's TV show, some of her guests were a tad too conservative. She had enjoyed the "Marry Me or Move On" segment with Sophie's friend, Maddie, though, and when Chase Holloway had proposed to Maddie onstage, Lucy had bawled like a baby. The "Dating Game" episode was great, too, all those yum-licious guys to choose from. How in the world had Sophie picked just one?

The flight attendant sailed by, indicating for people to buckle their seat belts and return their seats to the upright positions. Lucy did so reluctantly, patting the arm of the man beside her. On a plane, her nerves normally bounced like a rubber ball, but this time she'd tied a lucky charm around her neck, so she felt assured they wouldn't have problems.

"Thanks for letting me nap on your shoulder."

He gave her the once-over. "Anytime."

Honestly, she loved men. They could be so . . . easy. And this one was handsome, tall, dark skinned, and blond. Norwegian-looking.

He slid a business card toward her. "I'm Ray, here on business for a few days. I'm staying at the Hamilton-Turner mansion. Call me if you get lonely."

Lucy smiled, fluffing her wild strawberry blond

curls. "Thanks, sugar. I'm here on business, too, but I intend to explore Savannah's nightlife while I'm in town."

The plane hit the runway, jerking them slightly, and they both laughed. Lucy stuffed the card into the front of her silk blouse, grinning when his eyes followed the movement. The plane ground to a halt and everyone stood, gathering their overhead luggage.

The man retrieved his briefcase, then gestured toward the silver suitcase. "This one yours?"

"Yes, my work. I didn't want to take a chance on it not making it."

"I know what you mean. I'd lose a big deal if I showed up at my meeting without the papers in my briefcase."

Lucy laughed, wondering whether to reveal her job to the man and try to make a sale. If she did show him the contents of her case, he might think she was coming on to him, and get the wrong idea.

Then again, Lucy could handle herself. Besides, it wasn't like Sophie was at home waiting on her tonight. The house would be empty. She'd let herself in when she arrived and Sophie would never know how late she'd stayed out.

Businessmen/bachelors were an untapped market for her Sleepover, Inc., parties—the perfect gift for a wife, girlfriend, lover. . . . Maybe she and Ray could see the town; then she could show him some of her products and end the night by closing a sale.

"You know, Ray, I'm staying at my sister's, but she's not home tonight. If you want, we could get a drink somewhere."

Ray raked a hand over his chin. "Sounds great. Let's grab a cab and go down to River Street. I've heard there's great food and blues and jazz music."

Lucy latched onto his arm and they headed toward baggage claim, her body thrumming with excitement. Maybe while she was here, she'd shake up Sophie and make her realize singlehood was much better than getting married.

"Check out that knockout strawberry blonde with the tight ass," Reid said. "Wow, does she have some moves."

Lance grabbed the beer mug and glanced up, his eyes widening at the sight of the voluptuous woman writhing and gyrating to the music. Her spandex top and tight jeans would have to be peeled off of her. "Not my type, but go for it, brother."

"I would, but she came with that blond guy." Reid leaned back against the bar and scouted out the rest of the room. "Man, think what Chase is missing. I can't imagine giving up all this."

Lance nodded, although his head was pounding from the loud music, and the smoke was clogging up his nose.

He must be getting old. The dating scene felt odd, too, as if he'd gotten trapped in a wind tunnel that kept hurling him around and around in a circle. He was getting nowhere, still at the same place in his personal life as he had been at twenty.

"I'm going to check out that brunette in the red dress." Reid gestured toward a corner table, where two women sat sipping Cosmopolitans. "You interested in the one beside her?"

Lance shook his head. He'd heard her nasally voice when she'd passed him coming in. She must have a permanent sinus infection.

In fact, they'd been here for two hours, and he hadn't spotted one female yet in the entire room who appealed to him.

The strawberry blonde with the wild curly hair flitted past with her Norwegian-looking partner and Lance frowned, thinking she reminded him of someone, though he couldn't place who. He studied her as she and the man claimed a back booth. The man said something; then her peal of laughter floated over the sound of the music. She was Reid's type— flirty, fun-loving, and fancy-free.

He sipped the rest of the beer, hoping the alcohol would help him sleep tonight. He'd get an early start tomorrow, and install Sophie's new back door before she arrived home. Deciding to call it a night, he flicked a hand at Reid to wish him good luck, then headed out the door, but a commotion in the back drew his attention, and he hesitated. The security guard was standing over that strawberry blonde's table. She stood with her hands splayed on her hips, giving him hell. Some kind of silver case lay on the table.

He chuckled, grateful again that Maddie was safe and out of trouble. If that girl had an older brother or sister, they had their hands full.

Three hours later he lay on the sofa in Sophie's den again, counting the cracks in the ceiling in the dark, once again straining for sleep, but every time he closed his eyes he imagined Sophie in that string bikini with Rory Dalton's hand taking it off. He had already heated warm milk and tried that remedy, but he'd nearly gagged on the stuff. Then he'd tried some herbal tea he'd found in Sophie's too-orderly pantry—she really was an organizer, he realized when he'd noticed she shelved the items alphabetically—but he scalded his tongue and now it was numb.

A screeching sound erupted into the silence and he jerked up, scanning the interior. The cat? No,

Jazzy was upstairs, staked out on Sophie's bed again as if to dare him to enter her private territory.

Another sound, more like something sliding across wood, echoed from outside. The rocking chair being moved on the porch? Footsteps clattered next. He tiptoed to the sitting room and noticed the window sliding up. *Shit.* Sophie had a burglar.

He glanced around for the phone and something to use for protection. The phone was in the other room, but a two-by-four lay in the corner. He grabbed it, poised to fight, when suddenly the person pitched a silver suitcase through the window. It hit the floor with a thud, the latch sprang open, the contents spilled and rolled across the hardwood. Next, a body dove headfirst through the window, a hand raked around empty air for a place to land, and the person toppled onto the floor in a tangle of arms and legs, squeals flying from her. One high-heeled shoe sailed through the air and barely missed his nose.

"What the hell?" He hit the light, the piece of wood at the ready, and gaped at the leggy strawberry blonde with the wild hair—it was the same strawberry blonde he'd noticed earlier at the bar causing trouble. Had she followed him here to rob him?

She saw him and screamed at the top of her lungs. Swinging her fists at his legs to take him down, she caught his ankle. He yelped, dropped the wooden beam, and collapsed onto the floor, cradling his aching shin. Good Lord, the woman had nearly broken his leg.

She was spitting and cursing and flailing her fists at him. "Help, burglar! Help!"

He winced as her claws dug into his ankle, then grabbed her arms and pinned them to her sides.

"Why the hell are you screaming? *You* broke in!"

She stilled slightly and stared up at him, eyes wide with terror and temper. He loosened his grip. "Who are you?"

"Who are you?"

"I asked first."

Her lower lip quivered slightly. "I'm Sophie's sister, Lucy."

Sister? No wonder he'd thought the woman from the bar seemed familiar. They had the same dainty nose, the same fiery good looks, barring the hair color, the same great bod, but this one had a peculiar odor. . . .

"What's that smell?"

Lucy turned up her nose. "My lucky charm—it's garlic and a few natural herbs."

She was certifiable.

"Now, mister, if you don't release me, I'm going to scream bloody murder and grab your balls and twist 'em until they fall off."

Laughter sputtered from him, but the fierce wildcat eyes told him she'd try to fulfill her threat. He braced himself for control, difficult since he was running on forty-eight hours without sleep. "My name is Lance Summers. I'm the contractor your sister hired to renovate her house."

"Oh." She relaxed slightly, her eyes skating over him, recognition dawning. "Weren't you that guy who gave the dorky answers on her show, too?"

He gritted his teeth. Had everyone in the United States watched that ridiculous episode? "Yes."

"You need to work on your approach," she said, offering up a sweet smile as her gaze dropped to his hands where they still gripped her.

He released her and stood, then offered her a hand. "And you need to learn to use the door."

"I forgot my key."

"You could have knocked."

"I didn't think anyone was home."

Right. He explained his reasons for sacking out on the couch while she stooped to gather her suitcase. He had assumed they were her personal things, but he suddenly realized that the suitcase had been filled with sex toys. A rubber dildo had rolled to a stop beside his feet, a fake set of plastic boobs sat with jiggling nipples jutting heavenward in the corner, and chocolate-scented underwear fringed with licorice had caught on the lamp, looking oddly out of place next to the Victorian shade.

Of course, the phone chose that time to ring. He glanced in the den, then realized it wasn't the home phone. Lucy dug around in her mammoth purse, extracted a cell phone, and flipped it open just as he spoke.

"You can't stay here," he said. "I'll take you to a hotel."

Lucy gave him an odd look, then said into the phone, "Oh, hey, Soph. I just got here." She shoved a mass of hair from her eyes. "No, you heard right. Your contractor just offered to take me to a hotel."

Chapter Five

Sophie clutched the phone in horror, reminders of her past life with Lucy-on-the-prowl floating back. Not that she blamed her little sister for attracting men—lust and Lucy were synonymous. But still, her baby sister possessed a naive innocence, and Sophie had lost boyfriends to luscious Lucy before, and Lance was . . . Lance.

Damn it.

She cleared her throat to find her voice. "You're going to a hotel with Lance?"

"No." Lucy's voice sounded shaky. "After all, I just met the man. In fact, he attacked me when I came in."

"Lance attacked you?"

"Yes, well, actually I sort of fell all over him, but I couldn't help myself."

Sophie gulped. Of course she couldn't. Lance was big and strong and masculine and the sexiest man she'd ever laid her eyes on. Lucy would think the same.

"I had a few drinks earlier," Lucy babbled, "and later I danced with this cute salesguy I met on the plane, but then this security guard thought I was soliciting at the club; I mean, I only gave out a few business cards—"

Typical Lucy story, Ping-Ponging all over the place. "Did you say soliciting?"

"Can you imagine? Then I offered to give him some freebies from my kit, and the imbecile thought I was trying to bribe him."

Oh, heavens, add bribing a cop to the charges. "Lucy, you weren't arrested, were you?" She envisioned the headlines now: *Sophie Lane's Sister Arrested for Prostitution—Like Mother, Like Daughter.*

"No, of course not. I explained that I was showing off the stuff in my new kit to this man in the booth—"

"What man in the booth?"

"The hunky Norwegian one."

"I'm not sure I want to hear any more."

"It was perfectly innocent. Besides, there weren't any 'No soliciting' signs at the club."

"What club? What kit?"

"The . . . club, and the kit from Sleepover, Inc., party goods."

Why would the cop think Lucy was bribing him with aromatheraphy candles and lotion?

A big yawn stretched over the line; then Lucy giggled. "Don't be shy, Lance; go ahead and feel my boob if you want."

Sophie rubbed her temple where a headache pulsed. "What?"

"I told him to feel—"

"I heard that!" Sophie pinched her fingers over the bridge of her nose. "But why did you tell him to feel it?"

"Because he's staring at it," Lucy said on a sigh. "He might as well touch it if he's going to gape at it."

"Lucy, are you doing drugs?"

"Of course not."

"You're drunk then."

"Maybe a little tipsy." Her voice grew hushed. "Go ahead, Lance, play with it if you want. It's really firm."

"Lucy!"

"Well, he'll never buy it if he doesn't touch it and see how perky it is."

Sophie groaned. "Put Lance on the phone."

Lucy heaved another sigh. "All right, but ten more minutes, and I would have had him."

Just what she was afraid of.

Lucy would seduce Lance, then blab all of Sophie's secrets. . . .

Lance gripped the phone, his stomach plummeting as he realized how Lucy's one-sided comments must have sounded. He'd been too poleaxed by the sight of all this . . . paraphernalia to hear the first part. Lucy had explained about her toy box, hadn't she?

Did Sophie approve of her little sister carting around such outrageous stuff?

"Sophie—"

"Listen here, Lance Summers," Sophie lit into him without giving him a chance to speak, "if you lay one finger on my baby sister, I'll come back there and rip out your eyes."

He swallowed hard. One sister wanted his balls, the other his eyes. He'd be dismembered before they finished with him. "Your *baby* sister is the one throwing her boobs all over the place. You should be talking to her, not to me."

"Don't you dare put this off on her. She said you were looking at them."

He glanced at the floor where the fake boobs still lay, springy and perky and too damn real-looking for comfort. "How can I not? They're huge and . . . all pink. . . ." *And those nipples look so real. . . .*

Sophie's loud hiss echoed over the line, like a rattlesnake spitting poison. "I can't believe you're so crude. I really misjudged you."

Him? What had he done wrong? He'd been trying to sleep on her lumpy, too-short couch in her stifling-hot den while she was cavorting half-naked with strangers. . . . "Listen, Sophie—"

"You are not taking her to a hotel room, do you understand?"

"I was simply trying to be a gentleman, considering her safety."

"Safety? The only way she'll be safe is if you leave her alone."

"I won't leave her alone here." How could he with the door missing? Any Tom, Dick, or serial killer could walk in off the streets and kill her. And what if that man from the bar had followed her? They'd practically been humping onstage.

Static cut in over the line and Lance shook the phone, annoyed. "Are there any other siblings I should worry about dropping in?"

"No." Their mother probably decided Lucy was trouble enough. "By the way, someone named Deseree called; she sounded very interested in your weekend date." Not that he was fishing for information . . .

"Deseree called?"

"Yes. Who is she anyway?"

"Er . . . she runs a charity that I donate to regularly. I'll phone her back." Her last words came out garbled; then he heard, "Remember, Lance, forget the hotel. And keep your hands off Lucy."

He glanced at Lucy, who had knelt and was carefully organizing nude playing cards, body liqueurs, and edible G-strings in her silver case as if they were gold. Keeping his hands off her would not be a problem. The girl was a walking nutcase.

But where would Sophie's hands be while he was playing guardian to her little sister? And how dare she accuse him of trying to seduce Lucy?

What kind of man did she think he was?

The next day Sophie climbed into the limo to go to the airport. Lance Summers was the most infuriating man she had ever known. He'd rattled her so, she'd even resorted to lying about her own mother.

How had she misjudged him so badly?

Maddie.

Lance was her best friend's brother, so she had listened to Maddie's unbridled descriptions of how Lance had sacrificed for her and Reid, how he'd forgone college and started his own business to pay off debts, and Sophie had thought they shared a kinship. After all, she'd practically raised her little sister, too. She'd had to be the responsible one. She'd had to take jobs she hadn't wanted to take. The soul mate she'd sensed in Lance must have been a figment of her imagination.

Sucker.

While she was on vacation, he was in her house. Planting his scent. Making friends with her cat. Touching her things.

Lusting after Lucy.

She was never going on vacation again. Even though it had been bright and sunny with crystal-clear skies, a cloud of doom had settled over her.

She'd desperately tried to reach Deseree after she'd hung up with Lance the night before. What would she do if her mother suddenly showed up on her doorstep?

How had things gone awry in such a short time? While she'd been hundreds of miles away on a beautiful island with romantic music, heavenly breezes, and a testosterone-laden man ready to sweep her under the junipers for a gritty night of lovemaking, an earthquake had cropped up at home.

Worse, she couldn't circumvent the explosion because she was having too damned much fun. . . .

"Smile for the camera."

She resisted the urge to glare at the annoying cameraman, but Rory plastered a shit-eating grin on his face. Her smile had been frozen in place all day and felt as stiff and fragile as peanut brittle, while he'd had the time of his life, or so he kept claiming. They had snorkeled, sunbathed, Jet Skied, taken a tour of the Mayan ruins, wined and dined, and now, thank God, were on their way to the airport. For goodness' sake, she had even set her watch an hour early to avoid his last-minute attempt to frolic by the sea and get sand in all the wrong places.

She inhaled sharply to calm herself and leaned back against the plush leather seats with a diet Coke while Rory helped himself to the champagne bar. One plane ride and she would be at home, free of his smothering attention. But then she'd have to deal with Lucy's next adventure, her mother's ongoing saga of dramas, and the renovations to her house, sans Lance if she could arrange it.

But she still had a week's worth of the singles series to air. She twisted her hands around her glass and watched the coast rush by as she mentally planned the week. Monday: scenes from the various dates with all the couples. They'd hash over their first impressions. Tuesday: visitors from various singles/matchmaking services in the area. Wednesday: an episode on speed dating, the new concept of meeting in a room, rotating from table to table to interview someone for five minutes, then deciding if you wanted a date with them. Thursday: the social scene hot spots followed by Lucy and her new venture. And Friday: long-lost lovers.

Lucy's debut worried her the most. She had to find out more about Lucy's products.

Then the show was doing a special on mothers for Mother's Day. The June lineup proved to be just as depressing, with special features on June weddings and brides. A snore rippled from the seat beside her and she glanced at Rory, willing herself to see him as husband material. It didn't happen.

His head had fallen back, his mouth was hanging open, his tongue lolled to the side. Maybe he would sleep on the plane, too, and she could avoid any more kissy-kissy.

The driver pulled into the airport and parked near the entrance. "Here we are, Miss Lane."

Rory jerked awake and rubbed his chin where drool dripped (the hairy man was always sweating or drooling), then extended a hand to help her from the limo. She forced another gracious smile as she allowed him to escort her inside. Maybe she should have gone into acting instead of hostessing a talk show.

If she had convinced everyone she'd had a great time this weekend, she was ready for the big time.

Three sleepless nights now, and Lance stared at the new door he'd supposedly ordered, disgusted that he'd been shipped the wrong one. Obviously he couldn't do anything right. After he'd hung up with Sophie the night before, he'd phoned Reid to ask him to stop by and baby-sit Lucy with him, but his phone call had interrupted a night of hot sex between Reid and another woman. For a second Lance had been envious, but unfortunately the only woman he wanted to sleep with was in Cancún with another man.

Reid, looking for an excuse to escape any morning-after awkwardness, had leaped at the chance to come over and ogle another woman. Especially when Lance had mentioned that Sophie's sister was the knockout strawberry blonde with the tight ass Reid had fawned over at the bar earlier.

Of course, Lance had seen his brother's unadulterated look of lust when he'd walked through the door and spotted Lucy in her fluorescent pink T-shirt (it doubled as a nightgown, she announced), and Lance had realized the flaw in his plan. So he'd spent the better part of the night staying awake to make sure Reid behaved, and Lucy remained tucked safely upstairs with Sophie's psycho cat, who still hated him but adored his brother.

Now Reid had taken Lucy for a ride to show her the projects they'd recently built on Skidaway Island. At least, he'd better be showing her the houses and nothing more. Thank God, Lucy had left her silver case here at Sophie's.

Lance rubbed his tired eyes, then hauled the door to his truck. The warehouse where he ordered supplies was closed on Sunday, so he'd have to wait until Monday to pick up the new one. This morning he'd replaced the piping in the downstairs powder room so it was functional. He attacked the retiling project next. Maybe by the time Sophie returned he'd have her bathrooms accessible.

Ironic that while she'd been off gallivanting around nude beaches with another man, he'd had his head stuck in her bathroom plumbing.

Lucy twisted a strand of her hair around one finger as she watched Reid Summers describe the houses he and his brother had built on Skidaway Island. He had the biggest, sexiest hands.

She had always loved hands. Hands and feet and long toes on a man. Did Reid have long toes?

"Most of the estate homes are on five acres," Reid pointed out.

"My gosh, these are mansions. The owners must be rich."

"Most of them are; a lot of folks retire here. There's a section in back with smaller lots. We'll head that way." Reid maneuvered the Tahoe down the road toward the last phase of the development. "Lance and I work together on the construction. Chase Holloway, our brother-in-law, is the architect. My sister, Maddie, has a decorating service and furnished the interiors."

"It must be fun to work together. Sophie . . ." She itched to mention that she and Sophie had worked together, but remembered her promise not to talk about the Diva act. Pooh on Sophie for making her lie. "Uh, Sophie's show . . . I saw Chase and Maddie get married on Sophie's show."

"Yeah, they did." Reid gave her a wary grin, then shifted in his seat as if she'd produced a rope to hang him.

The M-word must be taboo. Hadn't Sophie mentioned that he and his brother had a bachelor pact? Well, he needn't worry. Marriage was the *last* thing on her mind. Lucy didn't intend to settle down; she didn't want to limit herself to one man. Although

Sophie wanted that security; it was the very reason she'd bought the house. Hadn't she said something about having a thing for Lance? It certainly didn't sound as if her sister was happy with him the night before. And Lucy didn't want her sister settling down, especially in Savannah, so far away from her.

"Maddie and Chase live in that one," he said, stopping his Tahoe in front of a long, winding drive that led to a smaller Southern plantation home.

"Oh, my stars, it has sleeping porches. I wonder if they use those in the summer."

He shrugged. "I imagine so."

"How romantic."

Reid grinned. "They can hear the water from the river on their back porch."

"Yum."

Reid laughed and angled his head toward her. "So are you moving here, Lucy, or only in town for a visit?"

"Just here for a visit," Lucy said. "I live in Vegas."

"Really? I've always wanted to go there. You gamble a lot?"

"Not really, I . . ." Er, she wasn't supposed to mention the act. "I hostess for a club there."

"I've heard it's a wild town. All those nightclubs and showgirls."

If he only knew . . . "Yeah, I love it. All the lights, excitement."

"We have excitement around Savannah, too."

Lucy toyed with her gold loop earring. "Is that so?"

Reid's lip twitched. He was probably a player, but he was sexy and easygoing, her kind of guy.

"Really." He reached out and twisted a strand of her hair around his finger. "Maybe I could show you around."

Lucy leaned into his hand. "I'd like that, Reid." After all, Sophie had warned her not to talk about the Diva act, but her sister wouldn't care if she had a little fun with Reid Summers, would she?

It was nearly midnight when Sophie finally made it home. She dragged herself from the limo, tipped the driver, who hauled her suitcase to the front door, and fished her keys from her purse with one hand while she visually inspected the premises for intruders, as she always did when she arrived home. Force of habit from living in low-rent, low-class neighborhoods her entire life.

Everything seemed in order, although barring the kitchen light, the house was dark and Lance's Blazer still sat in the driveway. Drat. If he had seduced Lucy, she'd kill him with one of his own tools.

What if Lucy seduced him? Could she really blame Lance for giving in to her vixen sister?

Shuddering at the possibility, she pushed open the door and barreled inside, clomping her heels as loud as she could to alert them that she had arrived. Swallowing her pride was one thing; actually having to witness the man she wanted—correction: *had* wanted—naked in bed with her sister was another.

Clip-clop. Clip-clop. "Lucy, I'm home!"

She dropped the bag by the steps, hesitating at the bathroom when she noticed the new tiles. *Wow.* Lance had made noticeable strides in the renovations already. Excitement budded in her chest, and she knelt to examine the work, running her hand over the sleek white ceramic. Jazzy loped in, turned up her nose, and rubbed against Sophie as she scratched the cat's back.

"Hey, baby, I can't wait to see the house finished. All my life I dreamed of having a real home, with a white picket fence, a walk-in closet. . . ." She let the sentence trail off, adding other requirements silently—a house with nice, clean furniture, everything neat and orderly, none of the ratty furniture or beer-stained rickety sofas and cigarette-scarred cheap tables she'd grown up with. A small yard for children to run and play—

"You're home?"

She swung around on her hands and knees, and Jazzy growled. Lance stood in the doorway, his gaze glued to Sophie's butt. She instantly slapped a hand over her rear, wishing she'd forgone the decadent desserts in Cancún.

Lurching upright, she nearly smashed her knee on the toilet as she stood. Jazzy darted through Lance's feet and raced up the stairs. *Smart cat.*

Lance steadied her but she pulled away. "You shouldn't sneak up on a girl."

"Sorry. I was so busy I didn't hear you come in."

Busy doing what? She skimmed her eyes over his torso, willing herself not to react to the fact that his denim shirt had come unbuttoned (or had he just put it on?) and his rolled-up sleeves revealed muscular arms covered in a fine layer of dark hair. "You're still here at midnight?"

"Working."

Sure he was. Her gaze cut toward the kitchen behind him. "Where's Lucy?"

He chewed his lip, shifting uncomfortably. "Out with Reid."

Sophie gulped. So if Lance couldn't have her, the other brother swooped in for the kill. "Lucy's with your brother?"

He shrugged. "He took her to see the property on Skidaway Island."

"What time?"

74

"They left around noon."

Her mind ticked away the hours. "And they're not back yet?"

"He called. Lucy wanted to see the sights."

And no doubt Reid had offered to show her. Sophie paced to the front window, pushed aside the curtain, and checked the drive. "You shouldn't have let them go off together."

Lance grunted. "What do you have against Reid?"

Sophie folded her arms and swung around. "He's a Summers man. That's enough."

He grabbed her arms and forced her to look at him, but his gruff voice sounded gentle when he spoke. "Listen, I know you're upset about the dating game thing—"

"I'm not upset; I had a wonderful time with Rory."

His jaw tightened. "I realize when you called last night that you misunderstood—"

"I didn't misunderstand anything." She tried to pull away, but he held her firmly in place.

"Yes, you did. I did not offer to take Lucy to a hotel to seduce her." He pulled her through the hallway to the kitchen, then pointed to the space where the back door had once been. Plastic flapped in the breeze from the fan Lance had brought over. "I didn't think it would be safe for her to stay here without the house being secure."

Sophie winced, still unforgiving. "But you were looking at her . . . her—"

"Her boobs?"

Heat flamed her face. "Yes."

"You misunderstood that, too."

She planted her hands on her hips. "How the heck could I misunderstand that?"

He crooked his finger toward the oak kitchen table

where a small silver case sat. "Look inside."

"What is it, a trap or something?"

He made an exasperated gesture with his hands. "Look and you'll see."

Determined not to let him off the hook so easily, she clip-clopped over to the table and opened the case. When a life-size fake woman's chest sprang up to greet her, she screeched in shock.

"Those are the boobs your little sister wanted me to play with."

Sophie glanced back at him, swung her gaze to the fake breasts again, then inched closer to the table, stumbling as she assimilated the remaining contents of the case. So this was the kit Lucy had been referring to, the reason the security guard had thought she was soliciting, then bribing him. Her new business?

What in the world had her little sister gotten into now?

Chapter Six

Lance hated the look of distress on Sophie's face. While she usually seemed so tough, so *perfect*, a soft vulnerability shadowed her eyes that made him ache to reach out and soothe away her worry lines. He actually found himself lifting his hand toward her, then remembered that she'd accused him of trying to seduce Lucy, and that she wanted marriage and family—her money pit of a house proved that. And he had been there and done the family part by raising his sister and brother. . . .

"I didn't ask any questions," Lance said, indicating the case. "And in spite of what you think of me, I am not into kinky stuff like *that*."

"I . . . this can't be right." Her hand trembled as she reached for the kitchen chair. He pulled it out for her and she fell into it, looking lost and pale. "She . . . told me she was working for a new company selling bath oils and lotions and other romantic products."

He quirked an eyebrow toward a package of

grape-flavored condoms sticking from one of the plush folds of the case. "Romantic?"

Sophie snapped the lid closed. "My sister has a vivid imagination."

"Maybe I should worry about Reid instead of the other way around."

He'd gone too far with that one. Sophie suddenly stood and pushed at his chest. "You'd better go, Lance."

He caught her hand, and her breath fanned his cheek. She was such a petite woman, so fragile-looking, yet so feisty. Her green eyes sparkled beneath the dim light in the kitchen, her milky-white skin tanned from her trip to the beach. His body thrummed with arousal, the sultry scent of her exotic perfume sending his senses into a dizzying spiral. He wanted to taste her, to touch her, to revel in the heat that spiked a fever in his body every time he was near her. Why her?

Why Sophie, with the big green eyes and the temper and the house that screamed for a husband and kids?

Her long black lashes fluttered, and he lowered his head anyway. Her rosy lips were just a hairbreadth away. Then they were touching. Gently. Softly. Tenderly. His lips just barely brushed against hers. It wasn't enough. His hand snaked into her hair, and he dragged her mouth to his. A breathy sigh escaped her as he claimed her mouth. Then he flicked at her lips with his tongue, nibbling at the edges, begging entrance. The sweet sensations of her kiss tortured him, the hunger that rose inside him raw and so primal that Lance growled and took the kiss to another level, searching, exploring, savoring each delicious foray his tongue made.

But then Sophie pulled away.

She stumbled backward, her eyes wild with emotions as she pressed a hand to her mouth. To savor his kiss or erase it?

"You have to go, Lance. I . . . I can't do this."

He swallowed hard, knowing she was right, although his heart pounded in his chest and his body throbbed with the need to have her. Restless energy and desire exploded inside him, irrational fear seeping through. He wanted her but he couldn't give her the things she wanted. The settle-down man she deserved.

He'd come here to repair her house. He had to keep his hands off everything else.

His voice sounded gruff when he finally collected himself enough to speak. "I . . . I can't let you stay here alone."

She shook her head, fluttering long red fingernails through her dark hair. "Lance, you made it clear you didn't want to date me. And I thought I made it clear that I felt the same way."

He closed his eyes and ran a hand over his neck. "I meant because of the door."

When he looked back up, hurt darkened the light green of her eyes to a shade near black. Guilt slammed into him again. He couldn't get it right with this woman.

Because you're not right for her.

He wanted different things in life, and being a Southern-bred boy at heart, he was too much of a gentleman to take what he wanted without giving back. And he didn't have enough to give. . . .

"I'll sack out on the couch. I—"

"No. I can take care of myself, Lance. I don't need a man to protect me." She gestured toward the cat, who rounded the corner, pausing to snarl at Lance. "Besides, I have Jazzy."

"Right, psycho cat. Some protection."

"We'll be fine."

He started to open his mouth to argue. Would she really jeopardize her and her sister's safety to get rid of him?

Muttering beneath her breath about not wanting his Southern macho type around, she snagged his arm and ushered him to the door. He had his answer.

He stalked to his truck, wishing like hell that he'd never kissed her. Because that one kiss made him crave another.

But even though he couldn't have that kiss, he couldn't leave her and Lucy alone to unsuspecting predators.

No, he'd park his Blazer a safe distance away but close enough to watch the house, and grab some shut-eye. At least if he fell asleep, he'd be close enough to reach her if something happened at her house. Surely he'd hear if someone broke in, if she screamed for help. He'd drive home early in the morning, shower, and make his breakfast meeting with Reid and the owner of the new development he and Reid were trying to win bids on.

And if he didn't sleep, maybe he'd figure out why Sophie was driving him crazy, and how to put an end to it.

"I had a great time today, Reid." Lucy toyed with the curly ends of Reid's hair, scraping her fingers into the thick mass. His six-foot muscular body in tight denim had driven her insane with lust all night.

"Me, too." Reid's gaze dropped to her mouth. "You sure you don't want to come back to my place?"

"I can't. Sophie will be home tonight. We need to

catch up." She ran a hand over his arm, smiling when his muscles bunched beneath her touch. "Girl talk."

"Right." Reid maneuvered the Tahoe down the street, and Lucy spied the pansies and day lilies dancing in the evening moonlight. The entire suburbia feel gave her the willies. Home. Responsibility. Kids. Boredom.

She already missed the excitement of Vegas, the bright flashing lights, the dinner shows . . . although the *Salty Breeze* had been a surprise. And River Street with all its shops and restaurants on the water was romantic. She'd actually envisioned herself and Reid taking one of the carriage rides. It really wasn't like her to be so mushy.

The front end of a Blazer caught her eye in the side mirror and she squinted, frowning when she noticed a man sitting inside. The vehicle was parked in the shadows of a huge Spanish moss–covered tree, the branches nearly shading it from view. Sophie had always told her to be careful and watch out for perverts in Vegas.

But a pervert had parked on Sophie's street here in Savannah and was watching her house.

"Here we are." Reid parked in the driveway to Sophie's house and killed the engine. "Thanks for the evening, Lucy." He curled his hand into a ball, then brushed his knuckles against her cheek. A shiver chased up her spine.

"Thank you. I'd like to see more clubs."

"Then we'll do it again while you're here?"

"Absolutely." She traced a finger along his jaw, intrigued by his husky voice. "You're pretty hot on the dance floor."

His voice grew even lower, humming with masculine want. "You have some great moves yourself."

If only he could come watch her show at the Palace. She bit back her comment, realizing she'd been on the verge of confiding in him her part in the Diva act. Sophie would kill her.

His eyes skated over her face, a heartbeat stretching between them before he dipped his head and claimed her mouth. Lucy gave in to the kiss, loving this bad-boy wildness. Reid was misplaced in Savannah; he needed to be in Vegas with the action instead of in this sleepy Southern town. One kiss led to several, the heat between them fogging up the windows. Reid was everything a lover should be, bold, wild, passionate, primal. She played a teasing game with his tongue, seeking, yearning, dancing around the flames of desire that erupted.

Too bad her older sister was waiting inside.

Already dreading the behave-yourself-Lucy lecture Sophie would no doubt greet her with, especially if she'd been watching through the window, Lucy slowly pulled away.

She finger-combed her tangled hair into some semblance of decency and tried to erase the whisker burns from her cheeks by licking her fingers and dabbing the moisture across the abrasions.

Before she climbed from the Tahoe, she kissed Reid one more time, this one long and slow, lingering with promises. A pebble caught in her red spike-heeled sandal as she tottered up the sidewalk to the front porch, and she paused and jiggled her foot to shake it free. But she caught her reflection in the glass windows flanking the door and winced. Her hair was sticking out in all directions, and the lickety-split job on her face had failed to erase the love bruises from Reid. *Oh, well.* Just because Sophie didn't want to have fun didn't mean she couldn't. Then again, maybe Sophie had had a fabulous weekend with her date and would be in a good mood.

She opened the door, but caught the reflection of the Blazer still parked in the shadows. Knowing she couldn't sleep with a pervert watching the house all night, she grabbed her cell phone and called 911. Later she'd work up one of her little protective spells to keep the other perverts away.

How could Sophie possibly be angry with her when she'd saved them both from a madman?

Lance hadn't expected to fall asleep, but exhaustion had finally gotten to him. Either that or the heat. He'd slumped down on the seat, his head thrown against the window of the driver's side, his legs sprawled in slumber. Minutes later, someone blammed on the door of his truck.

Jarred from the first stages of REM, he jerked upright, but he was so tired his head immediately fell backward. Good grief, he must be dreaming. He closed his eyes again and decided the blamming sound was a jackhammer. He'd fallen asleep on the job. Reid would have to oversee things; he needed to rest.

The blamming continued, louder, then a voice. "Open up, sir."

Sir? Who was talking to him? One of his workers? He had to wake up. He had something important to do . . . what was it? Pushing against the seat, he swiped a hand across his face and squinted through slitted eyes. A bright light blinded him. The sun? Was it morning?

He tried to crawl out of bed, but slid and his head hit the steering wheel. Through the rungs of the wheel he noticed a blue light swirling in the sky. A police car? What was a policeman doing at his house? His hand connected with the steering wheel as he dragged himself upright, and he realized he wasn't at home but in his Blazer. Sophie's. Right, he'd been watching her house to protect her.

The blamming started again. He swung his face sideways and squinted at the sunshine glaring through the window. It wasn't the sun, though. A beefy cop's face was pressed against the window, a flashlight aimed in Lance's eyes.

Blast it all to hell. Trying to orient himself, he rubbed at his bleary eyes, then threw up a hand to signal that he intended to roll down the window. The officer's hand went to his gun, his expression ominous.

Lance threw up both hands. "Don't shoot." He swallowed, struggling to unclog his sleep-deprived voice. "What's wrong, Officer?"

"License and registration."

Lance nodded and leaned sideways, digging through the crap on his front seat to reach the dash. A hammer and box of nails fell from the seat, nails flying in all directions. He scrambled to retrieve them, and wrapped his hand around the hammer, but too late, he realized the officer thought he planned to use it as a weapon, because he opened the door, his gun drawn.

"Drop it and step out of the truck, mister. Now."

The commanding voice brooked no argument. Lance released the tool and pivoted.

"Have you been drinking, sir?"

Lance shook his head. "No, just tired."

"Your words are slurred. How much have you had?"

"Nothing," Lance said, wishing he could drag his eyes open more than halfway.

"Step out of the car, sir. And do it slowly."

Lance stifled a groan, but opened the door and climbed out. A wave of dizziness washed over him from exhaustion, and he wobbled.

The man's hand clamped down onto Lance's with a steely grip. "Come on. You're going downtown, buddy."

"But I didn't do anything." Lance steadied himself to an upright position by holding on to side of the truck.

"A neighbor called and reported a stalker in the vicinity. Man in a Blazer watching her house." The policeman jerked Lance toward the squad car. "You're the only one on the street, buddy."

"No." Lance tried to extricate himself so he could look into the policeman's face, but the man's grip tightened.

"Do you want me to add resisting arrest to the charges?"

Lance balked. "I'm not resisting. I was just watching—"

"Tell it to the judge." Beefy hands slapped a pair of handcuffs on Lance, then pushed his head downward and stuffed him into the backseat.

The officer's accusations sank in as the door slammed shut, trapping Lance in the backseat behind the protective mesh wall. Someone had called and reported a stalker? Someone who'd seen his Blazer? Who?

Lance slid down into the seat, mortified as the answer splintered through his befuddled brain.

Sophie.

Had she called the police for revenge?

Sophie had unpacked, thrown on a nightshirt, and scrubbed her face free of makeup when Lucy wobbled in, humming "Forever Young" and dancing through the den with an invisible partner. Blue lights swirled outside, lighting up the foyer, and Sophie peeked out to see a police car rolling down the street.

"It looks like you had fun." She indicated the blue lights. "That car didn't bring you home, did it?"

Lucy frowned. "Of course not. In fact, you should be proud of me." Lucy hiccuped. "I scoped out the neighborhood and your house when I got home. Some pervert was hiding out in his vehicle behind some trees watching the house."

Sophie shivered. "You're serious?"

"Maybe you have a stalker from the show."

Sophie peeled back the curtain and watched the patrol car drive down the street. Tomorrow she'd ask the station manager if she'd received any unusual fan mail or phone calls.

Lucy vaulted toward her, her curly hair flying around her face as she enveloped her into a hug. Sophie recognized the scent of a man's cologne on her neck and alcohol on her breath. "It's okay, though, I'm here now, Soph. The two of us are back together, invincible."

Sophie hugged her sister, tears threatening at her vulnerable tone. How many times had she reassured Lucy that everything would be all right when she was younger? All the countless times they'd watched a patrol car haul their mother away. Lucy always cried, while Sophie hugged her, reassuring her that nothing could touch them as long as the sisters had each other. If they stuck together, they were invincible.

Suddenly glad for Lucy's visit, she took her hand and led her to the kitchen, automatically brewing coffee for her sister and pouring a diet Coke over ice for herself.

Lucy climbed on the bar stool, dangling her legs. "So how was the weekend?" Lucy asked. "I've been dying to hear. It looked like you were having a great time."

"Good, that's how I wanted it to look." Sophie joined Lucy at the table, then placed sugar and creamer on the counter for her sister. Lucy dumped both in the coffee, stirring and splashing it everywhere.

"You mean you didn't have fun in Cancún?"

Sophie shrugged. "The resort was fabulous, the ocean beautiful, the weather perfect."

"But Rory?"

"Edward Scissorhands."

"An octopus, huh?"

Sophie shook her head and sipped her drink. How could she explain when there was nothing concrete to criticize? "I didn't feel a connection."

Lucy rolled her eyes. "You mean that soul-mate thing?"

Sophie nodded, waiting for Lucy to laugh, as she usually did. "I know you don't believe in it, but I do, Lucy. I'm tired of the rat race of dating."

"I believe in karma between people, but not the one-person-for-everybody theory. How can you be tired of dating?"

"I want more than a different guy every night. After a while, dating starts to feel meaningless."

"Once upon a time you didn't need a man, Soph. We simply needed each other."

Sophie studied her sister, hearing her vulnerability and remembering that she had once felt the same way. Watching her mother flit from one man to the next had created a distrust for men in general. Sophie had vowed not to repeat her mother's mistakes. She wanted a meaningful relationship with one man—a man she could trust. "You're right. I don't need a man, Lucy." But she still wanted one—a big difference.

Lucy tapped her spoon on the counter. "So does this mean you're canceling the dating series this week on the show?"

"No." Misery laced Sophie's voice. "I can't cancel now. Besides, I'm on the show to dispense information. Some of the singles services might help lonely people meet one another."

"You have to join one, too, Sophie. Learn to have fun."

Sophie pressed a finger to her lips, the luscious taste of Lance's lips still lingering. She had found a guy, but he didn't want her.

"So I take it you and Rory didn't get it on at all, not even a little nooky?"

Lucy's expression was so forlorn that Sophie laughed. "No. I came up with excuses all weekend. The show. My image."

"The image thing. Good gracious alive, Sophie, you worry too much about perceptions."

And you don't worry enough. Sophie stifled the comment, refusing to start up their age-old argument.

"You need to learn to go with the flow. Have fun. Enjoy life."

"Like you're doing?"

Lucy pushed away the coffee. "Yes. Lance's brother is a hottie. He can dance and, man, can he kiss!"

"I thought those were whisker burns on your face. I wish you wouldn't get involved with Reid."

"I'm not involved. We simply went to dinner, went dancing. He showed me around Savannah."

"And you made out."

"All work and no play makes a girl boring." Lucy

twirled a strand of hair around one finger. "Did you know that having sex actually helps keep you younger? It's good for the heart and the skin and—"

"And working hard makes a girl successful, safe, and independent." Sophie shook her head and glanced at the silver case. "Speaking of work, Lucy, why didn't you tell me you were selling adult sex toys?"

"I told you I was selling products to enhance a romantic relationship. The Sleepover, Inc., parties are all the rage in the big cities."

"I can't let you show that stuff on my show. Savannah's more conservative than New York and L.A. and Vegas."

Lucy winced and stood, gesturing toward the front window. "Can we discuss this tomorrow? I'm beat."

"Sure." Sophie sighed. She had a show to do in the morning. The couples would return to discuss their dates. She had to face Rory again. Smile for the camera.

"You didn't say anything to Reid about our show life in Vegas, did you?"

Lucy kicked off her sandals and wiggled her bare toes. "Of course not, sis; I told you to trust me."

"I do." Sophie tried to ignore the mess Lucy was creating in her house. Her little sister was a whirlwind of chaos, with her sweet naivete and superstitions. "But I don't trust Reid Summers."

"Why not? He seems nice, and he's fun, and he likes to have a good time."

"He's a player, Lucy." And Lance's brother.

And Lance had hurt her too much already for Sophie to trust any of the Summers men.

* * *

By the time Lance reached the police station, any remnants of sleep had dissipated and cold reality stared him in the face. He had been given the Breathalyzer test and passed, but the cop insisted he'd been disorderly, so he'd been fingerprinted and thrown in a holding cell with a wino, a teenage punk strung out on God knew what, and some potbellied redneck bozo with a toothless smile aimed his direction. Across the way, a woman wailed as if there were no tomorrow.

He'd also heard the officer order his truck to be impounded. He felt fairly certain that in the light of day he could beat the charges, but by the time he paid an attorney and got his Blazer out, he would be out a small fortune.

The stench of sweat and urine floated around him. He and Reid and Chase had been called the Terrible Three in high school, but he had thought he'd long ago passed the stage where he found himself in the slammer.

Until Sophie.

Had she stood at her front window and watched the police haul him away? Was she sleeping like a baby in that obscene four-poster bed while he sat on this grimy, stained floor, huddled into a knot of nerves? Would he make it home in time to clean up for his morning meeting?

The redneck peered at him. "Hey, ain't I seen you over at Trade Off's?"

Trade Off's was the gay bar across town.

Lance shook his head, rubbed at his throbbing temples, and geared up for another sleepless night just as the woman across the way launched into an off-key version of "Folsom Prison Blues."

Chapter Seven

Reid Summers paced the front office of their company, his mind jumbled with memories of the night before with Lucy Lane. Was she as wild in bed as she was on the dance floor? Was her bare skin as silky as those unruly strawberry-blond curls?

What had she thought of him? She'd seemed attracted to him, but he could have been wrong.

Trying to banish the images from his mind, he approached Lance's desk. Lance would be here any minute for their breakfast meeting. Reid had to focus on work this morning, not let his lust for the gorgeous Lucy sidetrack him.

Lance never allowed a woman to mess with his head or interfere with his work. Why couldn't *he* be as focused and responsible as his brother?

Where was Lance, anyway?

Reid glanced at his watch and frowned. Lance was the most punctual man he'd ever known, especially in business situations. And Lance knew the importance of this meeting with Emmet McDaniels.

McDaniels was an investor from California who'd already purchased several of the dilapidated buildings on the east side of Savannah. He needed a developer to turn them into small businesses with lofts above the storefronts to purchase or rent, and Chase, Lance, and Reid desperately wanted the job.

Chase had left blueprints with him, and Reid would oversee the details of the construction crews, but his brother had the business mentality.

Reid had spent all his life trying to live up to Lance's expectations. He wouldn't disappoint him now. He'd file Lucy's luscious kisses away in his mind until he was off the clock.

But tonight, maybe, he'd see her again and maybe he'd—

"Mr. Summers."

He jerked his head up at the sound of Emmet McDaniels's voice. He'd been so preoccupied he hadn't heard the man enter.

"Mr. McDaniels, come on in." McDaniels removed his hat, and Reid shook the elderly man's hand. "My brother should be here any minute." Reid checked the message machine but it wasn't blinking.

The man's thick gray eyebrows shot up, accentuating his balding head. Reid automatically rubbed a hand across his own crown. "You mean he's not here?"

"I'm sorry, but no. I don't know what's keeping him; my brother is normally punctual. I'm sure he has a good reason for being late." He grabbed the phone. "Let me try his cell. He's probably on his way."

Reid quickly punched in the number, but agitation turned to worry when it didn't ring. He tried Lance's home number, too, but no answer.

McDaniels tugged at his tie, looking impatient,

and Reid asked about the man's trip, then routed the conversation to the changes in Savannah, and housing needs of the community. But a half hour later he was running out of steam, McDaniels was clearly agitated, they were both hungry, and Lance still hadn't made an appearance.

"Why don't we go to breakfast, then swing back here and see if Lance has shown up? He must have had some kind of emergency on one of the projects."

"Well, that certainly doesn't sound good."

Oh, hell, no, it didn't. But what other reason could there be? Unless Lance had had some kind of accident. Sweat beaded on Reid's forehead. "I'm sure there's an explanation. We really want this job, sir."

"Listen, Mr. Summers, I'm a very busy man." McDaniels started for the door. "I'm only here for the day, and I don't have time to wait around. I have two other developers chomping at this project. If your brother's absence is any indication of how you conduct business, I'll definitely go elsewhere."

"But . . . wait. Let me see if he left the bids and the blueprints. I can show you those over breakfast."

McDaniels checked his watch with a snort. "All right. But let's get on with it."

Reid scavenged the desk, the files, even the extra storage room and found nothing. Lance must have all the information with him.

Scraping together the charm that had saved him in high school, he strode back to the front office and pasted on a smile. Unfortunately McDaniels seemed immune, unlike his female teachers. "I'm sorry, he must have the bids and the blueprints with him. Please let us reschedule."

"I don't think so, Mr. Summers. If your brother was serious, he would have at least shown or phoned to explain his delay." McDaniels slid a hat over his bald spot, turned, and sailed out the door, firmly dismissing Reid.

Reid chased him outside, trying to apologize again, but the man climbed in his Mercedes and tore down the graveled drive. Reid fisted his hands in frustration and strode back inside, but the phone was ringing as he entered. He jerked it up, his foul mood spilling over in his clipped tone. "Hello."

"This is a collect call from Savannah Correctional Facility," a recorded message stated. "Will you accept the charges from inmate . . ." The voice paused and his brother's voice filled in the rest.

Reid gaped at the phone in shock. Lance was calling from jail?

"Reid, hey, are you there?"

"Yeah, man, what the hell happened? How'd you wind up in the slammer?"

"It's a long story," Lance said, sounding weary. "Last night I didn't want to leave Sophie alone in the house with the back door torn off, so I parked down the street in the truck so I could keep an eye on things, but I fell asleep. Next thing I know the police show up, claiming a woman reported a stalker in the neighborhood."

"You think it was Sophie?"

"Probably. I guess she wanted to get back at me. Anyway, can you bail me out?"

"Sure. I'll be there as soon as I can." Reid hung up, grabbed his keys, and headed to the door. But his mind replayed the evening before. He'd seen the blue lights of the police car entering Sophie's street as he had exited. Good God almighty, he'd had no idea they were coming after his brother.

Best not to tell Lance that—if Reid hadn't been so distracted by Lucy Lane he might have been able to prevent his going to jail.

*   *   *

An hour later Lance stepped into the daylight, wincing when the morning sunshine seared his blurry eyes. If he had to take sleeping pills, he'd do so tonight. He had to get some rest.

"Man, I was worried." Reid pounded Lance's back. "I can't believe they arrested you on drunk and disorderly conduct. Sounds like the old days, bro."

Lance huffed. "Thankfully, the Breathalyzer proved I hadn't been drinking."

"Yeah, too bad the cop locked you up anyway."

"He was a jerk. Said I was disturbing the peace."

"Bad break," Reid said, steering the truck toward the duplex they rented.

"So how did it go this morning? Did you reschedule?"

"Not exactly." Reid's hand tightened around the steering wheel. "McDaniels was pretty peeved when you missed the meeting."

Lance rubbed a hand over his face. "I have to talk to him."

Reid cut his gaze over him. "You'd better clean up first. You smell like rotten potatoes."

"My cellmate was a homeless wino." He rolled down the window to let some fresh air in and his own rancid odor escape. "So what did you tell McDaniels?"

"That we were interested, that you had the blueprints from Chase and an outline of our plans. He needs to see our bid, though. He's not a patient man."

"I'll contact him right after I shower and get my truck back." Reid parked in front of the duplex. Lance rented one side, his brother the other.

"So where are you headed?"

"To Skidaway to check on the projects."

"Good." Lance held on to the door of the truck, hesitating before he closed it. "Thanks for coming."

Reid grinned. "You've done it for me."

"I know, and it won't happen again. I'm going to finish Sophie's house and be done with her."

"She really gets to you, doesn't she?"

Lance saw her rosy lips parting for his invasion, remembered the salty passion of her kiss. "She's dangerous. And Reid?"

"Yeah?"

"So is her sister. Stay away from her. When we're finished with the house, I don't want any ties left to the Lane sisters."

Sophie gestured toward the screen, where highlights from the first two couples' dates had already aired. Apparently couple number one, Brenda and Larry, had enjoyed Paris and had decided to continue seeing one another. Shandra and Dwayne had hit it off as well and gotten hitched in Barbados.

At least two of the couples had experienced success.

Music played along with the last footage of her date with Rory. He sat onstage across from her looking confident in a designer suit, his grin feeding the audience's romantic ideas of happy endings. She hadn't yet broken the news to her winning date that she had not found him winning.

"So, Rory, do you want to give us your version of things?" Sophie's assistant, Eden, said. "Then we'll hear from our host."

"The limo ride was great, the water sports, the beach, the tour all ranked top-notch. And the food, wine, and atmosphere, I couldn't have picked a more romantic spot if I'd chosen it myself." He threw his arm across the back of the chair. "In fact, the weekend was nearly perfect."

"Nearly perfect?"

He gave Sophie a conspiratorial wink. "Yeah, nearly. But we have our secrets, don't we, Sophie?"

Sophie squirmed.

"How could a man not have enjoyed himself with a dynamite woman like Sophie Lane on his arm? And you saw her in that string bikini. . . ."

The audience laughed. Nerves skittered in Sophie's stomach as Eden turned toward her. A few more minutes and the show would end. "Cancún was everything I'd imagined and more. And Rory was a fabulous date."

"He looks pretty good in a bathing suit, too," Eden said, earning a round of applause from the crowd.

"Yes, and in a tux." Sophie accepted his hand graciously, although she was beginning to perspire beneath the hot lights.

"So is love in the stars for the two of you?" Eden asked.

Rory's gaze met hers and Sophie feigned a smile. "Only the future will tell."

His grin spread from ear to ear. "If I have my way about it, the romance has just begun."

The audience burst into applause and Sophie laughed, playing along, desperate to escape.

When the crowd finally died down, she gave a lead-in to Tuesday's show. "Tomorrow we'll hear from a singles service here in Savannah. So have your pens and pencils ready to learn how you can join and meet the man or woman of your dreams."

"I Will Always Love You" wafted over the speakers, and Sophie stood, waving to the audience.

"Sophie, I meant what I said." Rory slid his hands

in his pockets. "Can we see each other soon?"

"I . . . I don't know, Rory," Sophie hedged. "I'll be busy with this singles series this week, and my sister's in town—"

"No problem, I have to go to Atlanta for a couple of weeks. I'll call you when I return and we can get together."

Sophie nodded and let him kiss her cheek, then headed to her office to organize her thoughts for the next day's show.

Maybe by the time Rory returned, she'd have Lance out of her system, and she'd be more open to Rory's affection.

If I have my way about it, the romance has just begun. You saw her in that string bikini. The weekend was nearly perfect. Dalton's comments echoed in Lance's head as he hammered at the Sheetrock that needed replacing in the kitchen wall. *We have our secrets, don't we, Sophie?*

Just what the hell had he meant by that? Secrets as in that they'd had wild sex or romped naked on the beach?

Not that he cared if the two of them saw each other again or if they'd had wild sex or romped naked on the beach. But damn it, last night the woman had kissed him like there was no tomorrow, then sent him away with his gut in knots and had him arrested. He didn't care. He couldn't care.

He *wouldn't* care.

It was simply that he'd spent a terrible night in jail. And his day had gone downhill, too. When he'd finally showered and met up with McDaniels, the man had been aloof and condescending. Lance had practically begged him to take his bid and the sketches of their plans for the development with him. Finally McDaniels had agreed, although he had been emphatic that he expected perfection, not some half-assed job, and that he didn't tolerate a company missing deadlines.

Like developers could always control the weather or problems getting materials or workers who called in sick or any of the other million things that went wrong during a project.

Lance's head throbbed like the devil, but he slammed the hammer into the drywall anyway, discovered there was no insulation, and then began to tear out the rotten wood, determined to finish this renovation in record time.

The front door screeched open and he paused, wondering which one of the troublesome sisters had arrived. Sexy Sophie or her sex-toy sales sister, Lucy?

Heels clicked on the hardwood floor, the scent of an exotic French perfume greeting him before he saw the owner. Sophie. He'd recognize the sultry scent anywhere.

Jesus. He glanced up and caught sight of that black hair spiked up in disarray, and his fingers tightened around the chisel. She drove him crazy simply by walking into a room. All that porcelain skin and those big green eyes . . . it was enough to make him forget the hell she'd put him through the night before. . . .

Her cat darted from nowhere to slide against her legs, purring contentedly. The damn thing had hidden since he'd arrived.

"I see you've been busy," she commented, spying the shattered plaster and drywall on the floor.

She certainly wasn't acting as if she'd had him arrested; she was almost friendly. Maybe he'd been mistaken; maybe a neighbor had phoned. . . . "It'll be a mess for a while."

"I know. I guess I'll have to suffer through it."

And suffer through having you around too. He heard the unspoken message in her tone, and his anger from the night before returned. She really wanted to get rid of him. "I'll finish the house as soon as possible and get out of your way. I don't want you calling the cops on me again."

"Calling the cops?" Sophie's eyes widened. "What are you talking about, Lance?"

Was she playing innocent or lying? Or had he been wrong?

"Your phone call that I was a stalker—don't you think having me arrested went a little too far?"

Sophie gaped at him. "I . . . I . . . you were the pervert hanging outside the house last night?"

He ground his jaw. "I'm not a pervert, Sophie; I only wanted to protect you."

She dropped a bag of groceries on the counter, then began to unload the contents, avoiding his gaze. "I didn't call, Lance. I'm sorry." She angled her head up toward him. "You spent the night in jail?"

Humiliation crawled all over him. "Forget it."

She hesitated, started to say something, then seemed to change her mind. "Why are you still doing the renovations yourself, Lance? I thought you would just oversee things."

So she was changing the subject. He would play along. Anything was better than this god-awful tension between them, and reminders of his humiliating night. "Sometimes I do, but my crew's finishing up at Skidaway. Besides, renovations are my forte. That's how I got started in the business."

"I didn't know that."

He shrugged. "Had to fix up our old house to sell

it after Mom and Dad died." Plaster splintered down as he yanked at it. Why had he mentioned his folks?

She laid out lettuce and fresh vegetables for a salad, then removed a cutting board from the cabinet. Fatigue lined her face, and her television smile had faded. Dalton had obviously worn her out over the weekend, just as she'd said. Did she have a date tonight?

"Maddie talked about missing your folks. That must have been difficult."

He shrugged. "I was sorry Maddie was so young. She needed Mom around."

"Yes, girls need their mothers."

"Sounds like you're talking from experience."

She bit down on her lower lip. "Your brother and sister were lucky to have you."

"I could never take my parents' place."

"But you loved her; that's what she needed from you."

A pang settled in his chest. He had done the best he could, but he'd still known Maddie and Reid had both hurt for their parents, and he'd felt inept at filling their shoes. "Just like you love Lucy?"

Her shoulders lifted slightly as she arranged pasta ingredients on the counter and began to chop the tomatoes. His mouth watered. He couldn't remember when he'd eaten a home-cooked meal.

The burned toast in the jail cell this morning didn't count.

But all this talk of his parents and family resurrected past hurts and fears. Fear that he'd let Maddie and Reid and his parents down. Fear of losing his sister and brother.

He moved back to the plaster, anxious to end the conversation. He didn't want to know more about Sophie and her sister and the reason her green eyes looked so sad for a moment. If he didn't get to know her he wouldn't care.

And not caring was the only way to avoid getting hurt.

With the summer temperature outside soaring and Lance finishing her back doorway, the kitchen felt stifling as Sophie stirred the spaghetti sauce on the stovetop. She had been cooking since she was tall enough to reach the countertop. It had either been that or survive on dried-up peanut butter sandwiches, since Deseree's evenings had been filled with appointments.

Sophie hadn't understood what all those odd evening jobs were at the time. When she'd finally gotten old enough to figure out the truth, she had lived in denial, inventing elaborate stories for Lucy as to their mother's whereabouts.

Then Lucy had grown up, too.

Her heart tugged as she remembered the look of stolen innocence on her sister's face the morning she'd woken with an earache and tried to crawl into her mother's bed, only to be ousted by a stranger.

Sophie had vowed then that as soon as she was old enough, she and Lucy would move out on their own. Better to be alone than with a man for the wrong reasons.

A lesson to remember with Lance. And Rory and that singles service.

With Sophie's dancing gigs, she and Lucy had survived on their own. But Deseree had eventually popped back into their lives with promises that she'd mended her ways and lifestyle and wanted her daughters back in her life. Trouble was, Deseree meant well. Sometimes she lasted for months, working at a menial day job. But old habits were hard to break, and Deseree was no stranger to temptation. She'd meet an old client or flake out into one of her obsessive shopping sprees, and she'd run up her credit cards, and need a quick way out of debt.

In Vegas she could always find someone to oblige her.

Sophie had long since stopped blaming her mother for her weaknesses. She loved her in spite of them, and she worried about her like crazy.

Still, she prayed she didn't show up at her house while Lance was hanging around finishing the renovations. With Lucy coming, Deseree might be not be far behind. An explanation might get sticky.

Lance buffed the wood stain on the doorway and stepped back to examine his work.

Sophie couldn't help but admire him . . . er, his attention to detail.

"It looks fabulous, Lance."

"Thanks. I'm pleased." He turned to her with an odd look, a fine sheen of perspiration dotting his forehead. Odd how Rory looked grossly sweaty all the time, but on Lance a little moisture gave him a sexy bad-boy appearance.

She'd been so distracted watching Lance work that the sauce bubbled over. She jumped back to attention before she set the house on fire, and turned down the burner.

"That smells delicious."

The wooden spoon stilled in her hand. "It's pretty simple. I've been making it for ages."

"You enjoy cooking?"

"It's relaxing."

His eyebrow shot up as if he were surprised.

"You don't see me as the domestic type?"

A chuckle reverberated in his chest. "Maybe. Maybe not."

"It's Lucy's favorite." Speaking of her sister, where was she?

He crossed the room to wash his hands while she removed the pasta to drain it. They met at the sink at the same time. Steam oozed from the pot, curling around them. Or maybe the steam was oozing from her. Lance certainly made her hot.

Damn him.

She stepped aside, gestured for him to finish, then emptied the pasta in the strainer as he dried his hands. His gaze latched on to her, following her every movement. His stomach growled.

Oh, good heavens. She sighed. "Lance, do you want something to eat?"

His gaze met hers, the look in his eyes full of hunger.

But before he could open his mouth to reply, Lucy burst through the back door, dressed in workout clothes. "Yum, Soph, smells great."

Sophie dragged her gaze from Lance. "It's ready."

"Good, I'm starved." Lucy grabbed a glass from the cabinet. "Besides, we need to hurry. I invited a bunch of girls over for a Sleepover party tonight."

"A what?"

Lucy filled the glass with sweet tea, then plopped into the chair. "A Sleepover. I gave out business cards at the club the other night. The girls will be here any second."

Lance gathered his toolbox. "I guess I'd better get out of the way then."

Sophie nodded and let him go. Having him around was entirely too painful. Too tempting.

Too nice.

She did not want to want him this way. She wanted to be over him.

"Now," Lucy said, "let's eat; then I'll fill you in

on the games we'll play at the party." Her eyes lit up with excitement. "Wait until you see the party favors."

Sophie stared at the silver case full of goodies and grimaced. What in the world did Lucy have in mind?

Chapter Eight

You don't see me as the domestic type?

Hell, no, he didn't, Lance thought as he let himself inside his duplex. But he could imagine her in nothing except that damned apron and those clunky heels. And he had envisioned dotting sauce on her body and licking it off.

Frustrated, he strode to the refrigerator and scrounged through the measly contents. A half-wilted head of lettuce. Six-day-old pizza that had turned into a moldy brick. A soured carton of milk. An empty container of orange juice. Two beers.

Ahh, another night of a liquid diet or takeout. That is, unless he wanted to dress up and go out. Meet women. Flirt. Maybe bring one home.

Bachelorhood. The life he'd always wanted. The life he'd once loved.

Dirty clothes on the floor. His favorite sports magazines roosting on his scarred coffee table in the den. His bed unmade. His bathroom free of women's stuff.

Like the flimsy black teddy that had been draped over the shower rod in Sophie's bathroom.

His body thrumming with desire again, he phoned the new Philly cheesesteak delivery joint around the corner, jumped in the shower to chill his libido, then dressed in a pair of running shorts. Tired from lack of sleep but rejuvenated, he scrubbed a towel through his wet hair and tossed it to the floor. Another perk of singlehood—he didn't have to worry about a wife nagging him to keep things neat.

Grabbing a beer and the remote, he settled into his favorite rust-colored recliner. He'd watch TV while he waited on his food, then consider going out. He needed something or *someone* to distract him from Sophie Lane.

Or maybe he'd simply veg out and sleep. God knew he needed to catch some z's. With Sophie's door firmly back in place, she and her loony sister were safe. McDaniels had the bids for the contract. Maddie was content at home with Chase. And Reid . . . well, his brother would probably be on the prowl, but at least he wouldn't be out with Lucy.

Because she was entertaining a group of women to sell her sex toys.

Why would women want that stuff anyway, when they could have their choice of any red-blooded male instead? He didn't understand it. Then again, women had always been the world's biggest mystery.

He flipped the channels, grunting at the choices. Reruns of several sitcoms. A cooking show. Fishing tips. Mating patterns of some beetle. The best bathrooms in Vegas. Hmm, Chase and Maddie should be viewing it for ideas.

Right, the newlyweds would certainly be glued to a show on bathrooms.

He flipped again. A hundred and ten channels and nothing on worth watching. The doorbell rang and he dropped the remote, his mind conjuring images of Sophie's homemade spaghetti sauce instead of fast food. Sophie feeding him . . .

The doorbell dinged again, and he hurled himself forward. A few minutes later he banned Sophie from his mind while he chowed down on his cardboard cheesesteak, his gaze cutting toward the shopping bag from the mall. Afraid he wouldn't sleep again, he'd stopped by the mall and bought some ridiculous relaxation tapes the salesclerk suggested and had sprung for one of those rock garden waterfall thingies that were also supposed to be therapeutic.

Surfing the channels one more time, he sighed in relief when he discovered a sports channel. "Tonight we have an interview with Rory Dalton, one of the greatest football players to ever grace the field. We'll be hearing all about Dalton's favorite plays and his plans for the future now he's retired."

Lance frowned at the picture of Dalton that flashed on the screen, photographs of his past seasons filling the footage. Had Dalton used his favorite plays on Sophie?

Had they worked?

The phone trilled, cutting into his disturbing thoughts. He checked the caller ID—Tanya Whitson—he didn't recognize the name. Assuming it was a sales pitch, he let the machine pick it up.

"Hello, I'm calling for Lance Summers. My name is Tanya. I saw your name and number at the singles club." She hesitated, then lowered her voice to a breathy level. "I'd like to meet for a drink. If you're interested, call me at 555-2545. 'Bye."

Lance dropped his half-eaten sandwich onto his plate. The woman had a nice voice. She sounded pleasant. And he had nothing better to do.

But was he interested?

"Thanks for coming, Maddie. At least there's one sane person at this party." Not only had Lucy hung lucky charms around her place, but now a group of tittering women had gathered to examine Lucy's sexy products. And Sophie still hadn't told Lucy that she had actually had Lance arrested the night before. . . .

"Wow, look at all this stuff!" Maddie screeched.

Erotic massage oils and liqueurs, edible underwear, feathers, boas, Venus Butterflies, videos, pictures, artificial body parts, vibrators, posters, penis-shaped pasta . . . she had never seen so many types of romantic notions, as Lucy called them, in one place at one time.

"Are you kidding? I wouldn't have missed it." Maddie plucked a tube of grape lipstick in the shape of a male sex organ (the theme, it seemed) off the display and tested the color on her lips. "I may be married, but I'm far from dead, Soph. In fact, sex has never been better."

Tiffany, one of the guests, stole Maddie's penis-shaped drink charm from her martini with a grin. "Caught you."

"Drat, drat, double drat," Maddie said. "I just can't seem to hold on to my male organs tonight."

"It's because you can't stop saying the S-word." The object of the game, Sophie thought wryly, was not to say the S-word or you lost your stick. Difficult when every item on display conjured images of just that—sex.

Something Sophie had desperately done without lately.

"Okay," Lucy said as she lit a boob-shaped candle. "Time for another party game."

"Oh, heavens," Sophie said. "What next?" They'd already played Finish the Picture—essentially a picture of a man missing one important vital body part. Of course, Maddie had won with her sketch of Chase, which had every woman there anxious to meet Maddie's husband.

"All right." Lucy waved a glittery stick that resembled a magic wand—women were supposed to use it to make their partners deliver their fantasy. "This game is to stimulate your imagination. Everyone has to take the name of their first pet and combine it with the name of the street where they grew up. That will be your porn star name."

Several of the women squealed with delight. Sophie grimaced.

Maddie clapped her hands. "Okay, I've got mine. My cat's name was Too Cute, and the street I grew up on was Eaton Drive."

"Too Cute Eaton," Lucy said with a squeal.

Lucy passed the magic wand to the next girl in the circle. "I had a German shepherd named Tootsie and I lived on Poplin Avenue." Olivia twirled her olive in her glass. "Tootsie Pop."

The next girl snatched the wand with a mischievous grin. "Honey Lipton."

"Honey Lips," Lucy amended, bringing a round of laughter.

A stunning brunette lawyer joined in the fun. "Pepper Sprayberry—no, Pepper Spray."

"That sounds dangerous," Lucy said. "But exciting."

The magic wand continued, the game picking up speed. "Fluffy Main."

"Sticky Waters."

"Angel Ashton."

"Satin Butts."

"Furry Hornsby."

"Hotshot Sister."

"Blackie Humphrey—Blackie Humps."

Sophie rolled her eyes, quickly downing the rest of her martini as the spotlight turned to her. "My cat is Jazzy."

Lucy's eyes twinkled. "And your street was . . . ?"

She could not believe she was saying this; it was everything she had fought so hard not to be. "Bell."

"Jeezy Bell. You're our winner tonight." Lucy stood and handed over the prize, a pair of red fur-covered handcuffs and a black feather boa. Lucy gestured toward the refreshment table. "While we snack, ladies, look over your brochures and place your orders."

Sophie headed to refresh her drink while Lucy unveiled the treats—a seafood dip in bowls shaped like male body parts and a booty-shaped cake with chocolate icing. Several of the women congregated around the table, cracking jokes about their prospective orders while Maddie cornered Sophie. "Okay, what's up between you and Lance?"

"Nothing," Sophie said. "Absolutely nothing."

"Aren't you playing by the rules?"

"What rules?" Lucy asked, jumping into the conversation.

"The seven sacred rules for trapping a man," Maddie said. "Sophie's supposed to be using them on my brother."

"I am not," Sophie said.

"She is, too," Maddie argued. "He's a stubborn man. He doesn't know what's good for him."

"Your other brother is eye candy," Lucy said.

"He is, isn't he?" Mischief danced in Maddie's eyes.

"Yes, but I'm not looking for a husband," Lucy said, "so don't worry."

Maddie thumped her fingers on her hips, disappointment sliding across her features. "Hmm. Well, Soph, I know Lance saw the video of your date in Cancún."

"How do you know?" Sophie asked, suddenly suspicious.

"Because I made sure he did. Now it's time to turn to rule number three: Give him a nibble, then yank the line." Maddie tilted her head toward Lucy. "Translation: A little kissing is allowed, even a little tongue, but no heavy petting."

Sophie chewed her lip. "Well . . ."

Maddie narrowed her eyes, realization dawning. "You already did that?"

Sophie nodded, grabbed a cherry from the table, and popped it into her mouth.

"And how did Lance respond?"

Did she mean how was the kiss? Incredible. Hot. Tormenting. "He ran like hell afterward."

Lucy's eyes went buggy. "Typical male."

"I know," Sophie said in misery. "And this one doesn't want to be caught, so there's no use wasting my time." *Or putting my heart through the ringer any more.*

"Then it's time for rule number four."

"No more games," Sophie said. "I can't take it, Maddie."

Maddie ignored her. "Lance is still working on your house, right?"

"Yes."

"What's rule number four?" Lucy asked.

Sophie frowned at her baby sister. Lucy was probably mentally memorizing them.

"Make him swim in circles to catch the bait. Translation: Wiggle your butt and strut your stuff but don't let him touch . . . yet."

"Let your boobs hang out," Lucy added.

"She's right; show off the goodies," Maddie said.

Lucy snapped her fingers. "And I have the perfect thing for you to wear. Lance won't be able to resist."

Maddie threw an arm around Lucy's shoulder. "Hey, Soph, I like your sister."

"You two are trouble together," Sophie said. "Trouble, trouble, trouble."

Lucy flipped through the pamphlet and pointed to item number sixty-nine. "There, Jezzy Bell. If that doesn't entice Lance Summers, then I'll give up my business."

Sophie winced. Both Maddie and Lucy were wrong, but maybe if she proved it to Lucy, she'd follow up on her promise and give up the business. Then at least one good thing would come out of her infatuation with Lance.

Lucy pushed the pamphlet in her face and Sophie examined the picture. No, there was no way she'd ever wear *that*. . . .

"Come on, Chase. We have to get Lance out of the house and back into circulation."

Chase followed Reid next door to Lance's side of the duplex. "But what if he doesn't want to go?"

"Then we drag him. He's letting this thing with Sophie distract him so much he's not thinking straight." Reid raised his fist and pounded on Lance's door. "I had to bail him out of the slammer the other morning."

"What happened?"

Reid kicked dirt from his boot as he explained, then rang the doorbell. "And he missed the meeting with McDaniels. You know how important that account is to the company."

Chase nodded. "Why doesn't he go out with the woman? Get her out of his system?"

"I don't know. He even warned me to stay away from her sister."

"Her sister?"

"Yeah, her name's Lucy. A hot strawberry blonde with a body to die for."

Chase laughed. "And you're going to listen to him?"

"Hell, no. She's too much fun."

"Uh-oh, that sounds serious."

Reid roared with laughter. "Me, serious about a woman? That'll be the day."

Finally the door swung open. Lance had the phone in his hand and seemed surprised to see them. "What are you doing here, guys?"

"We're kidnapping you." Reid snatched his brother's arm. "It's time you had some fun."

Lance had danced with so many women he felt light-headed from their mingled perfumes and names. What had his little brother told them, anyway? That he was desperate for female companionship? Had Reid and Chase paid the women to be solicitous to Lance while they shot pool in the back?

He'd already been propositioned twice, his crotch grabbed and squeezed, and one woman had offered to give him sex in the men's room. Of course, she was already married, so she definitely wasn't looking for a commitment.

Every man's dream.

Or was it?

He had struggled not to lecture the woman on honoring her wedding vows, but realized he'd sound like an old fuddy-duddy.

Maybe he was an old fuddy-duddy. But he didn't believe in infidelity. If he ever did succumb to the dreaded M-thing, it would be because he loved a woman with all his soul, and he'd never think of deceiving her.

Another reason not to tie the knot. How many women actually kept their wedding vows? When the tough got going, how many of them got going and *kept* going until they were completely out the door? And if he loved someone so completely, what would happen to him when they left him? He knew from experience that people didn't stick around forever.

The leggy redhead who'd dragged him away from the woman with the spidery hair and toxic perfume stepped on his toe with her stiletto heel for the third time. He glanced at the pool table and salivated, wishing for a guys' night out without women. Or even the boring night in with the tube that he'd planned earlier. A hundred and ten channels and nothing worth watching sounded damn good right now.

She stumbled, stabbing his toe again.

"Sorry, sugar." Long red acrylic nails tapped a suggestive dance across his back, and she cuddled closer. "You must work out."

Oh, please. Some of their pickup lines had been worse than any man's he'd ever heard. And he'd never seen a woman down tequila shots like this redhead.

She purred into his ear, "Are you a bodybuilder?"

"A construction worker." He could have said 'developer,' which sounded more impressive, but he didn't particularly want to impress her. Pancake makeup coated her face, and her body felt like a bag of bones.

She gyrated forward, sinking her nails into his arms to regain her balance. "I like a man who works with his hands."

He nodded, twirling her toward the bar area.

"And I love a man with a big hammer."

He stiffened as she licked at his ear.

"I especially like to watch him with a screwdriver."

Lance pulled back and looked her in the eye, searching for an excuse to vanish. The only thing that came to mind was that he had to go to the bathroom.

A few seconds later he caught up with Chase and Reid at the pool table.

"So how's it going?" Reid asked with a grin.

Lance scowled at him. "I've never had so many women proposition me. One girl even grabbed my balls on the dance floor."

Reid grinned. "Great, huh?"

"Are you kidding?" Lance rubbed a hand over the raw flesh on his arm. "I feel so cheap. All they want is to use me for sex."

Chase gaped at him, while Reid's eyes bugged out of his head. "My God, bro, you've turned into a woman."

The telephone jangled just as Lucy began escorting the guests to the door. Sophie snagged it on the third ring. "Hello?"

"Hey, Sophie, it's your mother."

Sophie tried not to react to the word. "Hey, Deseree, what's up?"

"I saw the show, honey; it was great! Are you going to see that young man again?"

Sophie rolled her eyes and cleared the dishes. "I don't think so."

"Why not? He's gorgeous and athletic and he must be smart or he wouldn't have made it so far in his career."

All probably true. "He's not my type."

"What is your type?"

Big, strong, Southern macho men who were over-protective of their baby sisters and worked with their hands. Lance. "A professional."

"A professor?"

"No, a professional, Deseree. You know, a lawyer, doctor, maybe even a TV producer."

"Well, I hope it works out. Did Lucy arrive all right?"

"Yes, she's here." Sophie frowned at her sister as she danced back to the den with a red boa draped around her neck.

"She called and told me she's going to be on your show. That's great, honey. I'd love to fly up and watch."

Sophie dropped the plate with a clatter. "I'm sorry, Deseree, but it's too late to make arrangements."

"Oh, darn, I thought it would be fun to be in the audience, watch my two girls together."

Since when had Deseree gotten sentimental? "Maybe another time." Or century.

"All right, I guess I should have thought of it sooner. Anyway, I wanted you to know I'd be watching. Can I speak to Lucy now?"

Sophie glanced at her sister. She had her hands full of sample products, a banana-shaped toy to be exact. "Let me get her." She covered the mouthpiece with one hand. "Lucy, phone."

Lucy grabbed the portable one and connected,

then sat down at the table to tally up her orders while she talked.

Sophie attacked the rest of the mess, unable to stand the disorder another minute. She finished cleaning the kitchen, then scrubbed the floors and emptied the trash. Adrenaline surged through her as she put the den back in order. She'd endured the chaos as long as possible.

She had to have some control over her life. Deseree's suggested impromptu visit had reminded her just how desperately she needed it.

Sophie had normally exercised that control in the way she dressed, in her precision with her makeup, in her living area, maintaining neatness to the point of being accused of being obsessive. It had started when she was little; it was her way of sorting through her troubles and making their low-rent apartment look less embarrassing when a friend stopped by.

Then she had heard the names they'd called her mother and had withdrawn, not making friends so she wouldn't be forced to expose her secrets if they wanted to visit.

You are past all that, Sophie. You've matured. Deseree is trying to get her act together. Lucy has grown up. And you're on your own.

She organized the magazines on the coffee table, spreading them out in a fan pattern, then glanced up to see Lucy hang up the phone. She was toying with the feather boa again. Well, technically Lucy was grown-up. Except judging from the nightlights she'd brought, she still harbored her childhood fear of the dark.

By the time she'd started the laundry, Lucy approached her. "I made nine hundred dollars tonight in orders. Isn't that fabulous?"

Sophie frowned. "Yes, but I still want you to find something more reputable."

Lucy leaned against the doorjamb between Sophie's bedroom and the hall. "You didn't have fun tonight?"

"It's not that, but you can't have these Sleepover parties the rest of your life."

"You're always so serious, Soph. Why can't you lighten up and have fun?"

"I do have fun." Sophie kicked off her shoes to make a point, then couldn't stand it and set them side by side neatly. "But I also have to be responsible."

"I'm responsible; I pay my own bills; I live on my own." Lucy looked troubled. "In fact, I'm trying to work things out with Deseree. You're the one who keeps avoiding her."

Sophie removed her earrings and bracelet and placed them in her jewelry case. "I'm not avoiding her." *I simply don't want her to show up and interfere with my life.*

"Then you'll come to Vegas for Mother's Day and have lunch with us?"

Sophie swallowed. "Mother's Day?"

"Yeah, it would mean a lot to Deseree."

She doubted that. "Do we have to bring a gift?"

Lucy reached out to squeeze Sophie's hand. "Seeing her again would be gift enough."

Old pains surfaced, but Sophie fought against them. If Lucy was mature enough to forgive their mother, then maybe it was time she did.

"Let me think about it, okay?"

"Okay." Lucy hugged her. "Oh, and thanks for letting me have the party here tonight. I like your friend Maddie."

Sophie nodded and went into her bathroom to

brush her teeth. The white tiles Lance had installed beamed, the antique pedestal claw-footed bathtub the perfect addition, especially with the polished nickel faucet. She'd kept the headboard wainscoting but had Lance refinish it along with the built-in cabinetry. The only thing left to choose was wallpaper or paint, and Maddie would help her with those selections.

A denim workshirt lay on the floor. Lance's—it was so hot he must have removed it when he'd been working.

She picked it up and sniffed the fabric, inhaling Lance's scent. It lingered in the soft folds of the shirt, reminding her of the man who'd worn it. The man who'd stolen her heart and broken it.

Knowing she shouldn't but unable to resist, she slid her dress to the floor, removed her underwear, and pulled on the shirt. It swallowed her, the ends brushing against her knees, the soft fabric caressing her nakedness as if Lance had run his fingers over her bare skin. She slowly buttoned the buttons, hugging Lance's fragrance to her as she crawled into bed and turned out the light.

She had to forget Lance and move on. He was not some white knight who'd ridden in to save her from loneliness.

Tomorrow she would move on. But for tonight, she closed her eyes and pretended that his arms were wrapped around her. . . .

As soon as Lance got home, he showered the stench of the women off of him. Maybe something was wrong with him. Ten, even five years ago, he'd have been thrilled to have gone home with any one of the women who'd made themselves available earlier in the evening. So why tonight, when he'd had his pick, had he gone cold turkey?

Because he wanted Sophie . . .

No. That wasn't possible. Sophie might have bewitching green eyes and short black hair that drove him wild with the desire to thumb his fingers through it, but she could be replaced. And he would damn well find a replacement.

Tomorrow.

First thing after work, he'd haul his ass to that singles place, maybe call that woman who'd left a message on his machine. He'd even take Reid with him for encouragement. Sophie had given him the membership; he might as well use it to find someone who could destroy this insane obsession with her.

Exhausted, he set up the rock garden, then stretched out on top of his unmade bed, turned on one of the tapes, and closed his eyes. Tonight he would find blissful sleep without the tortured thought of Sophie's bed calling to him from the other room. Or her body beckoning him . . .

An hour later, just as REM sleep finally claimed him, a nightmare drew him into its clutches. He was being buried alive beneath a mound of sex toys, big plastic vibrators that were beating at his head and humongous plastic boobs that cut off his oxygen supply. . . .

No, the boobs weren't fake—they were his; he had grown breasts . . . he had turned into a woman. And the sound of that damn waterfall was making him have to pee like a racehorse.

He jerked upright, shoving at the sheets, panting and sweating. In his effort to survive the avalanche of paraphernalia and the nightmare of having a gender change, he'd knocked his alarm clock off his end table.

Rita Herron

Determined to put the ridiculous dream out of his mind, he collapsed against the pillows. But sleep eluded him again, and this time he realized that he was afraid to doze off for fear of being turned into a female or being suffocated by a pair of mammoth breasts and a dildo the size of a baseball bat. . . .

Chapter Nine

Unable to sleep again, Lance had finally crawled from his bed, booted up his computer, and researched insomnia. Various articles on its causes and treatments had been written, although none of them seemed to offer any concrete solutions.

Keep the same routine. Go to bed at the same time every night. Drink hot herbal tea. Avoid alcohol and caffeine in the evenings. Exercise regularly.

Hell, the night before he'd gotten up and exercised—a hundred sit-ups, a hundred pull-ups on his bar; then he'd jogged in place for thirty minutes. He'd literally run himself until he'd dropped but he still hadn't been able to fall asleep. Not after that crazy dream.

If stressed, consider ways to alleviate that stress.

Okay, all he had to do was alleviate Sophie from his life and he would sleep like a baby. But that was impossible. At least until he finished the job.

Or let someone take over.

But he wouldn't relinquish his responsibilities—

he wanted to refinish that house, make certain every detail was handled properly. Besides, Sophie was Maddie's best friend; he was bound to run into her.

The name of a sleep clinic flashed onto his screen, and he considered a visit, but envisioned himself being strapped down like a lab rat, and delegated that idea to the back burner. Surely he could conquer this condition on his own. It had to be temporary, didn't it?

Just like his infatuation with Sophie Lane . . .

Irritable and worried because he hadn't heard from McDaniels on the deal yet, he phoned the man, but his secretary informed him that McDaniels would call him back. *Great.* Lance would give him twenty-four hours.

He showered, then hurried over to Sophie's. Maybe she'd be gone and he could avoid seeing her.

He was out of luck.

Sophie had given him a key, so when no one answered the doorbell he let himself in and nearly plowed over her trying to reach the door. The first thing he noticed was that she'd recently crawled from bed. She looked sleepy and tousled and so scrumptious he had to fold his hands into fists to keep from grabbing her.

The next thing he noticed was that she was wearing his shirt. And she had been sleeping in it.

Heaven help him. Early-morning sunlight painted a golden halo across her ivory skin, while shadows from the doorway framed her face. He swallowed to unglue his tongue from the roof of his mouth while the rest of his body exploded in heat. She looked a whole sight better in his clothes than he did. She was so petite, the shirt nearly engulfed her. The top two buttons had come unfastened, exposing the creamy white curves of her breasts, and below the hem, sexy bare legs stretched down to toes painted in bright red polish. His breath caught.

Then she moved and sunlight played through the threadbare fabric.

Holy hell, she was naked beneath his shirt.

"I . . ." She flicked her fingers through her hair, spiking it even more and making his body thrum with desire. Suddenly realizing that he had noticed she was wearing his shirt, she drew the top together defensively, her face scalding. "Lance, what are you doing here so early?"

"I couldn't sleep." Damn, he hadn't meant to reveal that. "I mean, I wanted to get started early."

She backed away, looking wary. "I was getting ready to shower. I . . . I just grabbed this off the floor when I heard the doorbell."

Right. Now images of her naked and covered in hot, steamy water and soap bubbles would haunt him all day.

He reached out to pluck a feather from her hair. "From your pillow?"

She nodded, biting down on her lip. "I . . . they're the softest."

Now he would imagine her lying naked on those feather pillows. . . . "We . . . uh, need to discuss a few things around here," Lance said, struggling to sound coherent as he lowered his hand. The damn thing betrayed him, though, and slid along her cheek, brushing skin so soft it felt like silk.

"I made a list," Sophie said in a strained voice. "And I'm planning to meet Maddie to pick out colors. The material I ordered for the new kitchen countertops should arrive this morning. . . ."

A heartbeat of silence stretched between them. She leaned into his hand and a groan built in his throat.

"Why don't we have dinner tonight?" Lance suggested. "To review your plans."

"I can't." Sophie wet her lips, drawing him to the delicate pink skin. Her mouth tasted like sweetness and spice. He wanted to taste it again. And one flick and the third button on his shirt would pop open; then the cotton would glide down her slender arms and puddle at her feet.

"Soph." Lucy's voice cut into his consciousness with the force of a machete breaking glass.

Sophie stepped away from his touch. He dropped his hands to his sides.

Either oblivious to what she'd interrupted or choosing to ignore the tension hanging in the air, Lucy bobbed into the room. "What time are we going to the station?"

"A half hour." Sophie wrapped her arms around her waist. "We'll grab a bagel and coffee from around the corner so Lance can get to work."

"Great."

"About tonight?" Lance asked when he sensed Sophie was on the verge of running.

"She can't," Lucy interjected.

So she had been listening to their conversation?

"You have a date, don't you, Soph?" Lucy said.

Sophie's eyes widened like those of a deer caught in headlights. "Uh, right, I'm sorry, Lance. Maybe we can talk after work, before I go out."

Lance's jaw snapped tight. "Sure."

Sophie disappeared into her bedroom, and Lucy beamed him a smile. He forced a reciprocal one, although his gut had begun to churn. Who was Sophie seeing this time? Dalton again, or another man?

He rubbed a hand over the back of his neck. What difference did it make? Hadn't he decided to check out that singles service this evening?

And he would, as soon as he finished here. Then he'd finally be able to put Sophie Lane and *her* date out of his mind forever.

"Why did you have to say that?" Sophie asked Lucy as they rushed into Starbucks for coffee.

Lucy's innocent expression had to be fake. "Why did I have to say what?"

"That I had a date," Sophie said in a hiss, joining the mile-long line in front of the coffee counter.

"Because making a guy jealous is the best way to get his attention. Isn't that one of Maddie's seven rules for trapping a man?"

"No." Sophie strained her brain to remember them. "Well, maybe, sort of."

"It definitely should be."

Sophie released an exasperated sigh.

Lucy rolled her eyes. "Honestly, Soph, sometimes I don't think you understand men at all."

"And you're an expert?"

"No, but everyone knows that a man gets jealous only if he really cares."

"Lance doesn't care." Miserable and confused, Sophie moved up in the line, eyeing a double-chocolate muffin. To heck with staying slim. She needed comfort food in a bad way.

"Then you've lost nothing by going out with another man."

"But that's just it, Lucy—I don't have another date." Although when Rory got back from his trip, she could call and give him another chance.

Lucy planted her hands on her hips. Several men in line straightened their ties, coughed, and gave her the eye. "Aren't you interviewing several singles services on the show today?"

Sophie winced. "I hate to resort to those. They're for desperate women."

Lucy arched a brow.

"I'm not desperate." Although the clock was counting down until the big three-oh.

"Two beautiful women should go first." A handsome blond man wearing Ralph Lauren gestured for Lucy to step in front of him, and she batted her long eyelashes at him like a vixen.

"Thanks so much." Lucy winked at Sophie, then whispered, "See, Soph, go with the flow. Men are everywhere. We could get you a date right here if we wanted."

Sophie glanced around the crowd in horror. "You wouldn't."

Mischief gleamed in Lucy's eyes as she pivoted toward the man. "Hi, my name's Lucy,"

Sophie hissed a warning, but she was too late.

Lucy swung an arm around Sophie's shoulders. "This is my sister, Sophie. She needs a date tonight; are you busy?"

Lance worked all morning tearing out the faded and cracked countertops, cabinets, and the old stovetop. By lunchtime he'd started installing the new painted cabinetry, which was enhanced with decorative millwork, open glass fronts, and vertical plate racks. Later he'd add a kitchen island in the center, as Sophie had requested. She had ordered granite countertops in a Wedgwood blue with pewter hardware and a backsplash in a fruit motif. Even the Victoria faucet, dubbed the English Teakettle faucet, gave the feel of the rustic Victorian era. The combination of all the elements she'd chosen fit the time period, added color and charm, and, while giving the home an air of sophistication with the upgraded materials, still felt homey.

Reid had brought a crew to replace the rotten flooring on the back porch, which Sophie planned to enclose into a sunroom. Lance had to admit he admired her intentions. Realizing it was time for Sophie's show he flipped on the small TV in the corner, telling himself it would keep him awake while he worked. He really wasn't interested.

Reid strode in, wiping his forehead, and poured himself a glass of sweet iced tea Sophie had left for them. The music zinged for the lead-in, and Sophie pranced onstage wearing a dark blue suit that hugged her curves and showcased her dynamite knees.

He had it bad if he was noticing knees.

"Welcome to the *Sophie Knows* show," she said, smiling at the audience. "Today we're continuing our singles series by talking with two different matchmaking services in Savannah. Welcome our guests. . . ."

Lance hauled the broken countertop pieces outside, surprised when he returned and discovered Reid glued to the set. "Hey, man, isn't that the same service you won a membership to?"

Lance nodded.

"Have you filled out your résumé and checked to find your match?"

"No, but apparently Sophie put my name in, and I've already gotten some calls. I can't believe the women didn't wait until I'd filled out my profile or sent in a picture."

"Must be desperate or hungry for a man." Reid pulled out the chair to Sophie's computer and booted it up, then brought up the Web site. "Let's do it now, maybe narrow down the field and weed out any losers." Reid grunted as he studied the site. "Okay, answer these questions."

Lance pushed his hair from his face. "I don't have time—"

"It only takes five minutes."

"I'm not in the mood, Reid."

Okay, I'll fill in what I know. "Description. Likes, dislikes. Job. Salary?" Reid cut his eyes toward Lance. "Can you believe they ask about money?"

"Women want rich men."

Reid grunted. "What kind of woman are you looking for?"

Lance hesitated. One who looked like Sophie but didn't want commitment. "Dark hair, petite. Good-looking."

"Stacked. That's a given." Reid filled in the information. "Job preferences? Or do you want Suzy Homemaker, bro?"

Lance laughed. "I don't know. You answer for me."

Reid grinned. "All right." He typed in some information, then began to recite Lance's qualifications. "Attractive, professional, likes outdoor activities, enjoys dining out, wants to have fun . . ."

A few minutes later, the printer spit out several pages of potential matches.

Reid waved him over. "Take a look at these."

Single female seeking sexy male who makes $100,000 plus.

Lance tossed the printout in the trash.

Single female seeking single or married man who makes $100,000 plus.

Another toss.

Single female, forty-seven, seeking younger man who makes $100,000 plus.

Trash. "Geez, what is it with these women?" Lance asked.

"Hey, this one sounds great." Reid skimmed it. "Sexy, female, 40DD, professionally employed, athletic, likes all sports, especially sailing, looking for fun relationship—"

"Sounds good so far."

Reid read on. "Will meet anywhere, anytime, do anything." He choked, then handed it to Lance. "You have to read all the way to the last line."

Lance finished, "Recovering from recent sex change operation." Lance wadded it into a ball. "This is a waste of time."

"No, wait." Reid offered him another one. "This one sounds perfect. Single female, twenty-nine, dark hair, green eyes, employed, likes water sports—"

"She doesn't mention salary requirements?"

"Nope."

"And she's not a transvestite or a cross-dresser or a female serial killer?"

"Nope."

Lance accepted the listing. Maybe he would give her a try. At least she had the physical attributes right: dark hair, green eyes. . . .

"The show was great," Lucy said as she and Sophie drove back to Sophie's.

"I'm glad you enjoyed it." Sophie maneuvered through traffic, a twinge pulling at her stomach when she spotted Lance's truck still in the drive. "Uh-oh, I was hoping he was gone."

"All the more reason for you to check out the singles services you interviewed today," Lucy said. "You were right to agree to a few dates."

"I only did that because of the show." Sophie sighed. More cameras. More pretending. It seemed she'd been pretending all her life. Putting on a show . . .

"Right. But you'll meet a lot of men that way, get yourself out there, take a chance. The karma's completely off between you and Lance."

Lucy logic again. She'd gotten into all that New Agey stuff in the past year. Once Sophie thought she'd seen her sister singing to the moon. "I'm taking a chance tonight, Lucy." Sophie jammed her cell phone into her purse, parked in her drive, and opened the door. "I still can't believe you asked that guy in Starbucks to date me. For God's sake, you almost propositioned him. For a minute you sounded like . . ."

"Like Deseree?" Lucy's lower lip wilted.

A pang of guilt assaulted Sophie. "No, I . . . I didn't mean it like that." She squeezed her sister's hand. "I know you would never resort to some of the things Deseree did."

"Maybe Deseree was desperate," Lucy said in her typical naive mode. "She probably didn't know any other way to survive, and she certainly never had any help or support."

"Maybe," Sophie conceded. "But there are other ways, and we're not Deseree."

"You've been serious way too long, Soph. Don't worry; we'll both have fun." Lucy launched into a spiel about sneaking along a few products from her silver case to entertain the Hispanic man she'd met at the coffee shop, but Sophie shushed her when Lance appeared, dragging a box of trash toward his truck.

Sophie hopped out, stuffed her briefcase under her arm, and strutted up the sidewalk, pretending nonchalance as Lance watched her out of the corner of his eye.

"You'd better hurry to get dressed for your evening out," Lucy said a little too loudly. "Your date will be here soon."

Sophie wanted to throttle and hug her sister at the same time. Still, she took the opportunity to dash into the house to refresh herself before her date appeared.

What was his name, anyway?

A half hour later Sophie had half her closet spread on her bed, undecided what to wear. The mess in the house was driving her crazy. Her kitchen was torn apart, a small portion of the cabinets installed while Lance lay shirtless on the floor installing the rest. She'd wanted to ask him why he was half-naked, then realized that her air conditioner was on the fritz, which meant another repair—and endless nights of being haunted by the image of Lance without a shirt.

Lucy knocked, then vaulted into the room wearing a black leather miniskirt, a silver spandex tube top, a see-through black jacket/blouse over it, and sparkly eye shadow shimmering above her eyes. "Are you almost ready?"

Sophie eyed her wardrobe choices dubiously. "Not quite."

Lucy glanced at the bed and grimaced. "Oh, come on, Soph, you're not really considering that yucky green dress?"

"It's a designer knockoff. I want to downplay my role on *Sophie Knows*."

"It's hideous. You're not going to a Baptist revival."

"It's conservative."

"It's dowdy. Now get serious."

Sophie made a frustrated sound, then revisited her closet. A few minutes later, with Lucy's guidance, she emerged dressed in a slinky scoop-necked black cocktail dress that she'd bought for a party the station had hosted for local celebrities.

Lucy stepped back and whistled. "Fabulous."

Sophie scrutinized her reflection. "My boobs are hanging out."

Lucy pushed her own goods upward into her bra. "Perfect for Maddie's rules. Strut your stuff but don't let him touch."

"Don't worry about that; I don't intend to hop in the sack with this guy tonight." The doorbell rang and they both dashed from her room. "What was his name, anyway?"

"Jeremy—now be nice." Lucy teetered away for the door while Sophie paused to catch her breath.

Trouble was, Lance filled the hallway with a cabinet he was carting outside. They both paused and waited; then she rushed forward, wondering about could-have-beens. They met in the middle of the corridor, their bodies brushing against each other as they passed. Sophie felt the hard planes of his body and a thousand sensations slivered through her. Lance's intake of breath and the way he drew his shoulders away from her indicated he'd been affected as well. Feeling suddenly wicked, she drew in a deep breath, letting her chest expand and her taut nipples brush his naked, sweaty chest.

His gaze dropped to hers and he stilled, his lower body pulsing against the small of her stomach. Heat speared through Sophie. Hunger darkened the irises of his eyes. Her own breath quickened. His gaze dropped to her lips. She wet them with her tongue. He followed the movement.

"Yoo-hoo, Sophie, Jeremy's here."

Sophie released the breath she'd been holding. Disappointment mingled with desire. "My, er, date."

He shoved the cabinet out of the way and stepped aside. "By all means, have fun. I've got to get going, too—finally decided to try out that singles service you connected me with."

She pasted on a fake smile and headed toward the man waiting at the door, wondering who exactly Lance would be seeing tonight. Remembering Maddie's advice, though, she added an extra little sway to her hips.

She might be through with Lance, but she definitely wanted him to suffer. A tear threatened but she quashed it.

And she definitely wanted him to think of her while he was out with that other bimbette.

Lance didn't know if he could suffer through the remainder of the evening with this woman. Jamie James smoked like a fiend, ate like a horse, and so far had inhaled three shots of bourbon straight up without batting a false eyelash. And they were false, along with her nails, the nose job, and her boobs, which she had informed him cost thirty-five hundred dollars each, a gift from her third ex-husband in the divorce settlement. In return, she'd given him the Porsche, the second home in Denver, and the live-in-maid whom he was sleeping with.

Her only redeeming quality as far as he was concerned was the fact that she didn't have a police record. She'd told him that right up front, along with her personal and medical history, and a gynecological report that offered way too much information.

He tried to focus on his beer and ignore her inquisition.

"Now, Lance, do you have any serious medical problems?"

Was this first-date conversation these days? If so,

135

he'd been out of touch a long damn time. "No."

"Any venereal diseases?"

Weren't women supposed to be into all that getting-to-know-you chit-chat shit like, *Do you like football or romantic music?*

"Uh-oh, what—syphilis? Gonorrhea? AIDS?"

He coughed. "No."

"To all three?"

He yanked at his collar, sweat beading on his forehead. "Yes, to all three."

Horror streaked her face. "Yes, you have all three diseases?"

"No, geesh, I don't have any diseases."

"Thank goodness." She blew a breath between even white teeth, then waved for the bartender. "Prior children?"

His gaze shot to hers. "Definitely not."

"All right, then, I think this might work."

"Excuse me?" He cradled his beer and downed the rest of it. "What might work? You've just given me twenty questions."

"I know, and I'm sorry." She patted his hand, then reached into her purse and placed a plastic vial on the table in front of him. "But I had to know all those things before we could continue."

He eyed the vial with trepidation. "Continue what?"

"Making a baby."

"A baby?"

"Yes, I joined the singles service to find a sperm donor."

His hands began to shake. "You did what?"

"I want you to father my child." She finally gave him a smile. "Actually, consider yourself lucky. So far I've interviewed fifty-three candidates and no one filled all my requirements except you."

SLEEPLESS IN SAVANNAH

He gulped. He certainly didn't feel lucky. And he had no intention of fathering this lunatic's baby.

"Uh, excuse me; I have to go to the bathroom."

She grinned when he stood, then grabbed his hand. "Don't forget this." She slid the vial into the palm of his hand and closed his fingers around it. Heat scalded Lance's neck as he shoved his fist into his pocket and strode to the bathroom.

Surely he could find a back door. . . .

Chapter Ten

Sophie glanced at the door to the coffee shop where she and her date had stopped after dinner, surprised to see Lance peering through the doorway. What was he doing here? And where was this woman he'd planned to meet?

He strode in, his masculine presence suddenly filling the crowded shop and making Jeremy's lean build look almost feminine.

"Basically it requires a multitude of shots," Jeremy said. "Then I go in with the scalpel—actually some patients call it a gum knife . . ."

Sophie shivered. He had been giving her the basics on performing a root canal—in other words, boring her to tears for the last half hour. The only way she had survived was to people-watch and nod, neither of which he noticed due to his overinflated ego and obsession with himself.

But Lance glanced her way, and she jerked her head toward Jeremy, pretending interest.

As soon as they'd left dinner, Lucy and her date

had run off to go clubbing, claiming the coffee shop didn't quite meet Lucy's standards for excitement. At one time it hadn't met Sophie's either. Just last year she'd been content to attend new show openings and parties with Maddie. They'd even gone to that nudist colony. But the upcoming big three-oh—and seeing Maddie settled with a husband—had triggered her own desires for family, stability, love. . . .

"Last week I performed three root canals in a row; then I did an implant for this lady who bit into a caramel and lost her crown. That was a piece of work. I could show you the X rays, if you'd like; it's really fascinating. . . ."

Smile and nod. Maybe she should have gone with Lucy. At least alcohol might dull the drone of his monotone.

Jeremy's beeper sounded. "Sorry, forgot to tell you I'm on call."

Sophie sipped her mocha, praying he had an emergency. "No problem; go ahead."

He popped his cell phone off his belt and clicked in some numbers, his face animated as he spoke. "Okay, ma'am, calm down. Bring the teeth in. I can save them. . . ." Pause. His chest puffed out with pride. "Yes, all right. Meet me at the office."

He snapped the phone shut with a halfhearted sigh. "I'm going to have to call the evening short. A twelve-year-old knocked his front two permanent teeth out in a backyard baseball game."

"By all means, you should go," Sophie said, sorry for the poor child but grateful for the reprieve. "I'll get a taxi home."

"You're sure you don't mind? I can take you first." He squeezed her hands and she noticed his nails were manicured. His skin felt surprisingly soft, too, unlike Lance's work-roughened hands.

So she was odd—she much preferred Lance's calluses and wood-stained fingernails. "I'm sure. Go on; the child needs you."

"Let's do it again, Sophie. I had a wonderful time." He dipped his head and kissed her cheek.

She nodded and smiled again, accepting the obligatory gesture. Sure, he'd had a wonderful time. He'd talked nonstop about himself. Cradling her cup in her hands, she tried to ignore the fact that Lance was walking her way and that he'd seen her date desert her. Seconds later he slid onto the love seat beside her. In a typical manly move, he sat with his big legs spread wide so that they brushed her bare thigh. In spite of the air conditioner, hot air swirled around her, the scent of his body intoxicating. All she could think of was crawling in his arms and burying herself against his chest.

Unfortunately she'd have to settle for crawling into his shirt later on and burying her head against her own pillow.

He was wearing a hint of cologne, too, something slightly woodsy. Because he'd been on a date with another woman.

"Your date ran out on you?" he asked, a little too smugly.

"He's a doctor," Sophie blurted, tugging at the hem of her skirt as Lance's gaze fixated on her legs. "He had an emergency."

His smile faltered slightly. "A doctor, huh? Sounds like a good match."

For a doormat. "How about you? I thought you had plans tonight? Early evening?"

He cut his gaze away from her and sipped his coffee. "A disaster."

"Really?" *Too bad.* "So, what are you doing here? Following me?"

Lance shrugged. "I saw you come in, thought I'd drop by and tell you that that service you set me up with has some weirdos."

Poor baby. So he was blaming her for his date bombing. And had he really dropped in to tell her that, or did he want to see her? Her heart fluttered at the thought, but she refused to get her hopes up. "What kind of weirdos?"

Lance angled his head to peer down at her, his eyes grave. "Let's just say she wanted more than I was willing to give."

"Like you thought I did?"

His gaze darkened; then a low chuckle reverberated from his chest. "Not quite. She wanted a baby and wanted me to well, er . . . you know."

Sophie's mouth gaped open. "You're kidding."

He raised his hand in a pledge-type pose. "The gospel. Brought a little plastic cup with her."

Sophie laughed. "Okay, you win."

"Win what?"

"The worst-date contest."

Lance laughed, too, and they actually talked a few minutes, sharing the worst parts of their catastrophic evenings.

"Let me take you home," Lance suggested as they finished their coffee.

Sophie hesitated. She was enjoying their camaraderie too much. "That's not necessary, Lance. I'm a big girl; I'll call a cab—"

"I'm well aware of that," Lance said in a gruff voice. "But I'm still taking you home. My Blazer's down the street. We can discuss the renovations, since we didn't get a chance to earlier."

Of course, work. Nothing personal. "Right." She

stood and he lowered his hand to the small of her back, sending a delicious tingle up her spine.

They left the coffee and chocolate scents and chatter behind, only to be engulfed in the fresh fragrances of summer flowers and the sounds of Savannah tourists and the river in the background. The nearly full moon spilled soft light on the sidewalks, the Spanish moss draping the giant live oaks in the small parks creating canopies of privacy as they strolled back to his car. The simple sound of Lance's footsteps on the pavement and his breath in the quiet of the evening stirred her heart to an irregular beat. When she climbed into his Blazer, she couldn't help but notice he'd cleaned the inside.

For another woman.

A surge of jealousy snaked through her. Why couldn't the two of them be together? Why couldn't Lance love her?

He steered the truck away from the downtown area and she savored the short ride. She just hoped she didn't arrive home and find Lucy having sex with her date. . . .

Lucy had ditched her date after the second dance, claiming she'd spotted her old boyfriend on the dance floor and she didn't want trouble. Not that she hadn't been having fun, but she had something else she needed to do tonight while Sophie and Lance weren't around.

She was going to concoct a potion to help Sophie in the romance department.

Granted, Sophie had all the proper elements—sex appeal in spades, wit, intelligence—but she had obviously failed with Lance and that Dalton man because she wasn't putting out the right vibes. Lucy had a cure for that, although she was admittedly grateful Lance hadn't decided to pursue her sister.

Lucy wanted her sister to be happy; she really did. But Sophie harbored such a crush on Lance Summers that it worried her.

He was the wrong man for her sister. Wrong. Wrong. Wrong.

Sophie didn't need marriage. She needed someone fun-loving, exciting. A man able to tear her out of her self-imposed prison of responsibility and order and show her how to live. Lance was too solemn, too intense, too unable to loosen up. Lucy hadn't once seen him smile since he'd been working at her sister's. Not like his brother, Reid.

She desperately wanted to see that yum-licious man again.

Opening up her *Charms and Talismans* book, she found the perfect recipe, a spell to keep Sophie from making mistakes in love. Unearthing her caftan from her suitcase, she put it on, then draped beads around her head just as she'd seen a voodoo priestess do at a festival she'd attended in Vegas. Then she took a small piece of parchment paper, and with the Dove's Blood Ink she'd bought at the magic shop on her way home, drew the configuration of letters shown in the book. Next she blew on the parchment paper to dry the ink, then folded it and slipped it inside Sophie's day purse so she'd have it with her most of the time. The final step—she sprinkled Jinx Removing Salt all around the house, making certain to put it by all the windows and doors.

When she finished, she decided to add a spell to stir sexual desires and help Sophie find new sex partners. A new lover would be the quickest cure for her Lance lust. She hung the talisman over Sophie's front doorway. The charm was supposed to open up hearts at first meeting, allowing love to shine through or making the person want to go to bed with you. The smiling goddess on the talisman denoted the goddess of lust, passion and sensuality. Perfect.

She opened some incense, but a noise sounded at the door. Voices.

Sophie's and a man's? Not Jeremy's.

She sneaked to the window and peeked out, surprised to see Lance on the doorstep with her sister. Thank goodness they hadn't arrived home when she'd been sprinkling the salts around or the charm wouldn't work.

Now all she had to do was gather pebbles and arrange them around a pink candle, then burn it every night for seven minutes at sunset and Sophie would have all the new lovers she could handle. Then she wouldn't need to pine over Lance Summers.

And Lucy wouldn't have to worry about her sister getting married and leaving her alone. . . .

Lance stood on the front porch of Sophie's house, wondering if she'd bought his earlier story about dropping in the coffee shop to complain about the dating service. When he had passed the shop and seen her with the other guy, he'd had a total out-of-body, freak jealousy attack and followed her in, hoping to get rid of her date for her.

Now he was just damn mesmerized by her sultry presence. Although they'd already talked for over an hour, and he had developed a good understanding of Sophie's plans for the house he still hesitated, reluctant to leave less the good doctor show up to make up for running out on her by administering some mouth-to-mouth. "So you're going to keep the wood flooring?"

"Of course. In fact I want to strip away all the carpet," Sophie said.

He wanted to strip her, Lance thought, his gaze dropping to the low-necked slinky black dress she'd worn for her date. "And have them refinished?"

"That, too." Sophie's green eyes sparkled beneath the moonlight as he inched closer to her. Her back was pressed against the wood molding of the doorway, her delicate face angled upward so she could look into his eyes. Her mouth drew him, made him ache.

"I want the whitewashed look for the kitchen floors," she said.

"And Victorian accessories throughout."

"Absolutely."

He lowered his head toward her. "Craftsmanship is important to you?"

Her voice grew softer. "Only the best."

"It sounds as if you know exactly what you want."

A small smile curved Sophie's lips, triggering sensations inside him. "I do. Things that will last forever," she whispered. "But I'm not sure I can afford everything I want."

His chest squeezed as he feathered a strand of hair away from her cheek. "Cost too high?"

Sophie nodded and licked her lips. "I'm afraid so."

He cupped the base of her head in his hand, his entire body tightening at the way her breath whispered out. Hunger, denial, and need bolted through him. He forgot they were talking about her house and furniture and flooring. The cost of wanting her was too high.

The price of not having her was even more painful.

Unable to control his tortured body's response to

the flutter of desire in her eyes, he lowered his mouth and claimed her. The first touch of her lips sent fire burning through his belly; the second had his body hard and throbbing. And when she threaded her fingers in his hair and answered with a slow thrust of her tongue, he pressed her against the wall and kissed her as if his thirst would never be quenched. She dragged her hands over his shoulders and down his back, kneading his muscles with fingertips that urged him to deepen the torture. And he did.

Reason was forgotten.

He gently trailed kisses along her jaw, then up her neck to the sensitive shell of her ear, and lower. Unbearable need pulsed through him. She tasted like fire and sin, and sultry promises that turned his senses inside out with want. His hands tiptoed across her shoulders and down her torso, the pressure of her breasts against his chest intensely erotic. He wanted to touch her there, too, to taste her sweetness and hear her cry out his name as he suckled her. Another sip at her neck and he licked his way down to the curve of her breasts, but suddenly the porch light sprang on.

Seconds later the door burst open. "Sophie!" Lucy's head flounced through the opening. "Oh, my gosh, I didn't mean to interrupt. I heard voices and wanted to make sure that pervert wasn't back."

He stiffened, lowering his hands in front of him to hide his erection, while Sophie ran her hands through her hair trying to tame the wild ends. The gesture simply enticed him more.

Then Lucy's words rang through his sex-starved brain. *The pervert?* So Sophie hadn't informed her sister that he'd been arrested?

"Lucy," Sophie said in a warning voice. "Uh, there wasn't a pervert—"

"There was, too. I saw him, and called the police."

"You called the police?" Lance said.

"Yes, of course. What did you expect me to do, let him stalk us?"

"He wasn't a stalker," Sophie said.

Lance's anger cropped back. "You had me arrested?"

"You're the pervert," Lucy said.

"I'm not a pervert," Lance said tightly, "or a stalker." But before Sophie he was a legendary sleeper—eight to ten hours a night.

"It was a misunderstanding," Sophie said, trying to play peacemaker. "Lucy, Lance was watching the house because he was worried about us with the door missing."

Lucy wrinkled her nose. "Sophie and I can take care of ourselves. We don't need a man; for goodness' sake, we grew up in Vegas."

Sophie gently pushed her sister's arm, urging her back inside. "Lucy, that's enough."

Lance backed away. For some reason Sophie's sister didn't seem to like him.

What had he done to make her disapprove of him?

"What are you doing home so early? I expected you and loverboy to tie one on." Sophie closed the door, instantly annoyed at the sight of Lucy's things strewn across the den. Knowing her attempts to teach Lucy to be a neatnik were futile, she bit her tongue, more important issues rising to the surface.

Like Lucy's rotten timing. Why had she interrupted her and Lance? And why had she been so hostile?

"I started feeling guilty about leaving you with Jeremy, and decided to come home so we could spend some time together."

Guilt tugged at Sophie for being irritated. Lucy was in town for only the week. If she could give up a man, which was rare for Lucy, in exchange for time with her sister, Sophie shouldn't complain.

She threw her arm around Lucy's shoulders and they walked to the den. "Sorry, I didn't mean to snap. I was just surprised."

"And disappointed because I interrupted you two getting it on." Lucy gave her a curious look. "What exactly *is* going on between you Lance?"

Sophie dropped onto the sofa, perplexed herself. "I . . . I'm not sure."

"You were making out?"

Sophie shrugged. "He kissed me."

"I saw that."

Sophie narrowed her eyes. "You interrupted on purpose?"

Lucy winced. "No, I did hear a noise; then I opened the door and saw you." She toyed with the pillow on the sofa. "Are things moving forward with you two?"

"I don't know," Sophie said, miserable. "One minute we were talking about the renovations; the next we were tangled together in a lip-lock."

"He's a good kisser?"

Sophie pressed her fingers to her temple. "The best."

"You're in love with him, aren't you?"

Sophie groaned and dropped her head into her hands. "I'm trying not to be. After all, he did trick himself out of that date with me. And he's given me no reason to think he wants a relationship."

"Then stick to Maddie's rules." Lucy twirled a

strand of hair around one finger. "What was rule number five?"

"Make sure his teeth are sunk in; then reel him in."

"His teeth aren't sunk yet?"

"They only nibbled at the surface."

"So it was a good thing I interrupted. You indulged in some foreplay, but it's way too soon to consummate."

Sophie moaned again. She desperately had wanted to consummate things. "Right."

Lucy patted her back sympathetically. "How'd you end up together, anyway? I thought you and Jeremy were having coffee."

"We did." Sophie explained about his emergency. "But I have to admit that I was grateful when he left, Lucy. Jeremy is—"

"Boring."

Sophie laughed. "Dreadfully so."

"Sorry, Soph." Lucy clasped Sophie's hand, a wicked gleam in her eyes that Sophie didn't quite understand. "We'll do better for you next time."

"What do you have up your sleeve, Lucy?"

Lucy feigned innocence. "Nothing. But you're going to accept dates from that singles service for the show, right?"

"Did you have to remind me?"

"It'll be fun," Lucy said. "And who knows, you might just meet Mr. Right from one of the listings."

"And if I don't?"

"Then you'll have fun." Lucy pulled her into a hug. "After all, we don't need a man, Soph. We have each other. Together we're invincible, remember?"

Sophie hugged her. "Of course I do, silly. We'll always have each other."

Lucy nodded. "And no man will ever come between us."

Sophie heard traces of the fear she and Lucy had lived with as children. Deseree had let the men in her lives do exactly that, replace her time and feelings for her children. But Sophie and Lucy had vowed never to fall into that trap.

"No, Lucy, no man will ever come between us."

Emotions Ping-Ponged in Lance's head as he left Sophie's. He hated the fact that Lucy didn't like him, but adrenaline still surged through him from the steamy kiss he'd shared with Sophie. He had wanted more. Sophie had wanted more.

He would never sleep tonight for dreaming about having more.

Perspiration beaded on his forehead, and he cranked down his window to let some cool air inside. But the temperature had risen to the high nineties and the air felt sultry. Just as Sophie's touch had.

Maybe he should give in and sleep with her to purge her from his system. But what if that didn't work? What if one time only made him crave another and another and he became obsessed with her and needed her, and then she left him?

His sleep deprivation must be getting to him, making him crazy.

Because you're crazy over Sophie.

No, crazy in lust, maybe, but he and Sophie really had nothing in common. Other than the fact that they both liked restoring the house, and that she took care of her little sister just as he had with his . . .

His cell phone rang, jarring him, and he grabbed it off the console. "Lance here."

"Hey, man, it's Reid. Listen, McDaniels phoned

and left a message. If we're still interested in this deal, he wants us to meet him at seven AM at that new Pancake Palace."

Lance sighed in relief. "Don't worry, bro; I'll be there."

Reid agreed to meet him, then hung up. The local drugstore caught Lance's eye, and he veered into the parking lot and rushed inside. He wouldn't allow images of Sophie or the heat wave to keep him awake tonight. He'd find some over-the-counter sleeping pill and down it so he could spend the night in peace for a change and be fresh for his morning meeting.

A good night's rest, and he'd be able to put this insane attraction in perspective and get back on track.

Sometime around four in the morning, the sleeping pill finally took effect. Unfortunately, Lance had doubled the dosage out of desperation, and he slept straight through his alarm clock. A banging on the door finally woke him from his slumber. He dragged the pillow over his eyes, certain a bulldozer had attacked the house. The banging continued, the windows rattling from the force. Maybe it was an earthquake.

Cursing beneath his breath, he plastered both hands over his ears and burrowed further down into the bed. His limbs felt as if they'd been weighed down with concrete boulders, and pain sliced through his temple as if a chain saw had been unleashed on his skull.

Then a door slammed shut in the den, footsteps cut through the noise, and Reid appeared in his bedroom. Lance managed to tear one eyelid open enough to squint through the early-morning sun-shine.

"What the hell are you doing in bed?" Reid roared. "You missed the meeting. And this time McDaniels says he's finished with us for good."

Chapter Eleven

Sleep forgotten, Lance charged out of bed, sick to his stomach that he'd missed the meeting and let his brother down. For God's sake, his company's immediate and possible long-term future depended on him staying on his toes instead of on his back in bed, regardless of whether or not he'd had any sleep in the last decade.

"I'll fix it; I swear I will, Reid." He reached for the phone and began to punch in numbers.

"It's no use," Reid said. "He was pretty pissed. Let him cool down first."

Lance dropped the phone, disgusted with himself. He'd always been the responsible one. Reid counted on him. "I'll apologize. Grovel." Lie if he had to, but he'd damn well do everything he could to salvage this deal.

Reid made a *harrumph* sound. "I don't know what's gotten into you, Lance. Are you sick or something?"

Sick with lust. "Or something."

Reid eyed him with suspicion. "You don't have some disease, do you? Ulcers, a heart problem?"

Both. "My health is fine." Lance rubbed a hand over his beard stubble. "I just haven't been sleeping lately."

Reid folded his arms and leaned against the doorjamb. "A woman, right?"

Lance frowned and cut his eyes sideways at his alarm clock. At least he'd gotten three and a half hours.

"Sophie?"

Lance unrolled his fisted hands and stared at his stained fingernails, struggling to formulate an answer.

"Jesus, Lance, if she bugs you that much, why not go to bed with her and get her out of your system?"

Hadn't he contemplated the same idea the night before?

"Because she wants more than I can give."

"Maybe once you connect, she'll get tired of you."

Lance's head jerked up.

"It's happened before, hasn't it?"

Did Reid have to remind him of his other failed relationships? Not that he wanted a relationship . . .

"You take things way too seriously, man. It's obviously been too long since you've been with a woman." Lance opened his mouth to argue, but Reid raised his hand in warning. "Go on, get laid; then you can focus back on business." With that last bit of advice, Reid turned and strode out the door.

Lance stared at his retreating back, wondering if it could be a simple as his little brother suggested.

Either way, he had a lot to do to convince Mc-Daniels to give him a second chance. And he was going to call that sleep clinic and set up an appointment.

The getting laid part he'd have to think about. . . .

* * *

Desperate for help, Reid drove toward Sophie's to talk to Lucy. He had never seen his brother behave so oddly. If Lance didn't get his act together, their company might fall apart.

And all because of a *woman*.

But what could he do? He and Lance had interfered with Maddie and Chase and almost kept them apart. He wouldn't make the same mistake with his brother and try to keep him from someone he loved. If Reid could do something to help Lance get with Sophie, he'd give it a try. After all, he owed Lance everything.

If his brother hadn't taken care of him and Maddie, he would have been lost. No, not just lost; he might have floundered forever. Reid had enjoyed being part of the Terrible Three, Lance, Chase and Reid, the bad boys. He'd liked the excitement of living on the edge of trouble a little too much, and might have followed a path into complete destruction. A simple drunk and disorderly might have turned into serious jail time; hot-trodding on the highway might have escalated into joyriding with a stranger's car; and Reid would probably be making license plates now instead of building three-hundred-thousand-dollar homes.

He shuddered, grateful Lance had discovered his love of renovating houses and forced Reid to work with a hammer and nails to keep him off the streets.

He'd save his brother now.

He'd also heed his brother's advice and steer clear of a relationship with Lucy. Luscious, sexy little Lucy.

Still, he could use her help. . . .

Certain he had mastered control of his emotions and his attraction to Sophie's sister, Reid parked his

155

Tahoe in front of Sophie's, determined to speak with Lucy, then finish up over at Skidaway so he could help Lance complete Sophie's renovations.

He rubbed a hand over his face as he approached the house, admiring the woodwork as he rang the doorbell. Loud rock music vibrated from inside, and through the front window he noticed movements. He rang the doorbell again and waited, but the music drowned out the sound. Taking a step sideways, he glanced through the window to attract Sophie's or Lucy's attention. Lucy danced through the room, wearing a silky-looking, black, French-cut leotard. His throat closed.

Soft, voluptuous curves swayed and gyrated. Her dramatic hip movements amplified her sexuality as she slowly trailed the side of her hand down her body. Then she arched her back, presenting him with the silhouette of her profile.

Lord have mercy on his befuddled brain. He'd never seen anything so beautiful.

Strawberry-blond curls kissed her shoulders and hung down her back, her generous breasts were thrust upward, and her eyes were closed, her entire being thrown into the sultry seduction of the dance. And her legs . . . slender, shapely legs—spread slightly as if she were doing a back bend—ended with a pair of red stiletto heels. . . .

He felt like a voyeur but could not tear himself away from the window or drag his gaze from her as she traced the tip of a rose petal down the center of her face to her neck, then lower across her breasts and over her bare belly.

His throat went completely dry while his heartbeat jumped into record-breaking speed. The music finally slowed, and Lucy twirled around, spread her feet, and bent forward from the waist to touch the floor with splayed hands. In a graceful gesture that stole his breath, she tiptoed her fingers over her legs, up her body, and raised them above her head, ending with her body in a statuesque pose with her breasts thrust forward.

He was so rattled that it took him a second to register the fact that she'd opened her eyes and had caught him watching her.

Lucy had performed for thousands of strangers before, but knowing Reid was watching from the porch had stirred her own sexuality and heightened her awareness of every suggestive move.

What was he doing here, anyway?

All night she'd worried that she was doing the wrong thing by using the charms and talismans on Sophie, but she believed they'd help Sophie find romance. If anyone deserved to be happy, her sister did. She simply had to loosen up.

And find a fun man.

The rock music faded in the background, and she finally dragged her gaze from Reid, who hadn't yet moved from the porch. Had he enjoyed her performance? Was he as titillated by her moves as she was by dancing for him?

What would he think of her Vegas Diva dance?

You can't tell, Lucy; you promised Sophie to keep the act a secret.

Securing her riot of curls back into the clip on top of her head, she steadied her breathing and teetered to the door.

Reid smelled like an early-morning shower with a hint of seductive testosterone. She fought an odd moment of self-consciousness as his gaze raked over her body, but quickly dismissed it at the way his eyes darkened.

"I like to dance," Lucy said softly. "Great exercise."

"You *looked* great," he said in a thick voice.

Oh, heck. He looked sexy as sin himself.

"I . . . I wanted to talk to you about Sophie and Lance."

Did he know she'd used a charm spell to help Sophie find new lovers?

He shuffled back and forth, looking nervous.

"Come on in and have some coffee. I was about to have a cup myself. Sophie's a soda junkie, but I like my morning coffee."

"Thanks."

By the time they'd filled mugs and made their way back to the den, he'd composed himself. She kicked off her shoes and curled her legs beneath her on the couch, turning sideways so she faced him. His gaze followed the heels, then fell on her bare feet. Her stomach fluttered.

He seemed to like what he'd seen. And he certainly was utterly scrumptious eye candy. She loved his big hands, had fantasized about them. . . .

Heat engulfed her. It obviously permeated the room, because suddenly she and Reid were kissing.

She wasn't certain who started it exactly, but Lucy had always been impetuous, had gone after what she wanted, and she saw no real reason not to go after Reid. He wanted fun and sex; she wanted the same—how could it hurt anyone? Maybe Sophie could learn from her—a woman could enjoy romance without getting all tied down.

On the other hand, she might not mind Reid tying her down . . . at least for a little lovemaking.

He threaded his fingers through her hair, pushing her back on the sofa and running his hands all over her body. Lucy moaned and wrapped her legs around him, welcoming his heat as he rubbed his hard body against her. He tasted like coffee and man, and hidden hungers that she wanted to explore. The low growl he emitted as he drove his tongue between her lips suggested he wanted more, too.

Her hands snaked into his hair, then lower to his shirt, where she frantically freed the buttons, sneaking her fingers inside the fabric to stroke his chest. Hard work–earned muscles sprinkled with fine brown hair strained beneath her touch as he raised himself up to trail kisses down her throat.

"Oh, my God, Reid, you're wonderful."

He chuckled and nipped at her earlobe, making her writhe beneath him. She scraped her hands across his taut nipples as he licked his way down to her breasts. Then he moved lower still, suckling her through the thin material of the leotard. She ground her hips upward, moisture surging to her core, her insides quivering with need.

But the front door slammed and Reid jerked up. "Shit."

She didn't care. She framed her hands around his face. "Let's go upstairs."

"No, it's Lance."

"Reid!" Lance yelled from the foyer.

Reid jumped up and walked to the fireplace, pretending interest in the mantel woodwork as he refastened his buttons. Lucy frowned and wrapped the afghan around her shoulders to hide the damp spots on her breasts where only moments earlier Reid had given her divine pleasure.

Another reason not to like Lance. He had not only hurt her sister, but now he had spoiled her fun.

"Hey, man, what are you doing here?" Lance

asked. A suspicious look traveled between the brothers.

"I stopped by to see if you needed me today or if I should go to Skidaway."

"I thought we already talked about that."

"Yeah, right, I guess I'll get going." Reid shoved his hands in his pockets and darted toward the door. Lucy jumped up to follow, her body still humming with wicked desires.

"Don't you want that coffee, Reid?"

He shook his head. "Probably cold by now."

"We could warm it back up." Lucy smiled sweetly.

Reid's face contorted as if in pain. "Uh, rain check."

She followed him outside and closed the door to offer them privacy and him a chance to change his mind.

"Er, I'm sorry—"

"Don't you dare say it. The only thing I'm sorry about is that your brother interrupted us." Lucy dropped the afghan again and folded her arms across her bosom, well aware it enhanced her generous chest and that Reid could see the wet spots where his mouth had been earlier.

He jerked the afghan back around her shoulders to cover her. "Lucy, about Lance." His breath quickened; then his gaze dropped down to his work boots. "That's really the reason I came. I don't know if you realize it, but my brother has it bad for your sister."

Lucy chewed on her lip. "He certainly has an odd way of showing it."

"I know. He's confused and probably scared right now—"

"Scared of Sophie?" Lucy laughed. "Sophie's the

nicest, most fantastic woman in the world. And she's worked damn hard to get where she is—"

"Whoa." He held up a hand. "I didn't say anything bad about your sister."

"Good, because there is nothing bad to say." Even if Sophie had been a showgirl in Vegas and their mother had been a hooker.

"That's just it. I came by to see if you'd help me get them together."

Lucy coughed, shocked. "You want them to be together?"

Reid shrugged. "Well, I want Lance to get her out of his system."

"Excuse me?"

"You know, they've got this sexual chemistry stuff going on, so they might as well work it out."

"You mean like we were doing before your brother barged in?"

He actually blushed. "Well, yeah."

She ran a finger along his chin, wondering at the small scar underneath. "So we are going to finish?"

Reid rocked back on the heels of his boots. "That's probably not a good idea. Lance doesn't want me to get involved with you."

How dare Lance tell Reid to stay away from her? "What does he have against me and Sophie? Aren't we good enough for the Summers men?"

He looked completely rattled. "Uh . . . I, that's not what I meant."

She jutted out her hip, anger swelling inside. She'd been right: Lance was the wrong guy for Sophie. *The sexist, macho, overprotective, overbearing pig . . .*

"So are you going to do what Lance says?"

"I . . . I don't know. I need time to think."

Lucy seethed. Maybe he'd let his brother tell him what to do. But she had never allowed a man to order her around before, and she sure as heck wouldn't start now. In fact, she'd cast another spell tonight to sabotage Sophie's feelings for Lance. And maybe she'd seduce Reid to get revenge on his brother. After all, they didn't call revenge sweet for nothing.

And seducing Reid definitely wouldn't be painful. . . .

Sophie's station manager cornered her before the show. "Sophie, I have great news."

She glanced up from her notes. "What is it?"

"This singles series has increased ratings so much that *Sophie Knows* is going into syndication." He clasped her arms. "Isn't that wonderful? People all over the United States will be watching you!"

Excitement budded in her chest along with a moment of trepidation. More exposure meant . . . more exposure. The more people who saw her, the higher the chances that someone would recognize her from her prior life and spill the beans.

Still anxious a few minutes later when the show began, she became even more agitated when Lucy flounced in wearing a black leather miniskirt and red camisole top. "Hey, Soph, listen, you got a couple of phone calls after you left this morning. First, Rory Dalton left a message, said he'd be back next week and he'll call you."

Great.

"And then you had two calls from that dating service. Both guys sounded like possibilities." Lucy referred to the tiny notebook she'd extricated from her purse. "I went ahead and accepted on your behalf; hope that's okay—"

Sophie opened her mouth to argue, but Lucy rattled on in excitement.

"You're meeting date number one at Wet Willie's at six for cocktails." She paused and giggled. "He had some kind of science degree that I didn't recognize, so to be on the safe side, no dinner. Then at nine, you're meeting date number two, a yummy-sounding lawyer, at Windows on the River."

Sophie gaped at her sister. "You fixed me up with two men in one night?"

"Yeah, isn't it wonderful? You might meet Mr. Right tonight and be able to forget Lance."

She could only hope.

"Don't worry, though. I'll call midway through both dates, so if you need an out, I'll be your emergency excuse to leave."

Sophie grimaced. "I hate playing games like this."

"Hey, it's a great code. Heaven knows it's saved me from millions of horrific evenings." Lucy chewed her nail. "Oh, and Soph, I talked to Deseree. She wants to come and see us together."

Panic tightened Sophie's chest. "I'll call her tonight. Sounds important."

She was probably shacking up with a new man. The producer motioned at the time, so Sophie ushered Lucy toward the front of the stage to get seated. Over the next hour she suffered through the episode on speed dating. Each person essentially had five minutes to talk to someone before moving to the next. In that short time, they had to decide if they wanted to date the other person. She felt as if they were cattle being moved through a slaughter house. Scant seconds into the dating interviews, she wished for a crash course in marketing, since success with the service seemed to depend on the ability to sell yourself in a five-minute pitch to a stranger.

The bell dinged and she watched as the men chosen to participate in the session played musical chairs between the tables of women.

Guy #1: "Hi, Sophie. Evan Wainscott."

His smile was dazzling, his suit imported, his posture confident. She exchanged greetings and listened to his spiel, vying for optimism.

"I'm a stockbroker, own a house here in Savannah as well as one in Naples, where I vacation three months in the winter. I play tennis and golf every weekend, work late hours, and entertain business clients most nights. I enjoy spending time with a wide variety of women. I've been married twice, but neither worked out. I'm still open, though, and want to share my wealth with a companion who likes to travel."

Okay, he was wealthy—but cocky, to boot. A workaholic. Probably a womanizer. It was a plus that he'd been married, meaning he wasn't opposed to the institution, but he obviously couldn't make it stick. The womanizer part no doubt interfered. . . .

Guy #2: "Hey, Sophie, hon. Name's Billy Bob Waddel." He looped his thumbs around his suspenders and patted himself. "What you see is what you get."

What she saw was an overweight, uneducated man with smoke-stained teeth and a habit of adjusting his genitals.

"I'm an honest, hardworking man, drive a truck for a hospital, haul away wastes. You know, it's pretty specialized work when you deal with body parts that could be contaminated. . . ."

Sophie coughed and tuned out the rest of the gory details.

Guy #3: "Hello, Sophie. My name is Edward. I'm a talent scout. Visiting Savannah on a recruiting trip, doing auditions, combining work with a little sight-seeing. I'd love for you to show me around."

They chatted about Savannah for a minute or two; then Sophie commented, "Your job must be interesting. Do you represent anyone I might recognize?"

He shrugged his bony shoulders. "Not unless you're familiar with the Vegas showgirl scene."

Sophie pressed herself back into her chair, the need to run flooding her. She'd thought the man's name seemed familiar when she'd seen it on the program.

He leaned forward and narrowed his eyes. "As a matter of fact, you remind me of a dancer I used to watch out there, had this great act at the—"

The buzzer dinged, cutting him off. *Thank God.*

Five more minutes and the man might have recognized her. And that would have been disastrous.

Lance had worked all day finishing the cabinets in Sophie's kitchen. McDaniels hadn't accepted or returned his calls.

Sighing in frustration, he tried the man's office again, but the recorder kicked on. *Damn.*

A hissing sound broke the quiet, and he paused. It was the third time today he'd heard a strange noise from upstairs, almost like soft footsteps. The ghosts?

No, he didn't believe there were star-crossed lovers trapped in this house. The noise was probably Sophie's cat creating havoc somewhere. As if the little devil sensed Lance's thoughts, she appeared, perching herself at the doorway, her big, furry tail swishing back and forth, her eyes beady as if she were monitoring Lance's every move. His nerves tingled. Sophie's pet was a damn *watchcat.*

Speaking of nervous, he checked his watch. He had an appointment at the sleep clinic at seven, and had wondered all day what kind of tests he'd be forced to endure.

He'd best clean up for the night and face it. He didn't like leaving a mess behind him, especially in the kitchen. The clutter would make it difficult for Sophie to cook dinner, and what would he do if she tripped over a board or nail and injured herself? The rest of her house was so neat and orderly, the renovations must be driving her crazy. She'd be happy with the Victorian hardware, though. At least she should be; when the original stuff she'd ordered hadn't arrived, he'd managed to upgrade the hardware. In fact, he'd simply written it in at the same price, knowing a few cents here and there wouldn't make a difference to him, but the higher-quality materials would add to the house's value and appearance. And he could always use Sophie's house and Sophie as a reference.

He gathered the loose nails and his tools, nearly tripping himself over that silver case of Lucy's as he hauled things out the back door. Lucy obviously didn't believe in picking up after herself. The door swung back, though, and his foot hit the end of the case, sending it careening down the back steps. The lewd contents spilled everywhere. Shaking his head at the menagerie, he gathered the items quickly and stuffed them in the case, embarrassed to touch the cucumber-shaped dildo. A chocolate-scented pair of pasties lay at his feet. He bent to retrieve them when Sophie rushed around the corner. He jerked up and they bumped into each other. Her gaze fell to the pasties in his hand.

Heat seared his face. "I . . . they fell out of the case. I was picking them up."

She smiled and nodded as if he'd invented an excuse.

166

He dropped the pasties as if they were a hot potato, but his foot knocked the case and an odd buzzing noise reverberated from the inside. Blast it all to hell, what in the world was making that sound? "I'm cleaning up, going to get out of your way."

Her bright green eyes locked with his. "You're not in my way, Lance."

He focused on her mouth. "I . . . I have somewhere to be." He refused to tell her he had an appointment at a sleep clinic because visions of her were keeping him awake at night.

Her mouth tightened. "No problem. I have a date, too."

A date—he hadn't said anything about a date.

The buzzing continued, vibrating from the case, adding to the tension between them. Probably that ridiculous cucumber.

Disappointment momentarily flickered on her face; then she brushed by him. "I'd better get changed."

He nodded. "I guess I'd better go."

"Lance?"

He hesitated. "Yeah?"

"You're doing a wonderful job on the house. I can't tell you how much your attention to detail means to me."

He nodded. For some reason this project meant more to him than any in a long time. Maybe because the house was old and had fallen into disrepair; maybe because it held so much potential.

Certainly not because it belonged to Sophie.

An hour later Lance lay in a hospital-type bed naked save for his boxer shorts, socks, and the hospital gown the clinic had given him, several electrodes attached to his body. The clinic was sophisticated and his room wasn't nearly as sterile as he'd imagined it would be. They had given him a nice blanket and tried to make him cozy and comfortable, but Lance still couldn't relax. Maybe it was nerves, but he was freezing his balls off, and the bright lights pierced his eyes, giving him a headache. He had no idea how anyone could fall asleep knowing they were being filmed and monitored. And there were other staff members behind the glass window, making notes, hooking other patients up to the electrodes. . . .

Earlier he'd filled out paperwork, and had to admit the humiliating truth; that he was not only sleep-deprived but sex-deprived, and that the woman he wanted to sleep with but wouldn't allow himself to bed was the reason he couldn't sleep.

The doctor had given him a skeptical look, then described their standard procedure, although he'd admitted that Lance's condition might not warrant a complete study. He had given him a physical exam though, to rule out any obvious health problems, like a cold or fever.

They would test his breathing, his physical condition, heart arrhythmia, then determine whether his insomnia was related to physical problems or, as the doctor had subtly put it, some kind of psychological disorder.

He closed his eyes, and was grateful the assistant dimmed the lights. Simply thinking about trying to go to sleep exhausted him.

What was Sophie doing while he lay here haunted by her?

Chapter Twelve

Sophie had met date number one at Wet Willie's, an inexpensive but charming bar/restaurant. The outside temperature soared to record highs, yet her attitude about her upcoming date was chilly at best. She reminded herself to give the guy a chance. Sure, she'd shared one incredible kiss with Lance—well, maybe more than one—but he hadn't made a move since.

Maddie's rules flitted through her head: *Make him chase the bait.*

Trouble was, Lance wasn't chasing.

"The first thing you do when identifying spiders and insects is to determine their order," Tad Jeffries, an entomologist, said in a high-pitched voice that sounded as if he were passing through puberty. "Actually, most insects and spiders are nearsighted, so if you move slowly you can get a good look."

"I guess they've never heard of Lasik surgery," Sophie said.

Tad didn't get the joke. He merely squinted over

his bifocals with a dour expression—the same one he'd been wearing ever since she arrived at the bar. She had almost ordered the house drink, Sex on the Beach, but opted not to give Tad any ideas.

"The buffalo treehopper is one of the most interesting visually; it feeds on plant juices by drilling their bark with its beak, and looks like a miniature green buffalo."

Sophie twirled the swizzle stick in her martini, trying to pretend interest. Did this guy really think talking insects was romantic?

"Now, take the praying mantis; some people think it should be named *preying* mantis with an *e* because it really is a predator."

"Makes sense."

"Spiders actually are sexist, too," he said, drawing her head up for once. "The wolf spider doesn't live in a web, but she's a devoted mother, so she carries her eggs in a ball of silk on her back."

How odd that a spider would have more maternal instincts than Sophie's own mother.

"After they're born, they ride on her back until they're ready to fend for themselves." He sipped his Scotch. "They have to hurry, though, because the mother sometimes forgets they're her own babies and pounces on them as prey. Probably what happened to the male."

So maybe mama spiders weren't so devoted. "The poor babies."

"In fact, once the black widow female mates, she normally kills the male because he's served his purpose."

Yikes.

"I wrote my dissertation on the subject."

"Really?" Why wasn't she surprised?

He flexed his fingers. "It's important to know the

different types of spiders; recognizing which ones are poisonous and how to treat their various bites is an essential survival skill."

"Yes, it would be." Not that she planned to go trekking off into the unknown with this man.

"We could go camping sometime. I know a very remote spot on Tybee Island." His tone sounded somber. "Wouldn't you feel safe knowing that I could take care of you?"

Safe and bored to tears. And what a line.

Trying for a slick move, he slid his hand over hers, but he overcompensated for her short fingers and knocked over her glass, spilling her drink in her lap. Sophie jumped up, pouncing on the accident as the perfect excuse to escape yet another horrendous date.

One down, one more to go; then she could call it a night.

Outside, she wiped her skirt and made a mental note not to run any more singles series—unless she focused on the joys of being alone. Maybe the black widow was the smarter species after all. . . .

Lance finally dozed off for about an hour. Unfortunately he dreamed of Sophie. They were stranded on a deserted island wearing nothing but loincloths, her porcelain skin sun-kissed and dusted with a faint line of freckles, the ocean lapping at the sugar-white sand in the background. He had finally overcome his anxiety about being trapped by her—or *with* her, as the present case was—and given in to primal instincts.

He had to have her.

They had been on the island three weeks. Three agonizing weeks of watching her bathe in the crystal-clear waters, of watching those slender bare legs swim against the current, of watching her sleep beneath the makeshift cover they'd fashioned from palm leaves.

His body was so hard he thought it might explode from want. But he remembered the "Dating Game" show where he'd failed so miserably, and Sophie's comment that he wasn't romantic, so he gathered fresh flowers along the shore and picked ripe fruit, then peeled and squeezed the melon to prepare her a refreshing cocktail. Dusk had settled over the island, the sun slipping into radiant pink and orange lines, the early-evening shadows from the tropical trees offering a private sanctuary.

She had just emerged from the ocean, water droplets glistening off her skin and dripping from that raven-colored hair. He watched from the shadows, his body hardening and throbbing with desire.

Tonight she would be his.

She slowly walked toward the fire, and he smiled, then handed her the drink and retrieved the flowers from behind his back.

"What's this all about?" she asked in a soft voice.

"I want this night to be special." He stood and brushed her hair back with his fingers, inhaling the sweet scent of her hair mingled with the salty ocean breeze. "I want us to be together, Sophie."

A wicked gleam flashed into her eyes. Then she pushed the drink back into his hand. "I told you, Lance, I wouldn't go out with you if you were the last man on earth." She swept her hand across the darkening deserted island. "And I meant it."

With a final dismissive look, she turned and sauntered away from him.

Lance jerked awake and sat up, the electrodes pinching his temple, the monitor on the machine beeping into the silence.

* * *

Sophie met George Kirsch at Windows on the River, impressed by his choice. The Hyatt's adjoining restaurant served some of the freshest seafood in Savannah, and the atmosphere was unique. If a freighter passed by during diner, you found yourself in a three-dimensional wonderland—the mirrored walls reflected the magnificence above, behind, and around you.

"Hi, you must be Sophie."

An impeccably dressed, handsome man stared down at her. He offered her a rose, and her stomach somersaulted. His accent was slightly Northern, his voice rich and deep. He was almost six feet tall, with deepset gray eyes, dark brown hair peppered with streaks of blond, a kind face, and a sexy smile.

She was grateful she'd had time to dart home and slip into a cocktail dress.

"You look lovely."

"Thanks."

He slid a hand to her waist and escorted her to a table by the river. A bottle of fine wine sat chilling in a crystal decanter. She swallowed hard, realizing this man knew how to entertain a lady. Was it all for show? Would he be as full of himself as some of the others she'd met?

An hour later Sophie realized he was quite the gentlemen: intelligent, good-looking, and considerate.

"I'm a partner with Farley, Strauss, and Kirsch," he said.

Sophie tasted her salmon and smiled. "What kind of law do you practice?"

"The firm is a cross between business and corporate law. I'm a litigator." He shrugged and sipped his wine, his gaze intent on her. "I do take on a few pro bono cases."

"Really?" A generous, giving man to boot. Maybe he could help her forget Lance.

He shrugged again. "I came up through the trenches myself. Raised in Philadelphia, strictly working class." He leaned forward, an earnest expression in his eyes. "One should never forget where he comes from. Our past builds and shapes our character."

Sophie stared into her water glass, feeling a connection. "You had a tough childhood?"

"Somewhat." He cut into his steak. "But I don't dwell on it. A self-made man is far better off than one who is given everything and throws it away."

"I agree." Sophie wondered how much of what he said was an act, but sensed he was sincere.

He was too good to be true.

"Now, enough about me; let's talk about you, Sophie. I want to know your deepest desires."

Sophie tensed, her fingers brushing the stem of her wineglass. Her secrets rose to haunt her. What would he think if he knew the truth?

She wasn't ready to find out.

"I suppose you've seen the show."

"Yes, you're a natural on camera." He reached out and traced a finger over her knuckles.

A blush stole up Sophie's face. Oh, he was good with flattery.

"So you're enjoying the singles service?"

"I don't know," Sophie said honestly. "It's awkward meeting strangers." They ate, both sharing stories of past encounters. Some of his dates were almost as outrageous as her own. But none topped Lance's date where the woman handed him the plastic vial. What was he doing now?

Darn it, she couldn't think about Lance.

"I'm surprised you're using the dating service," Sophie finally said. "I can't imagine a man like you having trouble meeting women."

A teasing smile lit his eyes. "A man like me?"

Sophie laughed. "You're handsome, charming, intelligent, *employed.*"

He laughed this time. "I do meet women," he admitted. "But believe it or not, I'm not looking for a one-night stand. Most of the women I meet in bars are not what I'd consider for a long-term relationship."

He was looking for a *real* relationship? He must have been beamed in from another planet.

The waitress stopped by and he ordered the house specialty dessert, warm bourbon over ice cream with coffee. "You look surprised that I'm looking for a relationship?"

Sophie leaned her hand on her palm. "I guess I am. Most men these days just want . . ."

"Sex?"

She chuckled. "Yes."

"I didn't say I didn't want that," he amended with a mischievous grin. "But I'm a patient man."

Sophie's throat completely tightened.

He squeezed her hand, then scooped a bit of ice cream onto his spoon and fed it to her. "If you're up for it, we could take a walk down River Street, maybe stop in the Bayou Café and listen to some blues."

It was almost as if he could read her mind. "I love blues."

They finished off the dessert, Sophie savoring each delicious mouthful. He paid the bill and they left the restaurant, walking hand in hand along the river. The sounds of summer tourists, music, and laughter floated around them, creating a romantic atmosphere that was almost intoxicating.

Inside the café, they squeezed together at a small table in the corner and spent the next hour listening to the saxophone and piano.

Around midnight, he walked Sophie to her car.

"I don't want us to be strangers, Sophie." He turned her palm over and drew a circle in the middle. "Can I see you again?"

Sophie nodded and climbed in her car, feeling elated as she drove home. George was nice and handsome and a charming man. Yes, she would see him again.

Barring that one slip of insanity, he had helped her forget about Lance. She owed him another night simply for that.

The next morning Lucy let Lance into the kitchen to finish installing the new counters. She had already dressed and made coffee, and was waiting with her kit for Sophie to come downstairs. Lance looked rough and unkempt this morning, as if he hadn't slept. Dark circles rimmed his eyes, and his hair was tousled as if he'd run his hands through it a thousand times.

She fought sympathy for the man.

She did not care if he had troubles. He didn't think she and Sophie were good enough for him and his brother—that was reason enough to cast a hex on him. But she had restrained. She normally used the charms and spells to evoke positive energy, not for negative purposes.

And Sophie's love life had definitely needed a boost.

And since she'd heard Sophie come in after midnight, humming, she assumed the charm she'd slipped into her sister's purse had worked.

Sophie's heels clicked on the hardwood floor as she approached. Lucy handed her a diet Coke before she made it to the kitchen, then cleared her throat, making certain she spoke loud enough for Lance to overhear their conversation. She wanted to rub it in. . . .

"Soph, congratulations on the show being syndicated."

"Thanks, it's pretty exciting."

"I guess you celebrated last night with your dates. Tell me all about them."

Sophie sank onto the living room sofa and sipped her soda. "The first man was a complete dud, but George . . . George was nice."

"Details, sis, spill it all."

Sophie related the events of the evening. "It's hard to believe he's for real, he was so perfect."

Lucy clapped her hands together. "He sounds positively divine."

"He was charming, intelligent, well dressed, sophisticated but down-to-earth—"

"And he's going to call again?"

"He said he would." Sophie sighed and fluffed a sofa pillow. "And you know what the best part is, Lucy?"

"What? He's a great kisser?"

Sophie laughed. "He's real. He cares about other people enough to do pro bono work. He grew up in a humble home, and he's giving back."

"That is admirable."

"And he wants a real relationship."

Lucy lost her enthusiasm slightly. "It's a little early to get serious, isn't it?"

Sophie smiled. "I'm not serious with him. We'll have to wait and see if he calls back."

"Oh, he'll call." Notions of Lance being dust in the wind danced through her head.

"Now, tell me about your evening, Lucy. You didn't see Reid, did you?"

Lucy shook her head. "Not for lack of trying, but he told me yesterday that Lance didn't want him getting involved with me."

"He said what?"

Lucy fought a grin, knowing Sophie's motherly instincts would kick in. "The bottom line is, Lance doesn't think I'm good enough for Reid."

Lucy silently counted to ten, waiting on Sophie to jump up and pounce on Lance.

It took her sister only to the count of five. . . .

Lance wanted to disappear behind the walls. He'd been listening to Sophie and Lucy and had smashed his thumb when he'd heard Sophie describing her date. She obviously really liked this lawyer guy. And Sophie's show had been syndicated, meaning she would only become more of a celebrity.

Then Lucy had mentioned Reid. . . .

"Lance, we need to talk."

Bracing himself for the onslaught of Sophie's temper, he forced himself to face her. The hurt shimmering in her eyes stole his breath.

"You should get someone else to finish the restorations."

He thought he'd been prepared for her ire, but he'd never considered the fact that she might replace him.

"I . . . I can't do that."

Her dainty chin vaulted up a notch. "Why not?"

"Because the rest of my crew is busy." At least until the end of the week; then he had to convince McDaniels to use them.

178

He owed her an explanation, maybe an apology. Still, he couldn't let her know he'd overheard her conversation. "What's this really about, Sophie?"

The scent of her perfume greeted him seconds before she poked him in the chest with her fingers. "It's about the fact that you don't think Lucy is good enough for your brother."

"That's not what I said."

Her dark eyelashes fluttered. "Then what did you say?"

He caught her hands in his. She was trembling. "I simply suggested that Reid not get involved with your sister. I thought a relationship with them might complicate things."

"Might complicate what things?"

"My brother likes single life. Your sister is . . . well, your sister. I don't want her to get hurt."

"You and Reid have already managed to do that."

A sharp pang stabbed his chest. He instantly squeezed her hand, remorse filling him. "Sophie, I never meant to hurt you or Lucy."

The anger in her eyes faltered slightly, and a vision of her marrying that lawyer guy flashed in his head. The hurt that troubled her eyes compounded his turmoil. "I'm sorry. I . . . But don't you see, I'm not the man for you."

Her voice sounded breathy when she finally spoke. "Why not?"

Admitting his own insecurities clawed at his self-esteem. "Because you're famous. You're sophisticated and worldly and . . ." *More educated.*

She shook her head. "What difference does that make?"

"I would never fit in with your TV crowd. We're from two different worlds."

Her eyes flashed with emotions. "If you think that

the past makes a difference, or that our professions or our incomes make us who we are, then you're right." Sadness tinged her voice. "We definitely don't belong together."

Then, without another word, she dropped her head and walked back through the door. Lance had the oddest feeling he'd just failed some kind of personal test with Sophie.

That he'd lost any chance he might have had with her, and that he'd never be able to make amends for the pain he'd inflicted.

Chapter Thirteen

Later that night, Lance tried to get comfortable at the sleep clinic—they'd wanted him to spend at least three nights undergoing the testing. But thoughts of Sophie interfered. He felt like the biggest bastard in the world. He had been raised by his Southern mother to respect women, to treat them right, to protect them, and Sophie and Lucy had never done anything but be nice to him. Yet he had managed to hurt them both.

Damn it, he would never forget that haunted look in Sophie's eyes. It was the same deep pain he'd seen in Chase's face when he'd first met him years ago. Chase had been a gangly teenager with a chip on his shoulder, fighting for a place in the world. He had nowhere to call home but an orphanage. What would cause Sophie to look that way? It was almost as if she had secrets.

No. Sophie wasn't a gangly, abandoned child living in an orphanage—she was smart, sophisticated, beautiful, a celebrity, for God's sake—she could have any man in the world she wanted.

Why in the heck would she have chosen him?

It doesn't matter; you've totally blown any chance you might have had with her.

Did he want a chance with her?

He wanted to make the sadness he'd caused her disappear. Could he convince her that he was worthy of being her friend, maybe even her lover? Would that be enough?

He pictured Sophie making hot lip-prints all over his body after he'd brought her to ecstasy.

Was she fantasizing about doing the lip dance with another lover, or with him?

Sophie knows had featured a special on romantic nights in Savannah. The author of a popular book on the subject spoke, highlighting several restaurants, bars, hotels, and bed-and-breakfast inns along with various tours, romantic ghost tales, and excursions that would enhance a romantic evening. After his part of the program, Lucy highlighted the fine points of Sleepover, Inc.'s, romantic products, which could enhance a relationship, vaguely hinting at the more provocative items but tastefully eliminating any graphic details.

After the show, Sophie and Lucy met Maddie to shop for paint and wallpaper as well as a few decorative items for the house. Sophie was exhausted but exhilarated.

They finally decided to celebrate the syndication of Sophie's show with dinner out. They stopped at Tubby's Tank House for drinks and food, filling up on the shrimp salad and grouper fingers.

"Let's toast to Sophie's success." Maddie raised her Cosmopolitan.

Lucy clinked her margarita with Maddie's. "She's going to be a megastar."

"I'm not sure it's all good." Sophie hesitated before raising her merlot. "A lot of pressure comes with a move like that. I still want to air quality shows."

"No *Jerry Springer*–type episodes, sis?"

"Exactly." And no past secrets returning to haunt her. Like patrons of the Diva act. She instantly scanned the bar to see if the talent scout might be in the vicinity.

Maddie's eyes brightened. "How's it going with my brother working at your house on a daily basis?"

Sophie and Lucy exchanged knowing looks. "Not well," Sophie admitted.

"Lance told Reid to stay away from me," Lucy confided.

Maddie's face fell. "Those moron brothers of mine make me want to scream."

"Listen, Maddie," Sophie said, covering Maddie's hand with her own, "the last thing I want is to cause trouble between you and your brothers. Let's drop it, okay?"

Maddie pinched her lips, looking as if she might spit fire any second. "You are not the problem."

"I'm moving on," Sophie said.

"Yeah, Sophie's already met a dreamboat through that singles service. He sent flowers today."

Sophie glanced at her sister. "He did?"

"A dozen yellow roses. They're gorgeous." Lucy tapped the table in a drumroll. "Isn't that romantic, Maddie?"

But Maddie didn't respond. She was too busy staring at the door.

"What is it, Mad?" Sophie asked.

"Uh, too late, I sort of mentioned to Chase that

we'd be here, so if he and the boys wanted to stop by . . ."

Sophie swung her gaze to the door, where Chase, Lance, and Reid stood. The Terrible Three—they should have kept the nickname. They were undoubtedly the three best-looking men in Savannah, tall, rugged, muscular, hardworking men who wore jeans that fit like gloves and created a path of ogling women wherever they went. All they needed were black motorcycle jackets and tattoos to complete their bad-boy attitudes.

Sophie tried to remember George's face—what did he look like?

"Does Lance know you've been dating?" Maddie asked.

Sophie nodded. "Trust me; he's not losing any sleep over it."

Maddie tapped her glass with her fingernail. "I'm not so sure about that. Lance wants you, there's just something holding him back." There was a hint of worry in her voice.

"Do you think he's still hung up on that bachelor pact?"

"What bachelor pact?" Lucy asked.

Maddie rolled her eyes. "Lance, Reid, and Chase were buddies growing up. They signed this stupid agreement that none of them would ever get married, then renewed it right before they went into business together."

"They thought women would be a distraction," Sophie added.

"Duh?" Lucy laughed. "But a good distraction. How moronic are they?"

"They're men," Sophie said. "Need you ask more?"

Lucy laughed. "Hardly."

"Ditto." Maddie tilted her head, her earrings jingling. "But this isn't just about Lance or one date; it's the battle of the sexes." She leaned forward and whispered, "Now, Lucy, you do everything you can to seduce Reid. He'll cave in no time."

"I hope so. I have no intention of letting your brother tell me what to do."

"Be careful, Lucy," Sophie warned. "I don't want you getting hurt."

"Don't worry, sis. I can take care of myself."

"Good girl," Maddie said. "And Sophie, continue to make Lance swim in circles, strutting your stuff, but let's also play the aloof card."

"The aloof card?"

"Yes, men always want what they can't have."

"But he doesn't want me."

"Yes, he does; he just thinks he doesn't." She bit her lip and narrowed her eyes. "But he does like big-breasted brunettes who don't demand much, so let's give him what he believes he wants. See that girl at the bar?"

"You're going to fix him up with someone else?"

Maddie's look turned wicked. "He *thinks* he wants someone like her, but she's all fake, right down to her water bra."

"I'm not sure I'm following."

Maddie laughed. "Simple. We give her to him on a platter, and when he discovers she's a fake, he'll realize you're not, and that you're the one he really wants. Who knows, maybe her water bra will spring a leak."

Sophie tried to follow Maddie's crazy logic and failed. Besides, there was one flaw to the plan: She wasn't exactly the person everyone perceived her to be.

What would happen when he discovered she was a fake, too?

Lance wanted Sophie. But from the distressed look on her face she wasn't exactly ecstatic to see him.

"You going to talk to her?" Reid asked.

"I don't know. She was really pissed at me last time we talked."

"Maddie was pretty PO'd at me a few times, but we worked it out," Chase said.

Lance frowned into his beer as Maddie waved them over.

"Lucy's a real looker," Chase observed. "I can see why she's getting under your skin, Reid."

Reid and Lance exchanged uncomfortable looks. Sophie, Maddie, and Lucy were the three best-looking women in the whole damn city.

"All right, guys." Chase gestured toward the women. "Gear yourself up and let's go. The only way to combat the opposite sex is to get down and dirty."

If he had to fight to get Sophie's forgiveness, down and dirty sounded good to Lance. As though preparing for battle, the three of them squared their shoulders and fell into line, Chase leading the way as if he were the commander. Lance took center position, trying to read the situation as they approached.

Maddie launched herself into Chase's arms, the kiss that exploded between them steaming up the air. If his best friend hadn't already married Maddie, Lance would have pulled a shotgun and forced him to on the spot.

Fighting the awkwardness, Lance grabbed a bar stool and slid onto it. "Hi, ladies."

"Lance, Reid." Sophie's clipped response didn't sound promising.

Lucy, on the other hand, batted her eyelashes at Reid. His poor brother didn't know what hit him. He was completely sucker punched and immediately fell under her charms, leaving Lance to fend for himself.

"You look beautiful tonight," Lance said, figuring a compliment might break the ice.

"Thanks, we've been celebrating."

"Sophie's show's being syndicated; she'll be famous," Maddie exclaimed, dragging Chase onto a stool close to her. "She's even been offered a job in L.A."

"That's wonderful," Lance said. "You should be proud of yourself. You deserve the glory."

Sophie gave him a skeptical look. Okay, maybe he was laying it on a little too thick.

"Are you feeling all right?" Sophie asked.

"Sure, why?"

"You're being so nice," Sophie said with a tight smile.

His smile faded. But he wasn't ready to throw in the towel. "Maybe I've changed my mind about a few things." Actually the thought of Sophie moving away made him feel panicky.

Sophie sipped her wine, eyeing him over the rim of the glass. "What, you're going to find someone else to finish the renovations?"

She wished. "No, I'm going to finish them." He swirled his beer around in his mug. "Guess I'll be around for a while, after all."

"Too bad," Lucy said, then continued when Sophie gave her a questioning look: "I mean, too bad I'm leaving soon and won't see the finished product."

"You'll come back again, won't you?" Reid asked; distress laced his brother's voice.

Lance took another look at Reid. Was his brother falling for Lucy?

Lucy slipped her hand over Reid's. "Definitely. Vegas is only a plane ride away. And flights run both ways."

The bar was growing crowded, so Lance scooted his stool closer to Sophie's, struggling for something romantic to say that didn't sound ridiculous in front of his sister and the others. "What about you? Are you taking the job in L.A.?"

"I don't know."

Anxiety tightened Lance's throat. If she moved away, he'd never get a chance to hold her. . . . "Can I buy you another drink, Sophie?"

Her dark lashes fluttered in surprise. "I . . . thank you, but I probably need to go soon."

"Early day tomorrow?"

She nodded. "One more show in this singles series. I'll be glad when it's over."

"But at least you've met some nice men through the service," Lucy said.

"Speaking of the singles service," Maddie said, "how are you enjoying it, brother, dear? Met any women you want to tell us about?"

Lance gritted his teeth. "No."

"Ahh." Maddie slid her arm around Chase's neck. "There's someone at the bar I want you to meet, Lance. See that busty brunette with the halter top? She's one of my clients. I've been helping her redecorate her house for the last few months."

What the hell was Maddie doing? Trying to fix him up in front of Sophie? He thought she wanted the two of them together.

"Yoo-hoo!" Maddie stood and waved at her

friend. "Courtney, come here; I have to introduce you to my brothers."

The brunette wobbled toward them, her skintight miniskirt crawling up her legs. She gave Lance a slit-eyed look that said she was ripe for the picking. He inched closer to Sophie.

"Courtney, this is Lance and Reid. Remember I told you about them at the gym?"

"Right." Courtney ran long pink fingernails through her locks, shaking her hair over her shoulders. "Nice to meet you fellows."

For the next five minutes Courtney rubbed herself all over Lance. Much to his distress, neither Sophie nor Maddie made a move to rescue him.

Lucy stood. "Reid and I are going over to Bernie's."

A sheepish grin pulled at Reid's face. "They have the best songwriters in the south. Lucy should see the town while she's here."

"It's a pretty romantic city," Maddie said. "I still remember the first carriage ride Chase and I took."

Sophie pushed away from the table. "I have to be going."

"You need a lift?" Lance asked.

"No, thanks." She gestured for him to stay seated. "Stay here and enjoy Courtney."

Lance's hand tightened around his beer mug. He desperately wanted to escort Sophie home, talk some more, prove he wasn't the bastard she thought him to be. But Sophie said good-bye, dismissing him for the night.

And Courtney was pawing at his leg, telling him they'd find ecstasy together.

Or did she mean buy Ecstasy together . . . ?

* * *

Maddie and Chase walked Sophie to her car. "Trust me," Maddie whispered.

Sophie jiggled her keys. "If that's what he wants, let him go for it."

"He's probably trying to figure out a way to escape her as we speak."

"I doubt it." A wave of defeat settled over Sophie.

"Hang in there, Soph." Maddie hugged her. "Everything's going to work out; I know it."

Sophie nodded, although the only thing she knew was that Lance was chatting it up with Courtney, and she was going home alone while Maddie had Chase. And if Reid's smitten look told the story, Lucy had Reid, at least for the night.

What was wrong with her?

A late-evening summer breeze stirred the trees and brought a mixture of floral scents as she drove home. Late-night lovers strolled hand in hand along the riverbank, enjoying the moonlight, inhaling the salty air.

The night had been made for lovers, yet she had no love.

She parked in her driveway, loneliness echoing around her. All she'd ever wanted when she was a little girl had been a real home with a walk-in closet, birdfeeders in the yard, and a white picket fence.

With that house came stability and, of course, someone to love her. A family.

She had the house now. Had she thought the rest would follow?

Her heart heavy, she dragged herself inside. The message machine was blinking, so she replayed the messages.

"Hey, Sophie, it's Rory. Listen, I'll be back in town next week. Hope to see you then."

She checked the next one. "Hi, Sophie, it's George.

I really enjoyed our evening together. I've been thinking about it all day." A slight pause. "Anyway, I'd love to take you out Saturday. We could go for a drive along the coast, take a picnic over to Tybee, or if you want, we could try a dinner cruise. Call me."

Sophie noticed the roses on the coffee table and stopped to sniff them. There was no reason she shouldn't call George back and accept his date. No reason at all. He was handsome, intelligent, polite, interesting, romantic. . . .

So why couldn't she stop thinking about Lance?

Lance backed away, his back digging into the bar. Courtney was practically humping him like a dog in heat right in front of everyone. Hadn't her mother taught her any self-respect? He twisted sideways as a stranger passed by and he accidentally brushed her chest. A funny sound echoed, like water sloshing. *What the hell?*

He glanced at her chest—her boobs were jiggling. He'd thought they were fake, but how fake? Did she have water balloons in her bra? She ran her tongue down his neck, and he gently set her back. "It's been nice meeting you, Courtney, but I need to leave. I have an early meeting tomorrow."

"Ahh, sugar, really?" She traced a finger over his chin. "The fun's just getting started."

"I'm sure you can carry on the party without me."

She brushed a kiss across his mouth. "Will I see you again?"

"I'll call you." Disgusted with himself for being too chicken to be honest, he hurried away—he was going to kill Maddie for sticking this woman on him. Her smile was as fake as her boobs.

Not like Sophie.

Sophie seemed real in every way. Hardworking, serious, ambitious. She was obviously trying to provide a good role model for her lunatic little sister. And he had hurt her.

Heat suffused him as he walked outside, the music from the neighboring bar wafting toward him. He caught sight of a man and woman strolling along the riverfront, another couple embracing in one of the swings overlooking the water, and loneliness engulfed him.

What was he doing with his life? Building nice houses for other families and couples to grow old in? Putting up walls to keep them safe, yet keeping his own walls in place to protect himself? Going home every night to an empty duplex that he didn't own or bother to clean, much less decorate? Refusing to get involved with Sophie because he wanted to preserve his bachelorhood when he no longer wanted to play bachelor games?

He had lost the thrill of the hunt and the unknown. Or maybe he realized how empty nights with a strange woman felt in the light of morning.

His thoughts scattered. He walked down River Street to the florist, but found it closed, so he popped into one of the gift shops and picked up a silk rose. Then he headed back to his car. He had to see Sophie tonight, to tell her he was sorry for insinuating that she and her sister were not good enough for him or Reid, when all along he'd felt it was the other way around, that he wasn't good enough for her.

If she was still interested in him, he'd like to give it another try. And this time he'd prove that his answers on the "Dating Game" had been lies. He could be romantic. . . .

* * *

Sophie promised herself she'd wash Lance's shirt and return it to him—tomorrow. But she couldn't resist crawling inside the fabric that smelled of him one more time. She had slipped a jazz CD into the machine when the doorbell dinged. *Drat.* Who would be coming by this late?

Maybe Lucy had forgotten her key. Or she might be too smashed to find it in her purse.

Wrapping her arms around herself, she hurried to the door, expecting to find her sister teetering on the other side, but Lance stood on her doorstep holding a red silk rose. His dark eyes skimmed over her, sending a tingle up her spine. Silence stretched between them.

He touched the lapel of her—his—shirt. It was so hot outside that she'd rolled the sleeves up and left the top two buttons unbuttoned.

She was also very naked beneath.

Obviously Lance realized it, because an undeniable look of hunger flared in his eyes.

"What are you doing here?" Sophie asked. "I thought you'd be spending the night with Courtney."

"Courtney isn't the one I want."

Sophie's hands trembled. Oh, dear heavens, had he said that?

"I came to apologize for hurting your and your sister's feelings."

His softly spoken words brushed her nerve endings. "That's not necessary."

He pressed his hand on the door, pushing it open. "Yes, it is. Can I come in?"

Panic assaulted her, though she didn't know why. Maybe because she hadn't straightened up. And she had already removed her makeup. She felt bare, exposed—especially wearing his shirt. He must think she was foolish. . . .

"Please, Sophie. I can't stop thinking about you."

Oh, sweet Jesus. Desire splintered through her.

"We can just talk, if that's what you want." ·

Sophie struggled for a reason to say no. Her secrets . . . and Maddie had said to be aloof. . . .

"Please give me a chance." He lowered his hand to her cheek, and Sophie was lost. She backed up, allowing him to enter. His heady scent invaded her senses, tying them into knots of pure feminine need.

"I can make some coffee."

"I don't need coffee."

So what did he need? The question hung between them, asked and silently answered.

She turned and led him to the den. She'd already turned out most of the lights, so the dim light from the Victorian lamp painted the room in shadows. Sultry jazz flowed from her speakers, and the glass of wine she'd poured herself sat on the end table.

"Wine?"

"Sure."

Sophie retrieved the bottle and another glass from the kitchen, then poured him a glass, glad to have something to do with her hands. They were shaking now, her entire body engulfed in flames of hunger.

"I realized I've been unfair to you," Lance said. "I want things to be different."

"Different how?"

He accepted the glass from her, his hands caressing her fingertips. "I'm tired of pretending I don't want you. That I don't need you."

Sophie had no idea what to say. "What brought about this sudden change?"

A self-deprecating laugh escaped him. "Let's just

say I haven't been sleeping lately. It's given me a lot of time to think."

"I . . . I don't know, Lance. There's so much between us." *And still so many things you don't know about me.*

Lance set the glass down, then slid a hand to the nape of her neck. She leaned into his arm. "We don't have to rush anything. But I want us to get to know each other. For me to prove to you that I'm not the jerk you think I am."

Sophie opened her mouth to refute his statement, but he lowered his head and pressed his lips against hers, so tenderly that her breath lodged in her throat. Lance tasted like temptation and dark desire, an aphrodisiac too powerful to fight.

Passion overcame her, and she threaded her fingers in his hair, pulling him closer as he teased her lips apart with his tongue and delved inside. She met him thrust for thrust, a low mutter of yearning ripping from her throat when his hands slowly began to unbutton the shirt she wore. She rubbed her bare foot up his thigh and smiled at his moan of approval, cupping his head as he dipped his mouth to trail kisses down her neck, then lower to her breasts. And when he parted the fabric and licked at her skin, teasing her nipples to taut peaks with his tongue, she called his name and begged him not to stop.

Lucy and Reid had parked in front of Sophie's house for a good-night kiss. But one good-night kiss led to another, and like teenagers, they were about to get it on in the front seat of his Tahoe. "We could go inside," she whispered.

Reid cupped her hips in his palms, greedily sucking at her neck. "You don't think Sophie would mind?"

Lucy dodged the steering wheel as she climbed on top of Reid and yanked his shirt from his pants. "Who cares?" She panted into his ear. "Besides, your brother's Blazer is in the drive. What do you think he and Sophie are doing this time of night?" Was Lance there to wait up on her and Reid? She'd be damned if she gave him the satisfaction.

"Good point." A chuckle reverberated from his chest, then a low moan as Lucy's tangled hair tickled his bare chest. "God, that feels good, Lucy."

Lucy sighed and pressed her heat into him, flattening her hands on his jaw as she drove her tongue inside his mouth. Reid tasted like heaven, all male desire mingled with the essence of unbridled passion. When this man let go, he would be dynamite.

His hands kneaded her breasts, stroking and teasing, sending pinpoints of pleasure so intense it was almost painful rippling through Lucy's body. She arched her back, threw her hair over her shoulder, and groaned.

But a pair of headlights flickered in her eyes, nearly blinding her. She hesitated, her breath catching for a moment. Was it the police?

Oblivious, Reid began to inch her dress up her thigh, but Lucy spotted the car door opening. A tall, dark-haired man exited. *Dag-nab it. Peter.*

What the heck was her mother's old lover doing here?

Reid had her dress pushed up to her waist and was sliding aside her panties with torturous fingers. As much as she hated to stop, she had to. If Peter barged in, revealed his identity, and ruined things for Sophie, Sophie might think Lucy had had something to do with his arrival. Or she'd blame Deseree.

And what if Peter blurted out the truth about the Diva act?

She had promised Sophie to keep her secret.

"Reid, honeydoll." Sophie caught his hands. "We have to stop."

His hands froze on her bare thighs, his body jerking with need. "Why?"

"See that man walking up the drive?"

Reid nodded.

"I . . . I have to find out what he wants."

"I don't understand."

Lucy searched for a reply, opting for a half truth. "He's someone we know from Vegas."

Reid's face contorted with a mixture of emotions: anger, confusion, maybe a hint of jealousy? "An old boyfriend?"

Lucy bit her lip and smoothed down her dress, untangling her foot and searching for her shoe on the floor of the SUV. "Let's just say he could be trouble."

Pulling her pump on, she jumped from the Tahoe and teetered up the drive, hoping to catch Peter before he ruined things for her and Sophie. But Peter had already opened the door and was stepping inside.

She was so flustered she didn't realize that Reid had followed her until the three of them stood in the foyer together. A clunking sound echoed from the den, and Lucy glanced at the sofa.

No Lance or Sophie. Then a banging sound echoed from behind the furniture and a sock flew over the couch.

"Sophie?" Peter said.

"Lance?" Reid croaked.

Sophie's head bobbed up from behind the sofa. "Peter?"

Lance's head came next. "Reid?"

Then Lance turned to Sophie and asked, "Who the hell is Peter?"

Peter stepped forward, running a hand through his shaggy head of black hair. "I flew in from Vegas for Sophie's show on long-lost lovers."

Chapter Fourteen

Shock stole Sophie's breath. What the devil was Peter doing here? For goodness' sake and in those black leather pants and that silk shirt that made him look like some kind of Hollywood pimp?

Besides, he wasn't a long-lost lover. He was one of Deseree's live-ins, a stripper who'd danced with Sophie and Lucy in the Diva act.

And why had he shown up now, when she and Lance had finally gotten so close to making love?

Speaking of close, she shoved her arms back into the sleeves of Lance's shirt, vaguely cognizant of the fact that he was hastily redressing himself, and that his movements were terse and angry.

"I came about the show, Sophie." Peter's voice echoed with false hurt, but Lance stiffened, obviously believing Peter's act. "But it looks as if my timing is off."

"An understatement," Lance muttered.

Sophie spied his mutinous frown from the corner of her eye. He stuffed his shirt into his jeans in a hurried movement, not bothering to hide the fact that they'd been getting down and dirty. She inched up behind him, conscious that she was wearing a man's shirt, and that her legs and body were bare beneath, bare and still tingling with Lance's loving touches and kisses. Leaving that desire unsated was doing irritating things to her insides, too.

Compared to Peter, Reid and Lucy looked slightly unkempt, a fact that registered milliseconds before Lucy cheerfully offered to make coffee.

"I'm not here for coffee," Lance said in a dark voice, his intense look reminding her that he'd refused the offer earlier and said he wanted something else. That something had been her, and she desperately wanted the entire motley crew to disappear so she could give him what he wanted.

What they both wanted.

"Just exactly whose long-lost lover are you?" Reid asked in a voice that sounded surprisingly territorial.

Sophie caught the unprepared look in Lucy's eyes and they exchanged a silent moment of panic.

Peter's blue eyes twinkled. "Maybe you should ask the Lane girls."

"Lucy's," Sophie said.

"Sophie's," Lucy said at the same time.

The silence that yawned between them reeked of tension and lies. Peter had the audacity to chuckle.

"You both dated him?" Lance asked.

"You shared?" Reid added.

"No!" Sophie and Lucy shouted at once. Lance crossed his arms and glared at her, while Reid tapped his booted foot up and down.

"Actually, neither of us dated him," Sophie said.

The Summers men must have taken her comment the wrong way, because both of their expressions turned lethal. She couldn't blame them. After all, in his black clothing with his shoulder-length hair, shark tattoos, and biker jacket, Peter resembled a porn star.

Lucy jumped in to throw Sophie a lifeline. "It's not what you think, boys, so simmer down."

Sophie could not deal with this right now; nor could she deal with admitting the truth to Lance and watching disappointment darken his face. She had created a name for herself in Savannah, a decent reputation that she intended to keep by burying her past.

She had to in order to fulfill her goals.

"Lance, please try to understand," she implored softly.

"How can I understand when you haven't explained anything?"

Sophie gripped his arm. "Maybe you and Reid had better leave, so Lucy and I can straighten this out with Peter. Then I'll explain."

He turned to her and brushed a knuckle across her cheek, and she realized she was asking the wrong man to leave. But Lance would return tomorrow to work on her house. They could talk then.

Peter needed to be dealt with right away. She and Lucy had to get their stories straight before everything she'd worked so hard to achieve blew up in her face.

As soon as Lance and Reid left, Sophie cornered Peter. She liked order, wanted everything in her life in its place, and Peter disrupted that order to no end. "What in the devil's name are you doing here?"

Peter gave her mischievous grin. "I told you I came for the long-lost lovers episode tomorrow."

"You are not anyone's long-lost lover." She

skimmed her eyes over his outfit. "And did you have to dress like you were going to a Saturday-night pimp-and-ho party?"

"I like my clothes." Peter sat down in a chair and stretched out, leaning back and making himself comfortable.

Sophie stabbed a finger in his direction. "Don't get too comfortable; you're not staying."

"All right, I'll leave as soon as you give me what I want."

"You're here for money?"

Peter shook his head. "No, I want to be on TV. I heard about a new soap one of the networks is going to be filming. I want a part on it."

"You're leaving the Diva act?" Lucy asked.

Peter shrugged. "It's time for a change."

"You mean Deseree threw you out," Sophie said wryly.

"No, I want a career move."

"They don't film soaps in Savannah," Sophie said.

"My agent said there's a talent scout here looking for new talent. He was on your show the other day, and I want to meet him." Peter grinned.

Sophie closed her eyes and massaged her temple. "I don't have any contacts with that scout, and if I did, I wouldn't want to see him again. He might recognize me from Vegas."

Peter hooked his thumbs together and flattened his hands behind his head. "So?"

"So no one here knows about my life in Vegas, and I intend to keep it that way."

"Ahh." Peter tapped his head. "That's why you didn't want your boyfriend to know who I was."

"He's not my boyfriend."

Peter arched an eyebrow. "How about you, Lucy?"

"Reid was just showing me a good time."

Peter pointed to her tousled hair. "Looks like both of you were having fun." He winked at Sophie. "I've never seen you like this about a man. Are you going to marry him?"

"Marry him? He was barely speaking to me a few days ago."

"A man doesn't have to talk to get his message across."

"Wanting sex and marriage are not the same things, and you know it." Sophie paced across the room. "What am I going to do? He thinks you and I . . . that we . . ."

"I could talk to him."

"And tell him what? That you and my mother enjoyed a few nights together?" Sophie pounded her hand on her chest. "Oh, yes, that'll impress him."

"Why do you want to impress this guy, anyway? You don't think he'll love you for yourself?"

Sophie froze, his question hitting home. "It's not that, exactly." Or was it?

"You're ashamed of your mother?"

Sophie winced. "It's not that, exactly, either."

"Then what, Sophie? He won't approve of the fact that you used to dance in Vegas? My God, your act was famous in Vegas. Every man in the city wanted to jump your bones."

Sophie threw up her hands in frustration. "Exactly my point. Not only didn't I grow up with a *Cosby* mom, but my early career is not something I want to flaunt." Tears crowded her throat. "Don't you understand? I'm trying to make a serious reputation for myself here."

"At the expense of forgetting your family and your roots?"

Sophie stared at the door where Lance had left, a

silent war waging within her. She couldn't have it both ways, could she?

"What are we going to do about the model boy?" Reid asked the next morning. They had met for breakfast to review some additions Chase had made on the drafts for model homes in case McDaniels changed his mind and agreed to meet with them.

Lance growled into his coffee, an image of that black leather–clad milksop surfacing. He'd spent the better part of the night thinking about him at the sleep clinic. And this morning he'd watched the video they'd filmed of him when he'd finally fallen asleep. He'd been cursing the man. Sophie's name had cropped up several times, too.

"Lance?"

He'd forgotten his brother's question, then remembered he'd said *we*. "What do you mean, 'we'? Are you really interested in Lucy?"

Reid shook the packet of creamer against the counter. "Uh, slip of the tongue. I meant what are *you* going to do about Sophie?"

"What can I do?" Lance bit off the end of a bear claw. "If she wants to be with that wimpy-looking pretty boy or take another job and move away, I can't stop her."

Chase grunted. "You could if you wanted her bad enough."

Lance glared at him, tempted to mutter some blistering remark about the strangling confines of marriage, but remembered Chase was married to Maddie, and if Chase agreed with him, he'd have to pulverize him. "I wonder if he spent the night with them."

"I wonder which one he wants," Reid said, still thumping the creamer.

Chase grabbed the packet and tossed it across the table. "You two are pathetic."

"Thanks for your support," Lance said.

"Yeah, who asked you?" Reid snarled.

"If you want Sophie, Lance, don't give up so easily. Romance her. Wine her, dine her."

"I'm not the wining-and-dining type." He sipped his coffee. "That's the reason I stayed away from her so long in the first place. She would fit in L.A., not me."

"You can fit in any place you want. Go on; ask her for a date."

"I took her a rose, but she had a dozen already from some guy she met through that dating service."

"All right, maybe he has more money, but think of something else."

Lance finished his coffee, then hauled his butt up for a refill. The images that had tortured him the night before surfaced again—Peter in bed with Sophie, tasting and touching her skin the way he'd planned to do.

Chase was right. He had to do something. If Sophie decided to move away or hook up with that Peter guy, he might lose her forever. And he didn't want that . . .

He just hoped it didn't take him a month to think of an idea. He cut his gaze back to his brother, who had picked up another packet of creamer and started beating it to death.

What exactly was going on between Reid and Lucy?

Reid jumped into his Tahoe and drove toward the Skidaway site, his gut pinched. Maybe the coffee was getting to his stomach, or maybe something had been wrong with that sausage he'd eaten, because nausea gripped him in its clutches. In fact, the more Chase and Lance had talked about that Peter guy and Lance romancing Sophie, the more his stomach had cramped. Come to think of it, he'd felt sick the day Chase and Maddie had gotten married, had actually had a spell when he thought he couldn't breathe, as if the thought of being tied down to one person forever might suffocate him.

Not that he was considering it.

But he had a feeling Lance was heading down that track. *Poor guy.*

Not Reid—he was simply having fun with Lucy. He wanted to sleep with her in a bad way, but that was all there was to it.

So, why did a red-hot rage seize you at the thought of her spending the night with an old lover?

Irrational jealousy? No, protective instincts. The guy had seemed like a sleaze, the type to play on a girl's sympathies, sweet-talk her into the sack, then steal her cash out from under her.

And Lucy and Sophie both seemed naive, trusting.

He remembered the feel of Lucy's legs wrapped around him, the way she'd gyrated her rear into his sex, the way she'd looked dancing that day in that black leotard.

No, *naive* wasn't quite the word to describe Lucy. But sweet—yes, she was sweet. Sweet and delicious and the sexiest woman he'd had the good fortune to meet.

And he still hadn't bedded her.

His upbringing kicked in. Lucy and her sister were women, and women needed protecting, especially from guys who looked like Peter Wolf or whatever his name was. Maybe he'd talk to Maddie later, and see what she knew about the dude. Maddie and Sophie were close, so Sophie would listen to her, and Lucy would listen to Sophie.

His stomach eased up slightly now that he had a plan.

Maddie phoned Sophie before she could leave for the show. "Okay, spill all."

"What do you mean?" Sophie asked.

"Chase had breakfast with my brothers, and they're both out of sorts over this hunky guy Peter. I knew steering Courtney to Lance would do the trick."

Sophie dropped her head onto her arm and groaned. "Last night was a disaster."

Maddie squealed. "Tell me all about it."

"Well," Sophie began, "after Lance left Courtney, he stopped by here, and I was ready for bed—"

"You were wearing something sexy?"

"One of Lance's shirts that he left here."

"Oh, perfect."

"I couldn't resist." Sophie sighed. "It smells like Lance, Maddie. I'm so pathetic."

"No, you're not; you're my best friend, and I want you to be happy. Now go on."

Sophie wiped at a drop of condensation on her diet Coke can. "Lance said he came to apologize for hurting my feelings; then he acted all weird."

"Weird how?"

"Like he might have changed his mind about us being together."

"I told you." Maddie clapped her hands. "The rules are working."

"I haven't been trying to trap him, Mad, but he looked so handsome, and I was almost naked in his shirt, and then he kissed me, and, well . . . things got way out of hand."

"But I told you to play aloof." Maddie sounded distressed.

"I couldn't help myself. I poured him a glass of wine, and I had one, but we never got to it, because he is so hot and, well, he said 'please.' "

Maddie's laughter bubbled over the line. "Lance can be charming when he's not being all macho, overprotective, bossy, and big brotherly."

Sophie wanted to laugh, but the memory of Lance's hands on her stirred an ache deep inside her. Nothing brotherly about his touches . . .

"So how far did you go? Rule number five—getting sweaty and half-naked is allowed, but no consummation, right?"

"Actually, there would have been consummation if Peter hadn't shown up when he did. We were on the floor behind the couch, but I didn't care, and Lucy and Reid ran in behind him . . . it was so embarrassing."

"I can imagine Reid and Lance in a standoff with your friend Peter. A volcano erupted, huh?"

"Lance controlled himself, but he wasn't happy, and I had no idea how to explain Peter, especially when he claimed to have come here for my 'Long-lost Lovers' episode today."

"This just gets better and better." Maddie lowered her voice to a whisper. "Then what happened?"

Sophie chugged her soda. "I asked Lance to leave so I could talk to Peter."

Maddie roared. "Perfect. I bet Lance was awake all night wondering what you were doing."

"You don't think I made a major mistake, then?"

"Are you kidding? I couldn't have scripted it better myself, Sophie."

She hadn't been playing, simply trying to give herself time to concoct a believable story.

"Now, Sophie, just remember, stick to the plan. Keep making him swim in circles, and when you think the time is right, go ahead to rule number six: Snag him with the line, and don't let go."

"In other words, keep him sated."

"Right," Maddie chimed.

Sophie smiled, thankful for her best friend's encouragement. She desperately wanted to hurry up and get to the sated part.

Lance had finally come up with a plan. A corny one perhaps, but it was the best he could manage, considering he was sleep-deprived, sex-starved, and brain-impaired. He would set his scheme in motion tonight.

That is, provided the milksop black panther loverboy wasn't there to interfere. The mere thought of him cranked Lance's blood pressure up to the boiling point.

By the time he arrived at Sophie's house that morning, she had already left. He wondered if she'd intentionally done so to avoid him, but knew she had to prepare for the show.

"Long-lost Lovers."

Was Peter going to be one of the success stories of the reunion episode?

Needing to work his frustration out of his system, he installed the new thermal-pane windows in the kitchen. Earlier he'd stopped by Maddie's, reviewed some of the decorating plans she and Sophie had made, and picked up the special stained glass Sophie wanted installed in the kitchen bay window. Maddie had admitted that she and Sophie were on the fence about the decorative piece due to costs, but Lance decided he'd adjust the figures so it would work. If Sophie wanted the stained glass, she would have it.

She didn't have to know that he'd waive a fee or two. . . .

By the time Sophie's show aired, he had the stained glass in place, and had applied the first coat of paint on the kitchen walls. Sophie had chosen a pale yellow, which gave the room a bigger feel, especially with the bay window letting in natural light. She'd selected a Wedgwood-blue faux-marble paint finish for the dining room to match the blue granite counters, and he'd seen the mixture of blues, reds, and yellows she and Maddie planned to use in the living room.

Needing a lunch break anyway, he grabbed his bottled tea and sandwich from the cooler and sat down to watch the show.

The familiar music for *Sophie Knows* sang through the stage speakers; the cameras panned the audience, where he noticed Lucy and Peter sitting, and then zoomed in on Sophie as she entered. As always, she was stunning. Dressed in a silky-looking vee-necked black tank with a wide striped sash tied around her tiny waist and one of those funky black skirts that was split and angled up the sides of her legs, she sucked the wind from his lungs. Her makeup was always flawless, her appearance model-gorgeous. Once again, he wondered how a developer like himself would ever live up to her perfection.

"Ladies and gentlemen, today we have the final episode in our singles series—we're here to reunite a few long-lost lovers."

The audience clapped, and Lance bit off a piece of his dry sandwich, wondering how many long-lost lovers Sophie had in her past. After all, she'd never talked much about herself and her life before Savannah and the *Sophie Knows* show. On the show she played a part; here at home he'd glimpsed a more vulnerable woman. He'd seen her choices in her home, seen her without makeup, almost seen her without her clothes. What was the real Sophie Lane like underneath the show persona?

He made a mental note that if his plan worked and she accepted his date, he'd find out all he could about the real Sophie.

Agitation tightened Sophie's nerves as she forced herself through the show. Deseree had called suggesting she pop in to visit her and Lucy, then fly back with Lucy on Sunday. Sophie had stalled, claiming she was so swamped with the renovations she didn't have time for company. She'd also stalled Peter as a guest with the promise that she'd arranged a meeting for him with the talent scout. Actually, she'd asked her secretary to handle the details.

"Our first guest is Amy Price." Sophie gestured toward the thirty-year-old woman. "Tell us your story, Amy."

The slender mother of two fidgeted with her hands. "I'm here to reunite with my first love. He and I dated in high school, but when college rolled around, we went our separate ways."

"How long has it been since you've seen him?"

"Twelve years."

"And what's happened in your life since then?"

Amy chewed at her lipstick. "I dropped out of college when I got pregnant. I married the baby's father, but it didn't work out."

"You're divorced then?"

She nodded, staring down at her hands. "My heart was always with Jay."

"Did you try to find him?"

"I was afraid." A small nervous laugh escaped her. "We parted bitterly. I wanted to forget college, and marry him after high school, but he thought we should both get our educations."

"He sounds like a smart guy."

"He is, and he was right." Her head lifted a notch. "After my divorce, I went back to school and finished a business degree. Now I'm a computer consultant at a company here in Savannah."

"Well, let's bring Jay out and see what he has to say."

Seconds later, a tall, fair-haired man appeared with a rose in his hand and a smile on his face. "Amy, is it really you?"

Sophie's chest squeezed with emotions as the couple embraced. "I take it you're open to starting a relationship with Amy?" she finally asked.

"I've never forgotten her," Jay admitted as he pulled away slightly. Moisture filled his eyes. "And yes, I want us to see where it leads this time."

The audience clapped and cheered while Amy and Jay claimed side chairs and began to converse.

The next couple didn't quite work out. The man had recently gotten involved with another woman, so the timing was off. Sophie couldn't help but wonder if the timing had been off with Lance. Maybe ten years from now Lance would want to get serious. . . .

The third couple were in their eighties. Sophie had never seen anything so touching. They had apparently been lost to each other during World War II. He had been a soldier, and she'd been told he died in combat.

"I gave Erma a promise ring when we were fifteen," Horace said. "Took me four months to save up for it, making minimum wages back then."

Erma pulled a small valentine keepsake box from

her purse. "And I kept it all these years. I couldn't quite believe you were dead."

"I was a war prisoner," Horace explained. "Fifteen years. By the time I returned to the States, I was shell-shocked, broken down. Then I heard Erma had married. But I kept all the letters she wrote me while I was overseas."

Erma sniffled. "I had a few good years with my husband, but he died in a mine explosion in 'fifty-nine." She lifted a hankie and dabbed at her eyes. "But I still thought of you, Horace. You were my first love."

"And you never married, Horace?" Sophie asked, her own voice quavering with tears.

"No, my heart was set on Erma." He lifted her hand in his and kissed her gnarled fingers.

She lifted a shaky hand to touch the white hair at his temple. "And my heart still belongs to you, Horace."

The two embraced, and Sophie's heart squeezed. Their story reminded Sophie of the star-crossed lovers who were supposedly trapped within her house. What would it be like to have a man love you until you were old and gray?

Would she ever have that kind of undying love?

The remainder of the day Lance worked with a vengeance, determined to have the second coat on the kitchen walls and one layer of glossy white on the molding and trim. As usual, Sophie's cat had greeted him with a hiss, although he had brought along a cat toy. Jazzy had stared at it suspiciously and retreated up the stairs. Rome wasn't built in a day, he reminded himself. He wouldn't win the cat over in one either. But at least they had come to some terms: They tolerated the other being in the house, although their truce had yet to extend to sharing the same room.

A few minutes before five, when he expected Sophie home, he arranged his surprise, frowning when that Peter guy left a message saying he'd call back. He sneaked a peek at the card accompanying the flowers on her table and frowned—George. The man was definitely pursuing her. And the hulky football player had called three times.

Feeling foolish but determined to follow through with his plan, Lance wrote a suggestions for dates on six slips of paper, then slipped each of the notes inside a balloon, blew up the balloons, and tied one to each diet Coke in the six-pack. Each time Sophie popped a balloon, he'd take her on the date suggested in the note.

Whoever said Lance Summers wasn't romantic . . . ?

Chapter Fifteen

After the show, Sophie was exhausted, but she had to deal with Peter. Her secretary had phoned the talent scout who'd appeared on the show and arranged an appointment for him. She also had a message from her agent. The L.A. producer had phoned again about the reality-show offer, and a second offer from a producer at CNN sounded intriguing. They were looking for a special feature newscaster. Hmm. Maybe.

Still, she stalled and told her agent she'd think about it.

When Lucy popped in, she told her about the offers. "Lucy, you go with Peter and watch him."

"Sure." Lucy fluffed her curls. "I might get discovered myself."

Sophie pinched the bridge of her nose. "Make sure he doesn't reveal my identity."

"You're making way too much out of this, Soph. If your audience knew about your Diva act, it might boost your ratings. Have you ever thought of that?"

"My ratings are fine, I have job offers in L.A. and Atlanta, and I'm going into syndication, remember?" More people were going to see her, more people who might recognize her . . . her dyed hair might not be enough. "You really want to be on television?" Sophie asked, vying for another strategy.

Lucy scrunched up her eyes. "Why not? You don't think I'm talented enough?"

Heavens, she'd hurt her sister's feelings. "You're gorgeous and talented," Sophie said. "But making it in television is rough, Lucy." Sophie bit her tongue. "You've seen what it did to Deseree. After dancing, she tried making it in the acting world."

"Maybe she didn't have a choice," Lucy said.

"There are always choices," Sophie countered. "Deseree didn't look hard enough."

"And maybe you're not looking hard enough to see why she made those choices."

Sophie jerked her head up, surprised by Lucy's antagonistic tone. "What's that supposed to mean?"

Lucy twisted a strand of hair around her finger. "Deseree obviously didn't have the confidence you did. Maybe she felt trapped."

Sophie understood about feeling trapped—hadn't *she* felt trapped by circumstances when she was young? All those times when Deseree hadn't come home at night and she'd been left to soothe Lucy's worries. All those days she'd pretended to the other kids at school that her mother wasn't the call girl they knew her to be. Sophie had invented so many lies she hadn't been able to keep them straight. Just like now, her head was spinning from trying to continue the charade. "We've had this argument before," Sophie said. "I know she had it rough growing up, Lucy, but so did we. I simply want a better life for both of us. I want you to go back to school, get a degree—"

"You're on television; why can't I pursue a TV career? I could be one of those weather girls, or another Vanna White on a game show."

"Is that really what you want?" Sophie asked hesitantly.

"I don't know; you certainly don't like my Sleepover, Inc., job."

Sophie rolled her eyes, ready to launch into another motherly lecture, when Peter knocked at the door. He stuck his head in. "I need to leave now if I'm going to make that appointment."

Lucy nodded. "I'm right behind you."

Sophie grabbed Lucy's hand. "Please, Lucy, I realize you don't agree with me, but don't do anything rash. This scout already almost recognized me. If you tell him about the Diva act, he may put two and two together and figure out who I am."

"I still think you're making way too much out of that." Lucy squeezed Sophie's hand. "But trust me, sis: I won't do anything to hurt you."

Sophie's voice felt rough when she spoke. "I . . . I want a chance here, with the show, maybe with Lance."

Lucy hugged her. "I know, Soph. But remember, if Lance isn't the one, you'll find someone else. I'm sure of it."

Trouble was, she didn't want anyone else. Maybe soon Lucy and Peter would be back in Vegas and her secrets would all be safe. . . .

Why couldn't Sophie give up on Lance? Lucy wondered as Peter drove the rental car toward the Savannah Harbor Resort, where he was supposed to meet Edward Wormer, the talent scout.

Lucy's charms were supposed to help her find new lovers and sidetrack Sophie from this one-sided attraction. Maybe she needed a new spell, one to release Sophie. . . .

She shot an irritated glance toward Peter. Why did she have to baby-sit her mother's old boyfriend when she should be making that new spell, when she wanted to be seducing Reid? She had to return to Vegas tomorrow morning for the Saturday-night show, so tonight would be her last and only opportunity for a while. And when or if she ever saw him again, he'd probably have moved on to some other hot babe.

A dull ache throbbed in her chest, and she massaged it, wondering if that last chocolate doughnut she'd eaten this morning had been a tad too much. After the interview she'd drive Peter to the airport; then she'd do a little shopping, find herself something seductive to wear tonight, something that Reid couldn't resist. . . .

And before she left tomorrow, she'd figure out a way to convince Sophie to fly to Vegas for Mother's Day to meet her and Deseree. Granted, the three of them made an odd family, but it was the only one Lucy had, and she was determined that the three women stick together.

"It really wasn't necessary for you to tag along," Peter said as he parked in front of the hotel.

"Sophie insisted."

"She has issues."

"Maybe so, but you'd better do right by her, Peter, and not reveal anything about her past. She went out on a limb to line you up with this appointment."

Peter covered her hand with his. "Lucy, I know you don't believe it, but I honestly care about you and your sister. You are Deseree's daughters."

"You feel fatherly toward us?" Lucy laughed. "Peter, you're not old enough to be our father."

"But we've worked together a long time, and I love your mom."

As much as any man ever had, Lucy conceded slightly. "Thanks, Peter. If you really care, please honor Sophie's wishes."

Peter nodded and climbed out of the rental car. Lucy didn't feel it was necessary to accompany him inside. She trusted he wouldn't give away Sophie's past—not after her last warning. Instead she dug her book on charms from her purse while she waited. She had to make sure she hadn't done something wrong with the spells.

Maybe she'd even make up a new one to help Sophie fall in love with that guy George or that hunky football player, Rory, or maybe when she came to Vegas, Lucy could set her up with someone there.

She skimmed the charms and spells, but didn't find anything about releasing someone from an infatuation. *Hmm.* She'd noticed a voodoo-magic shop on the corner before they'd arrived at the hotel. Peter was safe inside; he would be fine. She'd hop over to that shop and pick up a few things she needed to help Sophie. . . .

As the day wore on, Lance grew more and more nervous about Sophie's reactions to his balloon idea. Twice he'd already taken the silly-looking display to his truck; then he'd imagine Sophie with that black-leather milksop or that football player, and he'd drag it back inside. On the third trip back and forth he'd dropped it, one of the aluminum cans had exploded, spraying all the balloons, and he'd had to redo the entire contraption.

He wiped at a bead of sweat on his forehead.

Who'd ever thought the idea of asking a woman out would make him so damn jittery?

I wouldn't go out with you if you were the last man on earth.

What would he do if Sophie rejected him?

His cell phone rang, and Lance laid down the paintbrush and checked it, wishing it were McDaniels. The Savannah Sleep Clinic's name appeared instead.

He clicked the on button. "Hello, Lance Summers here."

"Mr. Summers, this is Dr. Settleton at the Savannah Sleep Clinic. We have your test results back."

Settleton's tone sounded serious. Worried. Like a man preparing to deliver bad news.

Good grief, what if Lance had some kind of brain tumor pressing on his brain that caused his sleeplessness? Maybe a blood clot . . .

"Yeah?" he asked, hating the way his own voice wobbled over the word.

"Other than the occasional jump in blood pressure, our tests show that there is nothing physically wrong with you."

"That's good news, right?"

"Well, yes. Of course, it still doesn't explain why you're suffering from insomnia." His breath wheezed over the line. "But in my opinion, after our conversations, I'd speculate that your condition is triggered by stress."

Lance dropped his head forward and rubbed his neck. He'd paid God knew how much money for this doctor to tell him he was stressed. "Of course I'm stressed. I have a company to run." *And McDaniels to win over.*

"Work can create tension, but you might consider

seeing a counselor to talk about any unresolved problems, issues from childhood. . . ."

Christ, not that psychobabble about childhood repressions. "I didn't hate my mother or father, if that's what you're getting at. I loved my parents, and my brother and sister."

Settleton chuckled. "I wasn't going to suggest you hated your family, but often a loss, a sudden death in a family such as the one you experienced in your teens, can add pressure on a child that the child suppresses until later years. Given that you were left to be the sole caretaker, you probably experienced feelings of abandonment, fear of loss . . ." He hesitated. "Those unresolved issues might also affect your relationships today, or lack of relationships."

He'd never really examined his feelings. Hell, he hadn't had time. Maddie had been so vulnerable and erratic herself, and Reid had been headed for juvenile. . . . Begrudgingly, he admitted Settleton was making sense. But what did that have to do with Sophie?

He glanced across the counter, anything to distract himself, and noticed an envelope with the name Deseree written on it. Deseree, the woman who ran the charity Sophie supported.

"Think about it," the doctor continued, cutting off his thoughts. "Face your inner demons, whatever they are, and then you can move on."

"Eliminate the stress?"

"If possible. If not, learn to deal with it, and your fears."

He wasn't a fearful man, was he?

The back door opened, and Lance froze. The source of his stress had just walked inside, dressed in a slinky black sundress that hugged her curves and showcased that spiky black hair. She was so damn beautiful. Not only beautiful, but intelligent, a celebrity, and a generous one; no telling how much money she gave to this charity.

Had he been afraid to get involved with her? Afraid he'd love someone and then lose again?

His gaze flew to the balloons, nervous tension rippling through him. No, he refused to let fear rule his life. He'd face his issues and deal with them—starting tonight.

Sophie was so worried about Peter and the talent scout and whether or not to return Rory's and George's calls that she'd barely had time to think about Lance still being at her house when she arrived home. But as soon as she saw his face, the familiar tingle rippled through her to her toes, and heat charged up her body.

He looked different. She couldn't quite pinpoint *how*, but his expression, though guarded, definitely held an underlying note of hunger as well as mystery.

"Sophie," he said in a husky voice. "What do you think of the kitchen so far?"

Were they in the kitchen?

"It's hot," she said, then caught her lip between her teeth when he grinned.

"Yes, it is."

Twisting her hands together, she fought a nervous smile and tried to focus on the renovation. "The paint looks wonderful. I love the yellow."

"It does open the room up," Lance admitted.

"And the molding looks so much brighter."

"I need to apply another coat, and then touch up, but it's definitely coming along."

"Oh, yeah." He was watching her so intently, she turned to check the messages on the phone, but saw the light blinking and changed her mind. Sunlight flickered through the window, though, and the stained-glass window caught her eye. Hand-painted purple and yellow tulips danced in between blades of tall green grass.

"Oh, my gosh." Tears blurred her eyes.

"It's the one you wanted, right?"

She whirled around, blinking rapidly. "Lance, how . . . how did you know? I thought Maddie said it was too expensive—"

"We worked it out," he said. "I have arrangements with a few of the suppliers in town. We cut each other breaks."

"I can't believe you did that. I . . . I love it." She reached out to hug him, then restrained herself. "Thank you."

"It belongs here." A slow smile curved his mouth. "Your table will come tomorrow."

Her gaze dropped to the old rickety one she'd been making do with, and she narrowed her eyes at the six-pack of diet Coke with the balloons bobbing in the air. "What's that?"

Lance rolled back on the balls of his feet, his look sheepish. "I apologized the other night. Now I want to make up for the 'Dating Game' fiasco."

"What?"

"Each balloon has an idea for a date inside. Pop one each day for the next six days; the note inside describes what our date will be."

She gazed up at him in awe. "You want six dates with me?"

He nodded, then laid his hands over her shoulders, turned her to face him, and gently brushed a strand of hair from her cheek. Her breath caught at the restless desire in his eyes.

"What changed your mind, Lance?"

His finger touched her lip. "Like I said, I can't sleep for thinking about you."

Sophie pressed a kiss to the tip of his finger. "Really? I didn't think you ever lost sleep over a woman."

"I never did before." His reply rolled out on a husky sigh.

Sophie's heart banged around in her chest, her emotions boomeranging between hope and fear of getting her hopes up. "If this is about the other night, what we almost did on the floor, well . . ." She couldn't believe she had the courage to say this, but she went on: "I don't want a one-nighter, Lance." She glanced at the balloons. "Or even just six."

He cupped her face in his hands. "I know. And I can't make any promises, Sophie," he said in a rough whisper, "but I would like to see where this takes us."

While Peter had finished his interview, Lucy had skimmed the contents of her new charm book and written up a spell to counteract whatever lovesick spell had trapped Sophie in Lance's clutches.

Then she dropped Peter at the hotel and indulged in a shopping spree, emerging from one of the stores braless, wearing a silky red halter top with low-slung white cotton pants that dipped below her navel and white high-heeled sandals that showed off her new pedicure. Her belly button ring glittered in the fading sunlight, and the tips of her fire engine–red toenails matched her top. Dotting perfume between her breasts added the final touch.

She stopped by a small bistro she'd discovered while shopping, ordered a picnic dinner, grabbed a bottle of wine and glasses to complement the shrimp cakes and freshly baked breads, cheeses and fruits, and headed to Skidaway. Reid should be finishing up for the day. Tonight she intended to knock his socks off—literally.

When she arrived at the construction site, Reid's crew was packing up supplies. He patted his men on the back, making jokes and doling out orders for the next day. He was obviously in charge. The boss.

She admired his drive and skill. And she had never seen anything as fabulous as the antebellum house they had built. It was fashioned after the Elizabeth Henry House near historic River Street, and reminded her of castles and days gone by. Normally she wasn't a nostalgic person, but for some reason the huge white columns and sleeping porches on the back overlooking the water brought visions of Scarlett and Rhett, along with her own childhood fantasies of sharing a steamy romance with her own Southern hero.

Dusk was settling over the Skidaway River, a halo of orange sitting on top of the water. The air was filled with the sound of the river rushing over rocks and birds twittering in the tall trees bordering the riverbank. Reid's eyes lit up in surprise as she teetered toward him, but a black cat suddenly skittered in front of her, jarring her nerves. The black cat was a bad sign.

She silently recited one of her charms to ward off any bad luck.

Reid met her halfway. "What are you doing here?"

"I brought a picnic dinner, thought we might share it by the water." She tried to blink coyly while scanning the area for possible dangers. "That is, if you don't already have plans."

"Sugar, if I did have plans, I'd change them." His gaze skimmed down her top, making her nipples stiffen beneath the slinky fabric, then lingered on her navel. "And you have perfect timing; the last of the work crew just left."

So they were all alone. And no dangers, except for Reid. "I'll get the wine if you want to bring the basket."

He followed her and grabbed the basket while she removed a blanket from the backseat and tucked the wine under her arm. Her heels dug into the plush grass as they made their way around to the back of the house. Soon it would be sold, Lucy thought, a family moving in to occupy its massive rooms and fill it with memories. But tonight she intended to make her own memories with Reid to take back with her to Vegas.

"You look fabulous, Lucy," Reid said with a gleam in his eyes.

"Thanks, you look hot yourself." Lucy raked her eyes over his muscular torso in unadulterated appreciation. He wore a khaki shirt that had hints of dirt and sweat clinging to it, all a testament to the fact that he was a hardworking man who made a living with his hands.

Those big hands . . .

She spread the blanket onto the thick carpet of grass, imagining the pleasure they would bring her. Then she twined his fingers between her own and led him to sit down. His gaze locked with hers, fire breathing between the two of them as they sank down onto the blanket.

She reached for the corkscrew. "You can take out the food if you want," Lucy said. "I hope you like shrimp cakes."

Reid's stomach growled in reply, and they both laughed. "It looks delicious." Reid glanced down at his clothes for the first time. "I should probably clean up first, though."

Lucy's heart fluttered when he began to unbutton his shirt. Inch by inch the fabric fell away, revealing a solid wall of sculpted muscles dusted with light brown hair. She swallowed hard, nearly spilling the wine as she poured them each a glass.

"I'll be right back."

Lucy's fingers traced up and down the stem of the wineglass as he stood and strode toward the river. In a masculine gesture that robbed her breath, he knelt and rinsed his hands, then splashed water on his face and ran his hands over his chest to wipe away the dirt and sweat.

Oh, mercy. She wanted to run her hands over him.

As he strode back to her, she recognized the devilish glint to his eyes. The damn man knew he was turning her on, and he loved it.

Well, two could play that game.

She licked her lips, then ran her tongue around the rim of the wineglass. His gaze followed the movement.

"Are you hungry?"

"Starved."

"Ready to eat?"

"Oh, yeah."

Lucy laughed, enjoying their wordplay. But she wanted to prolong the pleasure, so she opened the cartons of potato salad and fruit and the plate of shrimp cakes, and gestured for him to partake. For several heat-filled minutes they nibbled on the food, enjoying the lull of the river rushing over the rocks and the sounds of nature in the woods beyond. Shadows danced from the trees, and the fresh scents of grass and wildflowers and the spicy shrimp filled the balmy spring air, while thunderclouds rolled in from a distance.

"I have to leave Sunday," Lucy said.

Reid sipped his wine. "It seems like you just arrived."

"I know. It's been a terrific week."

"You did a great job on Sophie's show."

"You watched?"

Reid licked his fingers, causing Lucy's stomach to tighten. "Lunchtime."

Lucy stuffed her plate in the garbage bag, frowning as the sky darkened with the onset of a spring thunderstorm. "Liar. You were curious about my Sleepover products, weren't you?"

Reid pushed his plate away and cupped his hand at the back of her neck. "Sugar, you don't need any of that fake stuff with me." He dipped his mouth to kiss her. "Don't you know the real thing's better?"

"Really?" Lucy traced a finger along his jaw. "Maybe you'd better show me."

Their mouths met, tasted, explored. Reid threaded one hand into her hair, drawing her closer into the vee of his spread legs, while his other hand snaked lower to tease the delicate nipples that stood begging for his attention. The suckling noises he made as he dipped his head to lick at her skin sent heat radiating through her body. She wanted him, desperately wanted to have him touch her in all those burning places.

She clung to him, digging her hands into his hair, then scraping her fingers along his bare back, urging him to hurry. He slowed the torture, though, pushing her onto her back and kneeling above her, letting his hands work their magic as he kneaded her breasts and slowly untied her halter top. As the material fell away, his gaze latched on to her breasts.

SLEEPLESS IN SAVANNAH

The warm spring air bathed her bare skin just before she felt his breath on her neck, and when he trailed kisses down her body and teased her nipples to stiff peaks again, she writhed and clawed at his arms.

"Goodness, Reid, I want you so much."

"I want you, too, baby, and this time nothing is going to stop us."

Chapter Sixteen

Sophie was stunned by the creativity Lance had shown in setting up the date choices. He had arranged an intimate personalized tour with the Victorian Lady on East Fifty-fifth Street. She flaunted a thick Southern accent and vintage Victorian attire, escorting them on foot to Monterey Square on Bull Street.

"The square was named to commemorate the Battle of Monterey during the war with Mexico. The monument honors Kazimierz Pulaski, a Polish nobleman who was mortally wounded during the Siege of Savannah while fighting for the Americans."

"Wasn't it removed and a fake one used during the filming of *Midnight in the Garden of Good and Evil*?" Lance asked.

Sophie studied Lance, surprised by his knowledge.

The Victorian lady nodded. "Yes, they removed it for repairs." She gestured for them to follow her. "This is the famous Mercer House," she said. "It was completed in 1871, and is one of the finest examples of Italianate architecture in the city. Some of the most stunning features include the ornamental iron-work accents, the eight balconies, and a sidewalk fence. There's also a lush garden with pond and fountain."

"It's magnificent," Sophie said.

"Yes, Berendt's work has drawn thousands of tourists to discover its elegance."

"The antiques dealer Jim Williams restored it?" Lance asked.

"Yes, he's also credited with restoring nearly seventy other Savannah homes."

"You like his work, don't you?" Sophie asked Lance.

The back of his hand brushed her waist as he guided her along. "Oh, yeah," Lance said with awe in his voice. "I've studied photographs, too, for ideas."

Sophie smiled, her admiration for Lance growing again. Although he seemed to enjoy hands-on labor, he obviously knew his history and studied his craft. One day maybe his renovations would be marked in the Savannah Historical Society's register.

Next they stopped to look at the Congregation Mickve Israel, which was the only Gothic synagogue in America, then on to the Victorian-style inn on Lafayette Square near the cathedral of Saint John the Baptist.

"We're going inside this one," Lance said.

Excitement mushroomed in Sophie's chest. Although she'd been in Savannah for almost a year, she'd never toured the historic homes or inns. As soon as she stepped inside and saw the dark red walls and rich gold hues, adrenaline surged through her. To the left sat a stately formal dining room where guests could enjoy Sunday brunch. Period paintings adorned the walls, and a red-and-gold tapestry rug stretched from one edge of the wood floor to the opposite wall. To the right a library stood with welcoming arms, boasting a collection of antique books available to guests for their pleasure, and were housed in antique bookcases that flanked a marbleized fireplace. The colors here were more muted—"bomber jacket" walls, a French armoire, and a liqueur service enhanced the comfortable atmosphere. Rococo revival love seats and two striped Empire chairs created cozy conversation areas, while the artwork of nymphs and clouds added style and personified the Victorian era.

"The entire inn is furnished with Empire and Renaissance revival antiques," the Victorian hostess said. "There are fourteen suites, all with luxury bathrooms with antique Victorian claw-footed tubs and Jacuzzis."

"It's absolutely breathtaking." Sophie envisioned ladies outfitted in their long dresses sipping afternoon tea and sharing idle chitchat.

By the time they left the inn and walked to Congress Street, a spring thunderstorm brewed on the horizon, and Sophie's head overflowed with ideas for decorating her house, all of which she'd have to discuss with Maddie.

"Now, for dinner." Lance opened the door of the East Café, and they rushed inside just as the first drops of rain splashed against the windowpanes. Sophie was immediately charmed by the Southern atmosphere and a guitar player serenading the guests beneath an ivy-covered trellis.

"Lance, this is too much," she whispered.

They followed the maître d' to a candlelit table in

the corner. "So am I digging my way out of the hole I got myself into?"

Sophie laughed at the teasing in his eyes. "You're above ground."

He chuckled and they claimed seats, the romantic atmosphere charged with the building chemistry brewing between them. Lance ordered a bottle of chardonnay while they studied the menu, each choosing one of the house specialties. Then Lance lifted his glass for a toast. "To date one. The beginning of six nights together."

A tear pressed against Sophie's eyelids. She sincerely hoped it was the beginning of a lot more.

Reid had one hand on Lucy's panties, ready to strip them and finally feel her naked flesh from top to toe, when a loud clap of thunder rent the air and rain burst from the sky. Lucy laughed and they both scrambled up, grabbing clothes and picnic supplies as they raced toward the car. Lucy clutched her halter top in front of her, her pants in the other hand, her breasts jiggling while she ran through the rain. Reid carried the picnic basket and wine, trying to cover her with the blanket at the same time, grateful no one had moved into the new development yet. He'd hate to get caught with his pants down.

Seconds later they fell into the front seat of her small rental car. She managed to grab the basket and stick it in the backseat while he pushed aside several packages from the passenger side. Apparently Lucy had been on a shopping spree. She poured them both another glass of wine while he examined the contents of the lingerie bag. He found racy black thongs, one of which even had a red zipper. *Wow!* He wanted to see Lucy wearing that later . . . then take it off. The hard edge of a book poked him in the crotch. He jerked it from the seat and sighed in sweet relief. Then his gaze fell to the title: *Charms, Talismans, Spells, and Voodoo.*

"You don't believe in this stuff, do you?" He quirked an eyebrow toward Lucy.

Panic brightened Lucy's eyes for a second; then she reached for the book. "It's fun reading."

He held the book away from her, teasing, then flipped open the pages. "You really think mixing roots and berries and chanting will improve your love life?"

She winced, looking suddenly vulnerable. "Give it to me, Reid."

"Ahh, sugar, you sure as hell don't need this garbage." He nuzzled her neck. "You're an incredibly sexy woman as it is. You've had me in knots ever since I laid eyes on you."

Lucy laughed softly, playing kissy with his fingers while she attempted to pry the book from his hand.

He turned her hand into his palm and sucked at her skin. "Maybe I should read further. . . ."

She rubbed her breasts against him, sidetracking him, and managed to extricate the book from his fingers, but a scrap of paper fell from inside and fluttered to the floor. He bent to reach for it at the same time she did and their heads collided. His arm was longer, though, so he snagged it first.

"Let's see, did you cast a spell on me? Is that why I've been so infatuated with you?"

She laughed and lunged for the book again, but he narrowed in on the scribbled words and frowned. Lance's name appeared in the spell.

"What is this, Lucy?"

She twisted her hands together. "It's sort of a love potion."

To make Lance fall for Sophie? Well, he had asked for her help.

He skimmed the spell and realized it wasn't a love potion at all, but some kind of spell she'd concocted to free Sophie from Lance.

"You're trying to keep them apart?"

She was tying her halter top back around her neck now, her breasts jiggling for attention.

He tried desperately not to notice, to focus. "Why don't you want them to be together?"

"They're not right for each other," Lucy screeched.

"Why? Because Sophie's a big celebrity with her own TV show and sophisticated friends? You think my brother isn't good enough for her?" Anger churned through Reid, destroying the last vestiges of his desire. Had their reputation as the Terrible Three returned to haunt them? "Lance was afraid of that, but I told him no. He's every bit as good as the two of you." He swung open the door. "I can't believe you lied to me, Lucy. I thought you were trying to help, when you were actually trying to sabotage them all along."

Furious at Lucy for deceiving him and at himself for being so stricken with desire for her that he hadn't noticed she'd lied to him, he stalked off to his truck. He sure as hell didn't believe in any of that nonsense. Chanting and candle magic and voodoo had nothing to do with romance or determining one's future. Lucy was a flake—it was time for her to go back to Vegas.

Man, oh, man, was he glad he hadn't gone and done something stupid like fall for her. . . .

For the longest time, Lucy sat in her car, staring at the rain and the river beyond the antebellum mansion, seeing Rhett Butler walking out on Scarlett, hearing him grind out those famous words that he didn't give a damn.

Well, she didn't give a damn about Reid Summers either. Let him walk away from her with his pompous, self-righteous attitude, acting as if he were all wounded, and leave her aching with unfulfilled desires when she'd only been trying to protect her sister.

So she believed in a little hocus-pocus. And she liked to dabble with charms and spells. That didn't mean she was stupid. Only he had looked at her as if she'd grown three heads and one of them belonged to a jackass.

Damn him.

She had her Sleepover, Inc., box at home with all those products—she didn't need a man.

Reid's words caterwauled through her mind. *The real thing is better.*

Would it have been?

A tear seeped from her eye and dribbled down her face, followed by another and another. Rain trickled down the windshield, a coat of fog enveloping her, shielding her from the world. She'd always liked rain when she was a child, she'd enjoyed the sound of thunder, the excitement, the drama of a storm. Unlike Sophie, who wanted everything in order, everything calm.

Yes, she had always played with danger, just like Deseree, while Sophie had lived on the cautious side. Always wondering what people thought. Trying to make a good impression. Putting on a show of her own to convince others she was worthy.

Well, Lucy liked to perform, too, but she didn't need to put on a show to know she was worth something. If it was up to her, she'd come right out and tell Reid and Lance Summers about their Diva act.

236

If the macho Southern boys didn't like it, they could lump it.

Irritated with Reid and with herself for being irritated with him, she snatched the charm book and skimmed through it. In true Ya-Ya fashion, she jumped out and danced around, chanting a hex to the thunderclouds. When thunder boomed in reply as if to say the spirits had heard her, she squealed with glee. She'd fix Lance and Reid for causing her and Sophie all this trouble. Lance would start having aches in his muscles, sharp shooting pains that would drive him crazy.

And his brother . . . Well, Maddie had proclaimed it a battle of the sexes, and if nothing else, Lucy Lane always came out on top. If Reid had given her another few minutes, he'd have learned that himself. In a most delicious way, too.

Maybe she'd write a spell, put that image in his mind, and make him suffer. . . .

"Lance, the evening was wonderful." Sophie leaned against the doorjamb on her front porch and gazed up at Lance. His face contorted with pain.

"I'm glad you enjoyed it."

"What's wrong?"

He rubbed at the back of his head. "I don't know; I suddenly had a shooting pain in my neck." He shook it off. "It's nothing, gone now."

Sophie smiled. "You didn't mind the tour?"

"Are you kidding?" He rubbed a hand along the door molding beside her. "It gave me some ideas for your house."

Sophie blushed. "Me, too. I'm not sure I can afford them all, though."

Lance brushed a knuckle across her cheek. "We'll

work something out. If I know Maddie, she'll find a way to help you out."

"I'm so lucky to have Maddie as a friend."

Lance nodded. Dusted in shadows from the porch, his dark features appeared even more masculine.

"Do you want to come in for coffee?"

"Sure." His hand dropped to his lower back. "Damn."

"Poor baby." Sophie turned and let them in, leaving only a single light burning in the fringed lamp in the den. Lance followed, kneading his lower back as she brewed the coffee and gabbed herself a diet Coke. "Let's sit in the den."

He nodded and followed her to the comfortable sofa, his hand rubbing at his chest now.

"You're not feeling well?" Sophie asked.

"I don't know what's up; I'm suddenly having these weird pains."

"All that physical labor," Sophie said softly.

"That's my job."

"Still, it has to wear on you. Turn around."

Lance obeyed, stretching out his broad shoulders and dropping his head forward, his posture rigid. Sophie pressed her fingers into the area around his neck, then slowly began to knead the tension from his muscles.

"Your muscles are tight," she said softly. His musky scent sent a burning sensation through her belly. She pressed her knuckles into the ridges between his shoulder blades, rotating them in a circular motion. Deseree had taught her the art of massage therapy, a trick her mother had used on many clients to relax them into paying her well. Sophie had almost forgotten she knew any of the techniques, but reveled in being able to relieve the knots she felt in Lance's muscles.

Lance rolled his head sideways on a groan. "You have magic fingers."

"Hmm, you've been working too hard on the house."

"I like doing it," Lance admitted in a husky voice. "You made a good investment here, Sophie."

"I didn't buy it to resell," Sophie said, hesitating. "I want to make my home here."

"What about your big opportunity in Hollywood?" Lance asked. "With your show being syndicated, you'll probably start raking in all kinds of offers."

Sophie squeezed his lower back so hard he flinched. "Sorry. I . . . uh, I'm really not interested in Hollywood."

"But if the money's right?"

Lance's body felt so wonderful beneath her fingers, Sophie was tempted to lay her head on his shoulder. If she'd wanted the big time, she would have stayed in Vegas. "I like Savannah. I have friends here. A good job. Life isn't all about money."

He caught her hands in his and turned around to face her. "You surprise me sometimes, Sophie."

Silence stretched between them. His breath whispered out to her, his masculine scent trapping her in his essence.

"Is that a good thing?"

"Oh, yeah." His voice sounded rough with desire. "That's a damn good thing."

He lifted her hands to his shoulders, then lowered his head, pausing an inch from her mouth. "In fact, I want to know more." His lips brushed her neck. "I want to know everything there is to know about Sophie Lane."

Lance had intended to start the conversational ball rolling and get Sophie to open up about herself, but the minute their lips touched his body erupted into flames. One kiss led to another, and conversation was forgotten as tongues mated and danced. His hands created a frenzy of their own, tunneling through her hair and then journeying along her cheeks to her neck and shoulder blades, where he dipped under the straps of her sundress. Sophie curled into his arms in perfect abandonment, her subtle moans of encouragement feeding the fire between them as he slid the straps down her arms. Her bare neck was too enticing to skip, so he trailed kisses along her porcelain skin, tasting sweetness and sin. He unfastened the front bra clasp, and plump breasts encased in a strapless lacy red bra spilled into his hands. For a moment he simply gazed at her offering, amazed at her beauty and the shadow of vulnerability he detected in her eyes.

"You're beautiful," he whispered.

A slow smile curved her mouth, and he lowered his head and flicked a tongue across her nipple, his sex hardening at the sight of the rosebud tightening beneath his tongue. Temptation tore away his restraint then, and he closed his mouth around the turgid tip and suckled her, the sultry rise of her hips triggering aches that only she could relieve. Abandoning her left breast with his tongue to torture the other, he cupped and kneaded her flesh, then pinched her nipple between his fingers and tugged it. Sophie writhed below him, pushing at his shirt. Anxious to feel his bare chest against hers, he yanked off his shirt.

Pleasure rode on pleasure as he stretched above her and took her in his arms. She wrapped a leg around his thigh and rubbed her bare foot up and down his leg in a teasing game that evoked all kinds of wicked fantasies in his mind. Then her hands lowered to his waist and tugged at his jeans, and his breath caught, his sex throbbing for freedom and sweet release.

But not yet.

This time he wanted to pleasure her first, to make certain he dispelled any lingering images of himself as the unromantic barbarian she'd thought him after that fiasco of a dating game. So he stilled her hands and shook his head, smiling with triumph at the look of utter awe on her face when he trailed kisses down to her breasts, then licked a fiery path to her navel. Emitting a low groan from deep within his throat, he slid her dress to the floor. Red lace thong panties greeted him, the slip of see-through fabric guarding secrets he intended to uncover.

But first he teased her with his tongue, biting and licking her inner thighs, tiptoeing his fingers gently inside the edges of the fabric to touch the soft folds within, and finally dragging the garment low enough to taste her sweetness.

One taste and she flew into heaven, clutching his arms and trying to drag him upward, but Lance had never tasted anything in his life so addicting. He spread her legs farther apart and plunged his tongue inside her, welcoming the flow of honey into his mouth as she cried out his name.

Sophie was just about to scream again with pleasure, flip Lance over, and offer him the same glorious treatment he had her when the front door opened, and Lucy tottered inside, muttering, "Damn men, dogs, freaking dogs, that's what they are." Her high heels clicked on the hardwood foyer as she came nearer.

"Lance!" Sophie tried to sit up, but he crawled on

top of her, his denim brushing her damp heat, which was still on fire from his kisses.

"I know." His mouth found hers, and she tasted his hunger and her own flavor and nearly forgot about the fact that her sister was just about to catch them doing the naughty, and that she almost didn't care.

"No, Lance, we have to—"

"For goodness' sake, have you two ever heard of a bedroom?"

Lance froze, covering her with his body as she lifted her head. "Lucy."

She jerked at the afghan on the couch and dragged it over them, miffed at Lucy's tone. "I've been living alone for a while."

"Obviously." Lucy stepped from the shadows to cross to the staircase, and Sophie noticed that her eyes were red and puffy, her skin blotchy. She'd been crying.

"Lucy, what's wrong?"

Lance dropped his head forward onto her breasts as if to shield her, and she wiggled, hating the fact that her nipples were tightening again, and that she was more turned on than ever, and her sister was standing in the same room.

"Nothing. Don't let me interrupt." With a stricken expression she vamoosed up the stairs. Lucy's comment about the sisters not letting a man come between them echoed in Sophie's mind, totally killing the mood.

Well, maybe not totally. It took a second for her body to lose its response and another second for her to realize that Lance had not. He shifted, wrapping the blanket around her before he stood and reached for his shirt.

"Lance." She pulled the afghan around herself

then rose and laid a hand on his back. "I'm sorry."

"Shh." He slowly turned to face her. His breath was slightly erratic, his bronzed skin flushed with passion, his eyes hazy with desire. "Don't be sorry, sweetness. I'm not."

A scalding red heat rippled up her neck. "I don't mean I'm sorry for that, just sorry we were interrupted." She traced a finger over the bulge of his jeans. "Sorry that you didn't . . . have the pleasure."

"Oh, baby, I had pleasure," he said with a growl, his dark gaze skimming over her again. "Don't think for a minute that I didn't."

"But—"

He pressed a gentle finger to her lips. "No buts. We have five more nights. It'll give us both something to think about." He dropped a kiss onto her mouth. "Something to look forward to."

Oh, mercy, he was such a gentleman. Then again, a few minutes earlier, he had not been gentlemanly. . . .

"Your sister sounded upset, and you're probably dying to know what's wrong and to make it all better."

Sophie smiled. "In some ways we're a lot alike, Lance—always looking out for our siblings."

Lance chuckled and headed to the door. "I know. I'll see you in the morning."

"All right."

He paused at the front door. "Oh, and pop another balloon after I leave; then call me and tell me what it says, so I know how to plan tomorrow."

Sophie nodded and watched as he went out the door, the scent of his touch still emblazoned on her skin, the memory of his promise about their having something to look forward to lingering in her mind. She was definitely looking forward to date two. . . .

*   *   *

Lucy heard Sophie enter but didn't bother to look up. She had already started packing her Sleepover, Inc., kit and then would start on her clothes. In went the catalogs, the cucumber and banana dildos, the fake boobs. . . .

"I'm sorry I interrupted. I'll be out of your hair tomorrow, and you and Lance can do whatever you want in any room you want, whenever." Dag-nab it, her spells and charms must be backfiring. Sophie and Lance were hot to trot, while Reid hated her.

"I didn't mean to imply that I wanted you to leave, Lucy," Sophie said in a low voice. "I love having you around." Sophie crossed the room, took her sister's arms, and forced Lucy to look up at her. "You know that, don't you?"

Lucy hadn't meant to sound so petulant, but realized she did by the wounded expression on Sophie's face.

She shrugged, hating the well of tears that puddled in her eyes. She was acting like a big fat baby, and she had no idea why. She'd never let a guy upset her before.

Sophie wrapped her arms around her. "Hey, sis, what's wrong?"

A sniffle escaped her and Lucy sighed. "Men suck."

Sophie chuckled. "Anyone in particular?"

"Reid Summers."

Sophie pulled back and studied Lucy's face. "What happened?"

"Nothing," Lucy said. "Not that it matters. I don't give a rat's ass about that construction worker."

Sophie nodded. "I see. You want to tell me about it?"

Lucy remembered Reid's reaction when he'd seen

the spell she'd written, and imagined Sophie going off on her. "No. I don't need for him to like me to be all right."

"You are all right, Lucy; you're special."

"Damn straight. And I'm going back to Vegas tomorrow. It's showtime for this Diva girl."

"Right. Tomorrow night you'll be dazzling thousands of men; what's one fish in the sea?" Sophie stroked a wild curl of Lucy's into place. "After all, it's not like you've fallen for Reid, have you?"

Sophie's tone was so tender that it made Lucy's chest squeeze. But she refused to feel anything other than lust for a man. "No, of course not."

She moved back to the bed, snapped the Sleepover, Inc., kit closed, and began to pack her clothes while Sophie said good-night and went to bed. Lucy suddenly couldn't wait to get back to Vegas, with its bright lights and music and the crowds who knew how to have fun.

She tossed her charm book inside her bag. Maybe it had been wrong to use the spells for personal gain, so now a curse had fallen over her.

She'd have to be alert for negative karma or signs of bad luck, especially before she boarded the plane. . . .

Chapter Seventeen

Sleep had once again eluded Lance. He might have to learn to live without it altogether. His promise to Sophie had haunted him all night—*something to look forward to.*

Even if they didn't wind up in bed, the anticipation of hearing Sophie's sultry voice, of touring the city or walking hand in hand along the river, or buying silly souvenirs exhilarated him.

He had never felt this way about a woman before. It was downright scary. No, terrifying.

Instead of staring at the ceiling all night, though, he got up and reviewed the plans for the deal they were putting together with McDaniels. Around four AM, he had a major brainstorm. Utilizing the details he'd noticed in some of the architecture books he'd studied and from the tour the night before, he jotted down ideas to give their project a slightly different slant. By six he'd phoned Chase and Reid and asked them to meet him for breakfast. Over heaping mounds of pancakes, he related his thoughts.

"We can add a historic flair to the new storefronts and lofts; that way the places would add to the ambience of Savannah, draw a higher class of clientele, and up the resale value."

"I like it," Chase said.

"Me, too," Reid agreed.

Chase stabbed another bite of hotcakes drenched with syrup. "I'll draw up the plans right away."

Lance funneled coffee down his throat, willing himself to stay awake now that it was work time. He wanted to finish the trim in Sophie's kitchen before lunch, so he could spend the rest of the day with her. The date she'd pulled from the balloon had included an afternoon of antiquing. Normally shopping wasn't his idea of a fun way to spend a Saturday, but if the antique stores inspired as many new suggestions for plans as the tour the night before, it would be worth it.

Besides, he would be with Sophie. It didn't really matter to him what they did, as long as he could see her.

Reid was stirring creamer into his coffee, sloshing it all over the table with a scowl.

"What's up with you?" Lance asked.

"Nothing."

"Did you strike out with the ladies last night?"

Reid shrugged. "You could say that."

"At the clubs?"

"I don't want to talk about it."

"That bad, huh?"

Reid simply grunted.

Lance polished off his food. "I gotta get to work on Sophie's house."

Reid caught his arm. "How's it going, man?"

Lance squinted, wondering at the concerned look on his brother's face. "Good." He remembered the way Sophie had come apart in his arms. "Actually, really good. Why?"

Reid shrugged. "No reason, just wondered."

Lance tossed some bills on the table and Reid stood. "Lance?"

"Yeah?"

"If you want Sophie so bad, don't let anything or anyone get in your way."

Lance froze. What would he do if Sophie decided to take the other job and move away? He had his business here, his family.... "Do you know something you're not telling me?"

Reid shook his head. "Just that you were right about Sophie's sister, Lucy. She's a nut. I intend to stay away from her from now on."

Then Reid turned and strode out the door. Lance remembered that Lucy had been crying when she'd come in the night before.

Exactly what had happened between his brother and Sophie's little sister?

Lucy tapped her heel up and down on the airport floor in front of the security camera, dodging suspicious looks from passengers and damning laughter from the burly security guard prowling through her carry-on bag—she definitely should have checked the Sleepover, Inc., kit.

"This could be considered a weapon." A skinny middle-aged woman pounded the cucumber vibrator in her hand. "We'll have to confiscate it."

"And this looks dangerous to me." The burly guard removed the banana-shaped one and waved it in the air, drawing numerous innuendoes and whispers from the crowd.

"You must be some lonely chick," a middle-aged woman behind her muttered.

"Man, she likes kinky stuff," a balding man with a birdlike nose yelled.

The mother of a four-year-old child whining for candy covered her daughter's eyes and coached her away as if Lucy were a pedophile.

Lucy sighed and gave the guards her best sweet dumb-blond look. "Those are a part of my home-shopping business; it cost me five hundred dollars, so could you please be a dear and let me through?"

The beefy man scowled. "I don't think so, lady."

"Pretty please?"

The hefty man lifted a candle from the kit, then a pack of matches. "You know these aren't allowed."

Lucy winced. "Sorry, I forgot those were in there. I just use them to light incense and those candles, of course. Did you know that burning incense can stimulate your sex drive?"

He cut his eyes upward as if she were a complete ditz.

The skinny man lifted a jar of sparkly massage oil. "This might be toxic. Better turn it over to the CDC." He dropped it into their collection of nail files, manicure scissors, and other dangerous confiscated paraphernalia.

"It is not toxic; it's lotion," Lucy snapped. "At least let me check the damn bag."

"Ma'am, we don't appreciate your tone." He gestured for her to step through the metal detector.

Lucy moved forward, but the light flashed and a buzzer sounded. "Oh, good gracious."

He pointed to the clunky gold necklace dangling from her neck to her waist. "Step back and remove all your jewelry. Make sure your cell phone's in your purse."

She did as they instructed and tried again, but once again the alarm sounded.

"Shoes, belt."

Sophie peeled off her heels and dropped them in the plastic bag they offered, placed her gold chain belt on the conveyor belt, and tried again.

A woman wearing bifocals gestured toward her blouse. "You wearing a push-up bra with wires?"

Lucy nodded, glaring at the woman. "I need the support."

Someone across the way snickered, while a teenage boy with purple and yellow hair offered a comment about her knockers.

"Brassiere's probably setting it off." The female security agent waved for another guard. "Got a check here!"

"You might as well bring your clothes in a paper bag and get dressed after you get strip-searched." Lucy reached inside her shirt, unfastened her bra, and tossed it on the counter. "There." She stepped through the security booth again, but it flashed and dinged.

"What now?"

The woman's eyes rose over the bifocals. "Guard!"

"Maybe it's my belly button ring," Lucy said. She twisted sideways, pulled up her shirt and unfastened the dangling chain, stuck it in the bin with the rest of her jewelry, then once again tried to pass through security. The light flashed again.

Heck, she might as well get naked. A few men surrounding her were actually salivating at her impromptu partial strip show. "Listen, could we please hurry? I'm going to miss my flight."

"Then you should pay more attention to how you pack and what you wear."

"Look at me." Lucy gathered her blond curls into a fist. "I'm not a terrorist."

"Did someone say there's a terrorist here?" an elderly lady squeaked.

Whispers and worried looks skittered across the crowd.

"I'm not a terrorist," Lucy said, raising her voice so the elderly woman could hear.

The woman cried out and ran toward the exit. Several passengers scurried away to the next line, while the beefy man stepped up, pulling at his pants. "Ma'am, I believe you'd better step over here."

He tugged her forward, and Lucy gave him an evil eye, promising retribution in a spell while he forced her to stand with her legs apart, her arms splayed, and ran the wand over her. A female guard frisked her and Lucy snarled. She was grateful for airport security and knew it was necessary, but last night had been the pits.

And things were going downhill today.

Five minutes later, her bra, jewelry, belt, belly ring, and shoes stuffed into her carry-on bag, along with the disheveled half-empty Sleepover, Inc., kit, Lucy jogged down the hallway to make her flight.

Nothing had better go wrong with the plane. She refused to stay in this hot, stuffy, humid city another night.

Sophie stopped by the station after she said goodbye to Lucy at the airport, still perplexed as to why her sister seemed so out of sorts. What had Reid said to upset her so badly? She didn't want to make waves with Lance, but she desperately wanted some answers. And if she didn't know better, she'd think Lucy didn't want her to be with Lance. But what could her sister possibly have against him?

Instead of questioning her, though, Sophie had held her tongue, determined not to pry into her sister's life. Lucy had accused her of behaving too motherly more than once in the past few years. Speaking of motherly, she phoned Deseree to inform her Lucy had caught a flight back to Vegas. Of course, Deseree didn't answer; she was most likely still in bed. It was, after all, only noon, and Deseree needed her beauty sleep.

Especially since she sometimes worked all night.

Sophie shuddered at the thought. Pushing the painful memories out of her mind, she gathered her notes on the upcoming week's shows. Rory and George had both called again, so she phoned them back and left messages, saying she was going to be busy for the next week, and she'd try them when she was finished with her project.

It was only a little white lie; they didn't have to know that her project was personal—five more dates with Lance. She'd also put off the L.A. producer who wanted to talk to her about hosting the reality show—she simply couldn't make a career decision right now.

The producer for *Sophie Knows* stuck his head into her office. She hadn't yet told him about her other offers. But she hadn't explored the details either. She wasn't that interested in hosting a reality show—she'd never really liked them. But a position as a newscaster held some appeal.

"Sophie, the show's ratings this past week were phenomenal. With the upcoming episodes leading into our June wedding series, the syndication is cinched."

"Great." She didn't want to move anyway. Did she? Not if things worked out with Lance. . . . They chatted for a few minutes about the game plan for the next few weeks; then she hurried toward her car, anxious for the afternoon. First she and Lance were going antiquing; then they planned to take one of the riverboat cruises.

She remembered the dreadful answers Lance had given in the "Dating Game" show and laughed. He had definitely redeemed himself by proving he had a romantic nature.

Guilt niggled at her. She needed to tell him about her past. Would he understand why she'd kept her secrets or would he look down on her, as the school kids had?

You're simply dating now, not engaged or involved in a serious relationship. You don't have to reveal your worst demons up front.

Maybe once they became closer, *if* that happened, then she could share more about her childhood and early career with him.

When she arrived at her house, Lance had finished painting the trim in the kitchen and had left a note that he'd gone home to shower. She hurried to refresh also, changing into a short denim skirt and tank top with a lightweight jacket. Layering would enable her to survive the spring heat while they shopped, but she'd definitely need the jacket tonight on the cruise. And the red top made her feel sexy, ready for fun and romance.

The doorbell rang, and she rushed down the steps, surprised to find Lance and Peter waiting on her front porch. The two men postured as if they were enemies. A florist's truck pulled up next to the sidewalk. A young man wearing a paper hat jumped out and ran toward the door.

"Lance, hi." She offered him a beseeching smile, then let it fade when she faced Peter. "I thought you'd already left town."

Before he could reply, the delivery boy waved a hand. "Sophie Lane?"

"Yes?" Had Lance sent her flowers?

"Sign here." Sophie opened the screen, heat climbing her neck as Peter strode inside. She was definitely going to put a padlock on the door. People were coming in and out as though she had a revolving door.

Speaking of the door, Lance held it open for her, but when she handed the young man the signed slip and reached for a tip from her purse on the table in the foyer, he was frowning at the flowers.

Drat. They weren't from him.

She skimmed the card attached to the roses. George.

Biting her tongue, she slid them onto the table in the foyer, stuffed a five-dollar tip in the delivery boy's hand, grabbed Lance's arm, and ushered him into the den. "Make yourself comfortable."

Peter loped in as though he owned the place. "Sophie?" Peter said. "We need to talk."

Sophie glared at him, stuck a finger in the air, and glanced at Lance. "Give us one minute, okay?"

His grunt was noncommittal, but at least he sat down and didn't barrel out the door.

Sophie dragged Peter to the kitchen. "What are you doing here?"

"I wanted to talk to you about Deseree before I left. And I had to thank you for the appointment with the talent scout. He's supposed to get back with me next week. I might get a few commercials."

"You're welcome, but I don't intend to discuss Deseree with you."

"You have to give her a chance." Peter countered. "Come to Vegas for Mother's Day; visit her; she's trying to change."

"I sent her a check, Peter. I talk to her on the phone—"

"It's not the same thing, Sophie. What are you, heartless?"

"Heartless?" A sharp pang settled in Sophie's chest. If only Peter had known how much Deseree had hurt her growing up, how many times she'd lain awake needing her mother, soothing Lucy's tears, wondering if they were safe or if one of her mother's boyfriends might be dangerous. . . .

"I think you'd better leave."

"But we're not finished."

"The lady asked you to go."

Sophie was startled at the sound of Lance's cold tone, her heart pounding at the sight of him standing in the kitchen doorway looking all protective of her. His eyes glinted with anger, his jaw was so tight she heard his molars grinding, and he'd fisted his big hands by his side.

How much of their conversation had he overheard?

Lance had finally given in to temptation and tiptoed to the door, but he'd heard Sophie ask the black-jacketed milksop to leave; then the man had moved closer to her, looking pushy and too damn tough to be anywhere near a soft, sophisticated woman like Sophie Lane, and he'd had to step forward.

"This conversation is between me and Sophie." The milksop glared at him as if he'd intruded, but Lance refused to budge.

"The conversation is over," Lance stated baldly. He took a menacing step forward and the hothead did the same, but Sophie pushed Peter toward the back door.

"He's right, Peter. Now go back to Vegas."

White-hot jealousy snaked through Lance at the sight of Sophie's hand touching the man. Sophie was not his to be territorial over, yet he felt territorial over her, and if the man touched her, he might not be able to restrain himself from tearing his arms completely out of his sockets.

"This isn't over," Peter said; then he slammed out the door.

Sophie turned, looking slightly shaken. "I'm sorry, Lance."

"What was that all about?"

She rubbed her hands up and down her arms. "Nothing."

He studied her posture, the slight nervous twitch of her hands as she fidgeted with her hair. She was lying. Somehow he had to get Sophie to trust him and open up.

Quickly collecting herself, Sophie gathered her purse, a big straw bag that she slung over one shoulder. "Do you still want to go out?"

The subtle worry in her tone triggered his protective instincts. He closed the distance between them, gently cradled her face in his hands, and pressed a kiss to her lips. "Yes, I want this day to be special."

Sophie squeezed his hands in hers and smiled. "So do I. I don't want anything to spoil it, especially an old acquaintance."

Lance nodded and followed her to the door. Was that all the milksop was? An old acquaintance? Or had he once been Sophie's lover?

If so, Lance intended to extinguish any lingering memory of the other man's hands on her body or his presence in her life.

And he did his best to do that as they strolled from one antique shop to the other.

Their first stop was the Arts and Crafts Emporium of Savannah, which showcased unusual artwork contributed by locals. Sophie gushed over a pair of hand-painted earrings made of crystals, so he bought them for her, his body stirring with desire when she allowed him to actually slide the earrings into the holes in her ears.

He must be too far gone for help if putting a pair of earrings on a woman turned him on.

Then again, he was sleep-deprived.

"Thank you, Lance; that's the first time a man has ever bought me jewelry." Sophie kissed him on the lips, her fragrance so enticing he wanted to take her right there. "And no man has ever taken me antiquing."

"I'm enjoying it," he said, thinking that last year he would have rather had his teeth yanked out with pliers than spend a Saturday afternoon traipsing through old dusty corridors and stacks of used furniture. Still, with Sophie, he didn't mind.

He wanted to be her first at a lot of things.

The thought momentarily panicked him, and he remembered his fear of losing his singlehood, purse holding all day while his wife shopped. But he wasn't purse holding, or getting married. He was simply dating Sophie. Seeing where and how they might fit in each other's lives.

After all, his attempt to avoid her had failed miserably.

Actually, he had a feeling they would fit together perfectly, at least in one way. Maybe in a lot more. They shared the same tastes in furniture, and although Sophie was a neatnik, she didn't choose items for their monetary value, but appeared to be interested in history and more sentimental pieces. That part surprised him. He'd expected more contemporary tastes, more expensive needs. . . .

They combed through a half dozen antique shops, laughing at old books and statues and a few children's toys that made Lance's heart squeeze. He'd had a little red wagon when he was a boy. He'd passed it to Reid, then Maddie. Maybe Maddie would have a child someday for them to pass it on to next.

Would he ever have one?

Sophie squealed over a French antique bracelet she discovered, cutting into his disturbing thoughts. "I'm going to buy this for Maddie as a thank-you gift for helping with the remodeling."

"She'll love it," Lance said. Maddie loved jewelry. She especially treasured the necklace their mother had left her.

After Sophie paid for it, they scavenged through a shop full of eighteenth- and nineteenth-century heirlooms, everything from porcelain and glass trivets, dressers, armoires, and art. Sophie raved over an old-fashioned Victoria that played while browsers lingered.

After they left the antique shops, they sampled homemade fudge from the chocolate shop and sipped on freshly squeezed lemonade while they crossed the street to the City Market. "My feet are killing me." Sophie paused to shake a pebble from her sandal.

"No problem." Lance had arranged for a pedicab to pick them up and drive them over to where the cruise boat docked.

"This has been a wonderful day." Sophie squeezed his hand.

"I'm glad you're enjoying yourself." And so was he. For the first time in years he felt lighter, less troubled. Except for the deal with McDaniels. First thing Monday morning he would knock on the man's door.

And he wouldn't take no for an answer.

But tonight was all about romancing Sophie.

Sophie had never been so romanced in her life. A thousand stars glittered above them in the inky sky as they climbed aboard the *Savannah River Queen*. Lance twined her fingers in his as they walked the ship, admiring the view of Savannah before taking off. Minutes later the ship cast away from shore, and they joined the other tourists for a romantic candlelit dinner. Folksy blues music floated around them and added romance to the evening's ambience.

Sophie sipped a martini and leaned into Lance's arms as the wind ruffled her hair. "This day has been spectacular."

"Have you taken one of these cruises before?"

Sophie shook her head. "It's hard to believe I've been in Savannah this long when there are so many things I haven't experienced."

"I grew up here, but I've never done a lot of the tourist things," Lance admitted. "And I didn't pay much attention to history and stuff like that in school."

"You weren't a good student?"

Lance's low chuckle reverberated through the wind. "Hardly. I'm sure Maddie's filled your ears with stories about me and Reid and Chase. The Terrible Three."

"Actually, she made you sound pretty wonderful." One reason Sophie had fallen in love with him. But she bit back the words, knowing Lance wasn't prepared to hear them. Would he ever be?

He nuzzled her neck. "What about you—were you a good student?"

Sophie smiled to herself. "A regular bookworm."

"Why am I not surprised? You're perfect now; you were perfect back then."

Sophie swallowed, uncomfortable. "I'm not perfect, Lance."

"Really?" He nibbled at her ear. "Tell me one bad thing you did."

She'd kicked one of Deseree's boyfriends in the shin because she hadn't liked his mullet haircut, but she didn't particularly want to share that experience. "I took Maddie to that nudist colony last year."

"I know." He growled and stiffened, then relaxed. "But I didn't mean last year; I meant as a kid."

"My childhood wasn't very interesting, Lance. We moved around a lot. That's one reason having a place to call home is so important to me."

"Makes sense."

The band slowed down to a love song, and people filtered onto the dance floor. Lance took her hand. "Dance with me."

Sophie nodded, grateful for the reprieve from sharing her past as she slipped into his arms. Their bodies swayed together seductively, every step and move heightening their awareness of each other.

Sophie didn't want the romantic cruise to end, yet at the same time she counted the minutes. *Something to look forward to.*

Nothing would ruin the night—no Peter, no Lucy, no Deseree. Nothing.

Not even the ghosts in the attic or the ghosts from her past.

Chapter Eighteen

By the time they arrived at Sophie's, Lance and Sophie were pawing at each other's clothes. "Do you want coffee?" Sophie whispered as he pulled at her tank top.

"No, nothing except you."

Her top landed on the foyer table, her skirt a puddle near the first step in the hallway, his shirt and jeans tossed somewhere along the staircase as they kissed and climbed toward Sophie's room and sweet oblivion.

Lance felt intoxicated from her heady kisses, his body thrumming with hunger at every soft moan and nibble of her mouth on his body. Sophie dragged him into her bedroom, but he hesitated, wondering if he was moving too fast.

Jazzy lay in the center of her bed, with that same snarl.

"Baby, you have to go out now." Without blinking, Sophie lifted the cat and set her outside the door, then shut them into their own private cocoon.

Ridiculous relief filled him that Sophie hadn't chosen her cat over him. Then Lance feasted on her near nakedness, a surge of emotion engulfing him at the look of unbridled passion in her eyes.

Sophie's nipples beaded at his hungry appraisal. "All day I've been thinking about what you said last night about anticipation."

Lance chuckled and reached for her bra strap, sliding it down inch by inch. "Honey, I didn't sleep a wink last night for imagining being with you."

Seconds later her glorious breasts bounced into view. Lance claimed his prize, torturing her again with slow, erotic kisses on her mouth and neck before dipping below to feast on the soft mounds of her breasts. Sophie wiggled and clung to him, moaning and tossing her head back in wild abandon.

Then he was kissing lower, trailing hot, fiery need in the wake of his tongue's delicious dance until he had her naked. He pushed her back on the mountain of pillows, crawling above her to slide his body against hers in torture. Sophie writhed and tugged at his boxers until he flung them to the floor. Then they lay naked, entwined in each other's arms. His erection pulsed between her thighs, aching for home, but he didn't want to rush the pleasure, so he stroked her folds with the tip, his heart pumping wildly at the way she thrust her hips in a plea for completion.

She flipped him over and Lance lay stunned as she coaxed his hands away, then climbed on top of him. Giving him a sassy look of pure feminine attitude, she lowered her head and teased him with her tongue the way he had her, starting with his mouth, then trailing hot kisses down his chest. She even paused and tortured his nipples, biting at them until he bucked up and nearly came. He groaned and tried to lift her, but she slid down his body and traced her tongue along the tip of his sex. His body damn near convulsed off the bed.

"Sophie, hon—"

"Shh, just enjoy."

A second later she'd taken him in her mouth, and he thought he would explode. He allowed himself only the briefest of pleasure before he stopped the torment by reversing their positions. Beneath him, she stared up at his face, breathless, her cheeks red with heat. He looked into her fiery green eyes then and knew he was lost, but he didn't care.

He sank himself inside her, thrusting gently until he filled her, cupping her hips into his palms and urging them closer together, until they were one. Sophie's moan of pleasure tore through the silence, their bated breaths splintering the tension as he rocked inside her. His tongue danced with hers as their bodies slapped together. Harder, deeper, faster, he moved them toward the gates of heaven until he felt Sophie's insides quivering with the first spasms of release. Then he drove himself harder, deeper, faster, claiming her mouth with his and letting his hands play along her breasts, riding out the storm until they both lay sated in each other's arms, breathless and elated.

Sophie settled into Lance's embrace, her body singing with joy, her heart bursting with love. He curved his arms around her, one of his legs thrown across hers, and she draped an arm over his chest, snuggling against him as they both fell asleep.

Sometime in the early hours of the morning, she woke to feel his lips trailing kisses along her face. She giggled and kissed him back, instantly coming awake with sensations when he climbed above her and slid inside her again. This time their joining was both gentle and quick, but so sweet that tears pressed against her eyelids. Then once again he cradled her in his arms as they fell into a blissful sleep.

Breakfast in bed a few hours later turned into a tempting feast of food and coffee and lovemaking. Afterward, they lay in bed and leisurely read the morning paper together.

"I should get up and work on the floors today," Lance said.

"But you look so comfortable."

"I am." Lance hugged her to him. "That's the best night's sleep I've had in weeks. But there's still a lot of work left to do on the renovations."

"You're not in a hurry to finish my house, are you?"

He chuckled and dropped a kiss on her nose. "Yes and no. I'm anxious to see the finished product, but I like hanging around here."

It was as much of an admission as she supposed she would get. Would a few more dates convince him that they belonged together forever?

"Then let's just hang out today."

He nuzzled her neck. "All right. We could go over to Tybee Island, take a picnic, charter one of the boats and see the marshland, eat at Williams Seafood."

"Is that one of the dates in the balloons?"

Lance nodded. "The yellow one."

Sophie kissed him. "Sounds perfect."

"Good, and while we lie on the beach, you can tell me more about yourself." Lance fingered a strand of hair from her forehead. "I want to know all about you, Sophie."

Sophie hesitated. "What kind of things do you want to know?"

"You've never talked about your family." He laid the paper aside and threw an arm around her. "Or how you came to Savannah to work on the show, what you did before."

Sophie clutched the covers, anxiety clawing at her as she struggled with how to answer him. The telephone trilled, sidetracking them both. Hoping it wasn't Peter or Deseree or George or Rory, she checked the caller ID. Maddie.

Sophie grabbed the phone, then pulled on a silky robe and sat cross-legged on the bed beside Lance. His hand moved to massage her neck, and she stifled a groan, then whispered for him to stop. "Hey, Maddie, what's up?"

"You tell me, girl. Are you and my brother doing what I think you're doing?"

"Probably. Well, not this second."

Maddie squealed. "I knew those rules would work. He spent the night; that's a good sign."

"It is, isn't it?" His hand slipped down to cradle her breast, and Sophie batted it away.

"Absolutely." She heard Maddie clapping her hands. "Now, remember the next rule. Keep him sated."

Sophie tugged at the sheet, lowering it so she could enjoy the view of male muscle in her bed. "Don't worry; I'll do my best."

She laughed, then hung up the phone and slid back onto the pillows to fulfill her promise. As long as she kept Lance happy in bed, he couldn't ask any more questions.

The next week flew by. Lance spent his days working on Sophie's house, his evenings taking romantic strolls along the riverfront with Sophie, trying out different Savannah restaurants, and discussing her house. Afterward, they'd share a nightcap at one of the local pubs, then return to Sophie's and make love.

He had never slept so peacefully in his life. Apparently his insomnia was cured. As long as he slept with Sophie. . . .

His mind wandered back to the busy week. Monday night they had taken the book tour based on *Midnight in the Garden of Good and Evil* and eaten breakfast at Clary's Café, just as Luther Driggers, the eccentric character in the book, had done. Plates of pecan waffles, sausage biscuits with gravy, and country ham had been delicious. Tuesday they enjoyed live music at an outdoor table at Malone's, then dropped by the Six Pence Pub for a nightcap. Wednesday they took a carriage ride tour and dined at the fabulous Oyster Bar. Thursday night they toured a special showing by the Savannah College of Art and Design. At a neighboring antique store, Sophie bought a replica of a revolutionary war painting to hang in the dining room. He had suggested taking one of the casino cruise ships out for Las Vegas–style gambling, but Sophie had opted for a walk in Wormsloe State Historic Park, claiming she wasn't a gambler.

His persistence had finally paid off that week and earned him a meeting with McDaniels. Lance had been a half hour early and wowed the businessman with the blueprints Chase had drawn up, as well as the ideas he and Reid and Chase had outlined. McDaniels was strongly considering giving them the job, a multimillion-dollar contract that would put their company on the map and assure them financial security. It was also a long-term commitment.

He and Chase and Reid had met for drinks to discuss the meeting.

"I think it's in the bag," Chase said. "No one else has given detailed thought to the historical aspects of the location the way we have."

"I agree." Reid raised his beer for a toast. "Let's have dinner and celebrate."

Chase squirmed on his seat. "I sort of promised Maddie we'd go out tonight. She's been working so hard this week, and she's been really tired."

"Sophie and I have plans, too," Lance said.

Reid made a clicking sound with his teeth. "How's it going with her, man?"

Lance sipped his beer. "We've been dating all week."

"Is she as good as you expected?" Reid asked.

Chase poked him, and Lance frowned. "A gentlemen never tells."

Chase raised a brow. "You getting serious with her?"

Lance stared into the amber bottle. Sophie had certainly welcomed him into her arms and her bed each night, and they'd had great fun together, and mind-boggling sex, but . . . "I don't know; it seems like she's holding something back from me."

Reid waved at the bartender for another beer. "What do you mean? She doesn't get into sex the way you do?"

"No, it's not that." Lance dabbed a spot on his shirt with his napkin. "I can't put my finger on it. She's great, and loving, and so damn sexy . . . but every time I ask her about her family or her past, she diverts my attention."

"You mean she changes the subject?" Chase asked.

"Actually"—Lance hesitated, knowing his complaint sounded weird—"she jumps my bones."

"And that's a problem?" Reid asked in an incredulous tone.

Lance gave a sardonic laugh. "I know it sounds strange but—"

"But you want more?" Chase said.

Lance sighed. "I guess so." He stared into his beer, wondering if he was crazy. Last year he would have been thrilled to have this kind of relationship. Sometimes he sensed Sophie really cared for him, maybe even loved him, but then she'd pull away. "There must be something wrong with me. I never felt this way before."

Chase slapped him on the back. "I understand completely."

Lance jerked his head up and stared at his friend. "What do you mean?"

"I hate to tell you this," Chase said, "but you're in love, buddy."

Lance realized he held his beer bottle in a death grip. Was it possible—could he be in love with Sophie? And if he was, what was he going to do about it?

As Reid watched Lance leave the bar, he scouted out the women, searching for one who sparked his interest. All week long he'd had these crazy dreams about Lucy Lane.

Lucy Lane on top of him, doing wicked and delicious things to his body with her tongue. Then Lucy sliding over him, him pushing into Lucy's warm, wet body . . . Lucy crying out his name in the throes of a mind-blowing orgasm.

He had tried to ban the images from his mind, but they came to him unbidden at the most inopportune times of the day. Yesterday he'd had a flash of her sinking onto his sex, and he'd nearly fallen off the roof of the house. This morning he'd seen her long strawberry-blond hair draped over his stomach and watched her go down on him, and he'd been so rattled, he'd almost walked through a plate-glass window. And on the way to the bar, he'd had fantasies of her naked and writhing beneath him. When reality surfaced, he'd nearly hit a semi, so he'd swerved, overcompensated and nearly run off the bridge into the ocean. The thought of becoming shark food over a woman was too much. . . .

"What's up with you, Reid?" Chase pulled cash from his wallet to pay the bar bill. "You're awfully quiet."

Reid shrugged. "Thinking about Lucy." Lucy having sex with him. Lucy chanting to the moon to hex him. Lucy destroying his sex life with other women. She was going to kill him. . . .

Chase threw his head back and laughed. "What the hell, you fell for Sophie's sister, didn't you?"

"No," Reid barked. "Hell, no."

"Then what's the problem?"

"She does all this hocus-pocus shit with charms and spells. I think she put a damn curse on me."

"What kind of curse?" Chase asked.

Reid chewed the inside of his cheek. "A curse to make me think about her."

Chase held his belly as laughter shook him. "You mean you believe in that hocus-pocus stuff?"

"No," Reid growled. At least he didn't think so.

"Then why would you think she put a curse on you?"

"Why else would she be on my mind all the time? It's not as if I really like her or anything." He lowered his voice to a whisper. "But I've even been dreaming about her. In the daytime, doing wild things to me."

"That the reason you're not trying to pick up

women today?" Lance leaned an elbow on the bar. "I thought you were off your marker."

Reid cocked his head in defiance. "I've been looking. But I haven't spotted anyone I wanted to flirt with yet."

"Right." Chase tossed some money on the table. "Take my advice: If she has you in knots like this, the only way you can get over her is to see her again."

"We . . . uh, didn't part on very good terms. That's another reason I think she might have cursed me." Although her other curse seemed to have backfired, because Lance and Sophie seemed to be getting along great.

He was the one dreaming about Lucy doing wicked things to him, then waking up and having to live with the fact that it was never going to happen.

Then again, maybe Chase was right. Maybe he should take a little trip to Vegas and surprise her. He'd force her to remove whatever kind of spell she'd cast on him.

Then he'd be free of Lucy Lane forever.

Lucy was cursed.

Everything that could possibly go wrong this week had done so. Her plumbing at her apartment had gone on the fritz, so her toilet had overflowed, not only ruining the carpet but half her collection of designer shoes and two feather boas she used as part of her Diva costumes. She was out five hundred dollars for the plumbing repairs and had to alter one of her numbers for the night until she found the right boas to replace the others.

Then, on her way in to the Palace, her car had died on the freeway, and she'd been forced to hitchhike a ride with a nice little family from Pasadena who acted as if they'd just escaped a time warp from the seventies. Worse, the teenage son had tried to snitch her watch, while the grandma described her deceased husband's hernia, her false teeth clacking for miles.

Now she'd arrived at the Palace for the early-evening show and discovered that someone had used her jars of creams and makeup, a major no-no. They'd also forgotten to store them properly, so now her blue eyeshadow had turned black and her powder had hardened into a brick.

She slammed the makeup drawer shut and borrowed her friend's. Sassafras was a college student, and unfortunately used the cheapest brands because she was too busy paying her slug of a boyfriend's way out of jail and into rehab.

She'd scavenged all the charm and spell books she could find for answers, and had no idea why her spells had backfired, unless she was being punished for being selfish and not wanting Sophie to be with Lance.

Was she being selfish?

Should she have looked deeper to see what qualities Lance possessed that had attracted Sophie to him? Should she have forgotten her own needs to have her sister close by and accepted that Sophie was grown and gone, and that she was alone and she always would be? Panic seized her. She'd never liked being alone; Sophie had always been there. . . .

For some odd reason, Reid's face materialized in her mind.

She banished it, certain she'd thought of him only because she'd been stewing about his brother and the two men were connected.

She did not want or need Reid Summers; she had

her Sleepover, Inc., playthings to keep her satisfied anytime she had the urge . . . er, the need . . . er, the desire. . . .

The real thing's even better.

Dag-nab it, his words haunted her like an incantation that hadn't worked but had been imprinted in her brain, because the words had been kind of pretty. Not that Reid was pretty, but he had been easy on the eyes, and he had great pecs and he had made her body hum with all kinds of decadent fantasies.

Lurching upward, she knocked her head on the mirror, caught her wingspan of red feathers in the doorway, and nearly choked herself when the door banged shut and her feathers got trapped between the hinges.

"What in the hell are you doing, Lucy?" Garrison, the stage manager, bellowed. "You're on in three."

The music that led off her first act of the night spilled through the speakers; the hundreds of Palace guests clapped in anticipation. The manager opened the door, freed her feathers, and shoved her forward. Lucy grappled for control, steadying herself as she adjusted to the thirty pounds of feathers and fifteen extra pounds of jewelry weighing down her arms.

Peter danced toward her, the shiny black outfit that hugged his body shimmering beneath the bright lights, and she glanced out to see Deseree wave from the front row. She'd meant to ask Peter what had happened with the talent scout and made a mental note to do so after the last number of the night.

But for now she was on. She only hoped that the curse didn't affect her onstage, turning her into such a klutz that she fell and ruined the dance.

Troubles or not, the show had to go on. For now, that was all that mattered.

Not Reid Summers or her crappy life, or the fact that her feet were aching in these spiked shoes, and that maybe, just maybe, Sophie had been right when she'd said that the excitement eventually dwindled, and that Lucy might not want to dance forever.

She held her arms high and strutted across the stage, pasting on her performer's face and diving into the music. But five minutes later, the show fell apart.

Sassafras, the girl who'd replaced Sophie, never showed, so Lucy had to do double duty trying to fill both their parts, leaping and twirling from spot to spot so quickly that she got dizzy and nearly fell off the stage. In between acts, the manager called her to the phone.

"It's Sassafras; she won't talk to anyone but you."

Lucy grabbed the handset. "Hey, honey, what's wrong?"

A wail greeted her. "You won't believe this, but I was helping Dicky into rehab tonight, and I fell and bruised my tailbone. The doctor says I can't dance the rest of the weekend." Another wail screeched over the line, this one louder and more miserable. "I'm sorry, Lucy; I know Garrison's going to fire me, but I can barely walk. I have to sit on a plastic doughnut; it's just so awful. I don't know what to do about work. . . ."

Lucy struggled for a way to help save Sassafras's job. After all, her friend's accident was probably a result of the curse on Lucy. Now she was bringing bad luck to everybody around her.

They had to find her friend a replacement. But all of the other girls had their own parts, and no one else knew the routine but Sassafras and . . . Sophie.

No, she couldn't phone her sister and ask her to fill in, could she?

"Please, Lucy, I can't lose this job. I need the money; I just found out I'm pregnant. . . ." She broke into another wail, and Lucy's heart tightened. "Dicky's promised to stay in rehab for the baby's sake, and my parents won't let me come home, and I want to finish college. . . ." Her blabbering trailed off into a hysterical sob.

"Don't worry, Sassy, I'll think of something. Now go home, put your feet up, ice your tushy or whatever the doctor said to do to it, and rest." She promised her she'd check on her later, then hung up and stared at the phone. Sophie had always taken care of her friends on the set, had always been the caretaker, and Sassafras had moved in with them when Sophie was still in town. She'd also taken Sophie's place at the last minute when Sophie decided to leave the act, so Sophie actually owed her.

But her sister had her own life now, and she didn't want anyone in Savannah to know about her past. Still, Sophie could fly out for the weekend. As the second part of the Diva act, she'd be in costume, so no one would recognize her—and she could return on Monday for her own show.

Really, she'd just have to convince Sophie to do it one last time, that no one would ever know. . . .

The *Sophie Knows* show had done a week's worth of programs devoted to motherhood, spouting the joys, triumphs, and tribulations of parenting in the modern-day world. Experts offering sage advice and women facing the daily challenges had all shared their experiences, insights, and knowledge. The series had wrapped up on Friday with a reunion show of mothers and daughters who had been estranged; the first half of the time slot had been devoted to mothers who'd given up children for adoption, the second to problem families.

Sophie had fought tears during the entire episode and had stayed late to chat with guests backstage and compose herself before she went home. The reunion had spurred her own troubled memories of her mother and their relationship, making her question whether Lucy was right. Maybe it was time to let the past go and try to build a friendship with their mother. After all, Sophie didn't blame her mother for her actions; she'd been young, foolish, had been cast aside by her own family, desperate, destitute, and pregnant at fifteen. She'd been little more than a child herself and had been forced to grow up fast. Of course, Deseree hadn't actually grown up, but she had taken some hard knocks.

Sophie contemplated phoning her mother all the way to her house. When she parked in the driveway, she was relieved to find it empty. Grateful for the time alone to sort through her emotions and freshen up, she gathered her purse and made her way inside. The phone was ringing when she entered.

She read the number for the Palace on the caller ID and frowned, her pulse clamoring. Was something wrong with Lucy? She hadn't talked to her all week, but her sister never called from work.

She grabbed the receiver. "Hello?"

"Sophie, I'm glad I caught you before you went out."

"What's wrong? Are you all right? Is it Deseree?"

"No, Soph, I'm fine, and so is Mom."

Since when had Lucy started calling Deseree Mom? "Oh, well . . . good. I was worried; you never call from work."

"I know and I can't talk long, but this is an emergency."

"What kind of an emergency?"

"Sassafras fell and injured herself and can't dance tonight or the entire weekend. I'm trying to cover tonight, but I can't keep it up for the rest of the weekend, and the crowd will complain if we skip the double numbers—"

"Lucy, why are you telling me this? Can't one of the other dancers fill in?"

"No, no one else knows the steps."

"You're kidding? When I left, I told you to get an understudy, that this might happen."

"I know, and you were right, and we did hire this girl named Jasmine. She subbed for me last weekend, but she has the flu and can't come in until Monday. We need someone now, just for the weekend show; you know Saturday night is our biggest night of the week."

Sophie's nails dug into her thigh as she realized the reason for Lucy's call. "You want me to come there and fill in? Lucy, you're out of your mind."

"No . . . well, maybe, but you're the only one who knows the dance, and Garrison might fire Sassafras, and she needs the money—"

"To take care of that no-account boyfriend of hers?"

"No," Lucy said, lowering her voice to a shaky whisper. "Soph, she's pregnant, and she can't go home. She has no one to help her."

Oh, dear heavens. Sassafras was such a sweetie, and she'd actually taken over for Sophie when she'd gotten the offer for the *Sophie Knows* show, dropping everything to help her. There was no question Sophie owed her. She pictured the young girl, alone, frightened, struggling with an alcoholic boyfriend, worried about her job. She'd seen the same desperate face on too many young girls in the past, one reason she'd wanted to get out of Vegas. She'd even felt desperate herself a few times.

Was that how Deseree had felt? Pregnant and alone, desperate, with no place to turn?

"I swear no one will find out," Lucy said. "You can come incognito to the set; we won't release your name, and with all the makeup and costumes you'll be wearing, you won't even recognize yourself."

Sophie squeezed her eyes shut, her emotions warring in her head. But she couldn't refuse to help this girl. And Lucy was right: If she went incognito the entire way, and avoided the press, they could probably pull it off.

"Soph, please, if you do this, I promise I'll sign up for night classes. I've been thinking about what you said about not dancing forever."

"You have?"

"Yes. Will you come? We could see Deseree together, too." Lucy hesitated. "Or wait, scratch that, I'm not trying to push you, Soph."

Sophie sighed. Hadn't she been thinking about Deseree? "All right, but make Garrison swear on his life that he won't reveal my name to the public, not even to the other girls. If he does, I'll sue his pants off."

"I promise," Lucy said. "And Sophie, thanks—I knew I could count on you."

Sophie said good-bye, then called the airlines. If she wanted to go standby, they could get her on a plane in a couple of hours. She'd have to cancel her date with Lance tonight, sleep alone. . . .

She hastily threw together a suitcase; then Lance's headlights flickered in the driveway.

How was she going to explain her sudden trip to him?

Chapter Nineteen

Lance took one look into Sophie's eyes and knew something was wrong. He kissed her tenderly first, then pulled back and clasped her hands in his. "What is it? You seem upset."

A faint flush crept onto her porcelain cheeks. "I didn't realize you could read me so well."

"Tell me what's bothering you."

"I . . . I have to cancel tonight," Sophie said, her voice filled with regret.

His first instinct was jealousy, but they had to build a trust between them. He wanted that as much as he wanted to take her in his arms and kiss her senseless. "Work?"

She shook her head.

"You haven't had some other long-lost acquaintance show up again, have you?" If she had, he'd have to pulverize him. He wasn't about to sleep with her, then let some other man put his grimy hands on her.

"No, it's not a man." Sophie laid her palm against

his cheek. "It's Lucy; she called, and there's an emergency with a friend of ours—"

His mouth tightened.

"A girlfriend," Sophie clarified quickly. "I have to go tonight, Lance. I hope you'll understand."

"Is she hurt? In the hospital?"

Sophie hesitated, her gaze dashing to their joined hands. "She's pregnant, and I need to take care of her." She kissed his fingertips, her lips lingering for a fraction of a second before she met his gaze. "Can we pick up where we left off when I return?"

"Of course. How long will you be gone?"

Sophie squeezed his fingers. "Only for the weekend. I'll be back for work Monday."

He waited for more, but she didn't offer it, and he knew he had no right to probe. They might be sleeping together, spending most of their evenings together, but he hadn't made any declarations of love or commitment, and neither had she.

Still, when she kissed him good-bye, he sensed she was lying to him. What secrets did Sophie have hidden in her past that she wouldn't share with him?

Were those secrets part of the reason she had to go to Vegas?

A few minutes later Lance crawled back onto the bar stool beside his brother. "I thought you might already have met up with some chick."

"I figured you were in bed with Sophie now."

Lance frowned. "Yeah, well, looks like we both struck out tonight. Sophie had an emergency."

Reid's hand froze on his glass. "Lucy?"

Lance grabbed a handful of peanuts and crushed them in his hand, almost laughing at his brother's worried expression. Did he really care for Lucy? "No, some girlfriend of theirs, said she was pregnant. Sophie had to go help take care of her."

"Sounds odd," Reid commented.

"Tell me about it," Lance said. "I can't figure Sophie out. One minute she's loving and all over me; the next she's secretive."

"Who can figure out women?" Reid asked. "I told you her sister was a complete ditz."

"Yeah, but Sophie's not ditzy; she just won't open up and talk about her past."

"Maybe there's nothing to tell."

"I think she's hiding something." Lance swallowed a sip of beer to wash down the peanuts and crushed another handful. "But she can't hide it forever, and sooner or later I'm going to find out what she's keeping from me."

Reid stood outside the airport in Vegas, grateful he'd caught a flight as soon as he'd left Lance. He was waiting on a cab, wondering why in the hell he had come and what he hoped to accomplish. Luckily Maddie had had Lucy's address in Vegas.

He hoped his suspicions proved wrong, that Lucy hadn't called Sophie to Vegas to get her away from his brother. He refused to let her mess up his brother's life.

His own was another story.

On the plane ride over, he'd fallen asleep and dreamed of Lucy's luscious lips creating havoc over his body and awoke, damn near humping the armrest of his seat. The airline attendant had glared at him as if he were a pervert, and the elderly lady sitting next to him with the bird-nest hairdo had screeched and jumped up, demanding to be moved. He'd gotten so riled, he'd knocked his beer over into his lap and soaked his jeans in an inopportune spot, so now he reeked of alcohol, which had earned him plenty of other odd looks.

The cabbie slowed and he hopped in, giving the address. Fifteen minutes later he was arguing with the landlord of the building while her teenage daughter looked on.

"She's not here," the woman said in a Midwestern accent, "and we don't want no drunken male hoochie-coochies bothering our tenants."

He glanced down at his disheveled shirt and jeans and wished he'd taken the time to change after his flight. Still, he turned on the charm. "I'm a friend of Lucy and her sister's from Savannah. I just got in and wondered where she was, that's all. Come on; I've come a long way."

The landlord's daughter fluttered acrylic nails through her orange-and-purple hair. "Lucy's at work."

"And that would be . . . ?"

"You must not be such a good friend if you don't know where she works," the mother said in a nasal tone.

"Actually, I'm more of a friend of her sister's. Lucy and I just met last week, but I got word there's some kind of emergency. I wanted to check on them while I'm in town."

"The Palace," the teen said. "I could ride over with you, if you want."

Reid gently declined, sensing that the teen was either looking for trouble or trying to escape her overbearing mother. As he took a cab to the hotel, he stared in awe at the glitzy lights and glamorous hotels. He'd never been to Vegas and realized he'd missed something. It was exactly as he'd pictured, the nightlife humming with excitement, the neon lights dazzling the clear, dark sky, the traffic and bustle of tourists and gamblers and showgoers charging the atmosphere.

Rita Herron

The Palace proved to be a huge establishment that offered extravagant nightly shows featuring something called the Diva act, with a restaurant that promised five-star dining, a casino, and a shopping mall built beneath. Something for everyone.

Glamorous showgirls and music filled the stage as he entered. "And now for our special feature, the Virginal Princess and the Virginal Vampiress." Reid's gaze shot to the stage, his interest sparked.

Although he'd missed nearly all of the show, the staff had allowed him to watch the last two acts. He was completely mesmerized by the various stages of undress. Some dancers were topless, while others wore skimpy sequin-studded outfits that hinted at nudity, and others wore thongs and feathers, boas and huge headdresses. Every costume, set, and prop was elaborate, creating a glitzy show that captivated the audience, men and women alike.

He remembered Lucy saying she was a hostess, but she hadn't seated him. Still, the place was so huge they had more than one, and she might not even be working tonight.

He ordered a beer from a waitress in a tight black bustier-type outfit and tipped her nicely. "Hey, sugar, do you happen to know a girl named Lucy Lane? She's strawberry blond, a hostess—"

"Hostess?" The waitress laughed. "No, hon, she's onstage. Don't you recognize her?"

"She's onstage?"

The waitress winked. "Uh-huh. Her sister used to work here, but she took off for some bigger job." The waitress slid the tip into her bustier. "Must run in the family; the mom was a stripper, too."

"Uh . . . really." Lucy and Sophie were strippers? His gaze shot to the stage, where a dozen beautiful women danced and paraded, all made-up and in costume. Shock filled him. Then memories rushed back—Lucy dancing at Sophie's. He slapped his forehead, feeling like an idiot. Why hadn't Lucy mentioned that she danced? And Sophie?

Was that the secret Sophie had been keeping from Lance?

To think he'd come here to try to keep them together, when Sophie was lying to his brother about everything.

He squinted, trying to pick her out. Two, no, three or four blondes at least were dancing in the first row; two were wearing masks; the other's face was practically covered in feathers. Which one was she? The one in all red? The silver-clad desperado figure? The one with the purple sequins? He decided she was dressed in black in the back row and forced himself not to watch her. Then a hot redhead in all white appeared, and he moved to the edge of his seat. The Virginal Princess. She was sexy enough to make him forget Lucy . . . at least for a while.

Anger started to mount inside that Lucy and Sophie had played him and his brother for fools, and he guzzled his beer, then ordered another. What should he do?

Confront Lucy? Call Lance?

And who was that knockout dressed all in white? He could have sworn she was watching him, too, maybe even playing up her act just for him. . . .

Lucy's body and feet ached, and she was dizzy from trying to double up and carry off two parts in the show, so dizzy in fact that she thought she must be having delusions when she first spotted Reid Summers in the audience.

But she danced closer to the front of the stage, gyrating her hips and swaying backward so her white feather boa fluttered enticingly toward the crowd. Kicking out her legs first, she swung around, strutted around the stage, then placed her back to the audience, bent forward, and touched the floor, peeking between her knees.

Oh, my God, it was Reid.

And he was contorted in his chair with a goofy grin on his face as if he were drunk, and as if it were the first time he'd seen a professional show. She added some extra sauce to her moves, wiggling her butt and dipping and leaning forward so her breasts jiggled and nearly popped out of the sequined top. He leaned forward, his tongue lolling out.

Did he recognize her?

Another maneuver across stage, and she pranced into the center arena for the grand finale, where male dancers lit a series of fiery handheld lanterns to surround her—their Virginal Princess. Of course, she was missing her partner, the Virginal Vampiress.

Every man's fantasy, a virgin princess and vampire. Sophie had been a genius to come up with the concept and the costumes.

Sophie . . . Oh, Lord, what would she do if she knew Reid was here? Somehow she had to get Reid alone and convince him to leave. Or maybe she should avoid him.

Fireworks suddenly exploded onstage, their glittery lights flashing a rainbow of colors around her, and smoke swirled into the air in a dramatic style. The last number finally drew to a close, and she watched Reid down another beer, his gaze feasting over all the dancers, then returning to her. Did he recognize her? Or was he lusting after someone he believed to be a stranger?

Only one way to find out.

Keeping her Diva mask, costume, and wig firmly

in place, she strutted toward him, first stopping to speak to Deseree. She told Deseree that Sophie would be coming in, so they could get together, perhaps before or after Saturday night's show.

Reid was still watching her, his smile raking over her as she approached. His eyes appeared slightly glazed over, his smile was lopsided, and from the wobble of his body as he stood to greet her, he'd been enjoying himself a little too much.

She shouldn't take advantage of the situation.

Then again, he had come here, perhaps to see her. To make up, maybe?

"Hey, sweetheart," he said in a slurry voice.

Lucy fluttered her white-gloved hand, playing the act for all it was worth. "Hi, handsome."

"Can I buy you a drink?"

Lucy nodded, the waitress appeared out of nowhere with her favorite, a Cosmopolitan, and she took his arm. "Did you come to Vegas looking for me?"

"Honey, of course I did. You're the woman of my dreams."

So he had come to see her! And he was being so romantic. "Are you stayin' here at the Palace?"

"Sure am. Wanna see my room?"

Lucy told herself she shouldn't, but his promise that the real thing was better than her Sleepover, Inc., products still haunted her, and she was in a forgiving mood, and he had come all the way to Vegas to be with her. No man had ever flown across the country for her.

What could one steamy night between the sheets hurt?

She'd screw his eyeballs out, then send him packing in the morning with some wild excuse, and he would never know that Sophie was here, or that Sophie had been involved in the Diva show. He certainly didn't seem to mind that Lucy had. In fact, he seemed completely turned on by her costume.

Five minutes later he was lying naked on satin sheets in a bedroom cast only in moonlight, and she was performing a strip-tease dance for him, one he'd requested.

As soon as her feathers hit the floor, she crawled on top of him and proceeded to have her way with him while he moaned and murmured that she was his fantasy come true. She had yet to remove her mask, though the thong had slowly been peeled from her body, and then came the heavy headdress and sequined top, her bare skin still glittery from the special costume makeup.

"You're all shiny, baby," Reid whispered as he took one pert nipple in his mouth and suckled her.

Lucy writhed and clawed at his arms, stroking his calf with her bare toes and kissing the sleek muscles of his chest. He tweaked her other breast with his fingers, pinching and rolling the nipple, and she moaned, folding her hand around his sex and stroking until he begged her to stop.

"No, let me touch you, baby." He flipped her to her stomach, slid his body on top of hers, and slowly tortured her with his hands and mouth. Lucy ground her hips into his erection, aching to have him inside her.

She had always liked sex, but she had never been so wanton with a man or wanted one as much as she wanted Reid. Cupping her hips in his hands, he lifted her to her hands and knees and slid his sex against her femininity, driving her wild with slow, grinding movements until she parted her legs farther and pleaded with him to take her.

Only then did he slide his length inside her and

take her to oblivion. His movements were passionate, strong, controlling, as if he held the power to satisfy her like no one else. She met him thrust for thrust, opening herself up to him as she never had before with another man. And when he drove himself deeper inside her, kneading her breasts at the same time his lips sucked her neck, she cried out his name so loudly she nearly shattered the chandelier above them.

Seconds later they collapsed onto the bed. She curled into his arms, spent and sated, then snuggled into his embrace and felt his breathing steady to a sleep rhythm. Blissfully happy, and so exhausted she couldn't keep her eyes open, she allowed sleep to claim her.

In the morning they would talk and everything would be fine. Maybe she and Reid would even fall in love and get married someday, too.

Sophie had worried about keeping their secret for nothing. . . .

Reid woke up with a pounding hangover headache, and his typical morning erection. But something was wrong with his arm. It was paralyzed, numb. He rolled over to see what had happened, and his pulse clamored. A glittery body lay next to him—the dancer from the night before.

Jesus, he'd spent an incredible night with the Diva woman, the Virginal Princess, no less, and she hadn't told him her real name. Lucy's face materialized in his mind, and he panicked momentarily, a tremor of guilt assaulting him.

Why did he feel guilty? He didn't owe Lucy anything. Nothing. *Nada*. She had lied to him and deceived him—just as Sophie had done to Lance.

Besides, who could have resisted this feminine

goddess, especially when she'd approached him? Had Lucy seen him leave with the center-stage act?

He tried to extricate his arm to shake the feeling back, but the moment he moved, the woman rolled over.

A scream lodged in his throat.

Lucy?

Lucy was the virginal goddess star of the show? Jesus Christ, he'd gone to bed with a masked Diva and woken up with Sophie's sister in bed beside him!

"What are you doing here?" He grunted.

Lucy opened her eyes, a sultry smile splitting her mouth. "Don't tell me you don't remember last night, Reid. It was pretty incredible." She traced sparkling silver fake nails over his torso and down to his sex, which had grown even more at the sight of her bare breasts swaying toward him.

"You . . . you're the Virginal Princess?"

Hesitation darkened her eyes; then realization dawned and anger robbed her smile. "You didn't know it was me?" She instantly grabbed the sheet and tugged it over her nakedness.

He suddenly realized the stupidity of his remark. "Well, uh . . . yeah, I just meant—"

"You liar!" Lucy grabbed the satin pillow and slammed it over his head, then leaped over the edge of the bed, jerking up feathers and her thong. Then, clearly thinking better of it, she rushed to the bathroom and came out wearing the white terry-cloth hotel robe. "You said you came here for me."

He pushed at the sheet to hide his hardened sex, which didn't seem to mind her temper, but instead had apparently enjoyed the view of her backside as she gathered her costume. She had the sexiest tush, all curvy and female. . . . "I . . . I did."

She narrowed venomous eyes at him. "You came here to see me?"

"Yes." God, she was so sexy he couldn't think.

"But you got turned on by the Virginal Princess and went to bed with her."

"Well, uh . . . she, I mean, *you* came on to me. For God's sakes, Lucy, you're the same woman."

"But you didn't know that!"

"But you did."

"I thought you knew it was me."

"You told me you were a hostess. I never expected you to be the star of the show."

Hurt and anger reddened her face. "Oh, so you didn't think I'd be talented enough to be the star?"

Why did women always twist a man's words? "That's not what I meant at all." Maybe he could turn the table on her. "Did you really think I knew it was you? Or were you trying to trap me into bed?"

Lucy slid her heels on, stomping around the room. "I do not have to trap or trick men to get them in bed with me."

"I'm sure you don't, not wearing that getup."

Uh-oh, totally wrong thing to say.

"What is that supposed to mean?" Lucy's nostrils flared. "You certainly didn't mind my getup last night."

"Of course not; I was drunk, and you looked damn sexy. What man wouldn't want to crawl all over you?"

"What are you implying by that comment? That I'd hop into bed with just anyone?"

"No." He remembered the way she'd danced to the crowd. "Would you?"

"You are an idiot, Reid Summers." Lucy's voice wobbled with emotion. Then a tear trickled down her cheek, totally sucker punching him. He hadn't meant to hurt her.

"Sophie was right; she said you wouldn't understand, that you and your brother would judge us. No wonder Maddie gave her those seven rules for trapping a man, and your brother is such a *male*, they're working!" Another pillow, this one from the chaise next to the window, sailed his way, hitting the painting above the bed and shaking it against the walls. Reid dodged, hoping the artwork didn't come down on his head. It probably cost a damn fortune.

"What rules for trapping a man?"

Lucy chewed the inside of her mouth. "Nothing, forget I said that, and don't change the subject. You're the jerk who came here and jumped in bed with a strange showgirl."

"The girl was you, Lucy!"

"But you didn't know that, so it doesn't matter."

He held up his hands to fend off another attack. The woman was insane! "Please calm down, Lucy. I was drunk and you were there, and somehow I must have known it was you under all that garb."

She planted dainty hands on her voluptuous hips. Unfortunately the robe slid open and those delicious breasts slipped into view again. "Somehow?"

"Somehow." He stood, wrapping the sheet around him, and stalked toward her. "And it was an incredible night." Although he wasn't sure how he felt about other men ogling her body while she strutted half-naked shaking feathers and sequins. And what would Lance think about Sophie's former life?

"Why didn't you tell me you danced for a living?"

"I promised Sophie I wouldn't mention it."

He raised an eyebrow. "Sophie used to dance, too?"

"How did . . . Who told you that?"

"One of the waitresses."

"Dag-nab it!" Lucy turned then and faced the window, staring out at the gray morning sky. "Is that the reason you came here, to cause trouble for Sophie?"

Reid rubbed a hand over his chin, feeling the bite mark Lucy had left there the night before. His sex throbbed relentlessly. "Hell, no, I came because I thought you'd called Sophie so you could break up Lance and Sophie. I figured you were up to your old hocus-pocus tricks."

Lucy turned to him, seething. "That's not the reason I called Sophie."

"So you haven't put a spell on them again?"

"No."

"What about me? Did you hex me with dreams about sleeping with you?"

Lucy's eyes widened to platter size. "You mean it worked?"

"You did; I knew it!" *The sneaky little witch.* She should have played the Virginal Vampiress instead of the Princess. She could cast a spell with her eyes and suck the blood from any man.

Lucy snatched the robe tighter around her. "Well, don't worry, Reid; now that you've lived out your fantasy with the Virginal Princess, I'm sure you've broken the spell." She grabbed the rest of her stuff from the floor and clip-clopped out the door, her head held high, her feathers and headdress and boa draped over one arm.

He wasn't so sure about the spell being broken. Even mad as he was, his body still wanted her. Lucy. The Virginal Princess. Whatever persona she chose to be.

Confusion pulled at him as he sank back onto the

bed. What was he going to do about Lance? He didn't want to hurt his brother.

But Lance had a right to know the truth before he got any more involved with Sophie. Wouldn't it be better if he found out now, before he did something dumb like propose to her?

Chapter Twenty

Lance's insomnia had returned. He had lain awake all night thinking about Sophie, worrying about the crisis she had in her life, and why she hadn't felt as if she could share it with him. He would have been there to support her, to take care of her.

Maybe he should call Maddie. . . .

No, he shouldn't pry. He had to be patient. Sooner or later Sophie would trust him enough to confide her secrets. Hell, they were probably nothing. He was probably imagining things because he'd let her mess with his head, and she'd been gone only one night, and he already missed her like hell.

If this was what love did to a man, he wished he'd never found it.

Love . . . Did he love Sophie?

Yes, he couldn't deny it any longer. In fact, he'd probably loved her for a long time, but he'd been too foolish and stubborn and scared to admit it. And it did scare him. . . .

What would he do if she decided to take that job

in L.A. and move away? He wasn't certain he could stand to live without her, but he couldn't ask Reid and Chase to uproot the company, especially with this multimillion-dollar deal in the works.

Good God, what was he going to do?

Rubbing his hand across his bleary eyes, he staggered toward the bathroom to shower, but he stumbled over a pair of sneakers. He kicked them aside, remembering how neat Sophie's house was, and how homey. His apartment was a mess, nothing remotely homey about it. The phone trilled, and he reached for it, hoping it was Sophie.

"Lance, it's Reid."

"Yeah, what's up?"

"I . . . uh, flew to Vegas last night."

"Vegas? What in the hell are you doing there?" Then the truth dawned on him. "You went to see Lucy?"

"Yeah, but I found a lot more."

His brother sounded upset. Nervous. "What do you mean?"

"I don't know how to say this, but . . ." Reid paused. "But I thought Lucy was trying to keep you and Sophie apart, so I wanted to talk to her."

"That's crazy." He sat down on the side of the bed, confused. "Why would Lucy try to keep us apart?"

"I don't know." Reid coughed. "But when I got here, I found out some interesting things about the Lane sisters."

Lance's heartbeat went into double time. "What kind of things?"

"Listen, man," Reid said in a worried voice, "I don't want to do this over the phone. You really need to come to Vegas."

"You're kidding, right?"

"No. You suspected Sophie was hiding something from you?"

"Well, yeah." He dropped his head forward, rubbing a hand over his beard stubble.

"You were right."

His imagination leaped onto a roller-coaster ride. Was she married? Did she have a separate life in Vegas? Was she some kind of fugitive?

"Just catch the next plane out, and I'll fill you in when you get here."

Lance hesitated. A few minutes earlier he'd told himself to be patient and wait for Sophie to confide in him. But he couldn't go through the day and the entire weekend wondering what had upset his brother so badly. Was Sophie's secret really that big?

"Lance, are you coming? I'm staying at the Palace."

Dread filled his chest. "Yeah, I'll see you in Vegas."

Sophie had caught the last plane out to Vegas the night before, and was so exhausted when she'd arrived at Lucy's that she'd crawled into Lance's shirt—she'd had to bring it with her to remind her of his scent—and fallen asleep. She'd expected Lucy to get home in the middle of the night after the show, and was shocked when she woke up and found the apartment empty. By the time she'd unearthed a diet Coke from Lucy's snake pit of a refrigerator, Lucy had sneaked in. Her sister's eyes flared in surprise; then she pivoted to make coffee.

"Soph, when did you get in?"

"Late last night."

"Sorry I wasn't here. I didn't expect you to come until this morning."

"I figured I'd need some time to go over the

dance; it's been a while since I've done the steps."

Lucy nodded, although she didn't quite make eye contact, arousing Sophie's suspicions. Lucy poured her coffee, twirling a strand of hair around her finger—another one of her sister's nervous habits.

"Where were you?" Sophie asked, wincing when she realized her question sounded a tad too motherly and judgmental.

The cup clattered as Lucy emptied a sweetener packet in it and stirred. "I . . . was worried about Sassafras, so I stopped by to see her. We started talking, and I decided to stay over." She finally looked up and Sophie noticed the remnants of tears. "Sassafras is concerned about the baby, and how's she going to make it and—"

"Lucy, why have you been crying?"

"It's just that time of the month, and Sassafras was crying, and you know how tenderhearted I can get. I cry over Kodak commercials. Have you seen that one with the grandma—"

"Lucy," Sophie interrupted her, "forget the commercial. Did you have a run-in with Garrett or Deseree, or is some old boyfriend bothering you?"

"No." Lucy's head bobbed as she shook it, but her eyes teared again. "Don't worry so much, Soph; everything's fine, just fine."

Sure it was. Then why did her sister look as if her best friend had just died? Other suspicions took hold. "Lucy, you did make Garrison promise to keep my identity quiet, didn't you?"

"Of course." She grabbed a bagel and started toward the door. "I'm going to hop in the shower; then we'll head to the club and practice."

Sophie nodded. "Sure. I'll shower after you. I have a feeling I'll need some extra stretching, or I'll be so sore tomorrow I won't be able to move."

Lucy disappeared into her bedroom, and Sophie snatched a bagel for herself, uneasiness stealing through her. For some reason Lucy had been lying to her. But why?

They had never kept things from each other in the past. . . .

When the shower water kicked on, Lucy let the flood of tears fall. She hated lying to Sophie, although technically she wasn't lying; she'd simply omitted a few truths. But Sophie would find out soon enough, unless Lucy thought of some way around it. Still, there was no need to admit up front that she'd made a complete fool of herself over Reid, or that he was here and he knew about the act . . . except that he would probably tell Lance, and then Lance would be upset with Sophie, and Sophie would hate her.

How had everything gotten so mixed up?

Her nose clogged, so she inhaled through her mouth, heaving with the mountain of tears welling in her chest and spilling over. She'd meant only to help Sophie by using those spells and charms—to save her from making a mistake by falling for Lance when he was so serious. But her spells had backfired, and now Lance and Sophie were all over each other. And she was alone, exactly as she'd been afraid she'd be. Worse, when Lance found out about Sophie they might break up. Then Sophie would be alone and miserable, and Lucy would be alone and miserable, and Sophie would never forgive her.

Unless she'd been wrong about Lance, and he really loved Sophie.

Then again, if he was anything like Reid, with all his judgmental macho-ism, he would hate the fact that Sophie had once been the Virginal Vampiress. He'd go off on her just as Reid had Lucy and think she had been a loose woman just because she danced, when dancing brought in good money. Heck, they had been two teenagers on their own, desperate and broke. And damn it, they hadn't been hookers or given lap dances. They hadn't even gone topless—and they could have upped their salary tremendously if they had. Any way around it, Lance would break Sophie's heart, and it was all Lucy's fault because she had fallen for that creep Reid Summers. She hadn't been able to resist when he'd said he'd come to Vegas to see her, and that she was his fantasy woman. And mercy, she had wanted to see if he really was better than her Sleepover, Inc., products, and dag-nab it, he was. But now she knew he'd meant The Virginal Princess was his fantasy woman, and although she hadn't been loose, she also wasn't exactly virginal herself.

Good gracious, she'd grown up in Vegas—how could she be totally innocent? And what man in the twenty-first century actually expected a woman to be a virgin?

A cretinous, backward Savannah boy, that was who. Not the man for Lucy Lane!

She and Sophie would both be better off without those insufferable Summers men.

Grabbing a towel, she dried off, wrapped it around her head with renewed resolve, and pulled on her robe. Her reflection caught her eye, and she grimaced. It would take a pound of makeup to cover up those dark circles and puffy red eyes. She hurried toward the refrigerator to find some cold cucumbers to press on her eyelids to stem the swelling. And then she'd find a couple of lucky charms for her and Sophie to wear tonight. They were going to need them.

After all, the show had to go on.

Now if she could just keep Sophie away from Reid for the next twenty-four hours; then she'd explain to Sophie what had happened, and how everything was going to be all right.

Really it was.

That was, unless she didn't have any cucumbers, and Reid showed up at the apartment before the show, or he called Lance. . . .

By the time Lance reached Vegas and the Palace, his stomach felt as though a fist had clutched it.

He regretted the trip. Then again, he regretted not asking Reid to spill this big secret over the phone, regretted not calling Maddie, regretted not trusting Sophie, regretted trusting her, regretted falling in love and having this sick feeling in his chest now, regretted that no matter what he did, he had a bad feeling tonight was going to get worse. Because Sophie would hate him for coming and not trusting her . . .

Blast it all to hell and back—he was an effing mess.

"Here you are, sir."

Lance paid the taxicab driver, jumped out, grabbed his overnight bag, and dashed up the steps. He'd been too discombobulated on the way from the airport to appreciate the magnificence of the city's architecture, but this hotel was stunning in its size and opulence. He read the glittery marquis: THE PALACE PROUDLY PRESENTS THE INFAMOUS DIVA ACT: THE VIRGINAL PRINCESS AND THE VIRGINAL VAMPIRESS.

Hmm, if he weren't so nervous over this meeting with his brother, he might like to catch a show. After all, he'd never been to Vegas.

Where were Sophie and Lucy? At the hospital with their friend? At her house?

Or had Sophie lied about that?

He walked through the revolving door, taking in the decorative ceilings, elaborate décor, and bustle of guests, but he was too anxious to note the details. He quickly checked his bag with the bellhop and told him to send it to Reid's room, then studied the floor plan, amazed at the size and variety of services offered in the hotel, as well as the different dining areas, workout room, bars, and photographs of the showroom.

Reid had insisted they meet at the bar—a drink to cushion the blow—so he stalked toward it. His brother sat on a stool staring into a half-full bottle of imported beer, looking miserable. The fist in Lance's stomach tightened.

Taking the stool beside him, he patted his brother's back. "You look like the world just came to an end."

Reid gave him the most pitiful hangdog expression Lance had ever witnessed.

"I'm sorry, man."

"What do you have to be sorry about?"

"For coming here." Reid dropped his head forward, picked up his beer, and took a sip.

"You wanna tell me what happened?"

"Not really."

"Then what am I doing here, Reid?"

Reid dropped a few bills on the counter and motioned for Lance to follow. "There's something you gotta see. Then we'll talk."

Lance frowned, but he followed him, surprised when his brother led him to the dinner/dance showroom. Reid had reserved a table near the front in the right-hand corner. Guests filled the room, the lights dimmed, and the music began for the first show.

"You wanted me to come out here to see a burlesque show?"

"It's not exactly burlesque."

"I don't get it."

His brother dropped into the chair, and Lance took the one opposite, annoyance mounting at his brother's cloak-and-dagger routine. "You're acting strange; why don't you just tell me what this is about?"

A waitress appeared wearing a skimpy little bustier and took their drink orders.

"Reid?"

"Shh," two older ladies next to them said. "The show's starting."

The main houselights went down, and suddenly dancers in various stages of dress or undress appeared. The sea of multicolored costumes complete with huge feathered-and-beaded headpieces, feathered wings, boas, thongs, and sparkly and sequined adornments made Lance's head swirl.

"Just watch; you have to see the Virginal Princess and the Vampiress."

Lance accepted the beer from the waitress and focused on the show. The music, singing, and dancing were unlike anything he'd ever seen, the dazzling costumed girls spinning and shaking and gyrating. Then a white carriage appeared, and out stepped a gorgeous redhead in a long white costume that sparkled with at least a thousand jewels.

On the opposite side a black carriage appeared, and out poured another seductress wearing blood red, except for the long blond curls.

Between them a man dressed in black leather with chains and whips appeared and summoned the Virginal Princess. The rest of the act was a song and dance between the three characters.

Lance was in shock.

The man was played by Sophie's old friend Peter, and if he was correct, Lucy was the Virginal Princess. "It can't be," Lance muttered.

"You recognize the Vampiress?" Reid asked in a thick voice. His brother's face had turned a ghostly white.

Lance frowned and squinted, trying to discern the face behind the heavy makeup, wig, feathers, and mask. It wasn't until the Vampiress bent to suck the blood from Peter that her head pivoted up slightly and recognition dawned. Those green eyes. "Oh, my God. Sophie's a vampire."

"I know," Reid said in a dark voice. "She and Lucy are the famous Diva act."

Amazement. Shock. Jealousy. Hurt. Anger. Betrayal. The myriad of emotions bombarded Lance at once, nearly suffocating him.

He barely found his voice. When he spoke, his voice sounded as if it were coming from far away, from someone else. "You . . . knew when you came here?"

"No," Reid said in a solemn voice. "I . . . Lucy and I had a run-in at home. I found this stupid spell book. She does these charms and spells, and she put one on you to try to break up you and Sophie."

"She did what?" Lance tried to drag himself from the sight of Sophie sucking at Peter's neck, that feathery costume billowing around her nearly naked body. The other men in the audience were just as mesmerized.

"I told you, she's a kook; she cast a dumb spell. When you said Lucy called Sophie to come here, I figured she had some scheme planned again, so I flew here to try to stop her." He swiped a drop of sweat from his forehead. "I never imagined this, but,

302

well . . ." He waved his hand around the room, gesturing at the festive atmosphere. "A waitress told me Sophie used to work here, too. Then today I saw her sneak in here to practice with Lucy." Reid turned to him. "I'm really sorry, man. I didn't know what to do, but I figured you had a right to know."

"Yeah." Lance nodded, still dumbfounded and glued to Sophie's behind twitching and swaying in that red lace. His heart was breaking into pieces.

"But Sophie should have told me."

Sophie stood, clasping Peter's hand to bow to the audience, with Lucy on his opposite side, her gaze scanning the audience. They were clapping wildly, reminding her of her past life. Then a man in the corner lurched to his feet and her breath froze.

Lance?

Peter whispered for her to take a bow, but she was paralyzed. The rest of the audience jumped to their feet, adding to the enthusiasm, but she couldn't drag her eyes from Lance and the awful expression on his face. He looked wounded, completely and utterly shocked.

She had to talk to him, make him understand.

She turned and ran, leaving Peter in the center waving to the crowd. The audience began to cheer, chanting for an encore by the Vampiress, but tears blurred her eyes and she was trembling all over, stumbling through the crowd of dancers backstage to reach the side door to the front. Dizzy with fear, she pushed past the audience, fending off people greeting her, wanting to shake her hand, men trying to paw her. She saw Lance standing ramrod straight, but when a middle-aged man grabbed her and pulled her toward him, Lance catapulted forward. Sophie recognized the man as the talent scout who'd come to Savannah, and her legs buckled. Her entire world was spiraling out of control. . . .

Lance shoved the man away, took her by the arm, and dragged her toward the back of the crowded room. The bouncer stepped forward, and Deseree, of all people, suddenly appeared, looking concerned.

"Honey, are you all right?" she asked.

Peter appeared with Lucy in tow, and then Reid dashed over, forming a circle around her.

Sophie was crying now, trying to catch her breath, wishing she'd grabbed a robe to hide herself from Lance's condemning eyes. "I . . . Lance, please let me explain."

"Why didn't you tell me?" His voice was hoarse with emotion.

She'd made a terrible mistake in keeping her past a secret. She couldn't escape it.

Secrets always came back to haunt you.

"What's wrong, Sophie?" Deseree asked. "Do you need us to throw this man out?"

"No, Deseree," Sophie whispered.

"It's okay, Mom," Lucy said. "He's Sophie's friend."

"Deseree is your mother?" Lance asked.

Another lie—she read the accusation in his eyes.

She heaved a shaky breath. "I'm sorry, Lance, but this was my past. I didn't think it mattered."

"Past?" He intentionally glanced at the French-cut costume and her bare belly, then to the low-cut top that amplified her cleavage. "You mean your second life?"

"No, it's not like that," Sophie said in a squeak. "I'm filling in for a sick friend—remember I told you one of Lucy's friends was pregnant and she couldn't perform—"

Lance's expression went cold. "You can stop with the lies."

"It's true."

"You have to believe her," Lucy said. "I begged Sophie to fill in, but she didn't want you to know."

"I can see why," Lance said in a biting voice.

"How did you find out I was here?" Sophie asked.

"From me," Reid piped up. "I came here to see Lucy."

Sophie turned to Lucy, hurt and bewildered. "You knew he was here, Lucy, and you didn't tell me?"

"I didn't realize he'd called Lance," Lucy said. "I thought I could fix things."

"Like you tried to fix it so they wouldn't be together?" Reid said.

Lucy glared at him. "Stay out of this, Reid."

"What is he talking about?" Sophie asked.

"She cast one of her charm spells on you and Lance because she didn't want you to be together."

"Lucy, is that true?" Sophie read the answer in her sister's eyes. "But why?"

"I didn't think he was fun enough for you."

"They're both liars," Reid said. "Tell him about the seven rules to trap a man." He shot an angry look at Sophie. "Lucy told me all about how you were playing this game to trap him."

Sophie gasped and turned to Lucy again. "Why would you tell him that?"

Lance's hands knotted by his side. "Really?"

"No," Sophie said, pleading now and reaching for him. He jerked away from her touch as if it pained him to be near her. "Those rules were a joke; Maddie was teasing about them—"

"So my little sister was helping set me up? 'Let Lance play the fool'."

"It wasn't like that at all," Sophie cried.

"Yeah and you've never been a call girl either, huh?" Reid said.

Sophie started to defend herself, but saw the crushed expression on Deseree's face and remained silent.

Deseree spoke up instead, her tone all fiery and motherly. "No, she hasn't, young man. And you'd better not insult her again or you'll deal with me."

Reid looked properly chastised, but Deseree clutched Peter's hand. "I think we'd better go."

Sophie's heart splintered in two. In spite of Deseree's past, Sophie loved her.

She turned to Lance, pleading for forgiveness. "I'm sorry I didn't tell you about my dancing. But I was afraid it would make a difference." Her heart sank at his closed expression. "And judging from your reaction, I was right."

He hesitated, that wounded look returning, mixed with anger. "You should have given me the chance."

Her old insecurities rushed back. Children chanting ugly words about her and her mother. The times she'd been too embarrassed to ask a friend to visit. Her dreams of starting over in a new place where no one knew. . . . "Why, so you could break my heart?"

"You don't get it, do you, Sophie?" Lance's voice dropped to a thready whisper. "The secret dancing life aside, the thing that hurts most is that you didn't trust me enough to confide in me."

She couldn't lose him, not now. "But I love you, Lance. I've loved you for a long time."

He shook his head. "No, if you'd loved me, you would have trusted me and told me. You wouldn't have let me find out like this."

He stared at her for a strained heartbeat, then whispered good-bye and walked into the crowd, disappearing from her life.

Chapter Twenty-one

A cold numbness settled over Sophie as she and Lucy drove back to Lucy's apartment.

"I'm so sorry," Lucy said in a low voice. "I never should have begged you to come here."

"It's not your fault," Sophie said. "Lance was right. I should have told him."

"But look how he acted when he found out." Lucy slapped the steering wheel with her hand. "He and his brother are both sexist pigs."

Sophie laughed sardonically. "You really like Reid, don't you?"

Lucy's stunned gaze swung to Sophie. "Like? He's the most despicable, infuriating, judgmental man I've ever known. I say good riddance."

Sophie propped her head on her hand and studied her sister. "I still haven't figured out why you cast a spell to try to keep me and Lance apart. You knew he wouldn't understand, didn't you?"

Lucy bit down on her lip. "I . . . I didn't think he would."

Sophie nodded, and Lucy guided the VW into her spot at the apartment complex. Weary and numb from pain, Sophie hauled herself up the steps, then went straight to the extra bedroom. Lance's shirt lay on top of the faded pink-flamingo bedspread, where she'd lovingly placed it this morning.

She picked it up, pressed it to her face, and sniffed his aftershave, savoring his scent. Tomorrow, when she got home, she'd wash and iron the shirt and send it back to him.

If they were going to make a break, she needed it to be a clean one.

But one last time, she undressed and slipped her arms into the soft worn fabric, then crawled into bed and tried to remember what it felt like to have Lance hold her and make love to her.

Even if the shirt had to be returned to the owner, her memories would be hers to keep forever.

Maddie had barely snuggled back into Chase's arms after making love when the phone rang. Knowing her brothers were out of town always made her nervous, so she grabbed the phone, laughing when Chase tried to pull her back down under the covers. She batted his hands away.

"Hello?"

"Maddie, it's Reid."

She shoved her mop of hair from her eyes and sat up. His voice sounded strained. "What's wrong?"

"Everything," Reid said. "Lance is a mess."

Chase dropped a kiss on Maddie's hand, and she mouthed that something was wrong with her brother. Instantly alert, Chase roused and propped up the pillows for her to lean back, then took her free hand in his and held it, as if to offer support for bad news.

"Tell me what happened; was there an accident?"

"No," Reid said, "nothing like that, but I flew to Vegas because I thought Lucy was trying to break up Sophie and Lance, and then I saw Lucy dancing in this Vegas show. Did you know she and Sophie were the stars of a famous act called the Divas?"

Maddie winced. "Well, er . . ."

"Lucy was this Virginal Princess and Sophie's a freakin' vampire; you should have seen them—my God, I would never have imagined it."

Maddie's stomach started churning like a washing machine. "And you called Lance out there to see for himself?"

"Maybe I shouldn't have, but I thought he had a right to know."

Maddie pulled the phone away from her ear and stared at it. Her brother was an idiot. "I gather Lance didn't take it very well?"

"That's putting it mildly. He and Sophie had a big blowup, and it turns out she was lying about other things too, like her mother. Did you know her mother used to be a stripper?"

Her stomach dipped and swayed to the mattress. "Well, er . . ."

"Anyway, we're coming back on the first flight, and I thought you might have an idea as to how to help Lance."

Maddie squeezed Chase's hand so hard he yelped. *Sorry*, she mouthed, then returned to the phone. "I'll definitely talk to him."

"And when you do, you might want to explain about those rules you and Sophie cooked up for trapping a man."

Fudgecake! "Er, I gotta go." Maddie slammed down the phone and rushed to the bathroom, her stomach pitching.

Chase knocked at the door. "Come in and take your life into your own hands," Maddie yelled.

He came in anyway. "Awww, baby."

His sympathetic tone brought tears to her eyes. She hated being this emotional. And her stomach protested again, ready to toss those measly saltines she'd nibbled on earlier.

"Please leave, Chase," Maddie said, waving him away. "I'm fine."

"You don't look fine, baby." He grabbed a washcloth, wet it with cold water, and pressed it to her neck. The pregnancy test she'd taken earlier sat on the counter.

"Maddie?"

She wiped her mouth and stood on shaky legs. "Huh?"

His voice was gruff. "It's positive."

Maddie brightened and gazed into her husband's eyes, then pressed her palm to his cheek. "So it is, handsome."

The overwhelming look of love in Chase's eyes made her throat close. "And I hope it's a little boy. I want him to grow up and be just like his father."

"I . . . God, I love you, Mad." Tears filled Chase's eyes as he picked her up and swung her around, laughing. "I can't wait to tell everyone."

Maddie's stomach sloshed again. "Uh, honey, if you don't set me down and stop spinning, it's not going to be pretty."

Chase halted and gently let her slip to the floor, then placed a tender hand over her stomach. "I'm sorry, sweetheart, but I'm so excited, I want the whole world to know."

Maddie held up a finger. "Me, too, Chase, but I think we should keep it a secret awhile. I don't feel right bragging about such wonderful news when the boys are in such pitiful condition." She explained about what had happened with Sophie and Lance.

"You mean she kept all that from him?" Chase asked as he led her back to bed.

Maddie glared at him. "I'm sure she planned to tell him sometime. It's not like he didn't have some wild days."

"Yeah, but—"

"Don't you dare say it's different for women than men."

He plumped her pillows, laid a blanket over her feet, tucked her hair behind her ear. "But she was a Vegas showgirl, and she lied about her own mother."

Maddie gave him a warning look but accepted his doting. "Don't go all Mars male on me, okay? If he loves her, he should understand."

Chase opened his mouth to argue, but Maddie swooned, feigning a dizzy spell to shut him up. She felt only marginally guilty at the pure panic on his face.

She loved her husband dearly, but she had to think of a plan to reunite Sophie and Lance.

Now her hormones had kicked in, she just couldn't scheme and argue at the same time.

Reid had never seen his brother so brooding before. They should have kept that damned bachelor pact intact.

He had no hopes about seeing Lucy again. Although while he'd lain awake, he had images of her on top of him again. Lucy as Lucy. Lucy as the Diva Virginal Princess.

A man's fantasy come true.

But Lucy hated him for bringing his brother there. Although he was surprised she hadn't thanked him.

After all, she had gotten what she wanted—Sophie and Lance were not even speaking, much less together.

The airline registration attendant gave him and Lance a suspicious once-over. They both looked rough. Lance hadn't slept the night before either, and this morning neither one had shaved or showered.

"Listen, you have to get us on this flight," Lance pleaded. "I don't care if it costs extra; I can't stay in town another minute."

The woman glanced up. "Is there an emergency? Death?"

Lance drummed his hand on the counter. "Not exactly. But please see what you can do."

"I can put you on standby, but I can't assure you that you'll both make the flight."

"Fine," Lance said.

Reid nodded. "No problem. If one of us gets on, take it, Lance. I'll catch the next one."

They turned to take a seat when Reid spotted Lucy and Sophie rushing toward the desk. "Uh-oh."

"Blast it all to hell," Lance muttered. "I can't believe this."

Lucy gave him a scalding look, then jutted her chin and hugged Sophie to her, steering a wide berth past them. Lance cut his eyes away from Sophie, but Reid saw the pain on his brother's face and wanted to choke somebody.

The Virginal Princess and the Virginal Vampiress—how appropriate. He wondered who had thought of the names.

"Dag-nab it," Lucy muttered. "What the heck are they doing here?"

"Probably the same thing we are," Sophie said in a desolate voice.

Lucy squeezed her sister's hand, worried sick. Sophie looked so pale, and she'd been so quiet, almost emotionless, that she was downright scared her sister had sunk into a trance. She'd have to consult her spell book and see if she could find something to revive Sophie's spirits. Really, she'd feel better if she would scream and yell at her, or cry and throw something, anything but this mind-numbing, pitiful silence.

"Well, if they're on the flight, we'll take the next one." She coached Sophie to the counter. "We have a reservation. I called this morning. Lucy and Sophie Lane."

"I told you not to come back with me," Sophie whispered while the woman checked their IDs.

"You shouldn't be alone right now, Soph."

"But what about the show?"

Lucy laughed. "The understudy is going to take over this week, and Sassafras will be fine by Wednesday. Garrison already had a special guest lined up, too, so he'll be fine."

The attendant handed them back their IDs. "You have the last two seats, ladies. Have a nice flight."

Lucy leaned over the counter, pointed to Reid and Lance, and whispered, "Are they on the flight?"

The woman quirked her head sideways. "Standby."

"Good."

"Is there a problem with those men?" the woman asked.

"Actually, I heard them outside talking. They sounded suspicious to me," Lucy answered in a low voice.

Sophie poked her, but she continued. "I think you

should have security check them out. They look dangerous, don't you think?"

The woman slid her glasses down her nose and peered over Lucy's shoulder. "Actually, I thought the same thing myself. Maybe I will call."

"Lucy, you are fiendish," Sophie said in a hiss.

"They deserve it." After all, she'd been harassed just because she'd had her Sleepover, Inc., kit with her. The boys should suffer simply for being men.

The woman punched a call button behind the counter and a security guard appeared. Lucy turned and grinned as the guard approached Reid and Lance and escorted them away.

Sophie desperately needed a diet Coke. A migraine had threatened all morning and she was starting to see spots, but had a flashback of the six-pack Lance had given her with the silly balloon dates, and ordered a real Coke instead. She might never be able to drink diet soda again.

While they waited for the flight to board, she and Lucy avoided Reid and Lance. When the boys had returned from security, they'd both looked furious. Reid had started toward Lucy with a threatening gleam in his eyes, but Lance had restrained him, earning another suspicious glare from the security guards.

She supposed she couldn't blame them for being angry, but told herself not to apologize.

Eventually they'd all wound up at the coffee shop, then the rest rooms, and now back in the waiting area. There were two empty seats beside her and Lucy, but Reid and Lance had opted to stand on the far side to avoid being near them.

Let them sit on the floor, for all she cared.

"Ladies and gentlemen, we'll begin boarding now," one of the airline attendants announced.

"We'll start with all first-class passengers and those who need assistance."

Sophie stared at their ticket and willed the process to move quickly.

Several minutes later she and Lucy had boarded and were settling in when a man and a rail-thin woman across the aisle jumped up. "You have to let us off; we have an emergency."

The chubby man waved his cell phone. "Miss, miss, my son called. They're having their baby and we have to get off the plane!"

The attendant rushed forward and cleared the aisle; the chubby man pushed forward, his wife shrieking, "I'm going to be a grandmother; the baby's two weeks early, but it's coming. Let us through!"

"We have to be there," the man yelled. "I told Geraldina not to push!"

Sophie laughed, but her laughter ended abruptly when Lance and Reid appeared, weaving down the aisle. She glanced at the two now-empty seats across from them and realized the Summers boys were going to nab them.

For the next five minutes she and Lucy combed the aisles, begging someone to change seats, but a teenage sports team who wanted to sit together filled the plane, and the airline attendant gave them the evil eye, her final warning to sit down.

Sophie slumped back into her aisle seat next to Lucy, who took the window, because Sophie got dizzy when she flew and couldn't look outside when the plane was moving. Across from her Lance sat like a pillar of stone, his big hands folded in his lap, his face turned the opposite direction.

She did the same, although she closed her eyes so she wouldn't get motion sickness, and hugged her pride. Pride was, after all, the only thing she had left.

Not only did Lance hate her, but she'd upset her mother as well. Maybe she should take that job and leave Savannah forever. . . .

Three days later Sophie had wallowed in misery until she was tired of hearing her own voice whine. Their special Mother's Day programming was extended for the following week—seeing all the families reunited only reminded her of her own divided one. She'd phoned Deseree a dozen times, but she hadn't answered or returned Sophie's calls. She probably didn't want to talk to her daughter who had treated her own mother so poorly.

Next week would be even more difficult. They were starting the series on weddings, with a featured couple who would marry on the show. Sophie had fantasized about having her own wedding with Lance, but that was merely a fantasy.

She still hadn't returned his shirt.

He had sent a crew to finish the renovations, though, a definite statement that he was finished with her.

And now she had to endure a birthday celebration: the big three-oh.

As soon as she entered the café, Maddie enveloped her in a hug. "Happy birthday, Soph."

"I don't feel much like celebrating," Sophie admitted.

"I know, sweetie, but we're going to anyway." Maddie dragged her toward a back table, where she had ordered a pitcher of Cosmopolitans. Sophie plopped down, anxious to have the evening over.

Maddie sipped a glass of water. "You look terrible. We have to do something about it."

316

"There's nothing to do," Sophie said, "but forget Lance."

"Ahh, you're not giving up, are you?" Maddie asked.

"Don't tell me you have a plan?" Sophie said. "Lance is still seething over the seven-rules-to-trap-a-man thing."

Maddie dipped a chip in the spinach-avocado dip, and Sophie poured herself a Cosmopolitan, then started to pour Maddie one, but Maddie shook her head. "I'm holding off tonight."

"Really, what's up?"

"Little stomach bug," Maddie said, although she didn't quite meet her friend's eyes.

"Has it been going on long?"

Maddie shrugged, her cheeks turning pink. "I'm fine, really; it's nothing."

But Sophie knew her friend too well, and she also knew Maddie and Chase had talked about having a baby. She put two and two together. "You're pregnant, aren't you?" Maddie nearly spilled her soda on her blouse. "Uh, whatever makes you think that?"

"You are," Sophie accused. "I can see that little light in your eyes. That's great, Maddie!"

Maddie giggled and leaned closer to her. "I know, I'm so excited. I want you to be the godmother, too."

"Oh, I'd be thrilled," Sophie squealed. "Does Chase know yet?"

"Yes, and he's so excited," Maddie whispered. "He wanted to tell everyone, but I'm making him keep it a secret. I don't want Lance and Reid to know just yet, not with . . ." Maddie lowered her voice, "with everything that's going on."

Sophie squeezed Maddie's hand. "Don't worry, Maddie, I won't tell Lance about the pregnancy. But

I can't wait to hold the baby! I can just see the little one now!"

Lucy couldn't believe her ears. She'd walked in on the tail end of the conversation, but she'd heard Sophie say she wasn't going to tell Lance about the pregnancy, then that she couldn't wait to hold the baby.

Dear God, was Sophie pregnant?

She wouldn't tell Lance. She couldn't wait to hold the baby. What else could she mean?

Now that she thought about it, Sophie had been sick all week, emotional, not eating, even sloughing off her usual intake of diet Coke—no wonder the break with Lance had upset her so badly.

Momentary disappointment trickled through her that Sophie hadn't told her first instead of Maddie, which meant that somewhere deep down Sophie still blamed her for the breakup with Lance. She was also aware that now Sophie was not only alone, but pregnant and alone, and that it was all Lucy's fault for being selfish.

But there was a baby to think about now. A tiny innocent life that had been created in love. And this tiny little life would be her niece or nephew. A niece or nephew she could not let be brought into the world without its father.

Not the way she and Sophie had.

She could barely contain herself from congratulating Sophie, and bragging that she couldn't wait to be an aunt. But both Maddie and Sophie clamed up tighter than a virgin in a male strip club when she approached, shutting her out. After she wolfed down most of the Cosmopolitan pitcher—not surprised when Sophie pushed her own away—she gave her sister the gift of the number sixty-nine item from her catalog.

"To help you get Lance," she told her. A few minutes later, she hopped a cab. She had made a mess of things before, and it was up to her to fix them now.

After the taxi dropped her off she stood, slightly woozy and light-headed, on Reid's doorstep banging on his door for all she was worth. She could have sworn he'd peeked out the window and seen her, then ducked inside and had refused to answer.

Damn, insufferable, infuriating, rat-fink man. Why God had created that Y chromosome was beyond her.

She banged again, and yelled, cursing him to the moon, then finally took her credit card from her purse and picked the lock. The door screeched open, and she clunked inside, scanning the dim interior as she yelled his name. The apartment reeked of stale pizza and beer. She was thankful she didn't see any woman's lingerie scattered inside.

Reid was slumped on a ratty-looking sofa, surfing the channels. "Where'd a Virginal Princess learn to pick locks?"

"Vegas, where else?"

He flicked her a quick glance, then returned to the TV. Some boring ball game blared from the set. He turned up the sound. "Well, pick your way back out and go on back there."

"Not until you listen to me."

He grunted and started to stand, but she tottered over to him, nearly falling over a pair of smelly tennis shoes. With a sigh, she snatched the remote.

"Hey, what the hell are you doing?"

Her bracelets jangled as she waved her arms

around. "We have a major crisis. We can't sit back and do nothing."

Reid sat up and rested his elbows on his knees. "What crisis? Did you lose your spell book?"

"This is not about me. Well, not directly. Actually, it affects both of us, and Lance and Sophie." Lucy rubbed at her head and paced. "No, it's bigger than all of us."

Reid folded his arms. "Lucy, did anyone ever tell you that you talk in circles?"

"Only an idiot wouldn't be able to understand me." She slapped her forehead. "Oh, wait, you're a man; you don't have a brain."

"Maybe if you just came right out and said what you mean . . ."

"I mean I'm concerned about the baby."

The color drained from Reid's face. He jumped up to grab her arms but swayed. "Oh, my God, you're pregnant?"

Lucy swatted at his hand. "I'm what?"

"You . . . I . . . we're—"

Realization dawned and nervous laughter bubbled inside Lucy. "No, Reid, I'm not pregnant."

"Then what baby are you talking about?"

Had she seen a moment of disappointment mingled with the panic? "Sophie and Lance's."

"Sophie and Lance are pregnant?"

"No, you idiot, Sophie is pregnant, and Lance is the father, and the poor kid is going to be an illegitimate baby if we don't do something."

Reid's mouth slacked open in shock. "What?"

"That's right. She'll be teased and called names and wonder why her daddy didn't love her. And who knows, Sophie has two job offers, so she may move away and the baby will never even see his daddy. Not that I could blame Sophie—"

"Just wait a damn minute."

"No, you wait." Lucy shook her finger in his face, her bracelets clattering down her arm. "I know what it's like to grow up without a father, and I won't let my niece or nephew suffer that, especially when I know Sophie and Lance love each other."

Reid's voice turned low, "I thought you didn't want them to be together."

Lucy sighed. "I didn't at first, but like I said, this is bigger than all of us." She snapped her fingers in his face. "Now are you going to sit there on your duff, or are you going to help me?"

Lance had closed the deal with McDaniels today and should have been celebrating. Instead he was brooding inside his duplex, trying to muster enough energy to work on the budget and forcing himself not to call the foreman of the three-man crew he'd put together to finish Sophie's house, when someone knocked on the door. He ignored it, hoping whoever it was would leave, but seconds later Reid appeared in the den.

"Lance, we have to talk."

Lance looked up from the paperwork on the table. "I'm busy."

Reid yanked out a chair and closed the folder Lance had been staring at for an hour. Reid's face was flushed, his hand shaking. "It's important, bro. I have something to tell you."

"What is it now?" His heart raced, his imagination going wild. "Has something happened to Maddie? Chase?" *Sophie, God, no, not Sophie.*

"It's about Sophie."

Lance's head swam.

"I just talked to Lucy, and you won't believe this,

but Sophie has two job offers and may be moving..."

He hesitated and Lance swayed.

"It gets worse, Lance, she may be...may be..."

Lance gripped Reid's collar. "May be what?"

"...well, she's pregnant."

Lance hit the floor with a thud, his last thought before he passed out the fact that Reid had once again told him something that should have come from Sophie.

Chapter Twenty-two

"Why didn't she tell me?" Lance asked from the floor.

Reid had squatted over him with a three-year-old bottle of vinegar, which had definitely woken Lance up, although he still felt too weak to stand. His head spun like a merry-go-round with thoughts of fatherhood and Sophie carrying his baby, and the two of them being together.

Reality intervened, though, like a lightning rod stabbing into the darkness. Sophie might be moving and he would lose her, and he might not ever see his own kid.

Reid shrugged and didn't reply, although Lance knew the answer. Why would she come to him after the way he'd treated her in Vegas? The hurt in her eyes when he'd walked away had haunted him for days. But he'd had a right to be hurt, too. . . .

Reid rubbed a hand over his chin, looking weary. "It's a mess, isn't it?"

"Yeah. A real mess."

"Women are too much damn trouble and work."

Lance had certainly never passed out because of one before. "Yeah, trouble and work."

"So what are you going to do, man?"

Lance grabbed the table edge for support, and Reid gave him a hand on the other side, helping him to stand. "I have to see her. I . . . She's having my baby." He should be furious, he realized, so why was his heart racing and a smile stretching his face? He was going to be a father. Get to ride his kid piggyback, play softball in the backyard, put up with one of those silly Slip 'N' Slid thingies that killed the grass . . .

Reid cleared his throat. "You want me to drive you over?"

"No." Lance searched for his keys on the crowded tabletop. "This is something I need to do alone. Just help me to the truck. I can make it from there."

Sophie had just settled into Lance's shirt for the night—okay, she hadn't washed it and returned it yet, but she would—when the doorbell rang. She let Lucy get it, then heard a man's voice.

Lance?

What was he doing here? Had he come to see the renovations?

Maybe he'd come for his shirt.

She clutched the hem of it, not certain she could part with it just yet, when suddenly he appeared at her bedroom door. Lucy, traitor that she was, must have let him in.

"Sophie, I . . . Can we talk?" He hesitated in the darkened doorway, and she drank in the sight of his big, muscular body filling the space. Memories crowded back, all the sultry touches and kisses, his body pulsing within her . . .

He moved inside the room then, bringing his masculine scent with him, and she tried to catch her breath. "Lance, I didn't expect you."

"I know." His voice sounded oddly shaky. Moonlight painted shadows across his face, but she saw emotions in his dark eyes, and her heart fluttered in her chest. Had he missed her? Somehow found a way to forgive her?

He moved even closer, and lifted a knuckle to brush across her cheek. She closed her eyes, remembering the times before when he'd made the same gesture, then when he'd undressed her and made slow, sweet love to her. If only they could turn back time and she could do things all over again. . . .

"Sophie, I want us to be together. To . . ." He paused and cleared his throat. "To get married."

Shock bolted through her. She opened her eyes and found him kneeling on one knee. He gathered her hand in his and held up a diamond ring that shimmered in the pale light of the room.

Sophie was breathless. She'd dreamed of Lance forgiving her, but not of a proposal.

"Oh, Lance . . ."

"Please, Sophie, I know we've had some problems, but there's chemistry between us, and I care about you, and I think you care about me. We'll make our baby a wonderful home—"

"Baby?" The joy Sophie had felt moments before disintegrated. Hurt welled in her throat, nearly cutting off the air in her windpipe. "What do you mean, our baby?"

He smiled then and laid his hand over her belly. She shivered and drew back from his touch.

"It's okay, I'm glad I know. I mean, I wish you'd told me, but still, I'm just glad I know." His voice was so calm, assured, determined. "We'll make it work, Sophie. We'll get past all this—"

"I'm not pregnant, Lance."

His fingers tightened around hers. "Sophie, you don't need to keep it a secret."

Tears pricked at her eyelids. "I'm not, Lance; I'm really not pregnant." She pulled her hand away, already missing his touch, then wrapped her arms around her middle to hold herself up. "What gave you that idea?"

His breath whooshed out and he stood, looking shaken. "Reid. Lucy told him she heard you and Maddie talking."

She pressed her lips together and saw the moment realization dawned.

"Not you, Maddie?"

Sophie nodded. "She didn't want to tell you right now, not with us . . . the way things are."

Lance gripped his hands by his sides. He glanced around the room, at the ceiling, his shoes, back at her. He clearly didn't know what to do.

"I think you'd better go, Lance."

"But Sophie, I . . . I'm sorry."

She turned and ripped his shirt from her body. Uncaring that she stood naked in front him, she shoved it at him. "Take it and go. I don't ever want to see you again."

Lance balled the shirt in his hands and backed away, his gaze glued to her until she shut the door in his face. As soon as she heard his truck crank, she yelled for Lucy.

The new job offers were looking better and better all the time. . . .

Lance picked up Reid on the way to Maddie's. If he had ever thought he might have another chance with Sophie, he had ruined it now.

"I was trying to be noble. To do the right thing," he argued. Which was obviously the wrong thing.

"I'll never understand women," Reid said.

Lance glanced at his crumpled shirt and nodded. "Me neither." And he would never forget the way Sophie had looked wearing nothing but that shirt. Then naked, handing it back to him with tears in her eyes. He had hurt her terribly, and he wasn't even sure what he'd done so horribly wrong.

Five minutes later he and his brother stood in Chase and Maddie's house.

"Why didn't you tell us the good news?" Lance pulled his sister into a bear hug, his throat thick with emotion. He was going to be an uncle; his baby sister was going to be a mother, his best friend in the whole world a father. "I'm so damn happy for you, you know that?"

Maddie hugged them both, then planted her hands on her hips. "How did you find out?" She slanted a suspicious eye toward her husband. "Did you tell, Chase?"

"No, er, it . . . just came out," Reid said.

Maddie's eyes narrowed. "Okay, something's up, boys; what happened?"

Somehow, between Lance and Reid's scattered explanation, they managed to spit out the gist of the story.

"Oh, good gracious, Lance." Maddie slapped at him. "Next time you have to deal with Sophie or any woman, check with me first. You and Reid both need lessons."

Chase chuckled, but Lance threw out his hands in confusion. "I still don't know what I did wrong. I thought I was doing the right thing."

"Which is exactly how it came across to Sophie." Maddie hissed and blew her hair away from her forehead. "I have to see her now and make sure you haven't damaged her for life."

Chase gently caught her hand. "Do you want me to drive you, honey?"

Maddie rolled her eyes. "You're sweet, but no, thanks, Chase. I'm pregnant, not an invalid."

He looked monetarily hurt, but Maddie kissed him. "Tell you what, though, you can give me a backrub when I get back."

Chase hugged her. "Of course, honey."

"Oh, for Pete's sake," Reid muttered. "Do you two ever stop?"

Maddie laughed, then fluttered a wave and ran out the door. Chase gestured toward the kitchen. "I've got some beer. Celebrate with me?"

Lance nodded, fighting envy at the nice home his best friend and sister had made, at the love they shared, and the baby they would bring into the world. They would be a real family.

Chase opened them all a beer and they sat at the breakfast bar. Reid tipped his bottle for a toast. "Here's to the first Summers-Holloway kid."

Lance raised his bottle. "Let's pray it's a male."

"Yeah, we don't need any more women in the family."

The other two members of the Terrible Three seconded that sentiment and clinked bottles.

"It was awful," Sophie said as Maddie and Lucy gathered around her with a chocolate layer cake, two quarts of ice cream, and a liter of diet Coke, which brought a fresh round of tears.

"I'm sorry; this is all my fault again," Lucy wailed. "I'm such a screwup."

"No, honey, it's not your fault." Sophie hugged her sister. "You meant well."

"I wanted to make it all up to you for putting a hex on Lance in the first place. It's all because I was so selfish that I didn't want to be alone. . . ."

Sophie brushed Lucy's hair from her damp cheek. "What do you mean? You're not alone."

Lucy hiccuped on a sob. "But I was afraid if you married Lance, you'd forget all about me, 'cause you'd be too busy with him and having babies and I'd never see you again—"

Sophie cut her off, the truth hitting her. "Oh, Lucy, honey, you're my sister, my favorite person in the whole world. I could never forget about you." She handed Lucy a hankie to dry her eyes. "No matter what happens, even if one of us does get married, we'll always, always have each other."

Lucy fell into Sophie's arms, and Sophie rocked her back and forth. She and her sister had both been affected by the way they'd grown up; they'd learned to cling to one another. She should have understood Lucy's feelings sooner.

"Well, I know my brother loves you," Maddie said. "Unfortunately he has mush for brains."

"Don't they all?" Lucy muttered as she blew her nose.

Sophie tried a laugh but failed. "For a moment I thought Lance did love me, maybe because I wanted it so badly, but then . . . I'll never forget the way he said we'd make it work. He didn't mention anything about love."

"Nothing?" Lucy asked.

"No. Oh, well, he said he cared about me," Sophie said in a sarcastic tone. "People care for their dogs; they don't care for the person they want to spend the rest of their life with. Maybe I should take that job and move."

"You're not moving," Maddie said emphatically.

"I'm just sorry that my pregnancy caused such a misunderstanding, and that it hasn't worked out." Maddie dabbed at her own eyes. "I really wanted you and Lance to be as happy as Chase and I are."

Sophie put her hand on Maddie's belly. "Don't be sorry for a minute. You should be celebrating now. I feel terrible for spoiling your news."

Lucy washed her hands, handed each of them a fork, and poured three glasses of milk. "I say we celebrate with Maddie right now."

They raised their milk glasses and clinked. "Let's just hope this baby's a girl," Maddie said.

"I thought you wanted a boy," Sophie said.

"I did, but I've changed my mind. We don't need any more men in the family; they're too much trouble."

With her big three-oh behind her, and after Lucy's comment about being afraid she'd lose her, and with Mother's Day only two days away, Sophie had done some serious soul searching. As an end to her Mother's Day tribute, she had phoned and arranged for Peter to bring Deseree to the show. Her mother had begged to come a few weeks earlier, when Lucy had appeared as a guest. Sophie had refused to entertain the idea then, but now she had a surprise for Deseree.

"Are you sure you want to do this?" Lucy asked.

"I'm sure." Lucy had been asking her questions all morning, as if she were afraid Sophie had gone off the deep end. She squeezed her sister's hand, grateful that Lucy had returned to Savannah with her. They had spent the last couple of days bonding, staying up late to watch old movies together, shopping, and debating Lucy's future with the Sleepover, Inc., company, the dance club, and a surprise offer from the talent scout who'd seen the Diva act in Vegas. Apparently he'd placed Peter on an MTV show, and the producer was interested in Lucy for another role in the production.

But Sophie had discovered a local arts theater that might be interested in her sister as a performer, and Lucy had an audition the following week. She was also considering going back to school.

"Did you see Peter and Deseree yet?" Sophie asked.

"Yes, I arranged for them to have good seats, right up front, like you requested."

"How does Deseree look?"

"Nervous but excited," Lucy said.

Sophie's heart squeezed. "I'm glad I talked to her yesterday and explained what I wanted to do."

Lucy hugged her. "It's going to be okay, Soph."

The producer stuck his head into Sophie's dressing room. "You're on in five."

"Be right there." Sophie took Lucy's hand and led her to the stage. She hoped this episode wouldn't cost her the career she'd worked so hard to build, but even if it did, she had to see it through. She'd kept her past and her present lives separate for too long; she didn't want any more secrets returning to haunt her or mess up her life.

Maddie pointed to her sofa. "Sit."

Lance and Reid exchanged confused looks with each other and Chase, but did as she said. They'd learned long ago not to mess with Maddie, especially when she had her mind made up. And she was pregnant now, which made her even more delicate and in need of their protection.

"What is it, honey?" Lance asked.

Reid leaned forward. "Do you need us to do something for you, Maddie?"

"Oh, good gracious," Maddie said. "I'm fine. But you two are going to sit here and watch the *Sophie Knows* show with me."

"I've got work to do." Lance instantly bolted up, and Reid started to follow, but Maddie pushed him back onto the sofa and Reid froze.

"Are you trying to punish me?" Lance asked. "It's bad enough I can't sleep for thinking about the woman without having to watch her on TV every day."

"It's not a punishment," Maddie said, although the gleam in her eyes made him wonder. "But you have to see today's show. You'll understand when it's all over."

She disappeared to the kitchen, and Chase jumped up to help her. Lance and Reid once again exchanged confused looks, but both were too worried about upsetting the pregnant Maddie to argue. After all, even if she didn't always act like a delicate Southern lady, her condition was delicate. And they had a niece or nephew to protect now.

Maddie and Chase swept back from the kitchen with an assortment of goodies, including a hot fudge cake with ice cream, and a pitcher of sweet iced tea, so the boys helped themselves. Maybe if he ate enough food, he'd distract himself from wanting to eat . . . lap up Sophie.

The music piped up and Sophie pranced onstage wearing a dark green suit that emphasized her eyes and hugged her figure. Lance mentally saw her naked, and wondered if he'd ever be able to ban that image. He still hadn't been able to wear that shirt she'd returned to him. . . .

Seconds later Lucy appeared. In spite of the fact

that Reid grumbled incessantly about Lucy being a kook, his little brother sat up straighter, his eyes glued to the TV.

"Today we end our Mother's Day special," Sophie said as the music faded. "All week long we've been reuniting mothers who have been separated from their children, hearing stories of troubled kids, and honoring the females who assume the matriarchal role to take care of their families. Today I have a special story to share with you. This is my own story. Mine and my sister's." Sophie hesitated, and Lance's breath lodged in his throat.

"My hope is that by sharing my past I can persuade others, especially troubled teens, who are in need of help to come forward and ask for it."

Maddie plucked a box of tissues from the table and hugged them to her. Chase massaged Maddie's back with a terrified look on his face. Reid seemed frozen to the spot.

"I'd like to start by telling you about my mother. Her name is Deseree." The camera panned to a close-up of the bottled blonde he'd seen in Vegas. She was decked out in gaudy jewelry and a bright orange outfit and had big hair, and seemed pleased to be on camera.

"My mother had a very difficult childhood," Sophie began. "She grew up with alcoholic parents who abandoned her when she was a teenager. With no family to help her, little education, and no money, she set out on her own. She survived, but she was desperate and resorted to working in a dance club in Vegas, and later, I hate to admit, to being a call girl."

The audience murmured a low rumble of whispers, but they were captivated.

"As a little girl, I didn't understand why other

children made fun of her or me, but I knew my family was different, and I closed myself off from others. By the time my little sister was born I was old enough to realize that the late nights my mother worked were not waitressing jobs. I was afraid of the men she brought home, protective of my sister, and basically ashamed of her life. I swore when I grew up I'd be different."

Lance knotted his hands into fists. "I don't want to hear any more."

Maddie was weeping now, tearing him in two even more. Chase cradled her to him. "We should turn it off, Maddie; all that crying can't be good for the baby."

"The baby's fine." Maddie snapped her fingers toward Lance and Reid. "You two sit down and hush. We're watching every minute."

Reid pressed his fists together while Lance pinched the bridge of his nose.

"Anyway," Sophie continued, "it wasn't until I met a special friend, Maddie Summers, and her brothers, that I learned about real families. I wanted that so desperately; all I'd ever dreamed of was a nice big old house with a front porch and my own bedroom with a walk-in closet and a white picket fence and maybe a pond out back. . . ." Emotions choked her voice, and she paused, making Lance's throat thicken. "I wanted that so badly I tried to hide my past, hide who I am."

Lucy cleared her throat and broke in. "You see, my sister and I grew up in Vegas, watching the showgirls walk the streets. We'd sneak into shows backstage to watch the girls dance, and eventually created our own show. When we got older we needed money ourselves, so we took our act to the

Palace. Some of you might have heard of it—the Diva act."

Again the audience murmured and whispered, but Lance saw their expressions. Sympathy. Compassion. Admiration.

He hoped Sophie saw it, too.

She composed herself. "Anyway, I realized recently that our past is very important; it shapes us and makes us who we are. We should never be ashamed of it; we should embrace it, treasure it, allow it to help us grow." She stood. "That said, I'd like for Deseree—my mother—to come up onstage." Sophie's voice wobbled. "You see, my mother may not have made all the right choices back then, but she loved me and my sister, and she did what she had to do to survive. And I learned from a very wise, smart girl"—she gestured toward Lucy— "about forgiveness. Today I'd like to honor my mother by introducing her to you."

The camera once again swung to Deseree, and the audience burst into applause as she wove her way up to the stage. "Come on up here, Mom."

Deseree waved to the crowd, then burst into tears. Sophie embraced her, and Lucy joined them in a group hug.

Lance exhaled, trying to steady his own emotions. Maddie was completely out of control, sobbing like a baby. Chase kept stuffing tissues in her hand, his expression of terror and sympathy almost comical. "I can relate to Sophie," Chase admitted gruffly, reminding Lance of Chase's life in the orphanage.

"I should never have let her go," Lance said in a husky voice.

"What a nightmare for Sophie and Lucy," Reid said.

"I love her," Lance said. "I thought she knew that."

Maddie blew her nose so loudly she nearly burst Lance's eardrum. But she was pregnant, so he didn't say a word. "I know you love her," Maddie said in a broken voice, "but maybe you don't love her enough. You never even told her."

Lance stared down at his shoes. Maddie was right. He had never told her. "It's too late now," Lance said, although he couldn't stand the possibility of her moving away and giving up the house she had worked so hard to buy. The home she'd put so much time and love into. "She gave me back my shirt." The fact that she'd rather be naked than wear it had said a lot.

Reid and Chase looked at him as if he'd gone alien on them.

"It's never too late," Maddie whispered. "Not if you really, really love her."

He did love her, more than anything. In fact, he wanted her so badly it hurt to breathe. But after the way he'd acted, how could he convince her?

Chapter Twenty-three

Lance had an idea, but he needed help, so he conferred with Reid, then called his work crew to set his plan into motion. Finally he left a message on Sophie's home machine saying that she and Lucy had to stay in a hotel for a couple of days so he could have the wood floors finished.

He had a couple of other things in mind, too, but they would be surprises.

Sophie's Mother's Day show had moved him so much that he stopped by to pick up some flowers and drove to the cemetery where his parents were buried. Odd how he had rarely visited their graves. The sight of the tombstones always evoked such a deep loss in him that he couldn't bear it.

But he owed his mother a visit. Besides, he needed to talk to her.

A warm spring breeze fluttered through the trees surrounding the property, and artificial flower arrangements swayed and danced in the wind. His chest felt tight as he forced himself along the path.

Finally he stood before his parents' final resting place. He had felt so young when they'd died, so scared of the future, so worried about Maddie and Reid.

So hurt and angry and alone.

Memories of his parents on various Christmases flooded him, their laughter and good-natured bickering over which tree to cut down and how many lights to add to the house. Birthdays, family dinners, church services, Easter, graduation—except his parents hadn't attended his graduation because they'd already been gone.

That night he'd walked onstage to accept his diploma, wishing with all his heart that his father and mother could have been in the audience. Instead of celebrating with his friends after the ceremony, he'd brooded and vowed never to get attached to anyone else again.

And he hadn't. . . .

Not until Sophie.

He knelt and placed the flowers in the vase at the head of his mother's grave. "Happy Mother's Day, Mom. I . . ." His throat choked as tears filled his eyes. "I miss you." He hesitated, gathering his control.

"I know I don't come to visit much, but it's hard, you know." He rubbed his hand over his eyes. "Anyway, I wish you could see Reid and Maddie, Mom. Reid's turned out to be a good worker; he's smarter than any of us ever gave him credit for, and . . . I think he might even be in love." He chuckled, remembering the stricken look on his brother's face when he'd seen Lucy on TV.

"And Maddie . . . well, you know Maddie's a handful, like always. She married Chase, and now they're expecting a baby, and her hormones have kicked in. Geesh, Chase has his work cut out for him." A smile came to him. "I wish you could be here to see your grandbaby, but I promise to watch over him or her, although Chase'll do that, too. He's going to make a great father, Mom, and he loves Maddie so much, you can see it every time he looks at her." He thanked the heavens his and Reid's interference hadn't kept them apart. "You'd be proud of her, too; she has her own business, and . . . well, you know I always thought I took care of her, but it's the other way around. Maddie takes care of me and Reid. She's the glue, Mom, that holds us together. You did good with her."

Emotions clogged his throat again. "Anyway, I came because I wanted you to know I've met someone. Her name is Sophie. She's . . . Maddie's best friend, and she's just the prettiest, brightest, greatest woman I've ever known, but I've screwed up with her over and over again. Frankly, I don't know why she didn't give up on me a long time ago." He cleared his throat. "I kept pushing her away, because I was scared of loving her and having her leave me like . . . like you and Dad did." He dropped his head forward into his hands, willing away the pain. "I hate to admit it, but I was angry when you left, mad at you and Dad for leaving me alone, for leaving me to take care of Reid and Maddie when I was just a kid myself." A tear escaped and trickled down his cheek. "That's the reason I haven't been by much, but that's going to change."

The wind whistled through the trees, stirring the grass and dirt over his parents' graves. He lifted his face to feel it caress his cheeks—was it a sign his mother could hear him?

"Uh, and there's one more thing." He stared up into the heavens. "I know you're up there, Mom, and I think you'd really like Sophie, so . . . I wondered if you could somehow flutter those angel wings and do something to help Sophie forgive me? And if she gets a job someplace else, well, maybe you could be there to tell me what to do then. . . ."

After she'd made peace with her mother, Sophie felt a weight lift from her. Not only had the show been a success and pulled in top ratings, but her agent had called and upped the money offer for that anchor news spot. She should be ecstatic.

But hearing Lance's voice on her answering machine had resurrected the pain of losing him all over again. She had packed a bag, and she and Lucy had driven to the hotel where Deseree was staying so she wouldn't have to face seeing him in person when he arrived to finish the flooring. They were getting dressed to meet Deseree for dinner, and had promised to show her some of the famous Savannah sights.

Sophie brushed her hair, wondering if she should let the natural blond color return or keep the black. There was no reason to hide anything now; she no longer needed to run from her past.

"You seem so sad." Lucy came up behind Sophie. "I wish I could do something, Soph."

"You mean you don't have a spell to vanquish heartache?"

Lucy fluffed her long curls. "I'm done with spells for a while."

Sophie laughed. "And I'm finished with that singles service."

"George and Rory both left messages. You could call one of them."

Sophie shrugged and dropped the brush. "Maybe later. But right now . . . well, it's not fair of me to go out with them when I'm thinking about Lance."

"I suppose."

"Do you miss Reid?"

"What?" Lucy gestured toward herself with her thumbs. "Me miss a man? Honey, there's lots of fish in the sea. Didn't Maddie's rules say to cast your line for another one?"

"Oh, my goodness, those rules..." Sophie laughed. "I think we need to chuck them along with your spells."

Lucy slid her arm through Sophie's as they walked to the door. "So if you're not into dating right now, you need to take a look at my Sleepover, Inc., catalog and stock up. I'm running a special closeout deal: Buy one item, get the second one free...."

Lance was shaking like a leaf in a tornado. He had no idea how Sophie would react to his plan, so he had divided it up into two stages. First he had to convince her that her dancing didn't matter to him.

Well, actually, it did matter, especially if she chose to continue it, but he loved her and somehow he'd learn to live with it. Surely the therapist who'd helped him with his sleep disorder could prescribe some medication to calm him enough so he wouldn't assault every male in the audience when he caught them looking at her. If not, maybe Reid and Chase could restrain him....

And if she wanted to move, well, he'd move, too. Maybe they could hire someone to help his brother and Chase here, and he could do some contracting work in a new city.

Trying not to dwell on that issue, he dressed in the vampire costume he'd found at a party store, and sneaked into the back room of Frosty's Bar. Although he hated public spectacles, the only way he knew to make Sophie believe he accepted her dancing—and the only way he could make himself believe he could fit in with her TV friends—was to face his fears dead-on. He'd asked Maddie to arrange an impromptu party for Sophie and her friends under the guise of celebrating the syndication of *Sophie Knows*, and he intended to surprise her.

Sophie and Lucy and Maddie were all hovering together in the back of the room while Sophie's friends mingled. He spotted Reid and Chase ordering beers from the bar. They looked up and saw him and laughed. He almost backed out. Then Sophie pivoted, and he saw her face. His heart did a strange flipflop, and he thought, Oh, hell, so what if he lost his pride? Without Sophie what did it matter?

He gave Chase the cue and rock music piped up. Inhaling for courage, he strode into the room, wove through the crowd, and began to dance for Sophie.

Sophie stared in stunned silence as Lance danced in front of her. He looked ridiculous in that vampire costume, and handsome as homemade sin, and incredibly embarrassed and delicious. . . .

So why in the heck was he doing it? To embarrass her?

He swayed and gyrated his hips and moved his feet awkwardly, and she had to bite her bottom lip not to laugh.

"Go, man," Chase yelled.

"Yeah!" Reid called.

"Oh, my gosh," Lucy whispered.

A few of her friends from the show giggled, some of the group began clapping and chanting, while her station manager simply raised his eyebrows in question. Lance flapped the vampire cape around his body, missed a step, and nearly crashed into the food cart. He desperately needed dance lessons.

Sophie almost felt sorry for him.

Finally the music trailed off, and he bowed.

"Great show!" Maddie squealed. "Now everyone can loosen up and dance." She waved her hands in the air, and Lucy caught on, grabbing the first available male near her, the maintenance man at the show, and they began to do the twist.

Lance pulled Sophie into the corner. "You owe me one more date," Lance said. "I popped the balloon, and the note said to dance for you."

"It did not."

"Okay, I added that part, but you still owe me a date."

"Is this a joke?" Sophie said in a strained whisper.

"You think I made a fool out of myself for a joke?" His voice sounded steely and serious.

Sophie swallowed. "I don't know what to think, Lance."

He traced a finger along her cheek. "When the party's over, meet me at your house. We'll finish the date then. . . ."

"Lance." Pain resurfaced as Sophie remembered his reaction to her Diva act. "Did you do this to embarrass me?"

"No, hell, no, Sophie." He gestured at the black vampire costume. "I did it to show you that your dancing doesn't bother me."

Sophie twisted her mouth sideways. "Really?"

"Really."

"Then if I want to go back to Vegas to perform that's okay with you?"

His eye twitched. "If that's what you want." He yanked at his collar as if he were sweating. "I'll take you any way I can get you."

Hope fluttered in Sophie's chest, but died when

she realized he was lying. Her dancing act would always bother him. Lance was old-fashioned, overly protective, a tad bit sexist. . . . "It's too late," Sophie said. "Too much has happened."

Lance brushed his knuckles across her cheek. "It's not too late, not if you love me." He pressed his lips to her cheek. "Meet me at your house. I'll be waiting."

And then he was gone, leaving Sophie confused and alone and wondering what else he had in store for her tonight. She was still hurting, too, because he'd said it wasn't too late if she loved him. But that had never been the problem.

The problem was that he had never loved her in return. . . .

By the time Sophie arrived, her nerves were strung tighter than a G-string. After Lance had left, she'd been too anxious to eat or drink and had finally begged off the party and hurried home.

She gaped at the white picket fence surrounding the house, astonished that Lance had had it installed so quickly. And how had he worked that into her budget? First there had been the upgraded hardware, then the stained-glass window. . . .

He waved to her from the porch, where he was pacing.

Good, at least he was nervous, too.

Sliding from the seat, she adjusted the straps of her sundress, wishing she'd worn a jacket. She felt naked and vulnerable and so needy for Lance that her body trembled from head to toe as she climbed the porch steps and walked toward him.

"Hello, Sophie."

"Lance." She gestured toward the fence. "How'd you do that so fast? And what about the cost?"

344

"Don't worry. It all worked out fine." His smile seemed forced. "There're still a few more things to do to the house, but I want you to see the progress."

She nodded, her gaze turning wary. "Is that what this is about, the house?"

He took her hand in his. "Partly."

Then he led her inside. Sophie ran her finger over the beautiful painted trimwork and molding, in awe that he'd discovered the natural wood beneath all the carpeting and had stripped and refinished the flooring so quickly. The kitchen island had been installed, the bright white trim and yellow paint giving the room an airy, sunny feel. He'd even added a contemporary sink with pewter hardware and a built-in pantry that she hadn't expected.

"Come on; there's a surprise up here." He pulled her around to the staircase, then up the steps. She smiled when she saw him bend to pet her cat. Jazzy barely snarled this time. Her cat must be getting used to Lance. Would Jazzy miss him, too, if things didn't work out?

Was she getting her hopes up that they would?

"We added some things to your bath," Lance said.

"Oh, my gosh." Sophie halted in shock. The Jacuzzi was working, but it was the big walk-in closet that caught her eye. She'd never mentioned a walk-in closet, thinking there wouldn't be room and that she couldn't afford it. She stepped inside, amazed at the customized shelving he'd designed.

"This is wonderful, Lance. What made you think ... How did you know?" Then realization struck. "You saw my show? The one with my mother?"

Lance nodded.

Sophie's throat closed, tears burning her eyes. "Lance, I didn't go on TV to get sympathy."

He winced at her biting tone. "I realize that."

She jutted her chin upward. "You're not giving me discounts because of it either."

"That's not what this is about. I . . . I made the changes because I want you to have the dream house you always wanted."

"But—"

"Shh." He pressed his lips to hers to silence her, then captured her hands between his and guided her down the stairs. "There's one more thing."

"No, there can't be; this is too much."

He guided her to the backyard. Tears filled her eyes when she spotted the white gazebo with built-in seats he'd added. A small round table sat in the center, draped with a tablecloth and candles, which were shimmering with soft light.

"Lance . . ."

"I didn't have time to build the fish pond yet, but"—he paused and gestured toward the left side—"it can go in right here, and we can add a flower garden and brick steps that lead out to the gazebo, and maybe a tire swing—"

"We?" Sophie clutched his hand and stared into his eyes, certain she'd misunderstood him.

"Oh, sorry, I'm getting ahead of myself." He dropped to his knees, took her hand in his, then lifted it and pressed a kiss to her fingers. Sophie's breath caught when he removed an antique diamond ring from his pocket. "I love you, Sophie. This ring belonged to my mother. I want you to have it because she would have loved you, too, and I know you like antiques, but if you want a new ring, we can shop for one—"

"The ring is beautiful, perfect, special." A small laugh escaped her. "But what did you say before that?"

He hesitated, then slid the ring on her finger and

pressed her hand to his cheek. "I said I love you, Sophie. I love you with all my heart. Will you marry me?"

Sophie fell to her knees, threw her arms around him, and knocked him over as she kissed him. "Of course I will." When she came up for air, she was breathless, her fingers beginning to toy with the buttons on his shirt. "Now can I have that shirt back, please? I'm sleepless without it."

Lance laughed and dared her to take it off, and Sophie gladly obliged.

Of course, she lost her own in the process . . .

Epilogue

As a prelude to Sophie's June wedding series, she and Lance were married the first week of June. Although her producer wanted her wedding to air on the show, Sophie refused, opting for a small private ceremony with friends and family. She'd also turned down both job offers, as she intended to build her life with Lance in Savannah with the home they'd restored together, surrounded by family and close friends.

Deseree and Lucy and Maddie bustled around her bedroom, fluffing her dress and veil.

"I want you to have these; they belonged to my mother," Deseree said. She placed a strand of pearls around Sophie's neck and hugged her.

"Did you know Mom enrolled in night school?" Lucy said.

Sophie gripped her mother's arms. "Did you really?"

"Yes, I thought I'd try my hand at cosmetology." Deseree lifted her big hair. "The dancers in Vegas always need classy hairstylists. And I can make a fortune doing wigs for the drag queen show over at Café Risque."

Lucy and Sophie laughed. The music started and they rushed down the stairs, straightening dresses and whispering. Sophie and Lance had both agreed to get married in her backyard in the gazebo. Lance had hired a crew to landscape the yard, and add the fish pond and a rose garden in honor of his mother. Reid and Chase had confiscated white wooden chairs and set them up, and Maddie and Lucy had decorated them with white ribbons and flowers.

Deseree hurried ahead and let Peter escort her to her seat. Maddie and Lucy, her two bridesmaids, were dressed in simple dark green cocktail dresses and carried fresh red roses. Sophie's assistant, Eden, sang "I Will Always Love You" to piano music supplied by the show's band, which had set up a stage in the yard.

Sophie followed, hanging on to Peter's arm as she walked toward Lance. Chase and Reid both stood beside him, but Sophie's gaze latched on to Lance's. His dark eyes sparkled with hunger, the kind that she trusted would never die.

Peter handed her over and the ceremony began with a simple prayer. "I believe Sophie and Lance have written their own vows," the minister said.

They nodded and Lance cradled her hand between his. "Sophie, I'm honored to be standing in front of you today, especially since you once told me you wouldn't go out with me if I were the last man on earth."

Lucy and Maddie giggled, along with the visitors.

"The truth is, I fell in love with you the moment I met you. But I had lost a part of my family when I was young, and I was afraid to love and lose again." He stroked her fingers with his and gently kissed them. "But even though I pushed you away, you stayed with me. Without you I couldn't eat, I couldn't think, and I was completely sleepless. In fact, you taught me not to be afraid, because life without love isn't really living.

"I love you, Sophie with all my heart, now, tomorrow, and always."

Tears burned the backs of Sophie's eyelids, but she blinked them away. "Lance, I dreamed of having a home when I grew up, a Victorian house full of antiques with a walk-in closet, a white picket fence, a gazebo in my backyard, and a pond. But I never dreamed I would find someone as wonderful as you.

"You gave me all those things I'd dreamed about in my house, but when I thought I'd lost you, I realized that a house was just four walls with things that didn't really matter. It wasn't a home until you added the loving touches with your own hands, until you stood inside with me." She kissed his fingers as he had hers.

"When I first met you, I sensed we were soul mates. Then I got to know you, and I knew I was meant to love you. I give you my heart, today and forevermore."

They exchanged rings and the minister offered a simple prayer; then it was time to kiss the bride.

Lance swept Sophie into his arms and claimed her mouth in a kiss so tender and erotic that Sophie felt faint when she pulled away. Maddie was crying and blowing her nose, but rushed to congratulate them. Lucy and Deseree hugged and squealed, then embraced her and Lance.

"You will be good to my sister, won't you?" Lucy asked.

Lance grinned. "Yes, of course I will. And I'll be your big brother if you let me."

Lucy twisted her mouth in thought. "As long as you don't boss me around too much."

Sophie and Lance laughed, while Peter came forward to hug them both. Chase pounded Lance on the back, and Reid looked oddly emotional. Then the party and celebration began. Everyone enjoyed the appetizers and champagne and wedding cake, then danced.

Lance dragged Sophie into his arms. "Were you really thinking about going back to Vegas to perform?"

Sophie nuzzled his neck. "No. Why, do you want me to dance?"

"Maybe later, for me. In private."

"I think that can be arranged."

Lance kissed her. "I hope so, Sophie. And if you want to take that job in L.A.—"

"We're not moving," Sophie said. "I love the show I'm doing now, Lance. I love Savannah and Maddie and you and our house. I don't need anything else."

Lance pressed her hands to his heart. "How about a family . . . someday?"

Sophie smiled. "Well, yes, I would like *that*."

"Do you think Lucy's really okay with us getting married?"

"I think so, but your brother looked kind of upset. Maybe we should check on them." Hand in hand, they maneuvered through the crowd.

"Where are they?" Sophie asked.

"I don't know. I hope they're not off arguing somewhere." He pulled her inside, and they searched the house. They were just about to give up when Lance heard a squeaking sound from the attic.

"Is there a ghost up there?"

"No." Sophie darted up the stairs and they tiptoed into the room to find Reid and Lucy kissing. "Oh, my gosh," Sophie whispered, grateful they were still dressed.

"Reid?" Lance stammered.

Lucy and Reid pulled away, their faces flushed, hair tangled, clothes disheveled.

"Lucy, I thought he was the most infuriating, exasperating, sexist pig you'd ever met," Sophie said.

Lucy grinned, her arms still looped around Reid's neck. "He is."

Lance quirked a brow. "And I thought she was a kook?"

Reid shrugged and tightened his hands around her back. "She is."

"Did you cast a spell on him?" Sophie asked.

Lucy shook her head, curls bouncing.

"It doesn't matter," Reid said in a goofy voice. "Because I think I love Lucy."

"Ahhh . . ." Lucy threaded her fingers through his hair. "I think I love you, too."

As soon as the guests left, Sophie and Lance raced up the steps to change. Seconds later Sophie emerged in a black G-string and pasties made of chocolate drops.

Lance's throat went dry. He'd thought the Virginal Vampiress was sexy; Sophie in this amazing getup was an orgasm waiting to happen.

"What exactly is that thing called?" he said in a thick voice as she began to slowly gyrate to the jazz music floating through the room.

"Item number sixty-nine from Lucy's Sleepover catalog. Chocolate kisses, the edible wonders." Sophie wiggled her fanny and dipped her shoulder so the chocolate kisses covering her nipples swayed. "Now, honey, you can have dessert."

Lance licked his lips and went to make his wife happy, something he intended to do the rest of his life. As he took the first bite, he feathered his fingers along Sophie's thighs. "Maybe your sister should hold on to that business," he whispered. "After all, we have anniversaries to come, and Valentine's Day...."

Sophie threw her head back and groaned. "Honey, I'll make sure we get a lifetime supply."

Marry Me, Maddie
Rita Herron

Maddie Summers is tired of waiting. To force her fiancé into making a decision, she takes him on a talk show and gives him a choice: Marry me, or move on. The line he gives makes her realize it is time to star in her own life. But stealing the show will require a script change worthy of a Tony. Her supporting cast is composed of two loving but overprotective brothers, her blue-blood ex-boyfriend, and her brothers' best friend: sexy bad-boy Chase Holloway—the only one who seems to recognize that a certain knock-kneed kid sister has grown up to be a knockout lady. And Chase doesn't seem to know how to bow out, even when the competition for her hand heats up. Instead, he promises to perform a song and dance, even ad-lib if necessary to demonstrate he is her true leading man.

___52433-3 $5.50 US/$6.50 CAN

UNDER THE COVERS
RITA HERRON

Marriage counselor Abigail Jensen faked it, and she is going to have to keep on faking it. She wrote *the* book on how to keep a relationship alive, and now the public is clamoring for more than her advice—they want her to demonstrate her techniques! But Abby has just discovered that her own wedding was a sham. Adding insult to injury, her publicist produces a gorgeous actor to play her husband, and with him Abby experiences the orgasmic kisses and titillating touches she previously knew only as chapter titles. Longing to be caught up in a tangle of sheets with her hunk of a "hubby," Abby wonders if she has finally found true love. She knows she will have to discover the truth . . . under the covers.

Improper English
KATIE MacALISTER

Sassy American Alexandra Freemar isn't about to put up with any flak from the uptight—albeit gorgeous—Scotland Yard inspector who accuses her of breaking and entering. She doesn't have time. She has two months in London to write the perfect romance novel—two months to prove that she can succeed as an author.

Luckily, reserved Englishmen are not her cup of tea. Yet one kiss tells her Alexander Block might not be quite as proper as she thought. Unfortunately, the gentleman isn't interested in a summer fling. And while Alix knows every imaginable euphemism for the male member, she soon realizes she has a lot to learn about love.

Wild About You

ROBIN WELLS

All Rand Adams wants is a ranch where he can train world-class quarter horses and the chance to lead an orderly, logical existence. But free-spirited Celeste Landry has moved in next door and opened the Wild Things Fun Farm, a children's petting zoo stocked with cast-off circus animals and misfit critters. There is about to be a problem.

The two couldn't be more different. Celeste believes in fate and destiny. Rand believes in self-determination. She thinks him headstrong. He thinks her a head case. But after they share one hot kiss, she is no longer driving him crazy; she is driving him wild. And there is only one path to true happiness: He has to start listening to his heart.
